AL AND JoAnna

Hannah of *Fort*

Bridger

Series

Under the
Distant Sky

Al & JoAnna La

Consider
the Lilies

JoAnna Lacy

No Place
for Fear

Pillow
Stone

Al & JoAnna Lacy

Perfect
Gift

Al & JoAnna Lacy

6
Touch
Compassion

Al & JoAnna Lacy

OTHER BOOKS BY AL LACY

Angel of Mercy series:
A Promise for Breanna (Book One)
Faithful Heart (Book Two)
Captive Set Free (Book Three)
A Dream Fulfilled (Book Four)
Suffer the Little Children (Book Five)
Whither Thou Goest (Book Six)
Final Justice (Book Seven)
Things Not Seen (Book Eight)
Not by Might (Book Nine)
Far Above Rubies (Book Ten)

Journeys of the Stranger series:
Legacy (Book One)
Silent Abduction (Book Two)
Blizzard (Book Three)
Tears of the Sun (Book Four)
Circle of Fire (Book Five)
Quiet Thunder (Book Six)
Snow Ghost (Book Seven)

Battles of Destiny (Civil War series):
Beloved Enemy (Battle of First Bull Run)
A Heart Divided (Battle of Mobile Bay)
A Promise Unbroken (Battle of Rich Mountain)
Shadowed Memories (Battle of Shiloh)
Joy from Ashes (Battle of Fredericksburg)
Season of Valor (Battle of Gettysburg)
Wings of the Wind (Battle of Antietam)
Turn of Glory (Battle of Chancellorsville)

Hannah of Fort Bridger series (coauthored with JoAnna Lacy):
Under the Distant Sky (Book One)
Consider the Lilies (Book Two)
No Place for Fear (Book Three)
Pillow of Stone (Book Four)
The Perfect Gift (Book Five)
Touch of Compassion (Book Six)

Mail Order Bride series (coauthored with JoAnna Lacy):
Secrets of the Heart (Book One)
A Time to Love (Book Two)
Tender Flame (Book Three)
Blessed Are the Merciful (Book Four)
Ransom of Love (Book Five)

BEYOND THE VALLEY

BOOK SEVEN

AL AND JOANNA LACY

Multnomah Publishers® *Sisters, Oregon*

BEYOND THE VALLEY
published by Multnomah Publishers, Inc.

© 2000 by ALJO PRODUCTIONS, INC.
International Standard Book Number: 1-57673-618-0

Cover illustration by Vittorio Dangelico
Design by Left Coast Design
Multnomah is a trademark of Multnomah Publishers, Inc., and is registered in the U.S. Patent and Trademark Office.
The colophon is a trademark of Multnomah Publishers, Inc.

Printed in the United States of America

For information:
MULTNOMAH PUBLISHERS, INC.
POST OFFICE BOX 1720
SISTERS, OREGON 97759

00 01 02 03 04 05 — 10 9 8 7 6 5 4 3 2 1 0

Blessed is the man whose strength is in thee;
in whose heart are the ways of them.
Who passing through the valley of Baca make it a well;
the rain also filleth the pools.

PSALM 84:5–6

Chapter One

Colin Wright woke suddenly, hearing only the cold Wyoming wind howling around the eaves of the house. His eyes took in the dying flames in the fireplace and the light and shadow flickering on the walls and ceiling. The wind-rattled windows were vague squares of blackness.

What had awakened him? It couldn't be the wind, which had been howling when he finally drifted off to sleep. Something else had invaded his sleep—loud enough to jerk him awake.

Then he heard the bawl of cattle.

Cougars! They were after more of his herd.

As he threw back the covers, Carrie stirred, then raised her head from the pillow.

"What is it, darling?" she asked in a sleepy voice.

"The cattle." Colin took his Levi's from a nearby chair. "They sound frightened."

"Cougars?"

"I think so. I'm going out to see."

"Oh, Colin, be careful." Her voice broke a little, then took on the edge of a whimper. "Cougars killed Bart Flaherty only a week ago."

He slipped into his shirt. "I'll be careful, honey. But I've got to kill those hungry beasts before they wipe us out."

The high-pitched wail of a cougar rose above the sound of

the wind, followed by the loud bawling of frightened cattle.

Carrie pulled the covers up to her neck as she sat up and watched her husband hurriedly button his shirt and pull on socks and boots.

He moved quickly to the fireplace, tossing a couple of logs on the fire, then looked over his shoulder at Carrie. "I'll be back as soon as I can."

She nodded, fighting the rising fear clawing at her insides.

As he hurried down the hallway, she whispered, "Please watch over him, Lord. And please let us put a stop to these cougars killing our cattle."

The moonless night was bitterly cold as Colin went out the back door, his Winchester .44 rifle gripped tightly in gloved hands. His hat was pulled low and the collar of his sheepskin coat turned up against his chin. The sky was a dark frozen vault scattered with stars that looked like glittering diamonds.

As he plodded through the foot and a half depth of snow, he could tell by the crunch beneath his feet and the way the wind popped the limbs off of the trees that the temperature was far below zero. The relentless wind only added to the cold.

Near the corral he saw two figures glide over the split-rail fence on the back side of the corral. They were little more than shadowy silhouettes.

He worked the lever of the Winchester, shouldered it and took aim, then squeezed off a shot. He worked the lever again and fired a second time. The shots pierced the night, and their echoes rattled off across the snow-laden fields, then faded into silence.

As he squinted against the snow pelting his eyes, he tried in vain to catch sight of the two mountain lions, but they were gone.

He went to the corral fence and could make out two dark

lumps lying in the snow. The rest of the cattle were milling about and bawling. He hastened to the barn door and flipped the frozen latch, then stepped into the dark interior. The small shelf near the door held a lantern and a small box of matches.

He snatched off one of his gloves and struck the match on the wall then touched it to the wick and turned up the flame for maximum light. As soon as he jacked a fresh cartridge into the Winchester's chamber, he picked up the lantern and went outside and plodded toward the corral gate.

The lantern light showed him that a cow was down, its blood spreading on the snow from her tattered hide. She was heavy with calf but would never give birth to it. She was barely breathing. A few feet away, already dead, was one of his best bulls. The cougars had at least partially satisfied their hunger by the time they had heard him coming from the house.

Turning back to the cow, he set the lantern down and raised the rifle, pointing the muzzle at her head.

As soon as she heard two gunshots, Carrie got up and put on her robe and slippers and went to stand at the kitchen window. A lantern burned on the cupboard next to her, and she cupped her hands to the sides of her face to get a better view of the barn and corral. She could barely make out Colin's dark form as he entered the barn.

Moments later, he came out and she lost sight of him when he carried the glowing lantern through the corral gate and moved to the far side of the barn. Then she heard another rifle shot.

Colin sighed as he walked away from the dead cattle, mumbling to himself, "Two more head killed...that makes twenty-seven—almost a third of the herd—since the first big snow hit us in November."

As he passed through the corral gate, he prayed silently, *Lord, what are we going to do to stop this? Please help us. Dear God, You know I tried staying up all night for a week in December, and another week in January, but the cats never showed up. It was as if they had some way of knowing I was sitting there in the barn, waiting for them.*

He paused at the back porch door and looked toward the corral. The cattle had stopped bawling and milling about.

When he stepped into the kitchen, Colin saw his wife of ten years coming toward him from the back window. Her face was pale and her hands trembled. He set the rifle next to the door and leaned it muzzle-upward against the wall, then folded her into his arms.

"I heard shots," she said, a quaver in her voice.

"Yes. I fired the first two at a pair of cougars that went over the fence as I was drawing up to the corral. They killed one of our best bulls and ripped up a cow that was carrying a calf, but she was still alive. The third shot was to put her out of her misery."

Carrie burst into tears. "Oh, Colin! When is this going to end? I know the beasts are only killing because they're hungry; but if this killing keeps up, we'll lose the ranch!"

He held her tight against his heavy coat and said, "We've prayed much about this, sweetheart. I know the Lord could stop the cougars from coming onto our property, but maybe by allowing the hungry beasts to come here, He's sparing our neighbors' cattle."

Carrie shook her head. "But we're about to lose the ranch. Doesn't the Lord care about that?"

"Of course He cares. Maybe He's just testing us to see if we'll stay close to Him in spite of our losses. Remember Pastor Kelly's sermon a week ago last Sunday…how it fit us so perfectly?"

"Yes." A small sob hiccuped through her. "I…I guess I just need more faith."

"Me, too, honey. This may be the Lord's way to put us in the Book more so our faith will grow. You know...Romans 10:17."

"You're right, Colin."

Turning her around and pointing her toward the doorway to the hall, Colin said, "We need to get some sleep."

"I don't know if I can."

"Well, let's try."

Colin woke at dawn and noted its frigid hush. The wind had stopped blowing. He moved slowly, trying to get up without disturbing Carrie. She seemed to be sleeping soundly, but when his weight left the bed, she stirred and opened her eyes.

"Did you sleep, darling?" she asked.

"I did all right. How about you?"

"Not too bad."

"Well, you just go back to sleep. I'll grab a little something from the pantry and be on my way."

"Where are you going?"

"To see if I can track down those two cougars."

She sat up. "Colin, you shouldn't go alone. That's what Bart did. You need to get one of the neighbors to go with you. After all, the beasts could start in on their herds at any time, just like they're doing to us and the Flaherty ranch."

"I know. But the neighbors are busy. I'll handle it myself."

"Why do you have such a stubborn streak?" she said, her brow furrowed.

Colin chuckled. "I learned it from the cute little blond I married ten years ago. I didn't have a stubborn streak till you taught me how to develop one."

Carrie sighed, threw back the covers, and slid off the bed. As she slipped on her robe, she said, "You men are all alike. You blame your faults on us poor innocent women."

Colin snorted. "Poor innocent women, eh? That's a good one!"

Carrie laughed and headed for the hall. "I'll get breakfast on while you feed the cattle and break the ice on the stock tank."

Colin's expression was grim as he stood over the dead carcasses in the corral. The bodies were already frozen stiff. He would have to hitch up one of the draft horses and drag them out of the corral tomorrow. Right now he needed to track the cougars.

After breaking the ice on the stock tank next to the barn, Colin primed the pump and worked the lever to draw water from the well. The cattle gathered around to drink.

From there he went into the barn and climbed the ladder to the hayloft. He forked sufficient hay into the corral to last the cattle for the day. Before closing the door of the loft, he looked down at his dwindling herd while they munched hay and felt a new determination to find those cougars and kill them.

A half hour later, Colin kissed Carrie at the back door and stepped off the porch into the brilliant sunlight that offered no warmth. He slid the Winchester into the saddleboot, adjusted the gunbelt on his hip, and swung into the saddle. Carrie had closed the door but was still peering at him through the frost-edged window. The sadness he saw in her dark brown eyes ripped at his heart.

"I love you!" he called loudly, his breath hanging in the cold, still air.

Carrie waved and tried to smile, but it barely curved her lips.

As he nudged the gelding forward, he twisted in the saddle and gave her a look to encourage her.

When Colin reached the back side of the corral, he leaned from the saddle and studied the snow-packed ground. The wind had all but erased the cougars' tracks, but there were still some traces left.

He slowly pressed toward the deep forest at the southern edge of his property, studying what the wind had left of the cats' tracks. There were definitely two cats, and the tracks were leading into the forest.

He pulled the rifle from its boot and jacked a cartridge into the chamber, then proceeded cautiously, relying on the horse to alert him of predators.

Carrie watched her husband until he and the bay passed from view, then let the curtain fall into place and finished cleaning up the kitchen. After placing a couple more logs in the cook-stove, she went to the parlor and added wood to the potbellied stove, then sat in her favorite overstuffed chair. With her head bent low she asked the Lord to help Colin put an end to the marauding cats.

Colin had been gone a little more than three hours when Carrie was in the kitchen kneading bread dough. When she heard a horse blow outside she rushed to the window and parted the lace curtains to see her husband riding into the yard. She watched him ride to the barn and dismount, then went back to her dough.

When he came inside moments later, he said, "Lost their trail in the forest. The wind had built drifts in that big open area in the middle of it and beyond, covering their tracks."

Carrie dropped the dough and wiped her hands while Colin leaned the Winchester against the wall and hung up his hat, then slipped out of the sheepskin coat. When he saw her coming toward him, he opened his arms.

As they embraced, Carrie said, "You did what you could,

darling. We'll just have to pray harder."

When Colin kissed her, she felt the icy numbness of his lips and took him by the hand. Leading him toward the cookstove, she said, "Let's get you thawed out, honey."

While he soaked up the fire's warmth, Carrie slid her arms around his slender waist and said, "I'm about to bake you some bread."

"I see that," he said, smiling. "Is that the last of the flour?"

"Mm-hmm."

"Since we weren't able to go into town for church because of the storm, we'd better go in soon and talk to Hannah."

"Yes," she said softly. "Before another storm comes. I really believe Hannah will understand and help us, especially after what she did for Chief Two Moons and his Crow village to keep them from starving."

Colin nodded. "We'd best drive in tomorrow morning and talk to her. These pantry shelves are getting pretty bare."

Even as he spoke they heard horses blowing at the front of the house. Colin went to the front door and peered through the curtains.

Frowning, Carrie called, "Who is it?"

"Karl Devlin and his brother. In a two-horse sleigh."

"Oh, no! You don't suppose—"

"I guess we're about to find out."

Colin opened the door and said in a friendly manner, "Come in, gentlemen. Plenty cold, isn't it?"

The Devlin brothers, who held the mortgage on Colin and Carrie's ranch, were in their late sixties.

Karl gave a sour look as he limped through the door and said tightly, "I've seen it colder."

"Yeah," said Kurt, "so have I."

"Good morning, gentlemen," Carrie said, doing her best to sound cheerful.

They did not return her greeting. Instead, Karl turned to

Colin. "I'd like to talk to both of you. Where shall we go?"

Carrie exchanged a glance with her husband, then met Karl's cold gray eyes and said, "How about the kitchen? There's a good fire burning in the cookstove. I could make some coffee."

"Not interested in socializing, ma'am," Karl said. "Just need to sit down and have a talk about your delinquency in the mortgage payments. Today is Thursday, February 2. When we closed this deal, you were to have each month's payment in the mail so I would receive it no later than the first day of each month. I keep thinking a check will come with the sufficient amount to catch you up. But it hasn't happened in spite of all your good intentions. So, when there was no check in yesterday's mail, I told Kurt I wanted him to bring me here today for this talk."

"Please come into the parlor, Mr. Devlin," Colin said. "Let us explain our situation. Believe me, being three months behind on our mortgage payments, we—"

"Four months now," Karl said.

"Uh…yes, sir. Four months. Come. Let us explain what's been happening to our cattle, which of course, affects our income."

An hour later, Colin and Carrie stood at the window of the front door and watched the Devlin brothers glide away in the sleigh.

"Honey," Colin said, "let's talk to the Lord about this some more. Our lives—as well as our cattle and our ranch—are in His hands."

Carrie nodded, then said, "Before we pray, I should tell you that when Mr. Devlin mentioned this is February 2, it came to me that the Jack Bower–Julianna LeCroix wedding is tomorrow evening. We planned to go, remember?"

"I do, now that you bring it up. With all this cougar business, it escaped my mind. As long as the weather stays like this, we certainly should go. So, maybe we could go to the store and talk to Hannah in the afternoon, then attend the wedding in the evening?"

Carrie shook her head. "No, honey. Even though Hannah is in her ninth month of pregnancy, she's going to help Rebecca Kelly and some of the other women of the church prepare for the reception in the fellowship hall."

Colin grinned. "That sounds like Hannah. From what we've learned about her since we moved here, she always thinks of others before herself."

"Mm-hmm. Oh, that I could be like her."

"Well, you come a lot closer than I do." He rubbed his chin. "I'm trying to remember…"

"Remember what?"

"Julianna, of course, is a widow and has that adorable little girl. But has the deputy marshal been married before?"

"No. This will be the first for Deputy Bower. Did you ever hear how they met?"

Colin shook his head.

"Well, it's quite a story. Rebecca Kelly told me about it that day I went to the church ladies' meeting in December. I'll have to tell it to you sometime."

"I'd like to hear it."

"But right now we'd best have our prayer session."

"That's right," said Colin. "Let's go to the parlor."

When they knelt beside the couch together, Colin took Carrie's hand and said, "Dear Father, we come to You in Jesus' name as Your children, asking for Your help in this very difficult time in our lives. You have told us in Your Word that You will supply all of the needs of Your born-again children.

"Lord, we need to stop those mountain lions from killing our cattle. And we need the money to pay Karl Devlin what we owe on the mortgage. We also need some credit from Hannah Cooper so we can put some groceries in our pantry."

Colin heard Carrie begin to sniffle as he went on to tell the Lord that they understood He had a reason for allowing these things to come into their lives so He could show His mighty hand of deliverance, in His own way and His own time. Colin's voice broke slightly as he told the Lord that no matter how much He tested them, like Job of old, even though He slay them, yet would they trust in Him.

When they rose to their feet, Colin held Carrie lightly in his arms and said, "Sweetheart, our heavenly Father has a plan for our lives, and these hard times we're experiencing right now are part of that plan."

She laid her head against his chest and said, "Remember that sermon Pastor Kelly preached a couple of months ago when he took us to the Twenty-third Psalm and pointed out the two times it speaks of the Shepherd and says, 'He leadeth me'?"

Colin squeezed her tight. "I'll never forget that sermon. What a mental picture he gave us! The tender Shepherd leading His sheep through this life. And since He's leading us, He's out front on our path. Nothing can get to His sheep unless the Shepherd causes it or allows it."

CHAPTER TWO

L ight snow fell from a leaden evening sky as the wedding took place inside Fort Bridger's church. Julianna LeCroix slipped her hand into the crook of Jack Bower's arm and moved forward with him. Before mounting the steps to meet Pastor Andy Kelly on the platform, they paused to gaze into each other's eyes.

The building was packed, and the overhead lanterns cast a mellow glow on the faces of the congregation. This glow paled, however, in comparison to the radiant eyes of the bride and groom.

Hannah Cooper sat on a pew near the front with Gary and Glenda Williams on one side of her and her four children on the other. She brushed a falling tear from her cheek as she thought about the bizarre way Jack and Julianna had met and fallen in love, and she praised the Lord in her heart for bringing them together.

Hannah's six-year-old daughter, Patty Ruth, sat next to her, wondering why her mother was crying. Next to Patty Ruth was her sister, thirteen-year-old Mary Beth. Sitting on her lap was Julianna's little daughter, Larissa Catherine, who was almost fourteen months old. Larissa was squirming in Mary Beth's arms, wanting down so she could totter to her mother.

Mary Beth tightened her grip on the wiggling child and

whispered into her tiny ear, "Larissa, I'll give you a special treat if you will sit still for me."

Larissa glanced at her mother, who was about to mount the steps to stand before the preacher, then looked up into Mary Beth's eyes.

"I promise," Mary Beth whispered.

As the decision was made, Larissa's chubby thumb found its way into her mouth, and she laid the back of her head against Mary Beth's chest. Though she didn't take her huge brown eyes from her mother, she sat perfectly still.

As bride and groom mounted the steps to the platform, Julianna's midnight blue velvet dress shimmered in the lantern light, and the gleam was reflected in her shiny black hair piled high on her head.

Hannah Cooper glanced across the aisle to two couples who sat together: town marshal Lance Mangum and Heidi Lindgren and Heidi's sister, Sundi, and Dr. Patrick O'Brien. Sundi was the town's schoolmarm, and young Dr. O'Brien had come to Fort Bridger just recently to become a partner in his father's medical practice.

Hannah smiled to herself as she focused on Lance and Heidi. Romance had budded between them, and they were obviously deeply in love. *It won't be long before they are at the altar.*

Hannah's line of sight shifted to Patrick and Sundi. A warmth spread through her, and she smiled to herself again. Though the doctor and the schoolmarm were just getting to know each other, it was obvious that romance was budding there, too.

When Hannah's eyes went back to Jack and Julianna, Pastor Kelly was speaking about marriage and its sacredness in the eyes of God.

Tears welled up in Hannah's eyes again, and as she used a hanky to dab at them, her peripheral vision saw Patty Ruth gazing up at her. Hannah smiled and patted the child's head, then sniffed and looked back at the bride and groom.

Patty Ruth sighed, then set her eyes on Jack and Julianna, wondering once more what there was to cry about.

When the pastor prompted them, Jack and Julianna gazed into each other's eyes and repeated the age-old wedding vows. Then Jack placed the ring on Julianna's finger and repeated the vows that went with it. When he was given permission to kiss his bride, there were oohs throughout the crowd as he held the kiss for some time.

After praying for the new home that had just been established, the pastor nodded with a smile, and the bride and groom turned to face the congregation. Julianna took hold of Jack's arm as Pastor Kelly said, "Ladies and gentlemen, it is my privilege to introduce to you Mr. and Mrs. Jack Bower!"

Patty Ruth looked up to see both her mother and "Aunt" Glenda crying and wiping tears. She shook her head, totally puzzled.

The bride and groom rushed up the aisle as the organ played a fast tune. When they were in the vestibule, Pastor Kelly announced that the reception would be held immediately in the fellowship hall.

After going through the reception line, Hannah Cooper looked for her children and saw them gathered in a group of other children on the opposite side of the hall. Nothing could have kept her from attending the wedding of her dear friends, but she was rapidly becoming quite tired, and she looked around for a place to sit down. She was now in her ninth month of pregnancy and felt uncomfortable most of the time.

Dr. Frank O'Brien happened to look across the room as Hannah eased herself carefully onto a wooden chair. He excused himself to the group and headed her way.

When Hannah saw the silver-haired physician in front of her with a question forming on his lips, she said, "I'm fine, Doc."

He bent over her and raised his bushy gray eyebrows. "You don't *look* fine, Hannah. You look peaked to me, and your eyes tell me you're worn out. I know you wouldn't have missed the wedding unless you were flat on your back, but it's time you were going home."

"Now, Dr. O'Brien, don't be an old grandma. I'll only stay a short while, then I'll have Chris walk me home. I won't overdo. I promise."

Doc sighed and shook his head. "All right, Wyoming's second most stubborn woman. But I'll be watching you."

"*Second* most stubborn? You don't mean Edie is more stubborn than I?"

Doc chuckled. "I've been married to her for nigh onto fifty years, Hannah. I'm qualified to name her just what she is…but you sure run a close second. Now, like I said, I'll be watching you."

Hannah gave him a mischievous grin. "Oh, I'm sure you will."

Doc shook his head, then walked away.

Hannah smiled after him and saw Abe and Mandy Carver coming her way.

When they drew near, Mandy said, "Hannah, dear, you look plenty worn out."

"She sure does, honey," said the town's blacksmith. "I'm a-thinkin' she should be headin' home. Do you want us to walk you home, Hannah?"

"Thank you, Abe, but I want to stay just a little longer. I'll have Chris walk me home pretty soon."

"Promise?" Mandy said.

"Honey, I've already promised the ancient doctor that I will, and he's got hawk eyes on me right now."

The Carvers turned to find Dr. O'Brien. Even though he was standing with a group of men, he was looking toward Hannah. When his eyes met those of the Carvers, he grinned at them and waved.

"See what I mean?" said Hannah. "A gal can't get away with anything when he's around."

The Carvers laughed and moved on.

Just then, Hannah saw Edie O'Brien talking to her husband while looking her way. Edie was nodding as Doc said something. She playfully slapped his arm, then headed toward Hannah, grinning. When she drew up, she said, "Honey, Doc just told me what he labeled you."

"You mean Wyoming's second most stubborn woman?"

"Yes."

"He's a case, he is," said Hannah with a sigh.

"I agree, but he does care about you and that baby. You *will* go home pretty soon, won't you?"

"I'll have to, or ol' hawk eye will be over here again."

Edie's portly body jiggled as she laughed, then she bent over and kissed Hannah's forehead. "Good. See you later."

"Yes. Later." Hannah smiled at Edie's back as she walked away.

As the people passed by the bride and groom in the reception line, many of them found their way to Hannah.

As the evening wore on, Pastor Andy Kelly and his wife, Rebecca, made it a point to compliment Mary Beth Cooper, who was keeping little Larissa occupied while her mother and her new husband were busy talking to friends. They noted that the baby was stuffing horehound candy in her mouth—a result of Mary Beth's promise during the ceremony.

People continued to come by and talk to Hannah. At one point, she saw Colin and Carrie Wright approaching. She managed a tired smile and said, "Well, there's the boss of the Box W and her assistant!"

The Wrights laughed, and Colin replied, "You've got that right, ma'am."

"How are you feeling, Hannah?" Carrie asked.

"A bit tired, but I'm all right. And how are things with the Wrights? Are you still having problems with the cougars?"

Colin nodded. "We are. We were hoping to be able to sell more beef to Cooper's General Store, but we just don't have it."

Hannah's brow furrowed. "I figured so. Have you had more head killed since we talked about it just before Christmas?"

"We've lost almost a third of the herd."

"Oh, I'm so sorry. I'm sure it's this severe winter that's got the wild animals running hungry. From what I've been told, they don't just kill cattle indiscriminately. It's only because their normal winter game have gone to other areas or have starved to death themselves."

"That's right," said Colin. "Ordinarily, cougars don't bother a rancher's cattle."

He paused and cleared his throat. "Hannah…Carrie and I would like to come by the store tomorrow and talk to you in private. It's very important."

"Why, of course."

"Is there a time that would be best?"

"Morning might be best, since I do tend to wear out by midday."

"All right. We'll be there in the morning. That is, if this storm doesn't get any worse. As long as it just snows it'll be no problem. Blizzard conditions could keep us from making it to town, like that storm did last week. We hated to miss church, but it was unavoidable."

"None of our farm and ranch people made it to church last Sunday," Hannah said.

Other people were drawing up now, wanting to talk to Hannah.

Before moving away, Colin said, "We'll see you sometime around ten o'clock in the morning, Hannah."

"That will be fine. It will give us a chance to get better acquainted."

"We'll look forward to it," said Carrie.

Hannah watched them walk away as Captain John Fordham and his wife, Betsy, drew up.

Hannah looked across the room and saw Dr. O'Brien observing her. *Uh-oh. Time to head for home before the O'Briens escort me themselves!*

Hannah was having a restless night. She could find no comfortable position, and the baby had decided to be active. She heard the old grandfather clock in the parlor chime 2:00 A.M., and then heard Chris leave his room to throw additional logs on the fire.

"Bless him, Lord," she whispered. "He's such a good boy. He has so marvelously shouldered the load, doing his best to fill his father's boots."

When she heard Chris return to his room, Hannah sat up and rubbed her swollen middle. "Baby Cooper, you just aren't going to let your mother rest tonight, are you?"

She rose from the bed and put on her robe, shuffling her feet into the slippers B.J. had given her for Christmas. She picked up a folded blanket from the foot of the bed and wrapped it around her shoulders, then moved to the rocker by the window and sat down.

By the vague light from a street lantern, she could tell it was still snowing. At least there was no wind.

As Hannah rocked and watched the falling snow, her mind went to the wedding. It had been such a blessing to see Jack and Julianna take their vows. That poor lady had suffered more than her share of heartaches. Hannah was glad Jack was so crazy about baby Larissa, and vice versa. He was going to make a good father.

These thoughts sent Hannah's mind to her own fatherless children, including the little one in her womb. A deep loneliness came over her as her heart yearned for Sol, who had been in heaven for some six months.

As was her custom since Sol's death, she talked to him when her heart was troubled, even though she knew he couldn't actually hear her. But opening her heart in this way always gave her a measure of comfort.

Hannah looked out the window toward the heavy sky and said, "Oh, Sol, I miss you so much. The children miss you so much, too. Chris is doing a marvelous job in his effort to be the man of the house. Mary Beth is maturing so quickly, Sol. It's more like she's nineteen than thirteen. And B.J. is so concerned about this baby. He can't do enough around here for me. If he had his way, I'd do nothing but sit all the time. Then, of course, there's our little redhead. I think Patty Ruth is about to lose a tooth or two. She hasn't said anything yet, but I've caught glimpses of her pushing on the two front ones."

At that moment, Hannah heard Patty Ruth talking in her sleep, and the sound of the family's pet rat terrier's claws tap the floor.

"Oh, yes, Sol. Biggie misses you, too."

The sound of the little dog padding down the hall met her ears. She smiled. "Biggie doesn't stay on P.R.'s bed when she talks in her sleep. He's no doubt on his way to the boys' room. Chris or B.J. will have a bed partner shortly."

Hannah sat in silence for a while. When the grandfather clock struck three times, she struggled out of the rocker and made her way into the hall. There was light in the hall from the fireplace. She went quietly to the boys' room and looked in. Sure enough, Biggie was snuggled up close to B.J., half of his body on the pillow. He raised his head and looked at her. "It's all right, boy," she whispered. "Go to sleep."

When she reached the girls' room, both girls were fast asleep, but Patty Ruth's feet were peeking out from under the covers. Her toes were wiggling slightly. Hannah moved up to the bed and smiled at those little feet that were never still, then gently covered them up.

Feeling a chill creep over her, she made her way to the parlor, placed another log on the fire, then went back to her room. She slipped between the blankets and sank down into the feather bed. Silently thanking God for His blessings, she closed her weary eyes, found the most comfortable position she could, and let sleep claim her.

Waking at her usual early hour, Hannah yawned and glanced toward the bedroom window. The sky was clear and quite bright, though the sun had not yet lifted above the horizon.

Struggling once again to get out of bed, she slipped into her cozy robe, pressed her feet into her slippers, and made fast work of straightening up the bed. Biggie was in the hall, looking up at her and wagging his tail. She patted his head, saying in a whisper, "You need to go out, don't you?"

Immediately, the little dog made a dash for the door and waited patiently while Hannah waddled after him. As soon as she opened the door, Biggie was outside like a bullet. Hannah tossed two logs on the dwindling fire in the parlor, then went to the kitchen. A few coals were still glowing in the cookstove. She stirred them up, tossed in some kindling, and went about taking things out of the cupboard and pantry to prepare breakfast.

As soon as the kindling was burning good, she dropped three small logs in the stove and went back to her food preparation. In her clumsy condition, it seemed to take her twice as long to do everything. But by the time she heard the children getting up, she had a hot breakfast almost ready.

Soon there was a scratching at the door, along with a whine. Hannah let Biggie in and he dashed to the fireplace, turning his shivering backside to the fire.

Mary Beth came into the kitchen and mildly scolded her mother for not awakening her to fix breakfast.

When the boys appeared, Hannah greeted them and asked if one of them would go downstairs and tell Jacob that breakfast was ready. Though Jacob sometimes fixed his own breakfast in his quarters, he had a standing invitation to eat breakfast with the family.

B.J. hurried to the coat rack, saying it was his turn to go down to "Uncle" Jacob, then dashed out the door.

Soon the little redhead put in an appearance and had to suffer playful persecution from her oldest brother for being a sleepyhead.

It was a happy group at the Cooper breakfast table as the children told Jacob about the wedding. They understood that as a Jew he was uncomfortable taking part in any activity that involved the church. He had visited the services twice as a favor to Pastor Kelly, and even though Hannah had given him the gospel many times, he still held to his faith and maintained his Jewish practices. Since this was the Sabbath, he would not be working in the store.

When breakfast was over, Jacob thanked Hannah for including him once again in their meal, then pushed back his chair. When Hannah rose to her feet, a wave of dizziness washed over her and she grabbed the back of the chair.

It was a race between Chris and Jacob to get to her first. Both of them took hold of her. "I'll be all right in a minute," Hannah said, then closed her eyes and waited for the dizziness to pass.

"We've got a good hold on you," Jacob said. "Come on. Sit down."

"You all right, Mama?" Chris asked.

She nodded. "Yes. It's easing off now."

"Should we get Grandpa O'Brien, Uncle Jacob?" Mary Beth asked.

Hannah was shaking her head mildly as Jacob said, "No need, honey. These dizzy spells come and go with having babies. At least that's what I've been told."

"Are you having pain anywhere, Mama?"

"No, Mary Beth. Everything's fine."

"Hannah," Jacob said, "maybe you shouldn't go down to the store today."

She met his gaze. "Oh, but I have to. I won't go till after lunch, but I get so lonely up here. I love talking to my customers, even though I have to sit on the chair to do it. And the children have plans for today. They'll be spending time with their friends."

"We could stay home, Mama," said Mary Beth. "Our plans can be changed."

"No, honey. I want you to have your day as planned. Besides, this is Glenda and Mandy's day to run the store for me, and I'd like some time with them. And—oh! I just remembered! Colin and Carrie Wright asked if they could see me in private for a while this morning. They'll be here about ten. Jacob, would you tell Glenda and Mandy that when the Wrights come in to send them up here?"

"I sure will."

"I appreciate it."

His brow furrowed. "Now, sweet lady, if you get to feeling better while the Wrights are here, and you really want to be in the store this afternoon, you tell Colin to knock on my door. Sabbath or no Sabbath, I'll come and help you down the stairs at whatever time you like."

Chris grinned at the little Jewish man. "But Uncle Jacob, you're not supposed to do any work on the Sabbath. Wouldn't that be work—helping Mama down the stairs?"

Jacob chuckled. "Of course not. Doing something for your sweet mama is pleasure, not work."

"Oh," said Chris, a hint of devilment in his eyes. "Then, since Mama has to go down the stairs out there, it would probably be a pleasure for you to shovel the snow off 'em, too, wouldn't it?"

Jacob's wrinkled face creased with a big smile. "Oh no, you don't, boy! It would be a pleasure, yes, but since that chore is yours and B.J.'s, I wouldn't want to rob you of it."

The boys looked at each other and laughed.

"I'm sure glad I'm a girl," spoke up Patty Ruth. "I'd rather do dishes, clean up the kitchen, and do housework than shovel snow, clean out the barn, and that kind of stuff."

"I'd rather be a boy, no matter what," said B.J. "I'd hate to wear dresses and petticoats and hair bows and that kind of stuff."

Patty Ruth laughed. "B.J., you'd look cute wearing a dress with petticoats, and with bows in your hair!"

B.J. turned to Chris and said, "We might as well go ahead and get the snow shoveled."

"Yeah. You can get started while I'm feeding Buster and breaking the ice on his water trough."

"And Patty Ruth and I will do the dishes and clean up the kitchen, Mama," said Mary Beth. "You just find your favorite chair by the fireplace and rest."

"Now that's good talking, Mary Beth," said Jacob. Then he said to Hannah, "You mind your daughter."

"Now, Mr. Kates, I've got Colin and Carrie coming. I'll get my rest while sitting in the store this afternoon. Right now I have things to do."

"But—"

"Jacob, please don't worry yourself about me. My girth may be huge, but I can still manage a few things."

Jacob left, saying he would tell Glenda and Mandy about the Wrights as soon as he heard them come into the store.

Hannah went to her room, intending to do some straightening up in the closet. Suddenly she felt a series of kicks and took hold of the dresser. She bent over a little, patting the mound beneath her breast.

"Not getting enough attention, little one? Well, sweetheart, you will soon make your most welcome appearance. Then Mama will be giving you a whole lot of attention."

CHAPTER THREE

I t was five minutes to ten when Colin and Carrie Wright entered Cooper's General Store. When the small overhead bell jingled, Mandy Carver and Glenda Williams, who were waiting on customers at the counter, waved a greeting.

As one of the customers finished her business and walked away, Mandy motioned to the Wrights, saying, "Miz Hannah told us you were comin' in to see her 'bout ten. She's feelin' a bit weak this mawning, so she didn't come down to the store. She asked that you go up to the apartment to see her."

"Maybe we should come back another time," Carrie said.

Mandy shook her head. "No need, honey. Jacob said Miz Hannah wants you to come up and see her."

"All right," Colin said. "How do we get to the apartment, Mrs. Carver?"

"Jis' go out the back door and you will see the wooden staircase that takes you right up."

Moments later, Chris Cooper opened the apartment door and said, "Good morning, Mr. and Mrs. Wright. Mama's expecting you. Please come in."

After Chris took their coats, Mary Beth ushered them to the parlor where Hannah was seated in her favorite overstuffed chair by the fireplace. In the midst of greetings, Biggie trotted over to the Wrights and looked up expectantly. He wasn't disappointed as Colin talked to him and petted him.

Carrie frowned slightly. "Hannah, we're sorry you're feeling a bit weak this morning. We can come back another time."

"Oh no, I'll be fine. The children are about to leave."

Colin ran his gaze over the faces of Hannah's brood. "We were hoping we'd be able to get to know them better while we're here."

"That will have to be another time," Hannah said. "They all have plans. Chris is riding with Lieutenant Dobie Carlin and a small unit of men to the Crow village north of town. Colonel Ross Bateman wants to know if Chief Two Moons and his people have any needs. Since the chief's son, Broken Wing, is Chris's best friend, Chris is riding along to spend some time with him."

"We were in the church service when Broken Wing was baptized," Colin said. "I recall that it was you who led him to the Lord, Chris."

The young man smiled and nodded.

Colin turned to Mary Beth. "So where are you going, little lady?"

"To spend the day with my teacher, Miss Lindgren. You probably don't know about the classes we teach at the Crow village, do you?"

"No, but it sounds interesting."

"Sure does," said Carrie. "Tell us about it."

Mary Beth explained that her desire was to one day become a teacher. Miss Lindgren had taken her under her wing by letting her teach some of the smaller children at school. And since Miss Lindgren was also teaching the Crow children to read and write English on Saturdays, when the weather was warm, she had asked Mary Beth to be her assistant.

"That's wonderful!" Carrie said.

Mary Beth nodded her head in agreement. "Anyway, I'm going to spend the day with Miss Lindgren so we can work on the lessons we'll be using come spring."

Colin looked at B.J. "And what's your day going to be?"

Hannah spoke up. "B.J. and Patty Ruth are going to the fort to Captain John Fordham's home for the day. Belinda Fordham is Patty Ruth's best friend, and her brother, Will, is B.J.'s best friend."

"Me and Belinda are gonna play with her dolls," Patty Ruth said, "an' with my stuffed bear, Tony."

"Belinda and I," Hannah corrected her.

Patty Ruth looked blankly at her mother. "Mama...*you* are gonna go to Belinda's house and play with her dolls and Tony?"

Hannah gave her youngest daughter a mock scowl. "No, P.R., you know what I meant."

Patty Ruth giggled. "Yeah, but it made Mr. and Mrs. Wright laugh, didn't it?"

The Wrights chuckled, and Carrie said, "Patty Ruth, you are a character!"

"Mm-hmm. That's what lots of people tell me."

Hannah glanced at Chris. "Shouldn't all four of you be going now?"

"You're right, Mama. Guess we'd better."

The children said good-bye to the Wrights and kissed their mother, then went to put on their coats and hurried out the door.

"Wonderful children," Colin said.

"They sure are," said Carrie. "I wish I could have some just like them."

Hannah struggled out of the chair and stood up. "How about some nice hot tea while we talk?"

Moments later, the three were seated at the kitchen table, each with a cup of steaming tea before them.

Hannah smiled at the couple. "Like I told you last night, I'm glad for this time so I can get better acquainted with both of you. How long have you two been married?"

"Ten years," Carrie replied. "That is, it will be ten years on February 25."

"Well, congratulations!" Hannah's voice softened as she added, "Solomon and I would have been married seventeen years this June 6. I was seventeen and he was twenty when we got married."

Carrie reached over and patted Hannah's hand. "Pastor and Mrs. Kelly told us about how your husband died on the way here from Missouri. Gave his life to save you and the children."

Hannah nodded, her lower lip quivering slightly.

Seeing that the subject was still a tender one, Carrie said, "I mentioned a few minutes ago that I wished I could have some wonderful children just like yours…"

"Yes?"

"We haven't been able to have any. The doctor in Laramie told me that I would never be able to conceive, and Dr. Frank O'Brien agrees with that diagnosis."

"I'm sorry," Hannah said. "Children are truly a heritage of the Lord. But in His wisdom, He has some reason for not giving you children. I'm sure you understand that."

"Yes. Our pastor in Laramie helped us to cope with the news, and Pastor Kelly has been a real help, too. It doesn't remove the natural desire for Colin and me to want children, but we've learned to let the Lord give us peace about it."

"That's good," Hannah said. "The Lord seems to give all of us reasons to find His grace sufficient if we'll let Him meet our needs."

"Of course, Hannah, I have considered kidnapping Patty Ruth and taking her home," Carrie said. "She's such a sweet little thing."

Hannah smiled. "Sweet, yes…and quite precocious. I'm amazed sometimes at the things she comes up with." After a brief pause, Hannah said, "But let's talk some more about Colin and Carrie. I knew you came here from the eastern part of Wyoming, but I wasn't aware it was Laramie. Tell me about it and what brought you to this side of the territory."

Colin leaned forward and said, "I worked on a ranch some five miles east of Laramie since about a year before we got married. Carrie and I dreamed about someday having a ranch of our own.

"Early last fall, I learned that a man named Karl Devlin, who owned a ranch some twenty miles southwest of Fort Bridger, was wanting to sell his ranch. Devlin had sustained a leg wound in the Mexican-American War, and it was getting so bad with arthritis that he decided he couldn't do the necessary ranch work anymore."

Hannah nodded. "I've heard of Karl Devlin, but I've never met him."

"So, anyway, I rode from Laramie to the Box D ranch—which is now the Box W—taking what little money Carrie and I had been able to save. Devlin had no other offers on the place and was quite eager to get it sold, so we struck a deal. I paid him some money up front and put a mortgage on the ranch. His cattle herd was part of the deal. We would make payments monthly until the debt was paid, which should take seven years. Devlin, who is widowed, moved to Rock Springs, Wyoming, to live with his widowed brother, Kurt."

"It seems I heard about that," said Hannah. "I recall that it was some rancher west of here who was in the store one day. He told me about Devlin selling his ranch and moving somewhere else to live with his brother. As I recall, the rancher had not gotten along very well with Devlin."

"I can understand that," put in Carrie. "We're having a problem getting along with him ourselves."

"Which brings up why we're here," said Colin. "Last night you asked about the cougars—and we told you that almost a third of our herd has been slaughtered by them. I've tried my best to track the cougars and kill them, but so far they have eluded me. They only come around periodically, and there's no pattern to the time of the attacks. I even stayed up all night, hiding in the barn with my rifle, for several nights in a row. But they never came around."

Hannah shook her head in wonderment. "They really are crafty, aren't they?"

"Hannah," Carrie said, "it's because of so many of our cattle being killed by the cougars that we've had very little beef to sell this past couple of months. As you know, we used to sell beef to Glenda Williams for her café, but we can't do that anymore. Neither have we had much beef to sell to our beef markets in Evanston, Green River, and Rock Springs."

"I believe I understand," said Hannah. "If you sell off many more cows or bulls, you won't have the new crop of calves you need in order to keep the herd growing."

"That's it," Colin said. "So we're in a real tight spot now. I mean, we're in serious financial trouble."

When Hannah saw Carrie's eyes fill with tears, she reached across the table and squeezed her hand.

"You see, Hannah," Colin said, "we are now four months behind in our payments to Karl Devlin. He and his brother showed up on our doorstep on Thursday. Devlin was anything but kind about all this, even though we explained the situation. When I told him I was trying to track the cougars and kill them, but so far had been unsuccessful, he commented that I was a pretty poor tracker. He said he wants the mortgage payments caught up very, very soon or he will sell the ranch to someone else, along with whatever cattle are left. We——" He choked up, then swallowed hard and said, "We just can't lose the ranch, Hannah. We have to come up with some way to pay him. But what we wanted to talk to you about is to ask if you would extend us credit so we can have groceries and the necessary household supplies. We'll find a way to get through this, but right now——"

"I'm not worried about you failing, Colin," Hannah said.

"Of course I will extend you credit. You can have all the groceries and supplies you need on credit until you can get back on your feet financially."

Tears filmed Colin's eyes, and Carrie let out a sob.

"Thank you, Hannah," Colin said. "I can't express how much this means to us."

Hannah nodded. "I understand, Colin." She turned to Carrie. "Honey, don't cry. Everything's going to be all right."

"I'm not crying because I'm afraid it won't, Hannah. I'm crying because of your sweet attitude and your willingness to help us."

Colin stood up and looked down at his wife. "Sweetheart, we need to go so this dear lady can lie down and rest."

Hannah let go of Carrie's hand and said quickly, "Before you go, may I tell you something that might be of encouragement?"

"Of course," Colin said.

"My Bible is on the table by my chair in the parlor. Would you get it for me, please?"

Seconds later, Colin was back with Hannah's Bible and sat down once again at the table.

She opened the pages to the Psalms. "I want to tell you about the sermon Pastor Kelly preached last Sunday evening. It was such a blessing."

"All of his sermons are a blessing," Carrie said. "Tell us what we missed."

Hannah flipped a few pages. "Let me read you his text. It was Psalm 84:5 and 6.

Blessed is the man whose strength is in thee;
in whose heart are the ways of them.
Who passing through the valley of Baca make it a
well;
the rain also filleth the pools.

"Pastor explained that *Baca* means "weeping," and that there is a massive valley in northern Palestine on the direct route south to Jerusalem. In Bible days, the valley was heavy with mulberry trees. Pilgrims who came down from the north country for the Passover feasts had to pass through the valley. The pilgrims would stop to rest in the heat of the day and would often spend the night there and sleep beneath those same mulberry trees for refuge in case it would rain. Pastor said that the mulberry tree, whenever one of its twigs or leaves is wounded by man or wind, exudes from the wound drops of thick saplike tears on the underside. Thus, the valley once dense with mulberry trees became known as the valley of Baca—the valley of weeping."

"My, what a beautiful picture!" Carrie said. "The mulberry trees weeping!"

Colin looked down at Hannah's Bible and touched its pages. "I never cease to marvel at the hidden treasures in this Book."

"The Bible couldn't have come from anyone but the Lord Himself," said Hannah. "It's God's love letter to the human race."

"Yes," Carrie said. "And that love letter is filled with marvelous wonders."

"That it is," said Hannah. "Now, let me tell you where Pastor went from there in his sermon. He pointed out that the valley of Baca in Psalm 84:6 is also used in a figurative way. It presents an image of human life in this world—our troubles and sorrows. God is showing that all believers go through the valley of Baca on their journey toward heaven.

"He said that in order to have a valley there must be mountains on both sides. Christians will have their mountaintop experiences while passing through this world, but at times they will find themselves loaded with heartaches, trials, troubles, and burdens that will take them down into the valley of Baca where they will shed tears of sorrow and grief."

Carrie leaned across the table and took hold of Hannah's hand. "Certainly you know about the valley of Baca…having lost your dear husband last year."

Tears blurred Hannah's vision as the memory of the events leading to Solomon's death entered her mind. "Solomon and I were indeed on the mountaintop the day we drove our covered wagon out of Independence, Missouri, with our precious children. We had stars in our eyes about living in the Wild West and doing our part to help settle the frontier." She drew in a breath and let it out slowly. "When Solomon so unselfishly gave his life to save ours, we came on to Fort Bridger, but our grief was so heavy that we were dragging the very bottom of the deep valley by the time we arrived here. But the Lord is now taking us toward another mountaintop. This little child I'm about to bring into the world is a special gift from God. With this baby in our home, it will be like having a very special part of Solomon still with us."

Then Hannah buried her face in her hands and wept. When she had brought her emotions under control, she looked at the Wrights and started to apologize.

Carrie jumped up from her chair, wrapped her arms around Hannah and said, "You don't have to be sorry for having a tender heart. You've been through horrible grief and sorrow, and I can't even imagine how lonely you must be without your husband."

Hannah nodded. "I didn't know my heart could hurt so much, Carrie. But in spite of the heartache and loneliness, the Lord has proven His grace to be sufficient. I have much to be thankful for. I not only have my four precious children to give me joy, but I'll soon hold this one in my arms, and he—or she—will give me more joy. In addition, the Lord has marvelously met our material needs. The store is doing well and making us a good living. The children and I praise Him every day for this."

"It's no wonder the store is doing well," said Colin. "We heard what you did for the Crows when you found out they were about to starve. And as quickly as you responded to our question about extending us credit, I know you've done it for others, haven't you?"

"Well…yes."

A wide grin curved Colin's mouth. "We reap what we sow, don't we! You've been sowing in a generous way toward people in need, so the Lord is being generous to you."

"That He is, Colin." Now that she had her emotions in control, Hannah said, "I want to finish telling you about Pastor Kelly's sermon. A few minutes ago, I told you that after Solomon died, the children and I came to Fort Bridger at the very bottom of the valley, but the Lord is now taking us to another mountaintop with this new baby coming into our lives."

"You're setting us up a beautiful picture, Hannah," Colin said. "I think you're going to tell us that we can't get to the next mountaintop without passing through the valley."

Hannah chuckled and said to Carrie, "That husband of yours is so smart!"

"Of course. He married me, didn't he?"

Colin grinned at her. "Other than getting saved, honey, that was the smartest thing I ever did."

Carrie shrugged but looked pleased.

"Well, anyway," Hannah said with a chuckle, "in his sermon, Pastor pointed out that in Psalm 84:6, God says, 'Who passing *through* the valley of Baca make it a well.' The Lord is saying that His children won't stay in the valley. They will get through the valley. And beyond the valley lies another mountaintop.

"So, you see, dear friends, right now you are in the valley. Your cattle are being killed by cougars. Karl Devlin is breathing down your neck for his money. Things are pretty bad. When you made the deal on your ranch a few months ago, you were on the mountaintop. Everything was smelling like wildflowers that grow atop the mountains. And then came the trail of sorrows that has taken you down into the valley of tears.

"But David wrote under the inspiration of the Holy Spirit, 'Who passing *through* the valley of Baca make it a well.' Your heavenly Father will take you through the valley. And beyond the valley is another mountaintop."

Colin took hold of Carrie's hand. "It's going to be all right, sweetheart," he said softly. "It's going to be all right."

"Yes, it is," Hannah agreed. "Pastor Kelly pictured Christians standing on top of a mountain, looking ahead on life's path. Suddenly they see another mountaintop ahead. And it's higher than the one on which they are standing. They want to get to that higher mountain, but there is only one way to reach it." She smiled at Colin. "And even as our brilliant rancher here has pointed out, the only way to do that is to pass through the valley."

"You make it sound better than I did," Colin said.

"You should have heard the way Pastor Kelly made it sound!"

"Either way," Carrie said, "it's wonderful."

Hannah looked back at her Bible. "Listen again to verse 5. 'Blessed is the man whose strength is in thee; in whose heart are the ways of them.' The Christian's heart is not like the trackless desert or the wild waste, Pastor Kelly told us. There are 'ways' in it. Ways of truth, righteousness, and holiness. When God's people pass through a time of suffering, disappointment, discouragement, grief, or calamity, they 'make it a well.' And with their faith settled deep in their Father's promises, 'the rain also filleth the pools.' Their faith turns the hard trial into a time of refreshing. Well, that's my version of the sermon."

"And what an encouragement it is!" Carrie said.

"Yes," Colin said. "Thank you for preaching it to us."

Hannah grinned. "Well, I'll leave the preaching to Pastor Kelly. Let's just say I *told* it to you."

Carrie said, "I'm so glad you asked us to stay so you could tell us something that might be an encouragement. Well, dear lady, what you have told us most definitely has encouraged us."

"I'm glad," Hannah said. "Let me add a little something that comes from my own heart. There are always blessings to be found while we're in the valley. We simply must search for them and God will reveal them to us. While you're passing through the valley of Baca, trust the Lord each and every day and let Him make it a time of spiritual refreshing. When you get beyond the valley and stand on your next mountaintop, you'll be able to look back and thank the Lord that in His wisdom He sent you into the valley, and in His love He took you through it."

Colin set appreciative eyes on Hannah. "Thank you, again, Hannah. Carrie, we must go and let Hannah rest."

Carried started to pick up some dishes. "I'll wash up these cups and saucers."

Hannah rose to her feet with some effort. "No, no. I'll just save them for when Mary Beth and Patty Ruth do the dishes this evening."

"Are you sure? It would only take me a few minutes to wash and dry them."

"I'm sure, honey. The girls will take care of them."

Carrie shook her head in amazement. "Hannah, you have such precious, wonderful children."

"Can't argue with that."

Colin went to the clothes tree to get their coats.

As the two women moved that direction, Carrie looked at Hannah's swollen middle and said, "I sure hope everything goes well when you deliver the baby." She paused, then added, "I so much want to be a mother, but the Lord has a reason for making it so I can't bear children."

Hannah wrapped her arms around Carrie. "Honey, the Lord has a mountaintop ahead that will make up for the fact that you can't have children."

Carrie kissed Hannah's cheek. "Thank you for being such a blessing."

Colin held Carrie's coat ready so she could slip her arms into it.

Hannah went to the peg that held her heavy winter coat and said, "Well! Let's take you down to the store so you can load your wagon with whatever you want. I'll rest later."

CHAPTER FOUR

T he team snorted as they pulled the wagon southwest-
ward. Colin and Carrie Wright sat close together under
a heavy blanket, squinting against a sunstruck world of
whiteness. Their wagon bed was well stocked with groceries
and supplies.

As the wagon rolled along, they discussed the truths of
the Scripture Hannah had shared with them and talked opti-
mistically of the day when they would find themselves beyond
the valley and on a new mountaintop.

Even as they talked, their eyes focused on the jagged,
snow-covered peaks of the Uintah Mountains. Their ranch was
near the northern tip of the Uintah Range and almost touched
the foothills. It was midafternoon, but still the temperature had
not risen to more than ten or fifteen degrees.

"Honey," Colin said, "I've been thinking about this financial
bind we're in. The Lord expects me to do everything I can to
bring in some money. It looks like I'll have to find a job and
spend my off time to do the ranch work. A couple of weeks ago,
when we were in town, and you were at the dress shop, I had
Abe Carver put new shoes on the team. Charlie Goodman came
in while I was there. He runs the saddle and harness shop…"

Carried nodded. "I haven't met him, but I've heard his
name."

"Charlie and Abe were discussing the town's growth, and

Charlie said his business was doing so well he was seriously thinking about hiring some help. He hoped he could find an experienced man."

Colin guided the wagon off the road and took the winding lane toward their ranch.

"As a rancher I've learned a whole lot about leather work—saddles, bridles, and harnesses. So what I've been thinking about is going into town tomorrow and approaching Charlie about hiring me. If I could get some income generated, we could catch up on the payments to Mr. Devlin. What do you think?"

"Well, honey, that might be the way to go. I hate to—" Carrie stopped midsentence when her glance took in the corral. "Oh, Colin, look! Cougars!"

Even as she spoke, Colin saw two cougars vault over the corral fence and race toward the woods. He yanked on the reins and jumped out, his nearly frozen fingers clumsily pulling out his revolver. He stumbled through the snow a few steps, then drew a bead on the cougars and fired. When he fired a second shot, one of the cougars stumbled, then rolled over but got up to follow its partner.

Carrie pulled the blanket up to her chin and watched as Colin continued to plow through the deep snow after the cats. When he reached the spot where the cougar had gone down momentarily, he saw crimson spots on the pristine snow and a thin trail of blood leading into the woods.

He returned to the wagon as fast as he could, his breath coming out in clouds as he said, "I'm going after them. There'll be a blood trail to follow now!"

Moments later, Colin guided the team to the back porch and pulled rein, then hopped out and went around to Carrie's side to help her down.

"You go inside, Carrie. I'll unload the wagon when I get back."

Without another word, Colin moved toward the corral. When he rounded the barn on the back side, he saw a dead cow lying in a circle of cattle. Anger welled up inside him. He looked around, but the rest of the herd appeared to be untouched.

When he headed back toward the house, he saw that Carrie was still on the porch, watching him.

"Honey, you're cold. Why didn't you go inside?"

"I wanted to hear what you'd found."

"One cow and her unborn calf are dead. Come on, let's go in."

When they stepped into the kitchen, Colin picked up the Winchester, checked the loads, and stuffed more cartridges in his coat pocket. "When I track down the wounded one, I hope his pal will be with him. I'll kill them both."

He reloaded the revolver, dropped it back into his holster, and picked up the rifle, then moved to Carrie and kissed her tenderly. "I'm going to end this cougar siege right now."

"Be careful, darling. Remember Bart Flaherty."

He kissed her again. "I'll be careful. Be back after I take care of those two beasts."

Colin tugged his collar up, closed the door behind him, and headed for the barn. Still in her coat, scarf, and mittens, Carrie watched him through the window in the back door.

She waited until he came out of the barn leading his horse, then she stepped out on the porch. "Darling, please be careful!"

Colin gave her a wave, then trotted away.

Carrie watched her husband ride off toward the dense forest and prayed for his safety and success in killing the cougars. A cold wind was coming up out of the west. Shivering, she wheeled and went into the house.

The fires in the cookstove and the parlor fireplace had gone out. As soon as she had rebuilt both fires, Carrie returned to the kitchen and stood in front of the stove, trying to catch what warmth the flames were giving off. After a time, she hung up her scarf and coat and took her apron off its peg, tying it snugly around her waist.

After filling the teakettle and placing it on a burner, she filled a large vat with water and placed it on the stove, then sorted the laundry. She hauled in a large galvanized tub from the back porch and filled it with rinse water. When the teakettle began whistling, she lifted it from the burner and poured boiling water into the pot, adding tea leaves.

While waiting for the wash water to heat sufficiently and the tea to brew, she decided not to wait for Colin and went to the wagon to carry in the groceries and supplies. When she had placed everything in its place in the cupboard and pantry, she began washing clothing, linens, and bedding on the old washboard.

Periodically she took a sip of tea, always with an eye toward the window, watching for Colin to ride in from the forest. A soft prayer formed on her lips for God's leadership and grace in their lives.

Colin Wright kept his horse at a trot until he reached the edge of the dense timber, then slowed to a walk, weaving the animal cautiously through the trees as he followed the wounded cougar's trail.

The forest density broadened ahead of him and climbed the foothills onto the sides of the Uintah Mountains. It remained dense until it reached the ten-thousand foot level. By the time the thinning trees were near timberline at eleven thousand feet, they played out, and the snow-capped peaks continued up to above thirteen thousand feet.

Colin glanced now and then at the mountains and saw the jumbled masses of ice-rimmed boulders glistening in the light. The frozen ice looked blue in the shadows, and streams of ice pitched steeply downward toward jagged walls of thinning timber that almost seemed to be creeping up the steep slopes, waiting for spring thaw to feed on the moisture from above.

Colin's horse nickered as they came upon a clearing. He pulled rein, glanced down at the bloody trail, then nudged the gelding forward. As they rounded a thick stand of birch and conifer, the horse nickered again. Colin drew to a stop and looked into the clearing some thirty yards ahead.

His heart leaped in his breast. The wounded cougar was bellied down in the snow, licking its right foreleg. As he slipped from the saddle Colin could feel the gelding tremble.

"You stay here, boy," he said in a low tone.

Working the lever of the Winchester as quietly as possible, he eased up to a huge pine tree, then threaded his way from tree to tree until he was at the edge of the clearing.

He raised the rifle to his shoulder, carefully drew a bead on the back of the cougar's head, and squeezed the trigger. The Winchester bucked in his hands as the sound of the shot clattered through the forest. The cougar's face dropped into the snow.

Colin jacked another cartridge into the chamber, then held the rifle in ready position and moved toward the crumpled body. When he reached the cougar and saw no sign of life, he said, "Ol' pal, I'm sorry this winter has been so bad that you and your partner were finding food hard to come by. But you went after it at the wrong place. You just about put me out of business, and—"

The gelding gave a shrill whinny and Colin's head whipped around to see the horse dancing nervously. Off to Colin's left, a cougar was coming at him at full speed and was already in the clearing.

Colin swung the rifle to his shoulder and fired. The forest echoed the shot, rolling like thunder, but the shot missed.

Before he could lever another cartridge into the chamber, the cougar was sailing through the air with a blood-curdling roar, fangs bared and claws distended. He hit Colin hard, knocking him flat in the snow.

The cougar's momentum carried him past his intended victim. While the cat skidded to a halt in the deep snow, Colin looked for his rifle. It lay a few feet away and he lunged for it. As his hand closed around the stock, the maddened cougar charged, blue frost billowing from his mouth.

Colin tried to bring the rifle up, but the cougar was on top of him, clawing at his clothing and flesh, its teeth tearing at his face.

He fought back with his bare hands, but it was a losing battle. *The revolver!* He tried to fend off the cougar with his left arm while he pulled the revolver from its holster. Blood was running into his eyes, and his body felt like it was on fire. But the will to live gave him the strength to ear back the hammer of the Colt .45 and press the muzzle against the cougar's belly. He dropped the hammer and the gun roared. The big cat let out a fierce wail, then ejected a grunt and collapsed on top of him.

Colin blinked at the blood pooling in his eyes and sucked hard for air as he struggled to push the lifeless body off him. When the dead cougar was finally off, he lay there a moment, waiting for some strength to flow back into his body. Finally, he made it to a wobbly standing position, but immediately his head began to reel and blackness poured over him like a liquid wave.

When Colin came to, he was lying face down. He groaned in pain as he rolled over to look up at the sun and noted that it was lower in the sky. By the amount of blood staining the snow, he would bleed to death if he didn't get home soon.

He struggled to his feet and stood for a few moments,

swaying. There was a moderate wind blowing, which helped to clear his head. When he looked back into the trees, he saw his horse eyeing him. Like a faithful friend, the gelding had remained where he'd been told to stay.

When Colin tried to call the gelding to him, no sound came out. He stumbled in the direction of his horse and fell about halfway to the edge of the trees.

Desperation filled him and he tried calling to his horse again. Although the sound was barely more than a squeak, this time the gallant animal's ears pricked up.

"Yes, boy!" Colin gasped. "Come! Come to me!"

The gelding bobbed his head and nickered, then trotted into the clearing. When he drew up to Colin, he snorted at the smell of blood.

"You gotta help me, boy," Colin gasped. "Move up a little so I can get hold of the stirrup."

The horse seemed to understand. He snorted again and took a couple of steps forward, lining up the saddle with his master.

Colin crawled closer and reached up toward the stirrup. Pain shot through his shoulder where the cougar's claws had ripped through his coat and deep into flesh. He gripped the stirrup and strained to pull himself to his knees, then used the stirrup strap to pull himself the rest of the way. When Colin was finally in the saddle, his head spinning, he took hold of the reins and said, "All right, boy. Take me home."

At the Crow Indian village some twelve miles north of Fort Bridger, Chris Cooper and Broken Wing were sitting by the fire inside the chief's tepee while Chief Two Moons and his wife, Sweet Blossom, stood at the center of the village, watching the unloading of food and supplies from the army wagon.

"It is a very good thing," Broken Wing said, "what Colonel

Bateman has done. But our people's hearts were touched the most when your mother gave us food when we were about to starve. My father told everyone in the village that your mother faced much opposition from people who thought she was giving us food they could have used."

Chris smiled. "The Lord gave me a wonderful, brave, unselfish mother, my friend. She would have given your people food off her own plate if it came down to it."

"I am sure that is true," said Broken Wing. "Your mother is a very good Christian. Sometimes when I look at her, I can almost see the Lord Jesus Christ in her face."

Chris nodded. "She's very much like Jesus. She walks close to Him. She sure knows her Bible, I'll tell you that."

"I want to know my Bible, too," said Broken Wing. "Ever since you showed me from the Bible how to be saved and I received the Lord Jesus Christ into my heart and was baptized, I have wanted to come to church so I can learn more about God. Every day I read the Bible you gave me, but I understand so little."

"That's because you're very young in the Lord, Broken Wing. And even though Miss Lindgren and my sister have taught you to read and write English, you still have many words to learn. You sure do need to be taught God's Word. That's what church is all about. Not only to get people saved, but to teach them the Bible afterward. I've been praying that the Lord will make a way for you to come to church regularly."

A smile captured Broken Wing's young face. "I asked my father not long ago if he would let me go to church."

"And?"

"He said something really good."

Chris's eyes lit up. "Tell me!"

"He said that when the bad weather goes away, he and my mother are going to come back to church themselves."

"Praise the Lord, Broken Wing! God is answering prayer!

My family has been praying ever since your baptism that the gospel your parents heard that day would sink into their hearts." Chris chuckled. "Talk about my wonderful mother...I've seen big tears roll down her cheeks when she prays for your mother and father to be saved. Just last night during our family prayer time, Mama was crying while she prayed for your parents. Afterwards she talked to us about how much she loves the Crow people. She told us that if the chief and his squaw would become Christians, it would open the door for the other Crows in the village to listen to the gospel."

Broken Wing nodded. "The people will follow Father's leadership. My parents have talked much about the sermon Pastor Andy Kelly preached the day they were in the service. They know there is something to it, because they have seen it in the lives of your mother and the doctors—Frank O'Brien and his son, Patrick. They talk very much about what your mother did for us to keep us from starving, and about the doctors who unselfishly came to the village when we had the influenza epidemic. Though some of our people died, many more would have died if the good doctors had not helped us."

"Have your parents noticed the change in your life since you became a Christian?" Chris asked.

"They have talked about it a lot. They both say I was a good son before, but becoming a Christian has made me even a better son."

As Carrie hung wash on the clothesline, she stood in snow that almost reached the tops of her fur-lined boots. Her fingers were numb and stiff from the cold, but wearing mittens made her hands too clumsy to work.

Every minute or so she glanced southwest where she'd last seen Colin ride.

After hanging one of his shirts on the line, she blew on

her fingers, then took another shirt from the basket, noting that the clothes and linens were frozen almost as soon as they were hung on the line.

Only two dresses left. *When they are hung up,* she told herself, *I can go back into the warmth of the house.* Then she realized the wagon had not yet been put under the shelter beside the tool shed and the team taken to the barn and unharnessed. *Well, after I take care of that, I can return to the house.*

She looked at her hands that were blue with cold. Blowing on them wasn't working anymore. She stuffed them into her coat pockets.

After a minute or so had passed, she bent over and lifted a half-frozen dress out of the basket, along with two clothespins, and moved to an open spot on the line. When the dress was secured, she went back to the basket and picked up the last dress. Movement caught her eye and she turned to see a horse trotting toward her.

Colin!

"Oh, dear Lord," she breathed, "he's just got to have good news!"

Carrie fixed her eyes on the horse and blinked as it trotted closer. The stiffened dress fell from her fingers.

Where was Colin? Why would the horse be coming back without—? "Oh, dear Lord," she wailed. "No!"

Suddenly Carrie was running as fast as she could in the deep snow, hurrying to meet the horse. Cold tears shimmered across her vision and trickled down her cheeks like drops of melting ice.

The gelding whinnied as he came to a stop in front of her. There was blood on the saddle and on the horse's coat.

Stroking the horse's face, Carrie said, "Where's Colin, boy?"

He whinnied shrilly and bobbed his head as he stomped a hoof.

She swung the reins over the horse's head and led him

inside the barn and removed the saddle and bridle. She was glad now that she hadn't unhitched the team from the wagon.

Carrie fought the panic rising in her. She went back to the house and hurriedly gathered clean cloths, a couple of quilts, and a bottle of chlorine.

She placed her load in the wagon bed and worked her way onto the seat, all the while begging God to spare Colin's life and help her find him. She snapped the reins and put the team to a run. In spite of the snow's depth, they bounded across the fields, the wagon bouncing and beginning to fishtail.

Over and over Carrie prayed, "Please, merciful Father, let me get to him in time."

Tears blinded her eyes and threatened to freeze on her cheeks, but she brushed them away with her mitten-clad hands.

She followed the two sets of Colin's horse's tracks and kept up the fast pace until she reached the forest, then guided the team into the dense woods, holding them to a walk. Her glance darted from side to side, scanning the snow, as she pushed the team deeper into the woods.

CHAPTER FIVE

Chris Cooper and Broken Wing stood close to Sweet Blossom and Chief Two Moons, watching the braves and soldiers put the last of the food and supplies in one of the tepees.

Lieutenant Dobie Carlin moved to the Crow leader and said, "We'll be going now, Chief."

Two Moons laid a hand on Carlin's shoulder. "Please give my thanks to Colonel Ross Bateman. And this chief's thanks also goes to you and your men for bringing these gifts to us."

"It was our pleasure, Chief."

Emotion moistened the chief's eyes. "It means very much that Colonel Ross Bateman and the people of the fort care that we have enough food and other necessary items."

Sweet Blossom smiled and nodded her agreement.

Dobie grinned, then placed a hand on the chief's shoulder in the same manner and said, "We have not forgotten how you and your people gave shelter to our soldiers during that blizzard several weeks ago. Some of our men would have died had you not taken us in. It is the army's pleasure to provide anything we can for you and your people."

Two Moons smiled, then took a step back to stand beside his squaw. "I must not detain you, Lieutenant Dobie Carlin. Go with my deep gratitude."

Dobie saluted and pivoted to face the waiting soldiers. "All right men...mount up!"

Broken Wing moved to his parents' side and set his gaze on his father. "Father, Chris Cooper and I have been talking about the church. How long will it be until we go to the church again?"

Two Moons smiled. "We will go soon, my son. In a few moons the weather will be warmer. It will be easier for your mother to travel to town."

Chris said, "It will make my mother very happy to see you and your family at church again, Chief Two Moons."

"Chris Cooper, I very much want to make your mother happy. She is the most generous person this chief knows."

Chris shook hands Indian-style with Two Moons and Broken Wing, made a slight bow to Sweet Blossom, then hurried to his horse and mounted. He looked down to see that Broken Wing had followed and was standing beside his horse.

"The Lord bless you, Broken Wing," Chris said.

"And may He bless you, too, my friend."

Chris rode away at the lieutenant's side. The other mounted men followed with the empty wagon bringing up the rear.

When they were about to pass from view, Chris turned around in the saddle and gave his friend a wave.

As Carrie guided the horses through the forest, the snow cracked beneath their hooves and the wagon wheels. She hunched her shoulders against the cold wind and pulled her coat collar up tighter, adjusting the scarf to better cover her ears.

Although the gelding's hoofprints led her on, the deeper she went into the forest without finding Colin, the more fearful she became. She would never forget how Bart Flaherty had been found dead, mauled by cougars. His widow had lost control of herself at his funeral service and screamed like an insane person. She had to be carried out. It took Frank and Patrick O'Brien three days to bring her to a place of reason again.

The gelding's hoofprints seemed to go on forever. A gust of wind came down from the treetops and sent a swirling funnel of snow particles into Carrie's face. She wiped them away and peered through the trees ahead.

The sun was near the peaks of the Uintahs now, and the temperature was steadily dropping. Each breath Carrie drew in was like a thin blade slicing her lungs.

Oh, Colin...where are you? Her throat went tight and she was curiously aware that her heart was growing heavy like a stone in her chest.

Through the trees she could see a clearing up ahead. The gelding's hoofprints led straight to it. A moment later, she noted a spot in the snow where a horse had been standing for at least a brief time. There were droppings, and the snow was packed down in a circle of hoofprints.

Suddenly Carrie's eyes fell on a dark mound at the edge of the clearing. Twenty yards beyond it, in the center of the clearing, were two more mounds covered with fur. Cougars...*dead* cougars.

"Colin!" she cried, and coaxed the team to the edge of the clearing.

As she climbed from the wagon her eyes stayed riveted on the form lying in the snow. Her stomach drew inward on itself until it felt like a clenched ball the size of her fist. She stumbled through the frozen depth and fell to her knees beside her husband.

Just as she took hold of his shoulder to turn him over, she saw the rise and fall of his back. "Oh, darling...you're alive!"

Her relief was cut short when she turned him over. Colin's face and neck had been horribly clawed. His upper clothing was in shreds, and his chest was soaked in blood.

Colin stared at her with glassy eyes. "C-Carrie…" The words emerged as a hacking whisper. "I found the one I shot. Killed him. The other one came from the woods…attacked me. I shot him with my revolver. I…I remember struggling into the saddle. Must have fallen off my horse."

"He came home," Carrie said. "Don't talk, darling. You're bleeding badly. I've got to get you in the wagon and take you to the clinic in Fort Bridger."

Carrie gripped Colin's coat at the shoulders and dragged him to the rear of the wagon. When she attempted to lift him, she couldn't do it. "Colin," she said, panic riding her voice, "can you muster enough strength to help me get you in the wagon bed?"

"I'll do my best. My strength is almost g—"

Colin's words were cut off when both horses whinnied shrilly. Carrie looked around and saw a cougar threading its way through the trees.

A deep growl came from its throat as it moved like a shadow to the edge of the woods and looked toward the dead cougars, then swung its eyes toward the wagon and snarled. The big cat's eyes were a golden amber color. It snarled again, showing fangs.

"My rifle…" Colin said, his voice coming out barely above a whisper. "My rifle's somewhere in the snow…by other cougars. It's our only hope…got to find the rifle and shoot…'

Carrie swallowed hard, her eyes fixed on the cougar.

"Move slow," said Colin. "Slow…steady. Crawl on your hands and knees. Not…as much…threat if you stay low."

Carrie's heart was banging her ribs as she began crawling toward the dead cougars, asking the Lord to keep the deadly beast where it was until she could find the rifle and shoot it. She had only moved about ten yards when she spied the rifle. It was another ten yards away.

Staying as close to the snow-covered ground as she could,

she moved steadily, keeping her eye on the cougar. It was watching her carefully, hissing and swinging its long tail back and forth.

Colin felt himself getting dizzy. He picked up a handful of snow and held it against his forehead and kept his other hand pressed tightly against the gash on the side of his neck, trying to stay the flow of blood. "Please, God," he breathed, "don't let me pass out."

The cougar still had not moved when Carrie reached the Winchester. She lay flat on the ground and picked it up with trembling hands. She slowly levered a cartridge into the chamber of the Winchester. "Help me, Lord, to shoot straight," she prayed in a low whisper as she swung the rifle into place, pressing it against her shoulder.

The cougar waved its tail, looking at the nervous horses and then at Carrie, as if trying to decide at which point to attack.

Carrie drew a bead on the center of the beast's chest, held her breath, then squeezed the trigger.

The rifle bucked against her shoulder as sound exploded the air. The slug found its mark and the cougar made a tiny grunt before dropping dead in its tracks.

The horses whinnied but stayed in place.

"Thank You, Lord," Carrie said as she jumped to her feet and ran toward the wagon. "I got him, Colin! I got him!"

"Good girl," he said, smiling faintly.

She laid the rifle on the wagon seat, then stepped directly in front of Colin and held out her hands. "Now let's get you in the wagon."

Summoning every ounce of his strength, Colin used Carrie's hands to make it to his feet.

"All right," she said, slipping an arm around his waist, "into the wagon."

As they moved to the rear of the vehicle, Colin's knees

gave way, and he sagged into the snow. "Honey…I can't…I can't…"

"Yes, you can," she said firmly, taking hold of his hands as before.

Once again Colin got to his feet, and this time he made it to the tailgate. With their combined strength they got him into the wagon bed face down.

"Can you crawl onto the quilt, darling?"

As soon as Colin was lying on the quilt, she covered him with another quilt. "It looks like your worst wound is on the side of your neck," she said. "I'll tie a cloth around it, then we've got to get you to town."

After tying the cloth, she closed the tailgate and hurried to the front of the wagon. The sun was partially behind the mountains now. She was on the verge of tears as she climbed onto the seat and took the reins.

"Hurry, Carrie," Colin said weakly. "Make the horses go…fast as they can."

"I will," she said, snapping the reins.

"I love you, Carrie," Colin said weakly. Then he passed out.

Carrie drove like the wind toward town.

Darkness had fallen when Carrie drove the wagon into Fort Bridger. She knew the clinic would be closed, but chances were good that Dr. Frank O'Brien and his wife would be in their apartment upstairs. It was suppertime.

She brought the wagon to a halt in front of the O'Brien Clinic, noting the lights in the windows of the apartment upstairs. There was also light showing through the shades of the office windows.

She glanced over her shoulder at Colin and saw that he was breathing but still unconscious. As far as she knew, he hadn't regained consciousness since they left the clearing in the forest.

Just as she climbed from the wagon and touched ground, the office door opened and Dr. Patrick O'Brien hurried across the boardwalk. "Carrie, is something wrong?"

"It's Colin! He's in bad shape!"

Patrick took one look at the bleeding man and dropped the tailgate to reach into the bed. He picked up Colin and cradled him in his arms like he would a child.

As Carrie followed the doctor into the clinic, she attempted to describe what had happened.

As soon as Patrick placed Colin on an examining table, he said, "Please go up to the apartment and tell my dad I need him. It's going to take both of us to stop Colin's bleeding. Hurry!"

Trembling all over, Carrie nodded and turned toward the back door.

Patrick was suturing the gash in Colin's neck when Doc, Edie, and Carrie entered the examining room.

Doc set his eyes on Colin and said, "Carrie told us what happened. Looks like the cougar really tore him up."

"Mm-hmm...bad," Patrick said without looking up.

Doc hurried to the medicine cabinet.

"Honey," Edie said softly to Carrie, her arm firmly around the young woman's shoulders, "let's go into the office and let the doctors do their work. We'll only be a few steps away."

Carrie looked at Colin for a moment, then nodded shakily.

Edie guided the young woman to the office and sat her down on a wooden chair, then stoked the dying fire in the pot-bellied stove and dropped in a couple of logs. She poured a cup of water from a pitcher on a shelf and said, "Drink this, honey."

When Carrie had drained the contents of the cup, Edie set it on the shelf, then sat down and took hold of Carrie's hands. "Now, child," she said in a loving tone, "Colin is not only in the hands of two excellent doctors, but he is also in God's hands."

Carrie's face pinched tight and her lower lip quivered. "But why, Mrs. O'Brien? Why?"

"Why did the Lord allow this to happen? Is that what you're asking?"

Tears spilled down Carrie's cheeks. "Yes. Why would the Lord let that cougar do this to Colin? All he was doing was trying to stop our cattle from being slaughtered. We'll lose the ranch if—"

Carrie bent her head toward her lap and broke into sobs.

Edie patted her head and said, "Honey, the Lord doesn't always do or allow things in our lives that our little finite minds comprehend. I can't answer your question, but I can tell you that our heavenly Father never makes a mistake. He had some reason for allowing the cougar to…to hurt him so bad."

"But we've tried so hard to be faithful to the Lord," Carrie said, raising her head up and wiping tears. "Why would He punish us like this?"

"Let's get you out of that coat, Carrie. It's finally getting warm in here."

Edie hung up the coat and scarf and took a clean hanky out of the desk drawer, then sat down in front of Carrie again and handed her the hanky. "You mustn't look at this incident as punishment, honey. When hardships come to God's children, it doesn't always mean they're being punished. As God's children, we have to learn this, even as Job did. You know Job's story, don't you?"

Carrie dabbed at her eyes.

"Well, Job was a faithful servant of the Lord, yet he lost almost everything he had and was smitten with horrible, painful boils on his body. If you recall, Job thought the same thing you're thinking. He wondered what terrible thing he had done to bring that kind of punishment on himself. And his three so-called friends tossed it into his face too, suggesting that he must have done something really bad. Remember?"

Carrie nodded.

"But it was a test to see if Job would stay faithful to the Lord and still love Him, in spite of the catastrophes he had experienced. It was also a test to see if Job would still trust Him, even though God had allowed it all to happen. It may be this kind of thing that you and Colin are experiencing right now. The Lord may very well be testing your love for Him and your faith in Him."

The door of the back room opened and both doctors entered the office, their faces ashen.

Carrie tensed. "Oh, no! No! Please, no!" she cried.

The older physician bent over Carrie and placed a tender hand on her shoulder. "Your husband…well, he had already lost too much blood. We weren't able to save him."

"No-o-o-o! No-o-o-o! It can't be!"

Edie embraced Carrie, holding her tight as she broke into uncontrollable sobs and buried her face against the older woman's shoulder.

Patrick cleared his throat and said, "I'll go get Pastor and Mrs. Kelly."

When the Kellys arrived at the clinic, Carrie was still sobbing. Edie moved aside and Rebecca folded the young widow into her arms while the pastor spoke in soft tones, trying to give her some measure of comfort. But Carrie was inconsolable in her grief, only crying out, "Why? Why, God? Why?"

When it became obvious that she wasn't aware of her surroundings or comprehending anything the pastor was saying, Doc O'Brien prepared a strong sedative and knelt in front of her. Carrie looked at him blankly through a wall of tears, but obediently swallowed the medicine. Her sobbing had diminished to sniffles, but she was breathing heavily. A trancelike expression came over her eyes.

Pastor Kelly looked at the doctors, deep concern showing on his face. "What can we do?"

"We'll keep her here with us," Doc said. "Right now, she's in a deep state of shock. She'll come out of it, I'm sure, once the initial trauma has worn off. We have a spare bedroom in our apartment and can keep a close eye on her."

"Good. Rebecca and I will feel better knowing that she's here with you."

"I'll take her up to the apartment and put her to bed right now," Edie said. "The sedative will take full effect pretty soon and she can sleep."

"I'll carry her upstairs for you, Mom," said Patrick.

"Would you like me to help you get her to bed, Edie?" Rebecca asked.

"Thank you, dear, but I'm sure I can handle it." She leaned over the young woman. "Carrie, honey, Patrick is going to carry you upstairs to the apartment, and I'm going to put you in a nice comfortable bed so you can get some rest. All right?"

Carrie tried to focus on Edie's face as she nodded.

Patrick picked her up and headed for the back room.

"Pastor," Edie said, "you'll understand when you don't see me in church tomorrow. I'll be right here with Carrie."

"Of course," he replied.

Edie hurried away to catch up with Patrick.

"Doc," Kelly said, "at church in the morning I'll talk to some of the ranchers who are members of the church and live toward the southwest. I'm sure they'll see to it that the Wright cattle and horses are fed and watered until we see what Carrie does with the ranch."

"That's good. When her mind clears up, I'll tell her the stock is being taken care of. That'll help her."

Upstairs, Edie followed Patrick into the spare bedroom where he placed Carrie on the bed and then quickly built a fire in the fireplace. When it had caught the kindling and was starting to burn, he headed for the door.

"If I can do anything else, Mom, you just holler."

"I will, dear."

Edie bent over Carrie, who was staring blankly into space, and said, "Honey, can you hear me?"

Carrie nodded slightly.

"What I need you to do is sit up on the edge of the bed so I can get you undressed and into a nightgown."

Carrie swung her legs over the edge of the bed and touched her boots, then gave Edie a helpless look. Her entire body was quivering, and her breathing was still labored.

"I'll take care of them," said Edie, and quickly removed Carrie's wool-lined boots. "Tell you what, Carrie. We'll dispense with the nightgown for now. Let's just get you under the covers. Can you stand up so I can turn the covers down?"

As she spoke, Edie took hold of Carrie's wrists. She guided one of Carrie's hands to the bedstead and said, "Hold on to this, dear, till I can get the covers down."

A few moments later, Edie was pulling the blankets over Carrie's trembling body. When she had her sufficiently tucked in, she pulled up a straight-backed chair and sat down.

"Sweetie," Edie said softly, "Doc and Patrick and I are here to help you. We know you've had a terrible shock and your heart is hurting. We love you, and we'll stay close by. Do you understand what I'm saying?"

Carrie closed her eyes, then opened them. Moving her lips silently, she mouthed, *Thank you.*

Edie caressed her cheek. "Let the sedative do its work now. Close your eyes."

Instantly, Carrie's eyes fluttered shut and in less than a minute her labored breathing became soft and steady. Edie placed a tender kiss on her forehead, then stood over her for a long moment. When she was sure Carrie was asleep, she glanced at the fireplace to make sure it was burning well, then tiptoed to the door.

She paused and turned to look back at the sleeping young woman. "Lord," she whispered, "this child is in much emotional pain. Colin is gone now, and she needs Your protection and Your merciful grace. We don't understand why you let the cougar attack and kill Colin, but we do know that You always know what is best. Take care of this sweet girl."

With that, Edie stepped into the hall and closed the door.

CHAPTER SIX

Mary Beth Cooper and her little sister were preparing supper when Chris returned from his journey to the Crow village.

When he saw his mother sitting by the fire, he quickly removed his cap and coat and headed that way.

Patty Ruth called out, "We thought maybe you'd stayed for supper with Mr. and Mrs. Two Moons, Chris."

He made a face toward the kitchen and drew up to Hannah, saying, "Mama! I've got good news about Broken Wing's parents. They're planning to come back to church!"

"Oh, honey, that's wonderful! Tell me about it."

Hearing the excitement in his brother's voice, B.J. came from the boys' room into the parlor. The girls were putting food on the table, but Chris also had their attention.

Chris's voice pitched higher and higher as he repeated what the chief had said about Hannah and the doctors showing what true Christians are like and that he and Sweet Blossom would come to church when the weather turned warmer.

"Oh, praise the Lord!" Hannah said, clapping her hands.

"And Mama..."

"Yes?"

"Before we left the village, I told Chief Two Moons it would make my mother very happy to see him and his family at church again. And he said he very much wants to make my mother happy. And something else..."

"Mm-hmm?" Hannah's eyes were dancing.

"Broken Wing said that his parents have noticed a difference in him since he became a Christian. They said he was a good son before, but now he's better than ever."

Tears filmed Hannah's eyes. "The Lord is answering prayer, honey. We're going to see Two Moons and Sweet Blossom saved—I just know it!"

"Praise the Lord!" said Mary Beth. "This is great news, Chris! And Patty Ruth and I have great news, too. Supper is on."

When B.J. had led in prayer over the food and the family dug in, Hannah said, "Pastor Kelly needs to know this about Broken Wing's parents, Chris. He just might want to go to the village and talk to Two Moons and Sweet Blossom before they come to church again. How about you and B.J. going over to the parsonage after supper so you can tell him?"

"Sure, Mama."

"Tell you what, honey. Would you tell him I'd like to talk to him before he goes to the village? It would help him to know the things I've told Sweet Blossom about salvation, and what her response has been."

"B.J. and I will go as soon as we get this awful food down," Chris said as he lifted a piece of fried chicken to his mouth.

Mary Beth's mouth fell open. "Awful food? Hah! I notice you're not making a face while you eat it!"

Chris chuckled and looked at B.J. "We're just trying to spare your feelings."

"Yeah," said his little brother. "That's it."

Mary Beth looked at Patty Ruth. "Well, I guess we could just let 'em starve."

"Yeah," said the little redhead. "Guess that would fix 'em."

"How about that, boys?" Hannah said with a smile.

Chris winked at his brother. "Well, we wouldn't want to

starve, so we'll act like the cooking is good."

"Yeah," said B.J., "we'll act like it's good."

Mary Beth grinned impishly. "You two had better be good actors, 'cause if I see anything on your faces that says you don't like the food, you don't get any more!" Turning to her little sister, she said, "Right, Patty Ruth?"

The six-year-old had her hand over her mouth, eyes wide.

"Honey, what's the matter?" Hannah asked.

Patty Ruth blinked, moved her hand enough to speak, and said, "Nothin', Mama."

"Why are you covering your mouth?"

Patty Ruth's features turned crimson. "Uh...jus' because."

Hannah frowned. "Is it a tooth? I've noticed the last few days that you seem to have a problem chewing sometimes."

Keeping her hand over her mouth, Patty Ruth swallowed hard. "Uh...it'll be fine, Mama."

"Come here," Hannah said. "I want to look at it."

The child's eyes widened. "But—"

"Come here, Patty Ruth."

She scooted her chair back and moved slowly around the corner of the table to her mother, still covering her mouth. Biggie was sitting on the floor near the table and cocked his head questioningly.

Hannah gently moved Patty Ruth's hand aside and said, "Open your mouth." She looked at the front teeth. "All right, is it upper or lower?"

"Uh...on top."

"Which one?"

"Both of 'em."

"Both your upper front teeth are loose?"

"Yes, ma'am."

"Open again."

The child winced as her mother pinched the upper teeth between her fingers and wiggled them.

"Honey, why didn't you tell me they were loose?"

"Cause it hurts to have 'em pulled. I know 'cause Belinda's papa pulled one of her teeth, an' she said it really hurt."

Hannah tested the teeth again. "Honey, they've got to come out so your new ones can grow in straight."

Patty Ruth swallowed hard. "How soon?"

"They're loose enough to come out right now."

"Maybe it would be best to wait till tomorrow."

Hannah shoved her chair back. "Let's go to the washroom. You can't eat with them so loose. Come on. It really won't hurt that bad. They're very loose."

"But I don't want it to hurt at all."

Hannah laid a hand on Patty Ruth's shoulder. "You have to be brave, honey. Come on. Let's go get it over with."

When Hannah and Patty Ruth returned to the kitchen some twenty minutes later, the boys had gone on their errand to the parsonage, and Mary Beth was washing dishes.

"Did the teeth come out all right?" Mary Beth asked.

Patty Ruth smiled, revealing a wide gap in the center of her upper teeth.

"She did fine, Mary Beth," said Hannah. "She was a brave little girl."

Mary Beth giggled. "I think she looks cute like that."

Patty Ruth grinned. "I never thaw you when your teeth were out. Did you look cute, too?"

"Papa said I did. And I lisped just like you, too."

"You go ahead with the dishes, Mary Beth," said Hannah. "I'll fix her some broth. She bled a little when I pulled the teeth, and chewing would hurt some right now."

When the broth was heated and Patty Ruth had taken her fill, Mary Beth took her to their room to undo her braids and brush her hair. Hannah was washing the bowl and spoon when she heard footsteps on the staircase outside. The boys came in but didn't say anything.

Hannah took one look at their faces and said, "What's wrong, boys?"

"Something bad happened today, Mama," Chris said. "Mr. Wright was killed by a cougar. Pastor Kelly told us about it."

"Oh no! What did he say about Carrie? Where is she?"

"He said she's taking it pretty hard. Grandpa and Grandma O'Brien have her at their house. Pastor and Mrs. Kelly were with her for quite a while. Pastor Kelly said Grandpa gave her a sedative and she's probably sleeping by now."

"Bless her heart. I'll go see her tomorrow. Did Pastor give you any details about the cougar attack?"

"No. He's coming over in a little while to talk to you about Two Moons and Sweet Blossom. He'll probably give you some details then."

"Did he say about what time?"

"No. He said he had someone to counsel in his office, then he would come and see you. He didn't think it would take very long."

B.J. hung up his coat and cap and went to the fireplace to add logs to the fire.

As Chris slipped out of his coat, he said, "Oh, Mama…"

"Yes?"

"In all the excitement over Two Moons and Sweet Blossom, I forgot to tell you what Colonel Bateman did."

"What's that, honey?"

"Well, you know he was sending Lieutenant Dobie and his men just to see if the Crows had any needs. Colonel Bateman decided to just go ahead and send them a wagonload of army food and supplies. It really touched the chief."

"I'll have to thank the colonel for being so kind to them."

Hannah sat down with the boys in the parlor. Moments later, when the girls came in, the boys asked to see the empty space where Patty Ruth's teeth used to be. Neither brother poked fun at her when she exposed the gap for them.

Hannah told the girls of Colin Wright's death and then asked them all to pray for Carrie.

The news of Colin Wright's death had changed the usual atmosphere in the Cooper home.

Afterward, the children talked about Christians dying, and why God would let Colin Wright be killed by the cougar. Hannah tried to help them understand that their earthly minds couldn't always comprehend God's reasoning—even as it had been hard to understand when their father had died on the journey to Fort Bridger.

Patty Ruth asked some questions about salvation, and the siblings remained quiet while their mother answered her. The six-year-old had been talking more and more about Jesus dying on the cross and about being saved.

When bedtime came, Pastor Kelly had not yet shown up. Hannah put her brood to bed as usual, then went back to the parlor to await the pastor's arrival. After adding another log on the fire, she sat down in her rocker and sighed. With four active children, there was rarely a quiet moment to herself. She laid her head against the back of the rocker and enjoyed the silence while thinking again of poor Carrie.

A soft glow came from the lanterns on the tables, and the rosy fire in the fireplace chased away the chill of the frosty night, in spite of the wind buffeting the outside walls.

The clock struck ten and Hannah's head was beginning to nod when a hesitant knock reached her ears. She used the arms of the rocker to get to her feet, picked up a knitted shawl from the couch, and wrapped it around her shoulders.

Moving in her rather clumsy way, she opened the door. A cold blast of wind whipped in and stung her face. "Come in, Pastor. I'm glad to see you."

"Sorry to be so late, Hannah. I told the boys it would only be a little while. The counseling session took much longer than I had anticipated."

"I know how those things go. Would you like some coffee? I still have some in the pot on the stove."

"Sounds good," he said, removing his hat and heavy coat.

"What a tragedy to hear about Colin."

"For sure."

When they were seated at the kitchen table with steaming cups in front of them, Hannah asked the pastor if he knew any of the details about Colin's death, and he told her what had happened.

"My heart is so heavy for Carrie," she said, shaking her head.

"Mine, too. She took it pretty hard. But then, you know how losing your husband in a violent death can affect you."

"I sure do. I'm planning to go to the O'Briens and see her tomorrow."

"I'm sure you will be a blessing to her. Especially since you were widowed so young and so suddenly, too."

Hannah nodded.

"I don't want to keep you up late," said Kelly, "so tell me about your talks with Sweet Blossom. Anything you can tell me will help. I've gone to the village twice since Broken Wing's baptism, wanting to plant some more gospel seed in their hearts. Both times the chief was gone. And as you know, the Crows have a custom that a white man cannot speak to a Crow squaw unless her husband is present. So I wasn't able to talk to her. I've been intending to go back again soon. I sure was glad when Chris told me Two Moons and Sweet Blossom are planning on coming back to church. But I agree with you that I should try to see them on a personal basis first."

At the same time Pastor Kelly was listening to Hannah explain about her witnessing sessions with Sweet Blossom, Chief Two Moons and his family were about to retire for the night.

A fire crackled inside the tepee, throwing its flickering shadows on the buffalo hide walls and shedding light on the Bible Broken Wing was reading as he sat on his straw pallet. He finished a chapter from the Gospel of John, then closed it, thanking the Lord in his heart that the Coopers had given him the Bible and that Miss Sundi Lindgren had come to the village over a period of time and taught the Crow children, including himself, to read and write English.

"Sleep time, son," said Sweet Blossom, standing over him. "Under the covers, now."

As Broken Wing slid under the blankets, Sweet Blossom knelt beside him, kissed his cheek, and tucked him in. Two Moons looked on.

Broken Wing looked up at his father and smiled. "Father, have you noticed that the sky is clear tonight? Even though the wind is blowing, there are no clouds. The moon is shining and the stars are twinkling."

Two Moons looked down at his son quizzically. "I did notice that it is clear tonight. Why is Broken Wing bringing this up?"

The boy grinned. "Since it is clear, there will be no snowstorm tonight. Even though it is very cold, could we go to church tomorrow?"

The parents looked at each other and smiled. Two Moons set loving eyes on his son and said, "Broken Wing is very eager to go back to church, yes?"

"Yes, Father."

"Then, since there will be no snowstorm, we will go to church tomorrow."

A wide smile lit Broken Wing's face. "Thank you, Father."

Sweet Blossom kissed her son again, readjusted the blankets to place them firmly around him and soon all was quiet in the tepee, except for the wind pelting the walls.

Broken Wing closed his eyes and whispered, "Lord Jesus,

thank You that I get to go back to church tomorrow. Please work in my parents' hearts like you worked in mine."

Sunday morning came with a clear, cold sky. The sun painted the dawn horizon a vermilion hue, then lifted its brilliant head over the edge of the world to send bright beams across the rolling, snow-covered hills around Fort Bridger.

A few minutes before Sunday school time, people began arriving from all over town and from the fort, the farms, and ranches. No one seemed to mind the cold. The hearts of the people were warmed by the friendships of Christian brothers and sisters as they moved inside the building to hear the Word of God.

When the Cooper family arrived, with Chris and B.J. steadying their mother on the snow-covered ground, Drs. Frank and Patrick O'Brien were standing in the vestibule, talking to Pastor Kelly. Patty Ruth showed the gap between her upper teeth in a smile and said, "Thee, Pathtor, Grandpa, Uncle Patrick: Mama pulled my teeth."

"Did it hurt, honey?" Patrick asked.

"Jutht a little bit."

"She was a brave girl," said Hannah, running her gaze to Doc, then back to Patrick. "How's Carrie doing?"

"She was still sleeping when we left the apartment," said Patrick. "Mom is staying with her, of course."

Since Doc was also the town's undertaker, Hannah asked him when Colin's funeral would be held.

"Pastor Kelly and I have set the funeral for Tuesday morning at eleven. He will be announcing it in the service this morning."

"Do you think Carrie will be able to attend?"

"We're sure hoping she will. Patrick spent most of the night with her. She didn't even stir."

"Which means she was resting well," put in Patrick. "We expect her to be awake by the time we get back from church."

"Would it be all right if I came to see her this afternoon?" Hannah asked.

"Of course," said Doc. "If she's awake, I'm sure she'll be glad to see you."

The children rushed off to their Sunday school classes, and the adults gathered in the auditorium for Pastor Kelly's lesson.

When Sunday school was over and the crowd was gathering in the auditorium for the morning service, Chief Two Moons, Sweet Blossom, and Broken Wing came in. They were welcomed by everyone they saw. Hannah invited them to sit with the Cooper family in their pew. The Williamses and their foster daughter, Abby Turner, always sat on the same pew, but there was room for all. Chris was especially happy. He had Broken Wing on one side of him and pretty Abby on the other.

During the congregational singing, the Crow family did their best to follow along, reading from their hymnals.

At announcement time, Pastor Kelly brought up Colin Wright's untimely death, made some comments about him being in heaven with the Lord, then announced the time of the funeral. He asked the people to be praying for Carrie, who was under Dr. and Mrs. Frank O'Brien's care in their home.

Later, when Kelly preached his sermon, he told of the bliss that all children of God know at the moment of their death, for the Lord Jesus is always there on the other side, waiting to fold them into His arms and welcome them into heaven.

Kelly told his people they should weep for Carrie, but they should not weep for Colin, for he was in the presence of his God, the saints, and the angels in heaven.

He read Revelation 21:23 to them: "And the city had no need of the sun, neither of the moon, to shine in it; for the glory of God did lighten it, and the Lamb is the light thereof."

Choking up a bit, Kelly said, "Folks, don't wish for Colin back. He is with the Lamb, who is the light of heaven's beautiful city. Once having looked into the bright face of Jesus, this world would be a dark place for Colin. Rather than wish him back, let us who are saved look forward to being with him in the bright presence of the Lamb."

Kelly turned to Luke chapter 16 and preached to those in the crowd who were not saved, showing them the awful experience of the man who died lost and woke up in the flames of hell.

Chief Two Moons and his squaw were very uncomfortable for the remainder of the sermon, and when the crowd was on its feet for the invitation, many people, including Broken Wing, were praying that the chief and his squaw would walk the aisle to receive the Lord. Two visitors—a rancher and his wife—did head down the aisle and were taken aside for counseling and prayer.

The invitation song was in its third verse when Hannah looked down and saw Patty Ruth crying. She bent down and whispered, "Honey, what's the matter?"

The child looked at her mother through shiny tears, and said, "Mama, I want to be thaved."

Caressing the child's head, Hannah said, "But Patty Ruth, you're a good little girl. Isn't that enough?"

"No, Mama. I'm a thinner, an' I need to be thaved. I don' want to go to hell. I want to go to heaven."

Hannah smiled. "All right, honey. We've talked about it lots of times, and I'm sure you understand it correctly. Do you want me to walk down the aisle with you?"

Patty Ruth shook her head. "No. Thath all right. I'll go by mythelf."

A wide smile was on Pastor Kelly's face as he bent down and talked to Patty Ruth when she approached him. He called for Rebecca to come and counsel the child, then smiled at Hannah, who was weeping with joy.

In a nearby pew, Betsy Fordham watched her own daughter, Belinda, who was not quite six. Belinda's eyes were wide as she observed her best friend at the altar with Mrs. Kelly.

Captain John Fordham leaned close to his wife and said in a whisper, "It won't be long until Belinda opens her heart to Jesus."

Betsy smiled and nodded, then patted Belinda's head.

Patty Ruth and the visitors who came for salvation were baptized. When the service was over, Patty Ruth got hugs and kisses from her mother and siblings, and many people made over her, expressing their joy in her salvation.

Just as Abe and Mandy Carver moved away after hugging her, Curly and Judy Charley Wesson stepped up. Curly let Judy hug Patty Ruth first, and people who stood around watched with interest, knowing the ritual Curly and Patty Ruth always played out when they got together.

When Judy stepped back, Patty Ruth looked up at the skinny, bald-headed little man and smiled.

Bending over her, Curly said, "So you got saved did you, little girl?"

"Yeth, I did," she replied, eyes dancing.

"Well, what's your name, anyway?"

"Patty Ruth Cooper."

Curly's eyes bulged in mock surprise. "Patty Ruth Cooper?"

"Yeth, thir."

"Well, how old are you?"

"Thix."

"Six? You're six years old?"

"Uh-huh."

"Well, do you know what I do when I meet a little girl whose name is Patty Ruth Cooper and she's six years old?"

"Huh-uh."

Dropping to one knee, Curly folded her in his arms. "I

hug 'er!" While he held her close, he said, "Darlin', Uncle Curly is so glad you got saved! I knew it was gonna be soon. I love you."

"I love you too, Uncle Curly."

Easing back, he looked into her eyes and said, "And you look so cute with those teeth missin'."

She giggled. "An' you look so cute with your hair missin'!"

Curly laughed and stood up.

Two Moons and Sweet Blossom stood close by, looking on. They saw the joy in Hannah's eyes over Patty Ruth's salvation and told her they were happy for Patty Ruth.

Pastor Kelly drew up to the Indians, and said, "Chief, I'm so glad you came today. Would it be all right if I come to the village and see you tomorrow?"

Two Moons smiled. "You will be most welcome, Pastor Andy Kelly."

"Thank you. I will be there about midmorning."

"We will be expecting you," said Two Moons, then took Sweet Blossom's arm and they headed for the door.

Hannah caught the pastor's eye and smiled at him. "I'll be praying," she said.

As B.J. helped Hannah out of her coat, she said, "Son, we're later than usual getting home from church. Uncle Jacob is supposed to eat with us today and is probably wondering what we've been doing. Will you go down and tell him dinner will be ready in half an hour, please?"

"Sure, Mama," he said and hung up her coat on its peg.

"Mama..." came Patty Ruth's voice from behind.

"Yes, dear?"

"Could I go down and tell Uncle Jacob about dinner? I want to tell him that I got thaved."

"Sure, honey," Hannah said. "You go tell him dinner will

be ready in half an hour, and while you're there, tell him what happened to you."

The child's eyes were bright. "Okay," she said and headed for the door.

Jacob's quarters were at the rear of the store on the opposite side from the apartment staircase. When Patty Ruth knocked on his door, it opened quickly. The little man smiled broadly and said, "Well, look who's here! The little girl with the teeth missing!" Jacob swept Patty Ruth up into his arms and kissed her cheek. "Are you here to tell me Sunday dinner is ready?"

She giggled. "Mama thaid to tell you it'll be ready in a half hour."

He planted her feet on the floor again and said, "Well, I'm glad she sent you to tell me. I'm getting pretty hungry."

Eyes gleaming, Patty Ruth said, "I came to tell you thomethin' elth, too."

"What's that, sweetie pie?"

"At church thith mornin', I got thaved! I took the Lord into my heart!"

There was dead silence, then Jacob pressed a smile on his lips. "Well, honey, I'm...ah...I'm happy for you."

"Uncle Jacob, will you let Him come into your heart, too?"

"Well, honey, you see, I...ah...well, my religion is different. In my religion, we don't ask Jesus into our hearts."

The child's face pinched. "Uncle Jacob, if you died like Mr. Wright did, would you go to heaven?"

Jacob cleared his throat and ushered her toward the door, saying, "Sweetheart, tell your mama I'll be up in a few minutes, okay?"

"Okay. Don't be late."

"Oh, do not fear. Your Uncle Jacob will never be late for a meal at your mama's table!"

CHAPTER SEVEN

Carrie Wright was sitting in a large overstuffed chair, staring into a crackling fire. Edie O'Brien had brought her food some two hours earlier, then returned to the kitchen to feed Sunday dinner to her husband and son.

Carrie had slept for a while, then left the bed to sit in the chair and think about Colin.

She heard footsteps in the hall, then the door eased open a few inches and Edie's plump face appeared.

"I'm awake," Carrie said.

Edie pushed the door open further. "Did you sleep some, honey?"

"About an hour."

"Good. Feel like company?"

"Who is it?"

"Hannah Cooper. She wants to look in on you."

A tiny smile tugged at the corners of Carrie's mouth. "Of course."

The door widened and Hannah stepped in, letting Edie close the door behind her.

Carrie rose from the chair and took a couple of steps toward Hannah, who folded her in her arms as best she could. "Carrie, I'm so sorry."

The new widow began to sob as she clung to her friend.

When she grew calmer, Hannah guided her to the small

horsehair sofa sitting beneath the window. When they were seated, Hannah pulled Carrie's hands into her lap and clasped them tightly.

"You didn't walk over here alone, did you, Hannah?"

"No, honey. Chris and B.J. escorted me and are waiting in the parlor with Doc and Edie."

"I feel better, then. I sure wouldn't want you to fall in the snow and hurt yourself...or the baby."

Hannah had prayed for wisdom, asking the Lord to give her the words to help Carrie in her grief.

"I won't pretend to know why the Lord took Colin home, Carrie, but I do know that our loving heavenly Father never makes a mistake. It was His will to do this, and we must accept it by faith, trusting Him completely. When we're in the deepest valley, the only way we can look is up. And always waiting as we look up is our precious Saviour. I urge you, Carrie, to let the Lord Jesus bless you with just Himself, cling to His loving promises, and trust His ever-sufficient grace."

Carrie's lower lip quivered as she nodded.

Still gripping her hands tightly, Hannah said, "I know what you're feeling, my dear. I too have known the overwhelming sorrow of losing my beloved husband. And everyday, oh, how I miss his sweet presence in my life!"

Hannah's tears spilled down her cheeks and splattered on their clasped hands. She sniffed and swallowed hard, then said, "You will gain comfort from your friends in your loss, but remember that Scripture calls our Lord the God of all comfort. Let the one who died for you—the one who knows all about you and loves you more than anyone else ever has or ever will—give you comfort. Let His blessed Holy Spirit abide with you and give you the measure of grace you need in these dark and frightening days. I know how He can give comfort and grace when your husband is taken from you. He never failed me, and He will never fail you, either."

Both women's heads were tilted low as Hannah spoke comforting words barely above a whisper. When they raised their heads and looked into each other's eyes, Hannah saw the sweet peace of the Spirit reflected in Carrie's countenance.

When Carrie stood up and bent over to hug Hannah, she said, "Thank you for being such a loving and loyal friend. God knew I was going to need you. Maybe…maybe someday I can bring comfort to one who is suffering, just as you have brought it to me."

Both women dried their tears, and a small, tentative smile brightened Carrie's visage.

"I'm here for you, Carrie," Hannah said. "Don't ever hesitate to come to me. You will be in my prayers, and my door is always open." Her voice was tender as she said, "Is there anything I can do for you right now?"

"I don't think so," Carrie replied softly. "The O'Briens are taking good care of me. And, praise the Lord, the ranchers from the church who live near the Box W are looking out for the livestock. So for the time being, I'm well taken care of."

"That's good. But don't forget that I'm here when you need me…for anything."

"I will remember."

"How about at the funeral? Would you like me to sit by you in the service?"

"That would be a great help, Hannah. I'm going to need all the help I can get."

Hannah rose to her feet. "Well, I'd better go. You need to get some more rest."

Carrie walked her to the bedroom door, hugged her once more, and said, "How can I ever thank you for coming to see me?"

"No need. It's thanks enough just to see you doing better. I'll drop in on you again tomorrow."

"Please do."

As Hannah stepped into the hall, Carrie said, "I love you, Hannah."

A sweet smile graced Hannah's lips. "I love you too, honey."

On Monday morning, the winter sun was shining out of a clear sky as Chief Two Moons and Sweet Blossom welcomed Pastor Andy Kelly into their tepee. Broken Wing was out hunting rabbits and squirrels in the nearby forest with a group of Crow boys.

Two Moons and Sweet Blossom provided a blanket for their guest to sit on, Indian-style, and Pastor Kelly placed himself between the chief and his squaw on the dirt floor of the tepee and opened his Bible.

Lovingly and tactfully, Kelly used Scripture to show Two Moons and Sweet Blossom what sin is in the eyes of God. After covering the subject from several angles, using illustrations to help them understand, both Indians readily admitted that according to the Bible they were guilty sinners before God, in need of forgiveness.

Kelly went on to show that in the eyes of God, every person is in one of two positions: in their sins or in Christ. To die in their sins meant to spend eternity in the flames of the lake of fire, which is hell in its final state and is called by God the "second death." But to die in Christ is to spend eternity with Him in heaven, never to know another pain or heartache.

As the pastor watched their faces, recognizing that the truth was making its impression in their hearts, he could also see them struggling.

Two Moons set his dark eyes on the preacher and said, "But Pastor Andy Kelly, what about the Crow gods? What about the faith the Crow people have in our medicine men and the religion they teach? Must we forsake our gods and our religion in order to have this forgiveness and salvation from hell?"

"Yes, Chief," said Kelly. "The Crows, like just about all

North American Indians, speak of the Sky Father, or sometimes speak of the Great Spirit."

Two Moons nodded. "We do."

"This Sky Father, or Great Spirit, is he different from your other gods?"

"Yes. He is the supreme one."

"All right. There is one God, Chief. But only one. He is the Creator of the earth and the universe. Let me read something to you."

Kelly flipped pages, stopped when he found what he wanted, and held the Bible so both of them could see it. "Right here. First Timothy chapter 2, verse 5: 'For there is one God, and one mediator between God and men, the man Christ Jesus; who gave himself a ransom for all.' It was God's only begotten Son, the Lord Jesus Christ, who came into this world from heaven, took upon Himself human flesh by the virgin birth—as I mentioned in the sermon you heard the day you came to church—and gave Himself as our ransom. Only by and through Him can we be saved."

Flipping pages again, Kelly said, "Jesus made this quite clear over here in John 14:6. Look at these words." With his finger on the verse, he read it to them: "'I am the way, the truth, and the life: no man cometh unto the Father, but by me.' Do you see it? Jesus is the one and only mediator between the Father in heaven and sinful men on earth. And He is the way to the Father. Not one of the ways, but the one and only way. The only way you can really know the one you call the Sky Father, or the Great Spirit, is through Jesus Christ.

"Jesus proved that He is the one and only way of salvation by not only dying on the cross for our sins, but by raising Himself out of the grave three days after He died. No one else has ever done this. No one. And He's alive right now, looking down at both of you, wanting you to put your faith in Him so He can save you."

A L   A N D   J O A N N A   L A C Y

Two Moons and Sweet Blossom exchanged solemn glances, then the chief looked at Kelly and said, "But our gods would be angry with us if we turned away from them."

"Chief Two Moons, Sweet Blossom, I do not say this to insult you, but to help you. There is only one true God. The gods of the Crow people do not exist except in their minds. Let me show you another Scripture." Kelly prayed in his heart as he turned to Galatians chapter 4. "In this passage, God has the apostle Paul writing to people who have been saved, like Broken Wing. Understand?"

Both nodded.

"Speaking to those people, Paul refers to the time when they did not know the true God, but trusted in false gods. Verse 8: 'Howbeit then, when ye knew not God, ye did service unto them which by nature are no gods.' See? Until we become God's children by faith in Jesus Christ, we all do service to some kind of gods. But Paul says that even by nature they are not gods. They do not exist, Two Moons. There is only one true God—and He is the God of this Bible."

Two Moons closed his eyes for a moment, then said, "But the Crow gods have been our religion since we were born. How can we turn our backs on them?"

"As the Bible says right here in Galatians 4:8, they do not actually exist. But since they do exist in your minds; this is part of what repentance is. I preached about repentance that day you came to the service. Jesus said, 'Except ye repent, ye shall all likewise perish.' Repentance means that you change your mind about your sin, your gods, and the direction you are headed, which is toward hell. You turn all the way around to the Lord Jesus Christ, believing that He died on the cross for you, was buried for you, and came out of the grave for you. That's when you call on Him, asking Him to come into your heart and save you. Remember? 'Whosoever shall call upon the name of the Lord shall be saved.'"

Two Moons and Sweet Blossom held each other's eyes for a long moment.

"Jesus is waiting, my friends. He wants to save you if you will let Him."

Two Moons took a deep breath. "Pastor Andy Kelly, Sweet Blossom and I appreciate your coming here to talk to us. We know you are very sincere in wanting us to become Christians, but this is a very difficult thing. We have believed in our gods all of our lives. We cannot give them up."

Kelly smiled. "I ask only that both of you think about what I've shown you today. Your eternal destiny depends on it."

Two Moons nodded. "We will think about it, Pastor Andy Kelly."

"And I would like to ask if I could come back and talk to you about it very soon."

The chief managed a thin smile. "Of course. You are always welcome."

"Thank you. And there is something else I want to ask of you."

"Mmm?"

"I will be preaching a funeral tomorrow morning for a man who was a member of our church. He was killed by a cougar a couple of days ago. I would like you to come for a special reason."

"What is that?" Two Moons asked.

"It would help you to understand better what I've been talking to you about if you could compare a Crow funeral with that of a man who has died as a Christian. Will you come? It will be held at the church at one hour before high sun."

Two Moons nodded. "Yes. We will come."

"Great!" Kelly rose to his feet. "Thank you for allowing me to come and talk to you."

Moments later, the chief and his squaw stood at the edge of the village to watch the preacher ride away. When he made a turn on the path and vanished from view, Two Moons looked at Sweet Blossom and said, "There has to be something to what Pastor Andy Kelly is talking about. We see something very special in Hannah Cooper and other Christians, which we do not see in ourselves or our people."

"Yes," said Sweet Blossom. "There is also something very special in the heart of our own son that we do not have."

At eleven o'clock on Tuesday morning, the church in Fort Bridger was packed. The sealed coffin rested on a wooden frame in front of the platform. The pump organ played as Heidi Lindgren stood behind the pulpit and sang a song about heaven. Her beautiful soprano voice served to bring the glory of the Lord Jesus Christ into each heart.

Seated close to the front was Carrie Wright, with Hannah Cooper on one side of her and Edie O'Brien on the other. Both women held tightly to Carrie's hands, giving courage and strength to the young widow whose body was trembling with sorrow and fatigue.

The Cooper children sat together. Next to Chris Cooper was Broken Wing, and beside him were his parents.

When Heidi's voice gently faded away on the last note, a holy hush descended over the crowd. As Pastor Andy Kelly stepped to the pulpit, Bible in hand, Carrie sighed deeply as though she had been holding her breath and relaxed against Hannah's supporting arm.

Kelly led the congregation in prayer, asking the Lord to be especially close to the young widow. Then he gave a clear gospel presentation and told how Colin Wright was in heaven at that very moment in the sweet presence of the one who had died on the cross of Calvary for him.

Both Two Moons and Sweet Blossom sensed that even though there was sorrow over Colin Wrigth's death…still there was an undercurrent of quiet serenity in the hearts of the people, something they had never felt at the Crow funeral.

Kelly then referred to the sermon he had preached on Sunday night the previous week on the valley of Baca and read Psalm 84:5–6. He emphasized the words "passing through the valley," and said, "God, in His wisdom, took Colin to heaven and left Carrie here on earth, in the valley of Baca…the valley of weeping." Then setting his eyes on Carrie, he said, "Your heavenly Father loves you, Carrie, and is with you right now in the valley of Baca. But He will not leave you there. He will take you through the valley and beyond. You will find another mountaintop."

There were some soft amens across the crowd. Carrie's eyes filled with tears, but she gave the pastor a gracious smile and nodded.

Two Moons and Sweet Blossom exchanged glances. Each knew what the other was thinking. Pastor Andy Kelly had spoken true words to them. This funeral service was much different than the Crow burials. When the Crows buried their dead, the medicine men chanted mournfully and the people wailed. These people had a peace that Two Moons and Sweet Blossom had never seen before.

As Kelly went on with his message, unchecked tears spilled down Carrie's cheeks. But the "peace that passeth all understanding" stole its way into her heart, and the gentle healing of the Great Physician began.

When the service was closed with prayer, the pallbearers carried the coffin outside and placed it in the bed of Dr. Frank O'Brien's wagon. Patrick O'Brien was at the reins.

The people followed and began the short walk to the cemetery. Carrie was transported in a carriage by Pastor and Mrs. Kelly, and because of her condition, Hannah was invited to ride with them. The Indians followed the crowd to the grave site.

At the grave, the crowd gathered. Pastor Kelly read some Scriptures about the first resurrection and briefly commented on them.

When the service was over and everyone had passed by to speak their words of condolence and encouragement to Carrie, Dr. Patrick O'Brien, with Sundi Lindgren at his side, helped Carrie and Hannah back into the Kellys' carriage.

The pastor was about to help Rebecca in when Chief Two Moons and Sweet Blossom stepped up to them.

"Pastor Andy Kelly," said the chief, "Sweet Blossom and Two Moons have seen the difference you spoke about."

Kelly smiled.

"Would it be possible for Pastor Andy Kelly to come to the village tomorrow? We would like to talk to him in the privacy of our tepee again."

The preacher's heart skipped a beat. "Of course I can come. Morning or afternoon?"

"Whichever is best for Pastor Andy Kelly. And if Rebecca Kelly can come, she is very welcome."

"We'll be there in the morning, Chief," Kelly replied.

It was midmorning the next day when the Kellys drew near the Crow Village in their carriage. When they topped a small rise and the long rows of tepees came into view, Kelly stopped the carriage and said, "Honey, let's pray one more time before we go in there."

Holding hands, they asked the Lord to make this the day He would draw Two Moons and Sweet Blossom to Himself.

When the Kellys sat down Indian-style on the floor of the tepee with the chief and his squaw, Two Moons looked across the small fire at them and said, "Sweet Blossom and Two Moons want to thank Pastor Andy Kelly and Rebecca Kelly for coming."

"It is our pleasure, Chief," said Kelly.

"Sweet Blossom and Two Moons have talked much about the difference we saw between Colin Wright's burial and the Crow burials. We Crow talk about our people dying and going to the happy hunting ground in the sky, but we have no assurance that there is a happy hunting ground. We only have an empty hope that we will ever see our dead again in another world.

"What you have shown us from the Holy Bible about heaven and what the Sky Fath—what the God of heaven says we have to do to go there...somehow we know is real. We have talked much about Jesus Christ and what He did when He sacrificed Himself on the cross for all sinners. We know in our hearts that we fall short of what the Creator expects of us, and that we have sinned before Him. In our religion, there is no sacrifice that has been offered for our sins, nor any way to have them washed away and forgiven. We see that you have shown us salvation, not just another religion with empty hope."

"I'm so glad you see that, Chief," said Kelly.

"You showed us in the Holy Bible that we must repent of our sin, which includes our gods, Pastor Andy Kelly. You showed us that the true Father's Book says the gods are not real. Somehow...somehow we have confidence that the Book speaks truth. We know now that the Crow gods are false. They do not exist except in the minds of our people."

Sweet Blossom's lower lip was quivering, and her eyes were brimming with tears. Rebecca rose to her knees, crawled around the fire to her, and took hold of her hand. Sweet Blossom smiled at her, then looked at Two Moons and said, "May I speak to them?"

Two Moons nodded.

"Chief Two Moons and his squaw were touched in our hearts by the funeral service. We want the same kind of peace

Christians have about death and beyond."

"You can become a Christian and have it, I assure you," said Kelly.

Sweet Blossom nodded. "Our son, Broken Wing, has made a powerful impression on us since he became acquainted with Jesus Christ. We want to become acquainted with Him, too. Is this not right, my husband?"

"Yes," said Two Moons. "We want to know Him, too."

"Then both of you are ready to receive the Lord Jesus Christ into your hearts?" said Kelly.

"We are," replied the chief. "Two Moons knows that by becoming a Christian, he will put a division between himself and the medicine men. But Two Moons is chief. He can keep this in control. And this chief will want to see his people become Christians, too. Show us what to do, Pastor Andy Kelly. We want Jesus Christ to save us."

Hannah Cooper was alone in the apartment when she heard footsteps on the wooden staircase. She was almost to the door when the knock came.

"Well, come in!" she said, swinging the door wide. "Is this a pastoral call, or is there something I can do for you?"

Andy Kelly removed his hat as he and Rebecca stepped inside. He flashed a smile and said, "Rebecca and I have some wonderful news! We just got back from the Crow village."

Hannah's eyes widened. "Yes?"

"You've been praying very earnestly for something big to happen there. What is it?"

Hannah laughed breathlessly. "That Two Moons and Sweet Blossom would be saved."

"Well, they're now your brother and sister in Christ!"

Hannah drew a sharp breath and her eyes moistened. "Tell me about it!"

"Let's get you off your feet, Hannah, and then we'll tell you every detail."

Andy and Rebecca told Hannah of their conversation with Two Moons and Sweet Blossom and of their clear understanding of their need for the Lord Jesus Christ.

When Hannah had asked all her questions and dried her tears of joy, she said, "Oh, I can't wait to tell my children! Especially Chris!"

"Honey, let's tell Hannah about Carrie," Rebecca said.

Hannah face took on a look of concern. "Carrie?"

"Yes…she's all right," the pastor hastened to say. "We went by the O'Brien apartment before coming here. We wanted to let Carrie know that it was Colin's funeral that finalized in the hearts of Two Moons and Sweet Blossom that the gospel of Jesus Christ is true. We wanted her to know that God used Colin's death as one of His means to bring Two Moons and Sweet Blossom to Himself."

"And did she ever shed some happy tears over that!" Rebecca said. "It was a real blessing to her. She said she understands now that the Lord had Colin's death in His perfect plan, and part of that plan was to help bring the chief and his squaw to Jesus."

"Oh, praise the Lord!" said Hannah. "I know this will be a great help and encouragement to her."

"And there's someone else the conversion of Two Moons and Sweet Blossom will encourage," Kelly said, winking at Rebecca.

Hannah gave them a blank look.

Rebecca giggled. "He's talking about you, Hannah, dear."

"Me?"

"Yes," said the pastor. "We spent some time talking to Two Moons and Sweet Blossom after they got saved. Sweet Blossom said it was you who first put it in her mind that Jesus was indeed the Son of God, and caused her to think about Calvary.

She had often discussed it with Two Moons, which also planted some questions in his mind as to why the Crow religion had no way of cleansing wrongdoing and bringing forgiveness from the Sky Father. Hannah, you had a whole lot to do with them coming to the Lord."

"And somebody else had a big part in their salvation," said Rebecca. "Two Moons and Sweet Blossom brought him up several times."

A smile spread over Hannah's lips. "You mean Chris?"

"Yes. Chris. It was his love for Broken Wing and his desire to bring him to the Lord that got the boy saved. The chief and his squaw couldn't say enough about how Broken Wing's testimony influenced them."

"Yes!" Hannah said, clapping her hands together. "That marvelous boy of mine! It was Chris who actually planted the gospel seed in the village by leading Broken Wing to the Lord. I can't wait to tell him about Broken Wing's parents. He's going to be ecstatic."

Late that afternoon, the Cooper children came into the general store, passing through it to the back door as they usually did. Jacob Kates was behind the counter with Nellie Patterson at his side. Both were waiting on customers but took the time to answer greetings from the children.

As they moved by the counter, speaking also to customers, Jacob called, "Hey, youngin's, how come you're so late getting home? School let out almost two hours ago."

Chris paused with his hand on the doorknob. "Miss Lindgren needed help putting some maps and pictures on the walls and rearranging some of the desks, Uncle Jacob."

"Well, bless your little hearts. Always willing to pitch in and help. I'm proud of you."

The children smiled at him, then went out back and

headed for the stairs to the apartment.

A short time later it was closing time. Jacob was locking the front door behind Nellie Patterson when he heard the back door open. Looking over his shoulder, he smiled and said, "Ah...Chris. Don't tell me. Your sweet mother sent you down to tell me supper will be at six, as usual."

Chris's eyes shone as he replied, "Mama did send me to tell you that, Uncle Jacob, but I wanted to tell you something else, too."

A big smile curved Jacob's lips. "Well, it's got to be good, the way your face is lit up. What is it?"

"You remember that my friend, Broken Wing, got saved a few weeks ago?"

The smile on Jacob's face drained away. "Oh...ah...yes."

"Well, Broken Wing's mother and father got saved this morning! Pastor and Mrs. Kelly led them to the Lord!"

Jacob forced a smile. "Oh, yes. That is really something, isn't it? I mean, with those Indians so steeped in their ancestors' religion, a thing like that doesn't happen very often, does it?"

"No, it sure doesn't. You were at church when Broken Wing got baptized, Uncle Jacob. Will you come Sunday and see Chief Two Moons and Sweet Blossom get baptized?"

The little Jewish man's features went a bit crimson. "Well, ah...I was there that day to sort of show God how thankful I was when those wagons showed up with our grocery supply, Chris. But I really have to get caught up on things here in the store. I'll do my worshiping in my quarters on the Sabbath. I don't think I'll have time to come on Sunday."

"But it really wouldn't take a lot of time out of your day, Uncle Jacob. Just an hour or so, and—"

"Hey, it's soon going to be time for supper, Chris. I've got to get washed up. Tell your Mama I'll be up shortly."

As Chris climbed the stairs to the apartment, he said aloud, "Dear Lord, I love Uncle Jacob, and I want him in heaven with us. Please work in his heart and life, and show him that Jesus is the true Messiah."

CHAPTER EIGHT

On Sunday Chief Two Moons and Sweet Blossom walked the aisle at church and gave their testimonies, then went into the baptismal waters. Two Moons asked the people to pray for him. His desire now was to show all of his people that they needed to worship the one true God.

Pastor Kelly assured Two Moons and Sweet Blossom that any time he went to the village to teach them the Word of God, any of the Crow people who would like to sit in would be welcome to do so.

When the baptism was over, there was hardly a dry eye in the building.

The next morning, Carrie Wright was sitting in Dr. O'Brien's outer office, waiting for Abe and Mandy Carver to come pick her up. Although Doc and Patrick were busy with patients in the examining rooms, Edie was sitting with her.

"Honey," said Edie, "are you sure you're up to returning to the ranch this soon? This is only the ninth day since Colin…"

Carrie dipped her head and took a deep breath, letting it out slowly. "Edie, the ranch needs me. The neighbors have been so good to feed and water the cattle and horses for me, but it's time I was taking care of my own stock. I have to get on with my life. So I might as well start now."

"I understand. But Doc and I want you to know you're welcome to stay longer."

Carrie smiled. "You've been so good to me, and I appreciate it. Since Pastor Kelly has lined up women of the church to stay with me, I'll be fine."

"How long will Mandy be with you?"

"Three days. Pastor has set it up on a three-day basis. Mandy will go home Thursday morning, and Marshal Mangum will bring Heidi to the ranch before Abe gets there to pick up Mandy. Heidi's leaving the dress shop in the capable hands of Julianna Bower."

"Who's coming after that?"

"I think it's Julianna, then Glenda Williams, Betsy Fordham, and Donna Carlin. That's as far ahead as Pastor has scheduled it. I told him by that time I'll be ready to stay alone."

"But if you find that you're not, Pastor will schedule more company, right?"

"That's what he said."

The rattle of a wagon and snorting of horses came from out front. Carrie went to the window. "It's them."

She slipped into her coat and was putting on her scarf when Abe Carver came in.

"Ready to go, Miz Carrie? Mo'nin', Miz Edie."

Carrie took her mittens from the coat pocket, put them on, then hugged Edie and thanked her for taking care of her.

"Now, honey," Edie said, "if you find that you just can't handle the ranch and have to sell it, you're welcome to come live with us. The spare room is yours as long as you need it."

Carrie kissed her cheek. "I appreciate that. You• pray for me, okay?"

"I sure will."

Abe opened the door and took Carrie by the arm, guiding her toward the wagon. Edie followed them outside and smiled up at Mandy. "Thanks for going out there to stay with her," she said.

"I'm happy to do it." Mandy's breath hung in the cold, still air. "Don't you worry now. Us ladies will take good care of her."

As the Carver wagon moved along the road toward the towering, snow-covered Uintah Mountains, Carrie talked about Chief Two Moons and Sweet Blossom becoming Christians.

"I wonder how the medicine men will take it when their chief no longer takes part in their religious ceremonies?" Abe said.

When Carrie didn't comment, Mandy turned toward her and noticed the tension in her body. She took hold of Carrie's mittened hand and asked her what was wrong.

"This will be the first time I've seen the ranch since Colin...since Colin died. I'm just a bit on edge."

"Would you rather not go on?" Mandy asked.

Carrie shook her head. "I have to go on."

Just then the Box W came into view. Carrie blinked and said, "There's smoke coming out of the chimneys."

"Looks like your neighbors have made it ready for you."

"Chad Tolman, no doubt. He's the one who's been doing most of the feeding of the stock. I told him at church last night that I'd be going home today."

As Abe guided the wagon off the road and headed down the lane toward the house and buildings, Mandy said, "You gonna be all right, hon?"

"I'll be fine." Carrie's chest was tight and her heart was pounding as she said, "Abe, would you swing over by the corral first? I want to get a count."

Abe hauled the wagon to a stop beside the split-rail fence, and Carrie ran her gaze over the herd and the horses. She was glad to see that the neighboring ranchers had removed the carcass of the cow. Her lips moved silently. When she finished counting, she sighed and said, "All there. It was definitely the three cougars Colin and I killed that were slaughtering the cattle. Maybe things will get better now."

"I hope so," said Abe. "You deserve something good to happen for a change."

"Her next mountaintop," said Mandy, smiling as she squeezed Carrie's hand.

When Abe drew the wagon to a halt at the back porch of the ranch house, he jumped out and ran around the wagon to help Carrie down, then Mandy, who carried a small overnight bag.

"Abe, darlin'," Mandy said, "I know you need to get back to town and open the shop. You go on now. We'll be fine."

"You sure? I'll be glad to go inside with you for a while."

"Thanks, but you go on now."

Abe kissed Mandy, then said, "Don't worry 'bout the children and this husbin o' yours. We'll be fine. I'll pick you up early Thursday mornin'."

The two women watched the wagon for a few moments, then moved onto the back porch. Carrie hesitated at the door. Mandy remained silent and let Carrie take her time. Finally, Carrie took hold of the knob and stepped into the kitchen. Mandy bustled inside after her and closed the door behind them.

"God bless Chad," Carrie said, feeling the warmth in the house.

"Amen." Mandy set the overnight bag on the floor and removed her coat and hat. As she hung them on wall pegs by the door, she noticed the .44 Winchester rifle leaning against the wall.

Carrie saw Mandy's glance at the weapon and said, "Chad brought our team and wagon back from town for me. That's the rifle I used to kill the third cougar."

Mandy nodded.

When Carrie had hung up her coat and scarf, she said,

"Mandy, I...I need to walk through the house alone. Do you understand?"

"Of course, honey. If you'll point me to the room I'll be sleeping in, I'll unpack my bag."

"I'll take you there. Come with me."

Mandy followed Carrie up the hall to the spare bedroom.

"You get settled in," said Carrie. "I'll be back in a few minutes."

She left Mandy and went to the small room that had been Colin's office. A lump came to her throat and tears misted her eyes as she looked at all of his things. She could picture him there, sitting at the desk. She rubbed the back of his chair, then leaned forward and picked up the letter opener with an eagle's head on the handle. She had given it to him for his last birthday. She could almost feel his presence. It took a moment to shake off the feeling.

She left the office and went to her sewing room. Even though this was her room, he had often come in when she was sewing and had moved up behind her to kiss the back of her neck. Her hand went to the very spot, and for a moment she thought she would break down, but managed to keep control.

The fire in the parlor was crackling pleasantly when Carrie walked in and ran her gaze around the room. Colin's Bible lay on the small table next to his overstuffed chair. Her throat tightened as she walked over and picked it up. She held it close to her heart and let her tear-dimmed eyes go to the other things in the room that were his.

Observing so much evidence of Colin's life here evoked a crushing loneliness within Carrie, but seeing and touching his possessions had a way of bringing comfort as well.

Finally, she entered their bedroom. Her heart lurched when she saw Colin's nightshirt lying across the foot of the bed. She had intended to take it to the kitchen and put it in the wash that morning but had forgotten it.

Her hands trembled as she picked up the nightshirt and pressed it to her face. Colin's scent was still there. Grief surged up within her, and this time she sobbed as if her heart would break into a million pieces.

Suddenly Mandy was in the room with her arms around Carrie, holding her tight and speaking in soothing tones.

After a few minutes, the sobs lessened. Soon Carrie gently pulled away from Mandy's arms, dried her tears with the night-shirt, and said, "You're such a dear, Mandy. Thank you for your comfort." She straightened her back. "But enough of this. I have a ranch to run now, and crying won't help me get the job done."

"You're only human, honey."

"How well I know. But this human has got to get hold of herself and move on with her life. How about some tea?"

"I could go for that."

The two women sat at the kitchen table, enjoying the steaming tea. After finishing a cup of the strong brew, Carrie said, "I'll be back in a couple of minutes."

She went to Colin's office and reached inside a desk drawer to take out a leather valise containing all the papers about the ranch and the mortgage. She returned to the kitchen and said, "Mandy, I've got to go over the ranch papers. Why don't you go sit by the fire in the parlor? Rest yourself. I'll join you later."

"I'd be glad to do some housework."

"Oh no, you don't, sweetie. The house is clean. You go sit down and rest. There are some books in the bookcase in the parlor. If you want to read, feel free to do so."

"Whatever you say." When Mandy reached the kitchen door, she paused to look back, and a smile flitted across her lips. It was good for Carrie to get her mind on needful things.

It was midmorning the next day when Mandy happened to be looking out the parlor window while Carrie was leafing through Colin's Bible. Over her shoulder, she said, "You've got company, Carrie. There's a rider coming toward the house from the road."

Carrie went to the window and focused on the rider, who was yet too far away to identify. "I think that's Chad," she said. "The horse is a gray roan like his."

The rider was trotting his mount along the snow-laden lane, and in less than sixty seconds, Carrie said, "Yes. That's him."

"Sure is," said Mandy. "Do you know how Leona's doing after her bout with pneumonia?"

"Chad told me Sunday that she's doing much better. He said Dr. Patrick went out to see her last week and said she was progressing well. It'll probably be spring before she can come back to church."

"Well, I'm glad to know she's improving."

Soon the tall, lanky rancher drew rein in front of the house. As he swung his leg over the saddle, he glanced at the window and waved at the two women.

Carrie had the door open before he reached the porch. Smiling, she said, "You were here earlier, weren't you?"

He made an innocent face and splayed his fingers across his chest. "Who, me?"

"Yes, you. Come in here out of the cold."

Chad Tolman, who was in his midsixties, removed his hat and displayed a thick mop of silver hair. "Hello, Mandy," he said.

"And hello to you," Mandy said, returning his smile.

"So you get the first three days with Carrie?"

"Yes. And it's my pleasure."

Looking at the young widow, Chad said, "Leona said to tell you she would be here to look after you if Dr. Patrick would allow her to leave the house."

"I appreciate that, but tell her I'm being well taken care of. I do want to thank you for taking such good care of my stock while I've been in town."

"I've had help," the lanky rancher said with a slanted grin. "Bill Chase and his sons have been here some, and Hank Weatherton, too."

"But it's been mostly you, I know. And it was you who came in here this morning and built the fires. That was very kind of you."

Chad nodded. "Glad to do it, Carrie. You're going to need help once in a while. Please don't ever hesitate to ask."

"I won't. You're very kind. Can you take your coat off and stay for a while?"

"Not very long. I've got plenty of work to do at home, but I came by to ask if you would sell me a few head of cattle."

Carrie's features paled. "Well, I—"

"Carrie, I know about your being behind on the mortgage payments. Colin shared it with me a few days before the Lord took him home. It was pretty heavy on his heart. I'll give you a good price so you can pay some money on the mortgage. I know you can't give up too many cows because you want a good calf crop this spring. But if you feel you can let a few go, I'd sure take them."

Carrie thought on it a few seconds. "Well, I guess I could sell a few and still have a decent calf crop, now that those cougars are dead. Let's go sit down in the parlor and talk about it."

Mandy excused herself and went to the kitchen while Carrie and Chad talked business.

When Chad made his offer, Carrie knew he was paying her more than the cows were worth, and told him so. He admitted it, saying he wanted to help, and from what Colin had told him, he knew that if he bought six cows at the amount he was offering, it would make two months' payment on the mortgage. They closed the deal, and Chad gave her cash for the agreed amount, saying he would come back the next day and get his cows.

That night, Carrie sat down and wrote a letter to Karl Devlin, which she would have Abe Carver post for her when he took Mandy back to town on Thursday.

She explained to Devlin that Colin had been killed by a cougar, but she was trying to keep his dream alive by staying with the ranch. She hoped the enclosed amount for two months' rent would show him that she was trying to get caught up. She assured him that if he would give her time, she would get the payments current. Thanking him in advance for his patience, she told him he would hear from her again as soon as she could come up with more money.

After addressing the envelope, she placed the letter and the money inside and sealed it.

On Wednesday afternoon, Carrie and Mandy were cleaning and dusting the parlor when Mandy looked out the window and said, "Honey, a buggy's coming. I don't recognize the two men in it."

Carrie moved up beside Mandy. Her face lost color as she said, "It's Karl Devlin and his brother. I'm sure Karl is here to demand some money."

"Well, he'll save you some postage."

Carrie headed for the door, and Mandy stayed on her heels.

"Hello, Mr. Devlin," Carrie said. "Please come in."

Karl limped past her, a sour look on his face, and Kurt

followed, looking the same way. Both of them frowned at the black woman.

Carrie closed the door and said, "Mr. Karl Devlin and Mr. Kurt Devlin, I would like for you to meet one of my dearest friends, Mandy Carver."

"We ain't here to be social," Karl said. "I had Kurt bring me here so I could collect some money. You people will soon be five months behind in your payments. I want no less than three of those payments, and I want 'em right now! Where's your husband?"

Carrie's emotions stirred, and tears surfaced. Her face pinched as she said, "Colin is dead."

Karl Devlin's eyebrows arched. "Dead? Well, this is a fine kettle of fish! So how are you gonna work this ranch and make it pay, lady?"

Sniffling, Carrie said, "I'm going to give it all I've got, Mr. Devlin. Some of my neighbors have offered to help me."

Karl snorted and shook his head. "Oh, sure. You couldn't make it when your husband was alive, what makes you think you can do it now? Especially with the cougars killin' your cattle."

"Those cougars are dead now. There were three of them. It was one of them that attacked Colin and tore him up so bad that he died."

"Okay, so the cougars are out of the picture. Even with some help from your neighbors, you ain't gonna make it, Mrs. Wright!"

Clenching her fists, Carrie said, "I can make it because it was Colin's dream!" With that, she broke into uncontrollable sobs.

Devlin sneered, waggled his head, and shouted above her sobbing, "Prove it! I want three months' payment right now!"

Contempt blazed in Mandy's eyes as she stepped close to Karl Devlin and snapped, "What's the matter with you, mister? Carrie's husband was killed! You must have a chunk of ice in place of a heart! Don't you have any decency in you?"

Devlin stepped around her and said to Carrie, "I want three months' payment on the mortgage. If I don't walk out of here with the money, I'm foreclosin' and takin' the ranch back. I'll sell it to someone who'll abide by his contract."

Carrie could only sob with her hands covering her face. Mandy walked away toward the kitchen.

"Stop the bawlin', woman! Are you gonna pay me or not?"

Suddenly Mandy reappeared, wielding the Winchester .44, her mouth hard. She aimed the muzzle directly at Karl, and her voice cracked like a whip. "Hey, you! Shut your mouth!"

Karl's jaw slacked at the threatening sight before him, and Kurt's eyes bulged.

"Now, wait a minute, lady. I—"

"If you'd back off and let Carrie get ahold of herself, she'd be able to tell you that she has an envelope with two months' payment in it she was gonna put in the mail tomorrow!"

Karl blinked and looked back at Carrie. "Is this true?" he asked loud enough to carry over her sobs.

Carrie took her hands away from her shiny, wet face, and nodded.

Karl looked at his brother.

Holding the rifle steady, Mandy rasped, "You need to have some compassion on this new widow, mister! Take the money and give her a chance to catch up on the payments."

Kurt eyed the black muzzle lined on his brother and said, "Karl, maybe you'd better let Mrs. Wright talk to you."

Karl tried to lick his lips, but there was little moisture left in his mouth. Clearing his throat, he said, "I will listen to her, but will you please point that gun another direction? It might go off."

Mandy looked at her friend. Carrie took a shallow breath and nodded her consent. The gun was lowered but still held firmly in Mandy's grip as she moved close to Carrie and set grim eyes on Karl Devlin.

"Mr. Devlin," Carrie said shakily, "I am asking you to accept the two month's payment and give me a little more time before you consider foreclosing on me."

"Why don't you sell more cattle and bring the payments up to date?"

"If I sell any more, I'll come up short on a calf crop in the spring, and then I'll lose everything. I don't know how I'll do it yet, but I will get caught up. I'll find a way."

Devlin let his gaze run over Mandy's stern face then looked back at Carrie and sighed. "All right, Mrs. Wright. I'll give you a month to catch up on two more payments and another month to get your mortgage payments up to date. If you fail on either of these dates, I'll foreclose. Do you understand?"

"I do," said Carrie. "Somehow I will meet your requirements."

Devlin nodded. "All right. Let's have the money you said you were going to mail to me."

When the Devlin brothers drove away, Mandy turned from the window and said, "Honey, how are you gonna meet his demands?"

"I have no idea at this point, but the Lord has the answer. He'll have to show me."

Early the next morning, Marshal Mangum and Heidi Lindgren arrived at the Box W. Abe Carver was with them. After Mandy had told them about Carrie's visit from the Devlin brothers and Karl's heartless treatment of her, Lance and Abe took Mandy and headed for town.

As Mangum drove his wagon over the frozen land, Mandy said to both men, "I want to go to the church first thing when we get back to town and tell Pastor Kelly about what Carrie is facing. He needs to know."

When they pulled into the church parking lot, Pastor Andy Kelly was just coming from the parsonage toward the church.

"Good morning," said Kelly. "So how was your stay with Carrie, Mandy?"

"My stay was fine, Pastor. But something happened while I was there that I would like to tell you about."

"Certainly. We'll talk in my office. Are you gentlemen coming in, too?"

"We have to move on, Pastor," said Mangum.

Moments later, Mandy sat down on a chair in front of the pastor's desk and told him what went on with the Devlin brothers at the ranch.

When she finished speaking, Kelly's features were stony. Shaking his head, he said, "How could Karl Devlin be so cruel to a grieving widow?"

"I guess because if he has a heart, Pastor, it's a chunk of ice. Carrie needs financial help."

"She sure does. On Sunday I'm going to tell the people what happened and what she's facing. We'll take a special offering both Sunday morning and Sunday night. It's hard to say how much we'll raise, but whatever amount, it will be a help to her."

Mandy smiled. "I knew you would want to do something like that, Pastor. God bless you."

When Sunday came, Carrie Wright was not feeling well. She had slept little since Karl Devlin's visit. Julianna Bower was staying with her.

At the morning church service, Pastor Kelly shared with the people about Carrie's situation. The people dug deep into their pockets...and again in the evening service. When the offering was totaled in front of the congregation, they had given a little more than enough to cover two more months' payments for Carrie.

Pastor Kelly ran his eyes over the faces of his people and said, "I know all of you have sacrificed to come up with this amount, and I appreciate it more than I can say."

Curly Wesson spoke up. "Pastor, I saw you drop a purty good chunk in the plate when it went past you. An' speakin' for the rest of us, I 'preciate how you and Rebecca sacrificed for Carrie, too. You've set us a perfect example."

Kelly grinned. "Thank you for those kind words, Curly. I'm wondering if all of you would let me lead you just a step further."

Many voices called for him to tell them what he had in mind.

Kelly pulled out his wallet and said, "Wouldn't it be wonderful if we could sacrifice a bit more and be able to give Carrie another month's payment? If we did that, she'd actually be a few days early making March's payment. What a blessing and encouragement that would be."

Kelly pulled out a ten-dollar bill, lifted it up, and said, "If I could get seven people to match this ten spot, we could do it."

Within a few minutes, the amount was raised.

Pastor Kelly and his people enjoyed the moment together, then he led them in prayer, asking God to bless his people for their generosity and to make the gift from the church a great blessing to Carrie Wright.

On Monday morning, Julianna Bower answered the knock at the door when Pastor and Mrs. Kelly arrived at the Box W.

"Pastor! Rebecca!" she said happily. "I'm so glad to see you. Please come in."

"How's Carrie doing today?" Rebecca asked.

"Much better."

"Will she feel like seeing us?" the pastor asked.

"I'm pretty sure she will. Sit down here in the parlor. I'll be right back."

Moments later, Julianna returned and found the Kellys standing in front of the fireplace, soaking up some heat. They both looked expectantly at her as she said, "Carrie is glad you're here, but she insists on getting dressed. She said to tell you she'll be out in a few minutes. It'll be a little faster if I go back and help her with her hair."

When Carrie and Julianna entered the parlor, Rebecca rushed to meet Carrie, embracing her as she said, "We missed you in church yesterday. I'm so glad to know you're feeling better."

"Thank you," Carrie said, giving Rebecca an extra squeeze.

"Mandy came to me on Thursday and told me about Karl Devlin's ultimatum," Kelly said.

Carrie nodded as her lips pulled into a pencil-thin line.

"I told our people about it in church yesterday morning. A special offering was taken in both the morning and evening services." As he spoke, he produced an envelope from an inside pocket and extended it to her. "Mandy told me how much your monthly payments are, and that within a few days you'll still be three months behind. So...your brothers and sisters gave enough to cover payments up to March. This will bring you up to date."

Carrie looked at the pastor in astonishment. When she found her voice she said, "I don't know what to say. I'm over-whelmed. I—" Tears welled up in her eyes. "Pastor, I—"

Rebecca went over to Carrie and took hold of her hand. "Honey, our people did this because they love you. Pastor and I love you. We want to be a help and a blessing in this very difficult time in your life."

Carrie wept for joy as she said, "There's nobody on earth like God's people. Pastor, thank you so very much for presenting my need to the people. Please convey to them my deepest appreciation until I can do it myself."

A broad smile lit up his face. "I will do that, Carrie. I most certainly will do that."

When the Kellys were preparing to leave, Carrie said, "Pastor, Rebecca, would you do something for me?"

"Anything," said Rebecca.

"Would you come back tomorrow evening and have supper with Julianna and me? It's the only way right now that I have of showing you my appreciation."

The Kellys exchanged glances, then Rebecca smiled and said, "It will be our pleasure."

CHAPTER NINE

O n Tuesday morning, February 21, Carrie was up at dawn. Her tender heart was still sore and lonely, but she had a purpose today. As she built a fire in the kitchen stove, she began planning her menu for the evening meal. When the fire was burning strong, she went to the parlor and built a fire in the fireplace.

Back in the kitchen, she found the stove getting warm, and by the time she had poured water into the coffeepot, filled the metal basket with coffee grounds, slid it into place and dropped the lid, the stove was hot. She set a pan of water on to boil for oatmeal.

While Carrie was rolling biscuit dough, she thought how good it was to get some normalcy back into her life. *There will always be a place in my heart for Colin,* she mused, *but he would want me to find some happiness, and that's what I'm going to do.*

In her room, Julianna stirred and opened her eyes. She instantly thought of Jack and little Larissa. Her little girl was in the care of Julie Powell, and Jack was playing bachelor at home. Julianna missed both of them very much but was glad she could spend these three days with Carrie.

She rose from the bed with a big yawn, put on her robe and slippers, and headed for the door. As soon as she opened it, she could smell the biscuits baking.

When Julianna drew near the kitchen door, she could hear Carrie humming a tune, and then she saw Carrie pouring oats into a pan of boiling water while humming almost merrily.

When Carrie looked up, she stopped humming and smiled at Julianna. "Good morning."

"And good morning to you," Julianna said with a lilt in her voice, giving Carrie a warm hug. "My, it's wonderful to see you so happy!"

"The Lord is good. He has given me real comfort in my loss of Colin, and I praise Him for it. Ready to eat?"

"Yes, who wouldn't be?" Julianna breathed in the tantalizing aromas of the kitchen.

Moments later, as the two women were enjoying their breakfast, Julianna said, "What can I do to help you today, honey?"

"Oh, just your company is enough."

Julianna frowned. "Come on, now. You're having guests for supper this evening. I'll help you here in the kitchen as much as you need me, then I'll spruce up the house."

"Tell you what," said Carrie, "if it's all right with you, I'll do the cooking and you do the sprucing. I do love to cook, and it will keep my mind occupied more than cleaning the house."

"Sure. Makes no difference to me."

"I'm really looking forward to the fellowship with Pastor Kelly and Rebecca, aren't you?"

"Very much so."

They finished breakfast, and together washed and dried the dishes and tidied up the kitchen, chatting all the while.

Julianna filled a bucket with hot, soapy water and several rags and took broom, dustpan, and feather duster with her, and started in her own room where she first changed the sheets on the bed, then went to work on the window and the floor.

Carrie went to her bedroom, made her bed up with fresh sheets, and returned to the kitchen, humming yet another tune, a tiny smile teasing the corners of her mouth. She replaced her plain white apron with a clean, colorful one, and while preparing the dough for bread she would bake for supper, she sent a prayer of thanksgiving heavenward for the gracious way her heavenly Father had provided the love of so many Christian friends and had given her such a loving pastoral couple in Andy and Rebecca.

When noon came, and Julianna saw how much Carrie had already prepared for supper, she insisted that Carrie lie down for at least a short rest.

Julianna did the wash and hung it out to dry under gathering clouds while Carrie rested quietly on the bed in her room. Carrie didn't nap, but rather let her mind wander back over the last several days. Slow tears coursed down her cheeks, and she brushed them away with a corner of her apron.

Sniffling, she thought, *I miss you so much, Colin. I'm doing the best I can to save this ranch that you loved and worked so hard to make successful.*

After two hours, she returned to the kitchen feeling refreshed. Already, delicious aromas were wafting into the warm air throughout the house.

At 5:30, Carrie and Julianna went to their rooms to freshen up before the company arrived.

When Julianna went back to the kitchen, she found Carrie checking on her simmering dinner, then they went to the parlor and sat in front of the crackling fire. Only a few minutes had passed when the sound of snorting horses and rattling buggy wheels met their ears.

Carrie welcomed her guests as they stepped inside, then excused herself, leaving the Kellys with Julianna in the cheery parlor. She hurried away to put the finishing touches on her carefully prepared meal.

Soon all was ready, and she and Julianna escorted their guests into the kitchen that was filled with mouth-watering fragrance. The windows were frosting over and a gentle breeze swirled snowflakes against them. In contrast, there was warmth from the fire in the kitchen stove, and even more dominant was the warmth of Christian love and friendship.

During the meal, the Kellys and the two women talked about Chief Two Moons and Sweet Blossom and gave praise to the Lord, agreeing that it took a lot of courage for them to leave the gods of their ancestors to turn to Jesus.

"They need a lot of prayer," said Kelly. "It won't be easy to convince their people they have done the right thing. They will need the Lord's power to get the light of the gospel into the darkened hearts of their people."

"Wouldn't it be wonderful if one day the entire village was in the Shepherd's fold?" Carrie said.

"It sure would," said Rebecca. "Ladies, this meal is delicious."

"Sure is," said the preacher.

"I can't take any credit for the cooking," Julianna said. "Carrie did it all by herself while I was doing other things."

Kelly took a sip of coffee, and said, "Carrie, Colin bragged about your cooking to me a couple of times. He said you had a special touch. Now I know what he meant."

"You're very kind, pastor."

Kelly shook his head. "I do try to be kind, but these words are spoken from thorough enjoyment."

When the meal was finished, Carrie suggested they take their coffee into the parlor and relax. The pastor tossed more logs on the fire; when he sat down beside Rebecca, he looked at Julianna and said, "Well, Mrs. Deputy Marshal, how have you found it, being married to a lawman? I recall that we discussed it in one of those counseling sessions before the wedding. You were worrying about the badge on his chest being a target for outlaws."

"Jack and I talked about it many times before we got married, Pastor. He even offered to resign and get another job if I was finding it too hard to face being married to a lawman. But I told him I would just have to trust the Lord to give me the grace and strength to take it.

"I know Jack loves his work, and I would never force him to give it up. So far, the Lord has helped me to daily entrust Jack into His hands, and He has given me peace every day when Jack leaves the house with the badge on his chest."

"Good," said Kelly. "I know Jack has been a great help to Lance. He would sure hate to lose him."

"Well, as for my part, Lance is going to keep him. They make a great team."

"They sure do," Kelly said. "And this town is a lot safer because of the two of them."

Carrie brought fresh coffee and refilled cups, then took the coffeepot back to the kitchen. When she returned, the pastor said, "Carrie, there's something I want to talk to you about while we're here."

"Mm-hmm?" she said, sitting down and picking up her steaming cup.

"I'm your pastor, and I care very much what happens to you, so I'm going to stick my nose into your personal business."

"All right."

"I'm concerned about your trying to maintain the ranch by yourself. I know your neighbors have offered to help—especially Chad Tolman—but they're limited in what they can do. There are always fences to repair, and the house and outbuildings demand continual attention. And then there's the branding of the calves, not to mention the hay and grain they have to be fed daily, and the water tanks kept filled, and the ice broken on the tanks in the winter. How are you going to do all of this?"

Carrie closed her eyes and sighed. "Pastor, I don't know. I

can't afford to hire someone to help me beyond what the neighbors will do."

Kelly cleared his throat. "I know you're desperately trying to carry on Colin's dream, but to me it just doesn't look feasible. Maybe you should seriously consider selling the ranch and taking a job in town."

Carrie's lips quivered as tears misted her eyes. "Pastor, I very much appreciate your concern for me, but I can't sell it and move to town. It was Colin's dream. I must carry it on, no matter how impossible it looks."

Kelly nodded but said no more.

Rebecca touched his arm. "Andy, we should be heading back to town."

Moments later, as the Kellys were putting on their coats and hats near the front door, Carrie produced an envelope and said, "Pastor, this is the money to catch up the mortgage payments with Karl Devlin. Would you mail it for me in the morning?"

"Of course. I'll do it first thing so it's sure to go out on the first stage."

On that same evening, Jacob Kates was having supper with the Coopers, which he did at least three or four times a week.

While Patty Ruth slipped morsels of food to Biggie under the table, Jacob ran his gaze over the faces of Hannah's children and said, "Everybody looks especially happy tonight. Has something extra good happened?"

"You could say that," Hannah replied with a broad smile. "We received a letter today from Adam and Theresa Cooper in Cincinnati, Ohio. You recall that I told you Adam is Solomon's younger brother."

"Yes. I remember."

"Well, I think I might have mentioned to you some time

ago that Adam has wanted to come to Fort Bridger and start a newspaper."

"Mm-hmm. Seems like you did."

"Adam is an intelligent and industrious young man, Jacob. Three years ago he became editor-in-chief of the *Cincinnati Post*. When I told Lloyd Dawson and Cade Samuels about Adam wanting to come here and start a newspaper—and I told them he had been promoted to editor-in-chief of the *Post* at age thirty-one—they both showed immediate interest in seeing him come and start a newspaper here.

"I put Adam in touch with them, and a short time later, Mr. Dawson told me he had corresponded with Adam several times by telegram and was considering having the bank loan Adam the money he needed to come and start the paper. Mr. Samuels also corresponded with Adam and told him if he came, he would try to find him space in a building on Main Street to house the paper, and he would help find him and his family a house to live in."

Jacob nodded. "And so I see happy faces around this table because in the letter you received from Adam and Theresa today, you learned it's going to work out. Is that it?"

"It sure ith, Uncle Jacob!" Patty Ruth said. "Uncle Adam, Aunt Theretha, and my couthinth, Theth an' Anna are gonna come an' live here!"

Hannah laughed. "In case you couldn't understand her, Jacob, Adam's son's name is Seth. He's six years old, and little Anna is just over a month old."

Jacob nodded. "So when are they coming?"

"Well, in the letter, Adam and Theresa said Mr. Dawson had confirmed the loan. Adam sat down with Claude Owens, the owner of the *Cincinnati Post,* explaining that he was coming to Fort Bridger to start his own paper. But of course, ethically speaking, he can't leave the *Post* until Owens has a man to replace him. Owens is working on it at present."

"So, there's really no way to know when they'll come?"

"No. But what a joy to know they're coming! And Adam is bringing his pressman with him. His name is Doug McClain, and he and his wife, Kathy, belong to the same church that Adam and Theresa do. Doug has been a pressman at the *Post* for several years. He'll be a real help to Adam. The McClains have a little daughter named Jenny who's just over a year old."

Jacob's eyes twinkled in harmony with the smile that lit up his face. "Hannah, I haven't seen you look this happy since I came here. I'm so glad to see it."

Hannah blinked at the moisture that flooded her eyes. "Jacob, I'm so delighted that Adam and his little family are coming to live in Fort Bridger. I love it here. And my friends are a constant source of joy. But I do miss my family, and it will be so good to have them close by. Adam is a lot like Solomon, and these children love him very much. My boys especially need Adam's strong male influence in their lives."

"That will be good," said Jacob.

"It sure will," said Chris.

Hannah sighed. "I only wish I could convince my parents to come and live here. My father is retired. There's no reason they couldn't. I've been gently working on them and praying about it. The Lord knows how to work it out."

"I really feel the Lord is going to bring them, Mama," spoke up Mary Beth. "Grandma and Grandpa would love it here, just as we do. And we need them."

"Well, I know I'd really like to have your grandma with me when this baby is born," said Hannah. "I had her with me when all four of you children were born. With this new baby about to arrive, I've been thinking about that, and missing her terribly."

"Mama," B.J. said, "you'll have Grandma O'Brien with you when the baby comes, won't you?"

"Yes, B.J. She'll be here to help."

"Will our new little thithter be born before Chrith'th birthday, Mama?" Patty Ruth asked.

"Patty Ruth!" said B.J. "How many times do Chris and I have to tell you? It's a little brother!"

Mary Beth rolled her eyes but didn't comment.

"According to Grandpa O'Brien, the baby's not supposed to be born till about a month after Chris's birthday, Patty Ruth," said Hannah. "And as you know, Chris's birthday is just three days from now."

"Yes!" said Chris. "I'll be fifteen on Friday. It was February 24, 1856, when the world was so blessed!"

Mary Beth made a face as if she were going to gag. "Ugh! Blessed? I think there's a better word for it!"

"Hey!" said B.J. "If our little brother gets born when Grandpa O'Brien says he will, that'll be just a few days after my birthday!" He thought about it a moment. "Know what? Our little brother could come a week or so early and be born on my birthday! Wouldn't that be neat?"

Hannah chuckled. "That's not likely to happen, B.J." Then looking at her other son, she said, "Chris, with all this talk about Uncle Adam and Aunt Theresa's letter, I forgot to tell you that Donna Carlin came by today and said they want to have your birthday party at their house Friday night."

Chris's eyes lit up. "Really? Hey, that'd be great! I love every minute I can spend inside the fort."

Hannah nodded with a smile. "She said it was Travis's idea. When he brought it up, both she and Dobie liked it. She said you can choose the people to invite, up to about twenty people. You'll need to run over to the fort before school in the morning and give her a written list."

"Great! I'll do it. Did Mrs. Carlin say what time the party will be Friday?"

"Mm-hmm. Eight o'clock."

"Can I ride up to the village after school tomorrow and

invite Broken Wing and his parents, Mama?"

"Only if you can find an adult to ride with you. You know I don't want you riding that far from the fort alone."

"I'll ask Dob—I mean, Lieutenant Carlin and Travis to ride up there with me."

"Fine," said Hannah.

Jacob ran his eyes over the Cooper family and saw that everyone had finished their supper. He looked at Hannah and said, "I have a little present for you, sweet lady. I'll be right back."

B.J. stared at the closed door and said, "Mama, what do you suppose he has for you?"

Hannah shrugged. "I have no idea."

"I've sometimes heard him working in his room during the past couple of weeks, Mama," said Chris. "He was using a saw and a hammer."

Patty Ruth said, "Maybe Uncle Jacob ith makin' a new bookshelf for you, Mama. He knowth the one you have ith too little for all your bookth."

"Maybe it's a new rocking chair," said Mary Beth.

They could hear Jacob's footsteps on the staircase.

"We're about to find out," said Hannah, adjusting her uncomfortable body on the chair.

Chris hurried to the door and pulled it open.

"Thanks, Chris," said the wiry little man as he came inside the apartment.

Hannah's eyes grew wide when she saw the beautiful cradle he was carrying. It was structured like the cradle he had made for Patty Ruth's doll for her birthday, but a larger version. The wood had been sanded and stained to a glossy patina.

His face beaming, Jacob carried the cradle to Hannah and said, "Do you like it?"

"Oh, it's beautiful!"

Jacob grinned from ear to ear as Hannah gently ran her fingers over the smooth wood. "Oh, Jacob, what a lovely surprise!" She leaned close and planted a kiss on his craggy cheek, then moved toward the hall and called over her shoulder, "Wait just a minute!"

The children were admiring the cradle when Hannah returned with a pillow covered in green and white fabric and a small fleecy white blanket. "Let's see how these go with it," she said.

"Here, Mama," said Mary Beth, taking them from her. "Uncle Jacob, would you set the cradle on the table, please?"

Mary Beth tested the pillow for size and found that it fit quite snugly on the bottom of the cradle. She draped the blanket over the pillow as if it had the baby lying on it.

"Perfect," said Hannah. "Just perfect."

Turning to Jacob, she kissed his cheek again and said, "Thank you so much for your kindness. It's going to be just right for the baby."

Again the little man grinned from ear to ear.

The next afternoon, when the Cooper children came home from school, their mother was sitting in the parlor in front of the fireplace. They removed their coats and caps and hurried to hug and kiss her.

Mary Beth was the last to do so, and after kissing her mother on the cheek, she said, "Did Glenda come and walk you to the clinic today as planned, Mama?"

"Yes."

"And did Grandpa O'Brien say he still expects the baby to be born the third week of March?"

"Mm-hmm. About ten days or so after B.J.'s birthday."

B.J. stuck his chest out. "Yeah. And Brett Jonathan Cooper is gonna be nine years old! Sure wish my baby brother would be born on my birthday."

"You mean baby sister," said Mary Beth. "It's going to be a girl, you know."

"Ain't neither! It's a boy!"

"No, it ain't!" said Patty Ruth. "It'th a girl!"

"I happen to know it's a boy," said Chris.

"Huh-uh-h-h!" countered Patty Ruth. "Mary Beth ith right. It'th a baby thithter!"

"No sense arguing, children," said Hannah.

Mary Beth looked at her mother. "Well, Mama, you have never told us which you think it is. A boy or a girl?"

"Honey, I'm pretty sure which it is, but I'm not going to declare myself on it. We'll just have to wait and see."

"Mama, what are you gonna name our new little thithter?" Patty Ruth asked.

"If it's a girl, I'm going to name her Betsy Lee, after a friend I had in school years ago."

"Since the baby is a boy, Mama," spoke up Chris, "what are you going to name him?"

Hannah grinned at Mary Beth and Patty Ruth, then said, "Well, Chris, if the baby is a boy, I'm going to name him after his papa—Solomon Edward."

"Hey, that's neat!" said B.J. "Will we call him 'Sol' like you called Papa?"

"No, honey. We'll call him Eddie."

"I like that, Mama," said Chris. "Eddie. Has a nice sound. Don't you think so, Mary Beth?"

"It would if it was a boy, but I like Betsy Lee."

Chris's eyebrows arched. "Betsy Lee for a boy?"

"Not for a boy, thilly," said Patty Ruth. "It'th a girl! An' it'th Belinda'th mama'th name, too!"

That night, when Hannah was tucking the girls into their beds, Mary Beth prayed first, then it was Patty Ruth's turn. Lisping through her prayer, she thanked the Lord for little Betsy Lee who was in Mama's tummy, then closed off by saying, "An' Lord, pleathe let little Betthy Lee have red hair like mine...an freckelth too!"

CHAPTER TEN

O n Thursday, February 23, some six miles east of Fort Bridger, farmer Rufe Imler watched his fifteen-year-old son ride out of the yard on his horse, heading for school.

It was a crisp morning. Rufe's breath clouded in front of his bearded face as he turned and mounted the porch steps to enter the old farmhouse. Scowling at his petite wife, who was wiping blood from her lip, the huge man growled, "Next time, Cordelia, keep your mouth shut."

Fear rode Cordelia's pale blue eyes as she said in a low voice, "Just because I asked you not to be so tough on Bob, you didn't have to hit me."

"It's the father's responsibility to discipline his son, woman! When I correct him, you stay out of it!"

Cordelia went to the water basin at the cupboard, wetted a cloth, and dabbed at the cut on her lip.

Rufe sat down at the kitchen table. "Gimme some more coffee," he said.

Without a word, Cordelia poured him a fresh cup, then started picking up the breakfast dishes and utensils from the table.

"I hope you've learned your lesson this time."

Cordelia did not reply as she carried the dishes and utensils toward the cupboard.

Rufe gulped the last of the coffee in his cup, banged it down on the table, and shoved his chair back. "I've got work to do in the barn." Shouldering into his sheepskin coat and dropping his hat on his head, Rufe went out the back door and headed through the snow toward the barn.

Cordelia heard hooves crunching in the snow and looked out the window to see a lone rider trotting toward Rufe.

Outside, Rufe's hard eyes were fixed on the stranger as the man said, "Mr. Imler?"

"Yeah," Rufe said.

"May I dismount?"

"Who are ya? Whattya want?"

"My name is Andy Kelly. I'm pastor of the church in Fort Bridger. Miss Sundi Lindgren, Fort Bridger's schoolmarm, is a member of our church. She told me that a family named Imler had moved onto the old Parkman farm east of town, and that their son, Bob, had enrolled in school last week. I came by to introduce myself, welcome you to the area, and invite you to come visit our services."

Rufe shook his head, spat on the snow, and said, "No need of leavin' the saddle. Just ride on."

"But sir, I—"

"You deaf? Get off my property! You weren't invited here and you ain't welcome! I ain't interested in your church, and neither is my wife. Now, I got things to do." With that, he wheeled about and stomped toward the barn.

Cordelia watched the scene through the kitchen window. She couldn't hear what was being said, but she could tell that Rufe was getting angrier by the minute. She wondered if the man was a neighbor, just trying to be friendly. *No doubt he has a wife,* she thought. *It would be nice if I had a friend to talk with.* Cordelia could tell the visitor was trying to be friendly, but Rufe was having none of it. Her mouth sagged as she saw her husband pivot in a rude fashion and head for the barn.

"Mr. Imler," Andy Kelly called out, "if there is ever anything I can do for you or your wife and son, all you have to do is let me know."

Rufe halted and turned around. His deep-set eyes grew dark with hatred.

Kelly nudged his horse forward and drew up again, looking down at the big man. "Sir, I'm here to help people if they ever need help. That's part of my job. I only—"

"I have no need for a preacher; I have no need for a church, and I never will!"

Speaking softly, with a gentle smile, Kelly said, "Mr. Imler, even people who are not church members die. And almost without fail, the family likes to have a preacher conduct the funeral…and they want the service conducted in a church. Right?"

Imler drew a deep breath and shouted, "It won't be true when I die! My wife knows I don't want nothin' to do with preachers and churches and all that religious stuff—dead or alive!"

"Let me ask you something."

"What?"

"When you die, where will you go? Heaven or hell?"

Rufe's face went crimson. Eyes flashing, he snarled, "Get off my property, and don't bother me again! Like I said, you ain't welcome here!"

Kelly turned the horse around and trotted toward the road. As he passed the house, he saw a female face peering at him through lace curtains from the kitchen window.

At the Fort Bridger school, Sundi Lindgren was stoking the fire in the big potbellied stove when her students began to arrive. She dropped the lid on the grate and turned to greet them. "Good morning, Sarah, Dorothy, Elaine."

The three girls returned the greeting.

Several more students arrived, receiving a welcome from their teacher. Suddenly the door opened and eleven-year-old Donnie Barker, whose father was an officer at the fort, hurried in and said, "Miss Lindgren, that new boy is picking on Ryan Fordham. I think he's going to beat him up!"

Sundi moved toward the door. Ryan was the same age as Donnie and no match for the fifteen-year-old who had been trouble since the first day he enrolled in school the previous week. Bob Imler was a big boy—much larger than any other boy in the school—and had already shown himself to be a bully. He had a short temper and had sassed his teacher on several occasions.

As Sundi bolted onto the porch, she saw Bob punch Ryan in the stomach, doubling him over. Other students were standing by, including the Cooper children. Chris Cooper was telling Bob to leave Ryan alone.

Bob set angry eyes on Chris. "You want some of the same, Cooper? Shut up or you'll get it!"

"Bob!" came Sundi's high-pitched voice as she drew up behind him. "Why did you hit Ryan?"

His mouth curved down in a thin slit, but he didn't answer. He gave her an insolent look as she bent over Ryan, who was holding his stomach and gasping.

"Are you all right, Ryan?" Sundi asked.

Ryan gritted his teeth and nodded. "I'm feeling a bit nauseated, ma'am. I thought for a minute my breakfast was going to come up, but I don't think so now."

"Why did Bob hit you?"

Ryan glanced at the big boy, then looked back at the teacher. "He was picking on Lulubelle and Marianne, ma'am. I told him to leave them alone. He got mad and hit me."

Looking at the Cooper children, Sundi said, "Chris, Mary Beth, will you take Ryan inside for me, please? Bob and I are going to have a talk. The rest of you go on in, too."

As Chris and Mary Beth guided Ryan inside the school-house, followed by the rest of the students, Sundi turned to Bob, who was a head taller than she, and said, "What's your problem, Bob? Why do you act like this?"

Bob stared at her with cold eyes but did not reply.

"Yesterday I had to lecture you for getting rough with two other girls, let alone the fact that you have made trouble with one boy or another since the day you started here. What is it, anyhow?"

He remained silent.

"Not going to talk, eh?" she said.

"Not if I don't want to."

"Listen to me, young man. In this school, I teach the boys to be gentlemen and the girls to be ladies. You're going to learn to be a gentleman, do you hear me?" When he didn't respond, she said, "Well, you will, or I'll be having a talk with your father."

Bob sneered, but remained silent.

"The first thing you need to learn, young man, is that a gentleman doesn't cause trouble in school. A gentleman doesn't cause trouble with any of the boys, and he most certainly does not pick on girls. Yesterday, you doubled up your fist at Abby Turner. Now you listen, young man, a gentleman would never strike a girl. Do you hear me?"

Bob only stared at her.

"I said, do you hear me?" Sundi's voice was sharp and ominous.

Bob blinked. "Yeah, I hear ya."

Sundi shook her head. "No! That kind of talk is not allowed. You say, 'Yes, ma'am. I hear you.'"

Resistance showed on Bob Imler's young face. The school-marm's eyes flashed fire. "Let me hear it, Bob!"

A tiny bit of surprise showed in Bob Imler's stony eyes. Nodding, he said, "Yes, ma'am. I hear you."

"That's better. Now, let's go inside so we can get started with our lessons."

As they walked side by side, Sundi could still feel the resistance boiling inside Rufe Imler's son.

That evening, Heidi Lindgren stepped out of her room smelling of perfume and powder, and noticed that the door of her sister's room in the small house they shared was standing open. Stepping into Sundi's room, Heidi found her sister sitting before the dresser mirror, brushing her hair, which she had washed an hour before. The brush made little crackling sounds as it sent static electricity through her hair.

"Is Lance here yet, honey?" Sundi asked, looking at her sister's reflection in the mirror.

"No, but he'll be right on time, so I thought I'd come and tell you I'll see you and Patrick at Glenda's Place. We've got to go by the Bowers' house for a few minutes. Something Lance needs to talk to Jack about. That's why he's coming early."

There was a knock at the door.

Heidi grinned. "See what I told you? The marshal of this town is quite punctual."

"I should say so. He'll be on time for your wedding, too."

Heidi blushed. "Honey, he hasn't yet brought up the subject."

"He will. See you at Glenda's."

Sundi heard Lance's voice, and seconds later the front

door clicked shut. She looked at herself in the mirror and said, "Well, schoolmarm, you've finally entered into some social life."

She thought about how her life had been so busy in the years she went to college to get her teacher's degree. Then, when she came to Fort Bridger—like Heidi—she found few Christian young men, and none who weren't already attached. The Lindgren sisters had known very little in the way of social life.

Marshal Lance Mangum had shown serious interest in Heidi before he became a Christian, but Heidi would let nothing develop between them. Sundi smiled at her reflection and said, "But since Lance became a Christian, things have been developing rapidly, haven't they, dear sister?" She sighed, smiled at her reflection again, and said, "And now, Miss Sundi Lindgren, Dr. Patrick O'Brien has come to town. Handsome, debonair, and interested in you. Mmm. Thank You, Lord. What a fine man."

Sundi's hair shimmered in the lamplight as she pulled the sides up, inserted silver combs to hold them, and let the back cascade down. It reached almost to her slim waist, curling naturally at the ends.

She got up from the stool and went to where her dress lay across the foot of the bed. She had chosen a soft woolen lavender dress that she knew deepened her blue eyes until they almost matched the color of the dress.

When the dress was on and buttoned, Sundi returned to the mirror and pinched her cheeks to add a rosy hue to them. She backed away, turned from side to side, and gave herself one last look in the mirror. She took her hat and coat from the closet and carried them to the parlor to wait for Patrick.

She had been sitting in front of the fireplace only a few minutes when she heard Patrick's footsteps on the front porch. She rushed to the door and pulled it open before he could knock. "Hello, Patrick. Come in."

A cold gust of frigid air followed him inside. When it reached the fireplace, it caused the flames to enlarge and flicker rapidly. Shivering with the cold, Sundi closed the door and smiled up at the man who stood almost a foot taller than she. "Thank you for braving the elements to take me to supper."

Giving her an admiring look, he said, "A man would be an absolute fool to let the elements keep him from a date with the loveliest young lady on earth."

The schoolmarm's complexion tinted. "You are very kind, sir," she said as she stepped to the sofa and picked up her coat. "I'm afraid I don't quite fit that description."

Patrick helped her on with her coat and said, "Dear lady, you more than fit that description."

"Thank you," she said, flashing him a smile as she put her hat on.

"It's really a cold night, Sundi. Better button your coat up tight and put your gloves on."

"Yes, sir," Sundi said with a twinkle in her eye. "You sound just like a doctor."

"Young lady, I remember just how sick you were when I first came to town not so long ago. We don't want a repeat performance of that!"

"You are so right, Doctor, even though I don't remember it as well as you do." As she spoke, she buttoned her collar all the way to her throat.

They stepped out into the cold night, and even though it was only a short distance to the café, Patrick put Sundi in his buggy and placed a blanket snugly around her. She was glowing with his attention and care.

"All set?" he asked, as he took his place beside her and picked up the reins. As he put the horse to a moderate trot, Sundi set her eyes on his profile, which was highlighted by the street lamps. Ever since Dr. Patrick O'Brien had treated her for a very severe case of influenza, she could hardly keep her mind off him. Each time she was with him, she found her heart doing some strange maneuvers, and her dreams had been filled with him. She wondered if she was having the same effect on him. There was something in the way he looked at her that made her think she might be.

When Sundi and Patrick entered the café, Lance and Heidi were already at a table and waved them over.

While the foursome ate, the conversation went first to Carrie Wright and how she was going to be able to run the Box W by herself, even with some intermittent help from neighboring ranchers. From there, they talked about other things, then the marshal looked at Sundi and said, "I understand that new boy, Bob Imler, has been giving you trouble at school."

Sundi nodded. "How did you find out?"

"Oh, some six or seven of your students have volunteered the information. They say he's been bullying some of the other students and that he's been talking back to you."

"Mm-hmm. Bob has been quite a problem since day one."

"Do you know about his father?"

A puzzled look captured Sundi's fine features. "What do you mean?"

"Well, Rufe Imler is a mountain of a man and has the look of a brute engraved in his face. He's quite unfriendly and very brusque. I saw Pastor Kelly approach Imler on the street this afternoon. Apparently, from what I picked up, Pastor had paid a visit to the Imlers sometime recently. The big man was really nasty to him when Pastor spoke to him. He told Pastor never to set foot on his property again and that he wanted nothing to do with him. He stomped away like a mad bull."

Sundi nodded. "Mm-hmm. Now I know why his son is like that. I have a notion the man is rough on his wife."

"Why would you say that?" Patrick asked.

"Because Bob not only bullies boys, he bullies girls, too."

"Well, you're probably right. You know…like father, like son."

"I'm hoping I can bring Bob into line."

"I hope you can too," said Lance. "If you run into anything serious, Sundi, let me know."

"I will."

"This food is really excellent," said Patrick. "Best I've had in here."

Lance grinned. "That's because Maude's back. She's Glenda's head cook, but she's been gone for about three months. Has an invalid mother back East somewhere. I think it was Maude's turn among her siblings to take care of their mother."

Even as he was speaking, Lance heard the kitchen door open and Heidi said, "There she is now."

Turning around, Lance waved at the middle-aged woman who was talking to a waitress. He caught Maude's eye. She smiled, said something to the waitress, then headed for the table. As she drew up, both men rose to their feet.

"Glad to see you back, Maude," said the marshal. "How's your mother doing?"

"Not real good, Marshal." She ran her gaze to the ladies. "Hello, Heidi, Sundi."

The sisters greeted her warmly, then Maude set her eyes on the tall, broad-shouldered man and said, "Is this our new doctor? He meets the description I've been given."

"Sure is," said Lance. "Dr. Patrick O'Brien, meet Maude Garvin."

Patrick smiled and did a slight bow. "Glad to meet you, ma'am. I was just commenting on how good this meal is tonight, and the marshal said it was because you're back."

Maude blushed. "Thank you, Doctor. And thank you, Marshal."

"I'm sorry to hear that your mother isn't doing well," said Patrick. "Marshal Mangum told me she's an invalid?"

"Yes. She has so many things wrong with her. I'll tell you about it some day when we have some time. Well, I have to get back to the kitchen. See all of you later."

When the couples had finished their meal and left the café, Lance and Heidi headed down the street toward Heidi's dress shop where she needed to pick up some things to take home.

Patrick helped Sundi into the buggy and drove her through the streets toward her neighborhood.

When they pulled up and stopped in front of the house, soft lantern light shone through the parlor window, and the porch lantern shed a yellow glow over the front of the house.

Patrick stepped out of the buggy and rounded it quickly, offering Sundi his hand. When her feet touched the snow-covered ground, he took hold of her arm and elbow and guided her safely onto the porch. Looking into her soft blue eyes, he said, "It's cold out here, so I won't keep you. Thank you for allowing me to take you to supper."

She smiled sweetly. "I'm honored that you wanted to take me."

"Could we do this again real soon?"

"Of course. I'd love it."

Patrick felt a warmth flow through him. His arms ached to hold her, but he told himself it was too soon. "Well, young lady, you need to get in out of the cold."

"Yes, Doctor," she said, turning to unlock the door. "Good night."

Patrick's heart was banging his ribs. "Good night. Rest well, and I'll see you soon."

"Don't make it too long," she said, then slipped inside and closed the door.

As Patrick climbed into the buggy and put the horse into

motion, he said, "Lord, she is such a sweet, warm person. I've never felt anything like this toward a young woman in my whole life."

Once inside with the door shut, Sundi leaned her back against it and sighed. Her heart was doing strange things. She had never felt this way toward a man before. Taking a deep breath, she said in a soft whisper, "Lord, he's everything a woman could want. Please let him feel toward me exactly as I feel toward him."

Half an hour later, Lance and Heidi arrived at the house. As he walked her up the steps to the door, the porch lantern cast a warm glow on her features. Her beauty took his breath.

Heidi's heart was pounding so hard she could feel the pulse throb in the sides of her neck.

As they looked into each other's eyes, Lance lowered his face toward hers. He paused and looked deeper into her eyes. When she didn't pull back, he ventured a kiss, and Heidi allowed it.

With stars in their eyes, they told each other good night.

On Friday evening, February 24, Chris Cooper had a wonderful birthday party at the Carlin home inside the fort. Broken Wing and his parents were there, as well as many of Chris's friends from church and school. Curly and Judy Wesson were in attendance, along with several other adults, including schoolmarm Sundi Lindgren and Jacob Kates.

There were so many gifts that Chris told the Carlins he would come by the next day with a wheelbarrow and pick them up.

When the party was over, and the Coopers were walking home with Jacob holding on to one of Hannah's arms and Chris the other, Patty Ruth walked alongside her big brother and said, "Chrith, you really have a big crush on Abby, don' you?"

The lamplights along Main Street showed Chris's red face as he said, "Little sister, I don't have a crush on Abby. I just like her a lot. But, then, I like some of the other girls who were at the party a lot, too."

Patty Ruth giggled. "Yeah, but you didn' hardly look at the other girlth. You were lookin' at Abby all the time!"

From behind, Mary Beth chuckled and said, "I noticed that, too, Patty Ruth. All the other girls could have suddenly disappeared and our big brother wouldn't have even known it."

Chris glanced back at her and gave her a mock scowl. "Aw, c'mon, Mary Beth."

"She's right, Chris," spoke up B.J. "What color dress did Abby have on?"

"Red and white," came the rapid reply.

"Okay," said B.J. "what color dress did Samantha Walker have on?"

When Chris couldn't reply, Hannah looked at Jacob and grinned.

"Well, I don't remember for sure," said Chris.

"How about Dorine Barker?"

"Her dress was…uh…well, I don't recall at the moment."

"It was dark blue, Chris," said Hannah.

"Okay, so I didn't notice. I still like her. She's a nice girl."

"How about Lila Montgomery?" B.J. said, enjoying his brother's discomfort.

"I…uh…well, I think it was brown."

Mary Beth laughed. "It was green, big brother."

"All right, so I don't remember. That doesn't mean I'm stuck on Abby Turner. I just like her a lot."

Patty Ruth giggled. "Well, Chrithtopher John Cooper, how

come you never thit by any of the other girlth at church? You alwayth thit by Abby."

"Well, I can't help that. Abby always comes and sits by me. It isn't that I always choose to sit by her. Sitting by other girls would be all right with me."

She snorted gleefully. "If you don't want to thit by her all the time, why don't you get up and move?"

There was dead silence except for feet crunching in the snow.

"Well, son," said Hannah, "answer your sister's question."

Chris set his eyes on his mother, then looked toward the star-bedecked sky and said, "Lord, what am I going to do with this family of mine?"

"How about tellin' uth the truth?" asked Patty Ruth. "You've got a great big crush on Abby, don' you?"

Looking down at her, Chris gave her what was supposed to be a mean look and said, "If you don't leave me alone about it, I'm gonna crush you!"

Everybody laughed—even the fifteen-year-old young man who had a huge crush on Abby Turner.

CHAPTER ELEVEN

When the examination was finished, Dr. Frank O'Brien glanced at his wife, Edie, then looked thoughtfully at his patient and said, "Well, dear lady, it can't be too long. The baby might even come a little earlier than I've been thinking."

"That would be all right with me," Hannah said. "I think this one is larger than any of my other children. Sometimes I think I'm going to burst."

Edie chuckled and patted Hannah's arm. "Pretty good sign that it's a boy."

"That's what I've thought for a couple of months," said Hannah, "but since the girls in this family want a girl, and the boys want a boy, I haven't told them what I think. Better if I keep it to myself and we just find out for sure the day the baby is born."

Doc smiled. "Well, it's natural that Mary Beth and Patty Ruth want a little sister, and it's just as natural that Chris and B.J. want a little brother. But knowing these youngin's as I do, whichever it is, they'll love him or her with all their hearts."

Hannah nodded. "Little Eddie…or little Betsy will be the object of plenty of love from this family."

That afternoon, when the Cooper four arrived home from school, they found their mother in her favorite overstuffed chair near the parlor fireplace. Mary Beth let the others hug and kiss their mother first, then she moved close to embrace her and said, "Did Grandpa O'Brien come and examine you today, Mama?"

"Mm-hmm." Hannah brushed aside a wisp of unruly hair that insisted on falling across her eyes. "Grandpa has now changed his mind about the baby waiting three more weeks to come. He says he thinks it will be sooner."

"Oh boy!" shouted B.J. "I've been prayin' the Lord will let little Eddie be born on my birthday. It's gonna happen! I know it is."

Patty Ruth stepped close to B.J. and said, "It really would be nithe if Betthy Lee would be born on your birthday."

"If it was a girl, Patty Ruth, it would be nice. But since it's a boy, it's very, very, very, very nice!"

"It really would be something if little Eddie was born on your birthday," Chris said.

"Eddie, nothing," put in Mary Beth. "I'm telling you, boys, it's going to be little Betsy Lee!"

B.J. opened his mouth to argue but was cut off when Hannah said, "Now look, children, this baby is already whatever it's going to be, and your wrangling about it won't make one iota of difference. Let's just continue to pray as we have for months that our baby will be strong and healthy. We all know we will love it, if it's a boy or a girl. Right?"

All four nodded.

Smiling, Hannah ran her gaze over their young faces and thought, *They are so precious—such a blessing. Thank You, Lord, for all of my children.* Then aloud, she said, "All right, sweet ones, let's not hear any more arguing. Let's just remember that whichever gender the baby is, it's what God wanted us to have. Shouldn't that be good enough for all of us?"

"Yes, Mama," said Mary Beth. "I'm sorry for arguing."

"I'm sorry too, Mama," said Chris.

"Me too," B.J. said in a hushed voice.

Patty Ruth crinkled her nose, grinned, and said, "I'm thorry about arguin', too, Mama. Little Betthy Lee wouldn't want uth to argue over her."

Hannah suppressed a laugh and frowned as she said, "Now, P.R., what if it's not little Betsy Lee? What if it's little Eddie? Won't you want him?"

Patty Ruth dipped her head, looked at her mother from the tops of her big blue eyes, and said, "Of courthe I would want him if it wath little Eddie, Mama. But I'm really sure ith little B—"

"Patty Ruth! That's enough."

"Yeth, ma'am."

The next morning, Hannah awakened just after sunrise and listened for any activity down the hall. It was Saturday, and all four of her children were sleeping in.

She got out of bed with effort and laid aside her nightgown. After putting on a clean maternity dress, she sat down in front of the mirror and brushed her hair. When it was pinned in place, she went to the closet and picked up her favorite pair of everyday shoes.

Patting her swollen middle, she said, "Baby Cooper, any day now would be fine. Your mother would rather hold you, bathe you, diaper you, nurse you, and everything else it takes than go on like this much longer, believe me." She sat down on a straight-backed chair and bent over to pull on her shoes. "Okay. Now the real task. Lace them up and tie them."

For several minutes she tried different tactics to accomplish the job, but the baby was squirming inside, and her hands simply couldn't sufficiently reach the laces anymore. She eased back on the chair and let out a huge sigh.

"I give up. I just give up. I'm so big, I can't even lace and tie my shoes, much less see my feet!" Hannah chuckled and looked toward the ceiling. "Oh, Solomon, if you could only see me now!" The chuckle turned into a laugh. "On second thought, darling, it's best that you don't see me! I'm really a sight. I was big with the other ones, but not like this."

She grew quiet and thought of how Solomon had treated her when she carried the other children. Speaking to him again, she said, "Sol, I know if you were here you would tell me I have grown more beautiful every day that I've carried your child. Then you would kneel down and lace and tie my shoes for me. Oh Sol, I miss you so much. How am I ever going to have this baby without you?"

Hannah's hand gently caressed the babe beneath her heart, and the child moved to her touch. Smiling, she said, "We won't be alone in this, baby Cooper. The Lord will be right there with us when you come into the world."

Giving the little one a final pat, she lumbered to her feet and walked down the hall, shoe laces dragging on the floor.

The aroma of breakfast cooking soon had the Cooper children stirring in their rooms, and Mary Beth was the first to put in an appearance in the kitchen.

"Good morning, sweetheart," Hannah said. "Sleep well?"

"Like Rip Van Winkle." Mary Beth said and covered her yawn.

"Little sister up and at 'em?"

When Hannah moved from the stove to the table, the loose shoelaces caught Mary Beth's eye. "Mm-hmm. She's taking care of the stuffed bear and the doll at present. Ah...Mama..."

"Yes?"

"Why aren't your shoes tied?"

Hannah looked down at the stringy laces trailing from beneath her dress and chuckled. "Honey, I just plain can't reach them anymore."

"You're not going anywhere today, are you?"

"Not since I have those dear ladies who so generously give of their time to help Jacob in the store."

"Then why don't you just wear the slippers B.J. gave you for Christmas, Mama? It would be better for your puffy feet to be in something more comfortable than those shoes, anyhow."

Hannah grinned sheepishly. "You are a very wise young lady, Mary Beth. Would you bring them to me?"

"Sit down, Mama, and I'll take off the shoes."

As soon as Mary Beth had removed the too-tight shoes from her mother's feet, Hannah sighed and wiggled her toes. "That feels better already."

In less than a minute, Mary Beth was back with the slippers. She knelt again and carefully put the soft slippers onto Hannah's feet.

"Ah-h-h. That's much, much better. Thank you, sweetheart. What would I ever do without you?"

Mary Beth stood up and kissed her mother's cheek. "You are most welcome, Mama. Now, what can I do to finish getting breakfast ready?"

On Monday morning, Sundi Lindgren was sitting at her desk, making notes in a history book while the students in seventh through twelfth grades were taking a test. The test questions were written on the blackboard.

Mary Beth Cooper sat between Keith Morley and Bob Imler. Very narrow aisles separated the desks. After concentrating on writing an answer, Mary Beth looked up to the board again and saw in her peripheral vision that Bob was looking at her paper then wrote on his. Turning to look at him, she used facial expressions to let him know she had seen what he'd done.

Bob turned his mouth down and glared at her.

Miss Lindgren, who saw the exchange, pushed her chair back and stood up, immediately drawing the attention of the entire class. She walked the narrow space between the student desks and stopped to look down at Mary Beth and Bob.

"What's going on here?" she asked, flicking her gaze between the two students.

Mary Beth set steady eyes on Bob, who shrugged and said, "Nothin'."

Sundi looked at Mary Beth. "Why were you two making faces at each other?"

Mary Beth held her teacher's gaze but remained silent.

"Don't want to get him in trouble, Mary Beth? Is that why you don't answer me? Was he cheating on the test by looking on your paper?"

Mary Beth swallowed hard.

Returning her gaze to Bob, Sundi said, "Were you, Bob?"

"Nope."

"The proper answer if you were telling the truth would be, 'No, ma'am.' Understood?"

Bob cleared his throat. "Yes, ma'am."

"Now, I will ask you again, Bob. Were you cheating on the test by looking at Mary Beth's paper and copying her answers?"

Again Bob cleared his throat. "No, ma'am."

Looking back at the pretty blonde, the teacher said, "Mary Beth, were you making faces at Bob to tell him not to copy off your paper?"

Mary Beth looked her teacher in the eye and said, "Yes, ma'am."

Sundi extended her hand to Bob. "Give me your test paper."

Sundi took the pencil from behind her ear and marked it with an F. Handing it back to him, she said, "You can turn this in when everyone else turns theirs in."

At recess, most of the children were playing in the snow and making repairs on the snowmen they had built several days earlier. Mary Beth was tying Patty Ruth's scarf tighter around her neck so she could return to play when Bob Imler spotted her.

When Patty Ruth rejoined her friends, Mary Beth heard a voice behind her say, "You're in real trouble, girl."

Pivoting, she looked into the stern face of Bob Imler.

"You could've told the teacher I wasn't lookin' at your paper. But you chose to make me look bad. You're gonna get it."

Arching her back, Mary Beth looked him straight in the eye. "I'm not going to lie for you, Bob. One reason is that it's wrong to lie. Another reason is that I'm a Christian, and as a child of God I must be honest. It would have been wrong for me to lie to Miss Lindgren for you. Besides, the fault is yours. You shouldn't have been cheating."

Bob's face had turned a dull red. "Like I said, girl, you're gonna get it!"

Mary Beth's voice was level as she replied, "I'm going to get it for not covering for you?"

Bob's lips thinned as he clamped them together, and his eyes burned with anger. Suddenly he struck her hard on the shoulder with the heel of his hand. The impact sent her reeling backward, and she slipped on the snow.

There was a rapid swishing sound in the snow, and Bob turned just as all 125 pounds of Chris Cooper hit him. They both went down in the snow, and Chris pounded him with both fists, shrieking, "You hit my sister! You hit my sister!"

Bob fended off the blows and jumped to his feet. He reached down, grabbed Chris by the front of his coat collar, and smashed him in the face. At the same instant, Travis Carlin tackled Bob, dropping him in the snow, then jumped on top of him, swinging for all he was worth.

Bob rolled over, punched Travis on the jaw, stunning him, then scrambled to his feet and started kicking him as he swore at him.

Mary Beth was screaming for Bob to stop when Chris got up and jumped on his back with his arms around his neck in a choke hold.

Other students were looking on, mesmerized by the scene. Mary Beth made a dash for the schoolhouse, calling her teacher's name. Before she reached it, Sundi came out the door.

"Miss Lindgren!" Mary Beth cried. "Miss Lindgren! Bob is beating up on Chris and Travis!"

Sundi bounded off the porch and slipped in the snow, then ran toward the boys with Mary Beth right behind her. Before they got there, Bob flipped Chris over his back, slamming him hard on the snow. This time, Travis leaped on Bob's back, trying to get his own choke hold on him. Bob swore at him and pulled him loose, lifting him over his head. He was about to slam him on the ground when he heard the teacher's voice, high-pitched and ominous, telling him not to do it.

Bob gave her a wild look as she drew up, as if he were going to slam Travis anyhow, but when she screamed again, he eased Travis down.

Mary Beth went to her brother, who was breathing hard and wiping blood from his mouth.

"All right, what happened here?" Sundi demanded.

"Chris jumped me, that's what happened," Bob said.

"Yeah, I did!" Chris said, still wiping blood. "But tell Miss Lindgren why I jumped you!"

Bob shrugged.

"He hit my sister, Miss Lindgren. Knocked her down!"

"You what? Bob, you hit Mary Beth?"

"Aw, I didn't hit her very hard. She just slipped on the

snow. That's why she fell."

Sundi's face went red. Fixing the big boy with blazing eyes, she snapped, "Didn't hit her very hard? Why did you hit her at all?"

Bob dropped his gaze. "Well, I...uh—"

"You hit her because she told me the truth about your cheating, didn't you?"

"Aw, she's one of these self-righteous Christians," he said with a sneer. "She had it comin'."

The flame in Sundi's eyes grew hotter. "A true Christian isn't self-righteous, Bob! And Mary Beth is a true Christian. You tried to frighten her into lying for you, but because she wouldn't do it, it made you mad, didn't it?"

Silence.

"Well, let me tell you something, boy. Mary Beth did right when she told me the truth. You're the one who's wrong. You were wrong to cheat on the test. You were wrong to try to frighten Mary Beth into lying for you. You were wrong to take it out on her by hitting her, and you were wrong to use the kind of language I heard coming out of your mouth. We don't use that kind of language at this school."

Bob shrugged his thick shoulders again and gave her a look of contempt.

He was taller than Sundi Lindgren and outweighed her by nearly a hundred pounds, but she was not intimidated by his size. She surprised him by suddenly reaching up and grasping his right ear and twisting it. He tried to pull his head away, but she pinched down harder.

"We're going inside, young man," she said sternly. "Move!"

When he resisted, she twisted his ear with more force and he let out a howl.

With his head bent toward her hand, Sundi guided him into the schoolhouse, telling the other students to follow. Once inside, she guided him to the front of the classroom, still keeping her hold on his ear. She told the students to sit down at their desks, then told fifteen-year-old Luke Patterson to go to the closet and get her hickory switch.

Bob's eyes bulged, but the grip on his ear was hurting too much for him to resist again.

When Luke returned with the switch, Sundi thanked him and said, "All right, Bob. Into the coatroom."

The big boy could do nothing but let her guide him to the coatroom, which was just off the front entrance to the building. When they stepped inside, Sundi used her heel to close the door, and still pinching down hard on the ear, said, "I'm going to whip you, Bob, for daring to lay a hand on Mary Beth. In my school, boys do not get rough with girls! And I am also going to whip you for the profanity you used on the school grounds. Nobody uses that kind of language here!"

Bob could only glare insolently at her from the corner of his eye. Seeing this, she twisted a bit harder and said, "Bend over and grab your ankles."

"I'm gonna tell my pa if you whip me! You better forget it!"

"I said bend over and grab your ankles!" As she spoke, she caused a little more pain in the ear.

When he had hold of his ankles, she said, "You stay in this position until I tell you differently. Understand?"

Silence.

"Understand?"

"Yes, ma'am," he said through clenched teeth.

Stepping behind him, Sundi took a good hold on the switch and lashed him across the posterior until he broke into tears. Then stepping in front of him, she said, "I hope this will be the only time I have to teach you about hitting girls and swearing. Now let's go back out with the others."

Sundi did not find it necessary to take hold of the boy's ear again. He stepped out of the coatroom ahead of her and went directly to his desk, sniffling and wiping tears.

The other students watched him, wide eyed, then looked at the teacher as she handed the switch to Luke Patterson and told him to put it away.

Bob was still sniffling as Sundi stood by her desk, ran her gaze over the class, and said, "Bob was not whipped for cheating on his test and lying about it. He was whipped for daring to strike Mary Beth and for swearing at Chris and Travis, who were trying to defend her. Bullying anybody will not be tolerated here, but the punishment will be most severe when a boy bullies a girl."

Setting her eyes on the chastised boy, she said, "Bob, I am not sorry for whipping you, but I am sorry I had to do it."

Bob sniffed and sat sullenly at his desk but said nothing.

The next day after school, Sundi Lindgren was coming out of Cooper's General Store, carrying a bag of groceries, and found herself facing Rufe Imler's hulking form. His eyes were red rimmed with anger as he blared, "I wanna talk to you, woman!"

People were passing by on the boardwalk and looked with disgust at the huge man for his brusque approach to the schoolmarm.

"We can talk, Mr. Imler, if you will lower your voice."

"My boy told me you whipped him with a switch at school yesterday!"

"That's right."

"I wanna know why!"

"He didn't tell you?"

"He said you whipped him because you thought he cheated on a test. Bob said he didn't cheat on no test!"

"Then he lied, Mr. Imler. And please lower your voice. Bob did cheat on a test by copying off Mary Beth Cooper's paper. He tried to bully Mary Beth into lying for him, but she told the truth. When the students went outside for recess, Bob got Mary Beth alone and hit her, knocking her down. Mary Beth's brother and another boy jumped your son to protect Mary Beth from any more abuse. Bob swore at them while fighting them off. I do not allow swearing on the school grounds, sir, nor do I allow boys to bully girls. Your son was whipped because he struck Mary Beth and because he used profanity. He knows this because I made it clear to him."

Rufe stared at her.

"You need to have a good talk with Bob, Mr. Imler. He needs to straighten up."

Rufe spit in the snow at the edge of the boardwalk and swore as he said, "You better not ever whip my son again, woman!"

People on the street were stopping to watch as Sundi snapped back at the huge man, "I will not tolerate any student breaking the rules, sir!"

At the same instant, Dr. Patrick O'Brien came out of the hardware store a few doors down the street. He caught Sundi's words, then heard Rufe swear at her as he repeated that she had better never whip his son again.

"If Bob breaks the rules again, Mr. Imler, he will get what he got yesterday. Like I said, you'd better have a talk with him. His insolence will not be tolerated."

Rufe ejected a string of profanity, then roared, "I don't like your rules, woman! Change 'em and you won't have this kind of problem anym—"

Rufe's words were cut off when a tall, muscular figure suddenly appeared in front of him and sent a rock-hard fist to his jaw. The blow put him on his back and sent the world to spinning around him.

Sundi grasped Patrick's arm. "Thank you for coming to my aid."

"Nobody's going to talk to you like that while I'm around," Patrick said. "He's going to apologize for it, too."

Rufe had raised himself to one knee. He was shaking his head, trying to clear the cobwebs.

Patrick moved close to him. "You are going to apologize to Miss Lindgren for your bad manners and your foul mouth, mister. She's a lady, and you're not going to speak to her like that!"

Patrick reached down, grabbed Rufe's coat collar, and lifted him to his feet.

Behind him, Patrick could hear two women telling someone what Rufe had done, and that Dr. O'Brien had put him down for it.

Rufe stiffened and batted Patrick's hand away. "I ain't apologizin' for nothin'!"

"It's apologize or get more of what you just got!"

An older man spoke up and said, "Better apologize like Dr. O'Brien said, mister! I got a feelin' the Irishman can handle himself purty good! You'll get yourself a real whippin'!"

Rufe glared at Patrick and was about to speak when a deep male voice cut in. "A whipping won't be necessary, Zeke. Mr. Imler is going to cool his heels in jail for a couple of days."

The huge man frowned and set his dark eyes on Marshal Lance Mangum.

"Jail! What for?"

"For accosting Miss Lindgren and for using profane language on her."

Patrick O'Brien shook his head. "Jail is fine, Marshal, but he's going to make his apology to Miss Lindgren or he's going to get a whipping before he goes to jail."

Mangum shrugged, looked at Imler, and said, "You going to make the apology?"

Rufe rubbed his sore jaw, then looked at Sundi, whose sister, Heidi, now stood beside her. "Miss Lindgren," he said, "I'm sorry for talkin' to you so rudely."

Sundi started to speak in response, but Patrick delayed it

by saying, "How about the foul language, mister?"

Nodding, Rufe said, "And I'm sorry for cursing you."

Sundi smiled. "You are forgiven, Mr. Imler. Now, take your son in hand and teach him to obey the rules at school."

Rufe nodded and looked at Mangum. "Do I still have to go to jail?"

"Yep. We have a peace disturbance ordinance in this town, and you violated it by your loud and boisterous behavior toward our schoolmarm. The penalty is forty-eight hours behind bars. Look around you. See the size of this crowd you've drawn? They all heard you shouting and swearing at Miss Lindgren."

Sundi stepped closer to Mangum, and her hand shook as she touched his sleeve. "Marshal," she said softly, "could Mr. Imler's sentence be abrogated if I asked for it?"

The crowd waited for Mangum's reply as he looked into Sundi's eyes and said, "Are you asking that he not be jailed?"

"Yes. I feel his apology to me is sufficient."

Rufe's deeply hooded eyes went to Sundi, then to Mangum.

"All right," said the marshal. He turned to Rufe. "Mr. Imler, because Miss Lindgren has pleaded your case and asked that your jail sentence be abrogated, you are free to go. I hope this will be a lesson to you."

"Thank you, Marshal. Thank you, Miss Lindgren." With that, he turned and threaded his way through the crowd and headed across the street toward his horse.

Heidi laid a palm against Sundi's pale cheek. "Honey, are you all right?"

"I'm fine."

"Then why are your hands shaking?" Patrick asked as the crowd began to break up.

Sundi put a trembling hand to her forehead. "I…I guess the emotional strain of this experience sort of got to me."

"Tell you what," said Patrick, "let me take you to the clinic and give you something to settle your nerves."

Heidi kissed her cheek. "I'll see you later, honey."

When Patrick opened the clinic door and ushered Sundi inside, there were no patients in the waiting room. He explained to Doc and Edie what had happened, and that he wanted to give Sundi a mild sedative. Edie went to the back room and moments later returned with a cup of mixture. When Sundi had drained the cup, both Doc and Edie thanked their son for going to Sundi's rescue, then went into the back room.

Sundi looked up at Patrick and said, "Thank you, again, for stepping in and coming to my aid." She raised up on her tiptoes and kissed his cheek.

Gently gripping her shoulders, Patrick said, "I would, of course, defend any lady against such treatment, but you are very special to me."

Sundi was overwhelmed at his words, and before they knew it, they were in each other's arms and enjoying their first kiss. When their lips parted, Sundi said, "Patrick, you are very special to me, too." She took a deep breath. "Well, I need to get home. Thank you again."

"Would you like for me to walk you home?"

"I know you have work to do. Thank you, but I'll be fine."

"You sure?"

"Yes. Knowing that I'm very special to you has settled my nerves already."

Patrick took her in his arms and kissed her again. She gave him a loving look and picked up her grocery bag.

After he closed the door behind her, Patrick watched her through the window for the few seconds it took her to pass from view. He was still gazing after her when Edie came in from the back room. Patrick turned and smiled.

The portly little woman moved toward him and said, "Son, I started out of the back room a few minutes ago, and

I…well, I happened to see…the kiss."

"Aw-w-w, Mom."

Edie laughed and hugged him. "Honey, both Dad and I have been hoping and praying that things would work out between you and that precious girl. We both love her very much."

Patrick grinned, pinched his mother's cheek, and said, "So do I, Mom."

When Sundi had taken no more than a dozen steps from the clinic door, carrying her bag of groceries, her knees almost gave way. She grabbed one of the supports that held up the roof over the boardwalk and clung to it for a moment. When the sudden weakness eased a bit, she took a few steps to a bench that stood in front of the boot and saddle shop.

Easing down, she looked at her trembling hands. She could feel the tremble running through her body from head to toe and wasn't sure if it was from the ordeal with Rufe Imler or from the kisses she had shared with the man who had stolen her heart. The elation going on deep inside her was a strong indication that it was the latter.

After a few minutes and a few deep breaths, she gathered her wits about her, picked up the grocery bag, and continued on down the boardwalk, a secret smile pulling at her lips.

CHAPTER TWELVE

Early on Tuesday morning, March 14, Chris Cooper was awakened by a sound of rustling in the room. By the time he could get his eyes open, his attention was drawn to his little brother, who was dressed and turning the doorknob.

Before Chris could ask B.J. what he was doing up so early, the boy was out the door and in the hall. He began hopping joyfully and shouting, "Hey, everybody! Time to get up! It's my birthday, and I'm nine years old!"

Chris could hear B.J. hopping and shouting all the way to the parlor.

By the time the rest of the family, still in their robes, appeared together in the parlor, the nine-year-old had a roaring fire going in the fireplace. He stood in front of it, grinning.

They all wished him a happy birthday, and then Chris put an arm around B.J.'s shoulders and said, "Nine years old! I remember my ninth birthday. A fella sort of grows up when he turns nine."

"Yeah!" said B.J.

"In fact, a nine-year-old boy is so grown up, he has to start going out to the barn every other morning so he can feed and water the horse, trading off with his handsome, mature, fifteen-year-old brother."

B.J. gave him a bland look. "Buster is your horse. Why should I have to do that?"

"You ride him, don't you?"

"Well, yeah."

"So we'll share and share alike."

B.J. shrugged. "Okay. I think Buster likes me best, anyway."

Chris laughed and cuffed him playfully on the chin.

Hannah wrapped her arms around her youngest son, kissed the top of his head, and said, "I'll never forget nine years ago today."

Looking up at her, B.J. said, "It was the most wonderful day of your life, wasn't it, Mama?"

Hannah laughed. "Well, honey, it sure was one of them!"

Mary Beth moved close and said, "Since it's my baby brother's birthday, I'm going to give him a big kiss!"

"Me too!" chimed in Patty Ruth.

B.J.'s eyes bulged. "Oh, ugh-h-h-h!" he said and turned away.

The girls laughed, and Mary Beth said, "What's the matter with sister kisses, little brother?"

"'Cause they're just exactly that! Sister kisses!"

"Someday when you're grown up, B.J.," Hannah said, "you'll feel differently about sister kisses."

"Hah! I'm almost grown up now, and sister kisses still scare me!"

Hannah was made to sit down by the fireplace while the boys went to the barn to take care of Buster and the girls prepared breakfast. She hadn't told the children, but during the night she had experienced a few pains and wondered at the time if her labor was beginning. She had dismissed that idea when she thought about how very irregular and far apart the pains were.

Still, she had felt quite restless but finally managed to get a little sleep.

At breakfast, Hannah wasn't feeling well, but made an effort to cover it. Though she was her cheerful self at the table, she noticed Mary Beth looking at her from time to time with a question in her eyes. Hannah and her children discussed the birthday party to take place that night. So that Hannah wouldn't have to go out, it was being hosted at the Cooper apartment by Glenda and Gary Williams.

Between bites of oatmeal, B.J. talked about how great it was to be nine years old. At one point, he said, "Just think, everybody! In a few years, I'll be a man!"

Patty Ruth laughed. "It will be at least forty yearth before you are a man, B.J.!"

This time, everybody but B.J. laughed.

When breakfast was over, Hannah went back to her over-stuffed chair in the parlor. She lowered herself awkwardly onto the cushion. Sighing deeply when she had accomplished the task, she put her head back and patted the mound that was her baby. The little one had been quite still for several hours, and Hannah knew this was often a precursor of labor.

While the table was being cleaned off by Patty Ruth and the boys, Mary Beth went to Hannah and said, "Mama, you're not feeling well, are you?"

"What do you mean, honey?"

"Mama, this is your oldest daughter speaking. I know you, don't I?"

"Of course."

"I know you well enough to know when you don't feel good, no matter how you try to hide it. I'm staying home with you today."

By this time, the other three were beside Mary Beth.

"There's no reason for you to miss school on my account."

"Well, I'm going to. You shouldn't be left alone."

"But you said yesterday that you have a big history test today."

"So? I can take it later. Miss Lindgren will understand."

Shaking her head, Hannah said, "I don't want you to miss school, Mary Beth. I'll be fine."

"I could thtay home, Mama," said Patty Ruth. "It would be all right, thinthe I'm not really thtartin' reg'lar thchoolwork till nex' fall."

Mary Beth smiled. "How about that, Mama? It really wouldn't hurt if she missed school today."

Hannah sighed. "All right. If something went wrong she could go down and tell Jacob."

B.J.'s eyes lit up. "Mama, maybe I should stay home with you since it's my birthday!"

"Don't you have a history test today, too?"

B.J.'s face tinted. "Well, yes."

"Nice offer, honey, but you go to school and take your test."

"I suppose you would say the same thing to me if I offered to stay home with you," said Chris. "Even though it's not my birthday."

Hannah smiled up at him. "You know the answer to that already."

Chris chuckled. "Oh, well, it was worth a try."

The kitchen was cleaned up and the dishes done just in time for the three older siblings to head off for school.

Standing beside Hannah's chair, Patty Ruth said, "Mama, can I get you anything?"

"How about a cup of water, sweetheart?"

The six-year-old dashed to the kitchen and moments later returned with the cup of water. She sat down on a small stool directly in front of her mother and sighed, saying, "I sure hope little Betthy Lee will be borned soon."

"Me too, honey." Hannah drained the cup and set it on a

side table, then leaned her head back.

Patty Ruth was rambling on about how much she liked the name Betsy Lee, and how much fun they were going to have together playing with dolls.

Hannah grew drowsy and was barely listening to the child when suddenly she came wide awake, grabbed her midsection, and ejected a gasp, ending in a soft moan.

Patty Ruth frowned. "What's the matter, Mama?"

Noting the worry lines on her youngest daughter's brow, she pressed a smile on her lips and said, "Nothing, honey. Mama's fine."

"You look sorta white, Mama. Should I go get Uncle Jacob?"

"No, P.R. I don't need Uncle Jacob. Tell you what...I think it would be real nice if you would go and do some straightening up in your room. When you get it done, play with Tony the Bear and your dolls."

The child nodded. "Okay, but you call if you need me."

"I will, sweetheart. You go on now."

Patty Ruth turned and headed toward the hall, but after a few steps she paused and looked back at her mother, uneasiness crinkling her brow. Mama was resting her head on the back of the chair and had her eyes closed.

Hannah was dozing when suddenly a sharp pain stabbed her in the small of the back, and with clawing fingers made its way around her middle. Her eyes popped open, and she drew a quick breath. Running her gaze to the old grandfather clock that stood near the mantel, she told herself she had better keep track of the time.

She settled back once more and closed her eyes.

In what seemed to be a very few minutes, an identical pain struck her. She bit her lips to keep from crying out, and when the pain receded, she checked the time. Actually, twenty minutes had passed.

I must have fallen asleep, she thought. *This could go on for a long time, so I won't send for Doc yet.*

She whispered, "Lord, please let my baby be healthy and normal."

Soon the gripping pain struck again, starting in her back and winding its way low in her abdomen. The clock told her it had been only ten minutes.

When the pain subsided, Hannah took a deep breath and fastened her eyes on the clock. The ticking seemed louder than usual. Her eyes followed the pendulum as it swung back and forth…back and forth… It was coming up on the ten-minute mark when another pain racked her body, more intense than the others.

She was about to call for Patty Ruth when the little red-head appeared. It took Patty Ruth only a second to know that her mother was in much pain. She knelt in front of her and looked up into her eyes. "Mama, are you all right?"

Hannah nodded, her breaths coming in short spurts. "Yes, baby girl. I'm fine. It's just time for our long awaited little one to be born."

The child's eyes widened and her mouth fell open.

Through clenched teeth, Hannah said, "Patty Ruth, run down and tell Uncle Jacob I need Grandpa O'Brien. And remind him that I promised Aunt Glenda I would send for her when the baby was ready to come. Ask him to send someone to tell her."

"But…but…I shouldn' leave you. Maybe I could go out on the deck and holler for him."

"He might not hear you, sweetie. Go on. Hurry."

As the child headed for the door, Hannah called, "Patty Ruth! Your coat! Don't go out without your coat!"

She dashed to the coat rack where her coat and scarf hung

on the lowest peg. Biggie came down the hall, watched her put on the coat and scarf, and whined.

"No, Biggie," she said, rushing toward the door, "you can't go with me."

Hannah watched the child plunge out the door, slamming it behind her. She could hear her pounding down the stairs and calling to Jacob before she got to the back door of the store.

When another pain had come and gone, Hannah hoisted herself out of the chair and waddled to the hallway, where she used the wall as support to get to her bedroom.

Between pains, she managed to put on a warm flannel gown. She tried to turn the covers down, but another pain lanced through her and she collapsed on top of the bed-spread.

Patty Ruth pounded up the wooden staircase, bolted through the door, and was already peeling off her coat. "Mama, Uncle Jacob—"

She saw that her mother was no longer in the chair. Looking down the hall, she noticed Biggie standing outside her mother's room. Patty Ruth dropped her coat and ran down the hall. When she entered the room, her mother was lying on top of the bedspread.

Hannah's teeth were chattering, both from the lower temperature of the room and from the unrelenting pain. She was moaning and moving her legs.

"Mama, Uncle Jacob ith on hith way to get Grandpa O'Brien, an' Major Barker from the fort wath in the thtore, an' he'th on hith way to bring Aunt Glenda."

Hannah nodded, closing her eyes as she gritted her teeth.

Patty Ruth dashed to the closet, took a heavy quilt from a shelf, and hurried back to the bed. She unfolded it and covered her mother as best she could, then kissed her cheek, knowing when her mother had done this for her many times in the past, it made her feel better.

"Doth that help, Mama?" she asked, taking hold of her mother's hand.

Hannah nodded. "Yes, sweetheart. Thank you."

Patty Ruth kissed her cheek again. "You're welcome. How come it hurtth to have a baby born?"

"I—I'll tell you when you are older, honey."

"Can I get thomethin' for you?"

"No. I j-just need Grandpa."

"Ith little Betthy Lee gonna be here thoon?"

Hannah managed a faint smile. "Yes. Very soon."

Biggie began barking and ran toward the front of the apartment. Immediately there was a knock at the door.

"That's probably Grandpa and Grandma, honey," said Hannah. "Go let them in, will you?"

Patty Ruth ran from the room, and when she reached the hall, she saw the O'Briens coming through the door.

"Grandpa! Grandma! Little Betthy Lee ith comin'!"

Doc set his black medical bag down, and while he removed his hat and coat, Edie hurried down the hall, peeling off her coat as she went.

Doc hung coat and hat on the clothes tree and said, "Patty Ruth, you wait here in the parlor. Your Aunt Glenda will be here in a few minutes."

"Yeth, thir," she said. "I'll let her in."

At the same time Hannah was having her labor pains, Carrie Wright was washing her breakfast dishes and cleaning up the kitchen at the Box W before going out to pump water into the tank for the cattle and horses. She had convinced Pastor Kelly that she no longer needed the church women to stay with her, so she was now by herself.

She put on her coat and scarf, then headed for the barn and corral. Something strange met her eyes as she drew closer. There was not a cow or bull in sight.

Slipping and sliding in the snow, she ran toward the back side of the barn. By that time, her heart was pounding, and it grew worse when the corral showed her no livestock at all. The back gate of the corral stood wide open. "No!" she breathed and ran out into the field, stumbling in the snow, her eyes searching in every direction.

"No-o-o-o!" she cried. "No-o-o-o! Please, God, no!"

Her eyes followed the myriad hoofprints in the snow that led off to the west, then turned north, but there was nothing in sight.

Tears filled Carrie's eyes as she hurried back to the barn and plunged inside. Both saddle horses and the wagon team nickered at her, swishing their tails. She felt a measure of relief, knowing she still had her horses.

She quickly bridled and saddled her bay mare and led her out of the barn and through the corral gate. She was about to mount up when she saw a wagon rolling into the yard, bearing three men. It took only seconds to recognize Karl and Kurt Devlin. She had never seen the third man before.

When the wagon halted in front of Carrie, Karl fixed her with stern eyes and said, "I want to talk to you."

Thumbing tears from her cheeks, she said, "I don't have time to talk right now, Mr. Devlin. I have to get to town."

"We have to talk, Mrs. Wright," Devlin said evenly. "So you came up with enough money to catch up on your payments. Donations, right? Well, what about when it comes time for April's payment? It's due April 1, you know. If the money isn't in my hands by that date, you are behind again. Face it. You're not gonna be able to keep makin' the payments. This man with us is Dean Driskell. He wants to buy the ranch. Let's go inside, sit down, and talk about it."

Carrie's eyes flashed as she said, "The ranch is not for sale! There's nothing to talk about. Now excuse me, but I have to leave."

Even as she spoke, she stepped into the stirrup, swung aboard the mare, and put the horse to a gallop, leaving the three men gawking after her.

Karl Devlin swore as he said, "If she's one day late on the next payment, you'll be able to buy the ranch, Dean. In the contract, I made no provision for late payments. I've gone along with this situation for too long already."

Marshal Mangum and Deputy Bower were at their desks doing paperwork when Jack happened to look out the window and see Carrie Wright skid her mare to a stop at the hitch rail and slide from the saddle.

Lance noticed his deputy looking out the window. "Something got your attention, Jack?"

"Mm-hmm. It's Carrie Wright, and she looks pretty upset."

Both lawmen were at the door and had it open when Carrie reached it.

"Come in, Carrie," said the marshal. "What's wrong?"

Carrie told them about finding the back corral gate open, that all the cattle were gone, and of her search for the herd.

Mangum ran his fingers through his hair. "Carrie, this can mean only one thing. Your cattle have been rustled."

Tears were welling up in Carrie's eyes. "Then I'll lose the ranch. Karl Devlin was there just before I left. He had a man with him who wants to buy the ranch. Karl told me I can't make it and might as well sell out. I'll lose it back to him for sure if I don't get my cattle back."

"I'll go out and take a look, Marshal," said Jack. "Maybe they've left a good enough trail to be followed. I would think so, with the snow on the ground."

"I'll go, Jack," said Mangum. "You've got that farmer and his wife coming in to see you, remember?"

Lance put a comforting hand on Carrie's arm and said, "If I can find a trail, we just might get those cattle back for you."

When the marshal and the young widow arrived at the Box W, they rode to the spot where the back corral gate had been left open. Dismounting, Lance carefully studied the snow-packed ground and the hoofprints. Nodding to himself, he said, "Let's follow the tracks a ways."

Carrie silently rode alongside the marshal while they guided the horses into the field where she had been earlier. She watched his expression as he leaned from the saddle, scrutinizing the prints in the snow. They were almost halfway to the backside of the Box W property when the tracks turned northward, dipped into a draw, and were lost to their view.

"Let's stop here," he said, pulling rein.

Carrie remained in the saddle while the marshal dismounted again and bent low, examining prints in the snow. He moved from one side of the path of tracks to the other, twice kneeling down to make careful inspection.

He was shaking his head when he returned and looked up at her. "Carrie, it wasn't rustlers who took your cattle. It was Indians."

"Indians! But, Marshal, those cattle had to have been stolen during the night. They were there when darkness fell last night, and if they had been taken while I was cooking and eating breakfast, I would have heard them bawling. I've been told that Indians don't travel, roam, or do their fighting at night. It couldn't have been Indians."

"Well, ma'am, what you just said is generally true. However, there are some Indians who don't pay any attention to those customs. Let me show you something." He took hold of her horse's bridle at the bit and led her to some hoofprints at the edge of the path. "Look here, Carrie. See these horses' hoofprints?"

"Yes."

"They aren't wearing horseshoes. The only people who don't shoe their horses are the Indians. I figure it was Blackfeet or Shoshoni."

Carrie's features lost color. "Then my chances of getting the cattle back are nil."

"Well-l-l...don't give up yet. I'll head back right now and talk to Colonel Bateman at the fort. He'll send a unit of cavalry-men to follow the herd and see who has them."

Carrie nodded. "I'd like to go with you to the fort and talk to Colonel Bateman. I'm already on the verge of losing the ranch. If the army doesn't get my cattle back, I'll lose it for sure."

At the Cooper apartment, Patty Ruth was in the kitchen, draw-ing and coloring pictures. Glenda Williams was in the bedroom with Hannah and Doc and Edie.

Patty Ruth's mind was never far from her mother. Every few minutes, she left the table with Biggie at her heels, walked down the hall, and silently stood outside her mother's room, her eyes riveted on the door. Each time, the voices inside were subdued, and Patty Ruth couldn't make out what they were saying. After listening briefly, she made her way back to the kitchen and resumed her coloring.

Hannah tried to catch her breath between the almost constant pains while Edie dabbed at the perspiration on her face and Glenda held her hand. At one point, she gasped and said, "Doc...this isn't like...any of my other...deliveries. It started so suddenly, and…escalated so fast."

Doc smiled. "This is going to be a very special baby, Hannah. Remember all of your comments on how different this pregnancy was from the other four?"

Hannah experienced another sharp pain and looked at the silver-haired physician through anguish-filled eyes. "Doc, does that mean you think there's something wrong with this baby?"

"Oh, of course not, dear girl. I just meant that regarding the circumstances of this birth, the baby you are about to bring into the world is a very special one."

Hannah's pinched features relaxed. "Oh. Of course. I agree. You're so right, Doc. You're so right."

Another pain demanded her attention and Glenda squeezed hard on her hand. Edie dipped the cloth into cool water and gently wiped Hannah's shiny face, all the while speaking in low comforting tones.

When the next pain eased, Hannah let out a pent-up breath and said in a soft whisper, "I'm so tired."

"I know you are," said Edie, "but you can't stop working with Doc now. That baby is almost here."

Glenda gave Hannah a sip of water, then Edie bathed her face with cool water once more. Glenda smoothed Hannah's wet hair back from her forehead.

Almost overcome with the hurting in her pain-racked body, Hannah let her mind wander to Solomon. In her weary mind, she could hear him say, just as he had when he was with her through the other births, *You can do this, sweetheart.*

Another pain took her thoughts from Solomon. When it eased off, she thought, *I'm so tired. I want this to be over with. Lord Jesus, give me strength.*

Solomon came to mind again. *I miss you so much, my darling husband. I need you. This is your baby…the part of you that I still have. But you're not here. With the Lord's help, I can do this, though. I know I can.*

Another sharp stab lanced through her body. Fog seemed to fill her mind. And then she heard a loud slap, followed instantly by the welcome cry of her precious newborn baby.

The fog cleared up instantly.

Oh, thank You, Lord! Thank You! We did it!

Patty Ruth was putting the finishing touches on a picture she had drawn of Biggie when she heard a loud slap and a weak little cry that rapidly built to a strong one.

Slipping off the chair, she ran down the hall and stood before the closed door. Other than the baby's cry, there were some sounds she did not recognize, but she waited patiently for someone to come out the door and tell her that her mother and the baby were all right...and if little Betsy Lee Cooper looked like her six-year-old sister.

CHAPTER THIRTEEN

As Dr. Frank O'Brien finished his work on Hannah, she said, "Oh, praise the Lord! My baby's healthy and normal. Thank you, Doc! Thank you for taking such good care of us."

Doc's Irish eyes twinkled. "That's what I'm supposed to do, Hannah."

Glenda turned from Edie and the newborn infant and leaned over to kiss Hannah's forehead. "Such a perfect little baby, honey. Solomon would have been so proud."

Hannah nodded. "Yes, he would."

"While Edie's getting the baby ready, honey," said Glenda, "I'll bathe you a bit, then change your bedding."

When Hannah was finally sitting up with pillows at her back and clean sheets and blankets enfolding her, she reached out her arms toward the portly little woman holding the bundled infant and said, "I'm ready now."

Edie nodded. "Can't blame you for being eager to get this little bundle in your arms, Hannah. This is one beautiful child!"

Hannah's heart seemed to turn over within her breast as the baby was placed in her arms and she gazed at the tiny face. Her lips quivered as she said, "Oh, he looks so much like Solomon!"

Little Eddie moved his mouth silently and seemed to

focus on the face of his mother with eyes the same shade of blue as Solomon's.

"And that means he looks a lot like B.J.," said Hannah. "This is going to make B.J. so happy!"

Tears spilled down Hannah's cheeks as her heart enlarged to make room for this special little child.

While Doc, Edie, and Glenda looked on, Hannah carefully folded the blanket back and examined every inch of him. "Yes, you are one perfect little boy."

Once again wrapping the downy blanket snugly around him, Hannah held little Eddie close to her heart and placed a tender kiss on top of his soft, fuzzy head. "Eddie, I'm your mother, and I love you so very much. You have already stolen your mama's heart. Now, precious little boy, I want to tell you the same thing I told your brothers and sisters right after they were born. There is a name I want your ears to hear now, and for the rest of your life. The name is Jesus. He is God's Son, Eddie, and when He was born into the world, His mother wrapped Him in swaddling clothes and laid Him in a manger.

"That precious little boy didn't have a mortal father like you, honey. His mother was a virgin, and God was His Father. Listen to these words. 'For God so loved the world, that he gave his only begotten Son, that whosoever believeth in him should not perish, but have everlasting life.' Eddie, you will hear this truth over and over and over again. You will hear the gospel, precious son—how that Christ died for our sins according to the Scriptures; and that He was buried, and that He rose again the third day according to the Scriptures. And one day—when you're old enough to understand about sin and salvation—you will turn to Jesus and ask Him to save you. Mama has prayed for this since she first learned that God was going to bring another child into our family."

Holding the tiny bundle close to her face, Hannah closed her eyes and said, "Thank You, Lord, for giving me this perfect baby. And even though he's only a few minutes old, I give him back to You. Please care for him, bring him to Yourself at a young age, and use him for Your glory. Please give me wisdom as I raise him. There will be difficulties, as I must be both mother and father to him, but with You, Lord, all things are possible. Thank You, heavenly Father, for this blessing. All of this I pray in the precious name of Jesus. Amen."

As Hannah bent her head and kissed the baby's forehead, Doc, Edie, and Glenda were wiping tears.

"Oh, Hannah," Glenda said, "that was so beautiful. What a wonderful thing to do—to tell your newborn about Jesus before he has been in the world thirty minutes."

Edie dabbed at her wet cheeks and Doc used a bandanna from his hip pocket to blow his nose.

Hannah kissed her newborn son again, and said, "I love you, and I will do my best to raise you in the nurture and admonition of the Lord."

As though the babe understood what his mother had just told him, he cuddled down with a contented sigh. A wistful smile flitted across Hannah's tired but beautiful face.

Biggie could be heard making little whining sounds in the hall.

Hannah looked toward the door and said, "I'm sure there's a little redheaded, freckle-faced girl just outside that door. It's time she was allowed in to see her new baby brother."

"Can I tell her, Hannah?" Doc asked, his eyes dancing with joy.

Hannah nodded. "Yes, Doc. You tell her, and bring her in."

When Doc opened the door, Patty Ruth was standing there, her big blue eyes shining with anticipation.

"Well, Patty Ruth," said Doc, "you have a new little baby brother, and he wants to see you!"

The little girl looked at Doc in disbelief. She cocked her

head, squinted at him, and said, "Grandpa, you're joking, right? It'th really a little thithter."

Doc took her hand and led her into the room, then bent down and hugged her, and said, "No, honey. I'm not joking. Come on. Little Eddie wants to see you."

Patty Ruth shot a glance around Doc to her mother. Seeing the bundle in Hannah's arms, she said, "Mama, it'th really Betthy Lee, ithn't it?"

Hannah smiled. "No, honey. Jesus gave you a new little brother."

A shadow of disappointment started to darken the child's face, then suddenly her eyes lit up over a big smile, and she clapped her hands as she hurried toward the bed. "Oh, Mama! I want to see my little brother!"

Hannah smiled at Glenda and Edie, then pulled the blanket away from little Eddie's face and held him so Patty Ruth could get a good view of him. "Here he is, honey. What do you think of him?"

Having never seen a newborn, Patty Ruth studied her little brother for a moment, then said, "Ah...he'th cute, Mama, but—"

"But what?"

"He'th awfully wrinkled."

"Sweetie," said Doc, "you were wrinkled like that too, when you were born."

The child looked at her mother. "Really, Mama?"

"Yes, honey." Hannah reached out and patted her cheek. "But your wrinkles went away, didn't they?"

"Mutht have. I ain't got none now."

"Eddie's wrinkles will go away, too."

Patty Ruth nodded, her eyes fixed on the face of the baby. "Know what, Mama?"

"What, sweetie?"

"He looks like B.J."

Hannah smiled. "He sure does, P.R. And he looks like Papa, too. Do you see it?"

Patty Ruth squinted, studying Eddie some more. "Mm-hmm. I thee it. He hath a chin like Papa'th."

"Yes." Hannah's eyes misted. "I wish your papa could be here to see his new little son."

Edie stepped up to the bed, put an arm around Hannah's neck and said, "Solomon is in that great cloud of witnesses who are looking down to earth as we run the race, dear. Maybe the Lord is letting him look down at little Eddie right now."

Hannah nodded. "Yes. Yes, He probably is."

"Why not?" said Glenda.

Hannah blinked at her tears and said, "Glenda, would you do something for me?"

"Name it."

"Would you go to the school and ask Sundi if she will let my children out of school so they can come home and see their little brother?"

"Be my pleasure. Do you want them to know it's a boy before they get here?"

"Yes. You go ahead and tell them."

"I'll hurry," said Glenda, and went into the hall.

Patty Ruth looked at her little brother again. "Mama?"

"Yes, honey?"

"Could I give Eddie a kiss?"

"Sure, honey. You're not disappointed that it's a brother instead of a sister?"

The child shook her head. "No, Mama. The Lord wanted uth to have a brother, tho it'th all right."

Colonel Ross Bateman was at his desk, reading a letter from U.S. army headquarters in Washington, D.C., when there was a tap at his door.

"Come in, Corporal."

His adjutant, Corporal Barry Morse opened the door, took a step into the office, and said, "Sir, Marshal Lance Mangum is here with Mrs. Carrie Wright. They would like to talk to you."

"Certainly," said Bateman, dropping the letter and rising to his feet. "Show them in."

Carrie came in first, with Mangum on her heels. The colonel welcomed them, and invited them to sit down.

When all three were seated, Mangum told Bateman about Carrie's stolen cattle and that the horses ridden by the thieves wore no horseshoes.

"Which direction were the cattle taken from the Box W?" Bateman asked.

"North. I figure since there are both Blackfoot and Shoshoni villages due north of there, it has to be one tribe or the other."

Bateman nodded. "I agree."

"Can you help, Colonel?" Carrie asked.

"I'll do my best. I'll assign Captain John Fordham to take a cavalry unit and see who has them. I'll send them right away before new snow covers up the tracks."

At his words, Carrie's composure broke and tears of relief welled up in her eyes as she said, "Thank you, Colonel. If I don't get my cattle back, I'll lose the ranch."

The colonel leaned forward and said, "I can't tell you exactly what we'll do at this point, Mrs. Wright, since I don't know for sure who has your cattle. Captain Fordham will be instructed to take whatever action is judicious, once he has found them. I'll tell him to come to the ranch and fill you in as soon as they find the cattle."

Carrie thanked Colonel Bateman for his help, and as she and the marshal were passing through the outer office, they heard the colonel dispatch his adjutant to fetch Captain Fordham.

As they mounted up and headed for the fort's main gate,

Mangum said, "I'll ride back to the ranch with you. I want to make sure you get there all right."

Carrie gave him an appreciative look and said, "That won't be necessary, Marshal. I'll be fine."

Mangum shook his bead stubbornly. "I insist, ma'am."

Carrie smiled. "You are very kind, Marshal."

They spoke to the soldier who opened the gate, waved at the two in the gate tower, and trotted out of town toward the ranch.

At the Fort Bridger school, Sundi Lindgren was sitting quietly at her desk while her older students were taking their history test and the younger ones were doing a reading assignment. Her attention was drawn to the door as Glenda Williams stepped in and beckoned to her. Every child had heard the door open and turned around to look.

"Everybody stay with your work," the schoolmarm said. "I'll be right back."

When Sundi and Glenda stepped into the coatroom and closed the door, all but Bob Imler went back to work. Leaning close to Mary Beth, Bob whispered in a friendly voice, "Could we talk for a few minutes after school? It's important."

Surprised at his friendliness, Mary Beth said, "Of course."

Soon the class heard the door to the coatroom open, followed by their teacher's footsteps. Sundi moved to the front of the class and said, "Chris, Mary Beth, and B.J., you are excused. Mrs. Williams is here to see you and she will be going home with you. I'll give you special time tomorrow to finish your work."

The Cooper three put their papers and pencils in their desks, and as Mary Beth stood up, she said in a low voice to Bob, "I guess our talk will have to wait until tomorrow."

The boy actually smiled at her and said, "Okay. Thanks, Mary Beth."

At the door, Glenda said in a whisper, "Get your coats on. I've got some wonderful news for you."

"The baby?" Mary Beth said.

"I'll tell you outside. Hurry!"

When they were out the door, still buttoning up their coats, Glenda said, "Congratulations. You have a new sibling at your house! Both mother and baby are fine."

As they started across the school grounds, B.J. beat the other two by saying, "It's a boy, isn't it, Aunt Glenda?"

Smiling, Glenda said, "Yes, B.J. Little Eddie is waiting for you to come and see him."

Chris clapped his gloved hands together. "I knew it all along! We got us a baby brother!"

"I'm glad Mama and little Eddie are all right," said Mary Beth. "I just don't understand how I could have felt so sure it was a girl."

Glenda laid a hand on her shoulder. "Well, honey, sometimes what we want is what gives us our inward inclinations."

Mary Beth nodded and said, "It really doesn't matter, Aunt Glenda. The Lord gave us a boy, and I love little Eddie already and can't wait to see him and hold him."

"Me too," said B.J. "Aunt Glenda, would you care if we run on ahead of you?"

Glenda laughed. "Of course not. I know you're eager. Go on. I'll be there shortly."

"Thanks!" said Chris, over his shoulder as he bolted across the school yard. Mary Beth and B.J. took off after him.

Mary Beth shouted ahead to her big brother, "Chris! Chris! Don't you dare get there before B.J. and me! You wait up for us!"

"Yeah!" shouted B.J. "Wait up!"

Chris slowed until the other two caught up with him, and then kept a steady pace, staying just a few steps ahead of his brother and sister.

When they reached the apartment, they bounded up the

stairs, each trying to be first to reach the door. Chris rushed ahead of them, turned the knob, and burst inside with the other two on his heels.

They rushed headlong down the hall, but were met by Edie O'Brien, who came out of Hannah's room and closed the door. "Whoa!" she said, throwing up her hands.

All three skidded to a halt, anticipation showing on their young faces.

"Hold on," said Edie. "I know you want to see your new little brother, but you need to get your coats and caps off first."

As they began removing their wraps, Edie said, "Where's your Aunt Glenda?"

"She'll be along shortly, Grandma," Chris said. "We asked her if we could run on ahead."

Edie nodded. "You'll have to wash your hands, children—in warm, soapy water. I have some waiting on the stove. We don't want to bring any germs to the baby."

While the Cooper three were hanging up their coats and caps, Glenda came in, puffing slightly.

Edie smiled at her and said, "Oh, to be young again, eh, Glenda?"

Peeling out of her coat, Glenda said, "Uh-huh. But that's not going to happen till I get my new body in heaven."

Edie chuckled. "We'll both be glad for that, won't we?"

"Yes, ma'am! I'll go see if there's anything I can do for Hannah."

Under Edie's directions, the Cooper three made quick work of the hand washing, and when they were through, B.J. said, "All set! Can we go in now, Grandma?"

"All right," she said, leading them down the hall, "but don't go in there like a thundering herd of buffalo. You don't want to frighten little Eddie."

Edie opened the door and stepped aside. Three eager faces peeked in.

Their mother was sitting up in the bed, her back braced with pillows. Patty Ruth had placed herself on the bed as close to her mother and baby brother as possible. In Hannah's arms was the tiny newborn, wrapped in a blanket. She smiled at the trio who seemed frozen at the door. "Come in! Come in! There's somebody here who wants to meet you!"

In awe, they drew up to the side of the bed, opposite from Patty Ruth. Their eyes were fixed on the fuzzy little head that protruded from the blanket.

Hannah turned the baby so they could see his face, and his tiny blue eyes seemed to focus on them.

"Look, Mama!" said B.J. "He knows me!"

Mary Beth laughed. "Hardly, B.J."

"Well, he does! He's lookin' right at me!"

Hannah chuckled. "Well, what do you three think of him?"

"Mama," said Mary Beth in a hushed tone, "he...he looks like Papa!"

"He does!" agreed Chris. "And he looks like somebody else."

"Uh-huh," said Mary Beth. "He looks like B.J."

B.J.'s chest swelled and his face lit up. "I wondered how long it was gonna take you two to see that! Did you see it, Patty Ruth?"

The little redhead nodded.

The nine-year-old's eyes were sparkling. "Since he looks like Papa and me, can I hold him first, Mama?"

"Where are your manners, son?"

"Huh?"

"Isn't it supposed to be ladies first?"

"Well, uh...yeah."

"Then Mary Beth should get to hold him before you and Chris."

All eyes were on Mary Beth as Hannah placed little Eddie

into her eager arms. Mary Beth's eyes glistened with tears as she held him close to her face and said, "Hello, little brother. I'm your big sister, Mary Beth." She kissed his forehead. "I love you."

Hannah grinned. "Even though he's not Betsy Lee?"

"Yes. Even though he's not Betsy Lee." She kissed him again.

"My turn now," said B.J.

Doc stepped up and said, "I think it would be best if I supervise this a little."

B.J. grinned up at him. "You mean since I've never held a baby before, but Mary Beth has?"

"Something like that."

"Let's go over here and have you sit down on this chair, B.J.," said Doc. "I think it'll be safer if you have a lap."

Patty Ruth watched as B.J. sat down on a straight-backed chair. Doc put his hands under B.J.'s as Mary Beth handed the baby to him. Patty Ruth turned to her mother and said, "Mama, where doth your lap go when you thtand up?"

Hannah smiled. "Well, it just disappears till you sit down again, honey."

"Oh."

When Doc was sure the nine-year-old boy had the bundle safe in his arms, he stood back and observed as B.J. smiled down at the baby and said, "Hi, Eddie. I'm your next to biggest brother. But you already know that, don't you? You already know that my name's B.J. And you know what? You and me are gonna be real good buddies."

B.J. rubbed his thumb over the baby's tiny hand, and as if he had practiced the move before, little Eddie grasped B.J.'s thumb in a tight grip.

"Look, Mama! He's holdin' my thumb! He's tellin' me that we sure are gonna be good buddies!"

"I'd say so," said Hannah, her countenance beaming with joy.

"My turn now," said Chris, moving directly in front of the chair.

"Okay," said B.J. He kissed the baby's cheek and allowed Grandpa O'Brien to help him place the infant in Chris's hands.

B.J.'s eyes followed little Eddie as Chris took him.

Hannah watched the emotion play across B.J.'s face and felt a warmth glowing in her heart.

While Chris was holding the baby, Mary Beth stood next to her mother and said, "Mama, he really does resemble Papa. Look at that chin and the shape of his forehead."

"Yes," Hannah said, a lump forming in her throat. "And I think his hands are going to be like Papa's."

There was silence for a moment, then Mary Beth said, "Mama, the Bible says the people in heaven are a great cloud of witnesses..."

"Yes?"

"Well, Miss Lindgren told us once in our Sunday school class that since the people in heaven are watching us run our race down here, that she believes there are certain times when God lets them look in on their loved ones. Do you suppose the Lord is letting Papa look down on us right now, so he can see little Eddie?"

"I believe He is, honey."

"Really?" spoke up Patty Ruth. "Papa'th lookin' down at uth right now?"

"I think so, honey."

The child looked heavenward but did not utter a word. "Mama, can Papa hear uth?"

"I'm not sure, honey."

"Well, then, I'll jutht thmile up at him." As she spoke, she smiled toward heaven.

Hannah's lips were quivering. She blinked at the tears that filled her eyes and wiped them away with a corner of the sheet.

"Mama, am I too little to hold the baby?" Patty Ruth said.

"Not if Grandpa will help you."

"Be glad to," said Doc. "You ready to give him up, Chris?"

"Not really, but for P.R., I'll do it."

Before he let Doc take the baby from him, Chris kissed the little wrinkled cheek and said, "Your big brother loves you, Eddie. You sure do look like Papa."

"And me," put in B.J.

"And B.J.," said Chris.

Doc let Patty Ruth sit right where she was, next to her mother, and placed the baby in her arms, keeping a firm hold with his hands.

She looked down at the baby and said, "Eddie, thome-body will tell you that I really wanted little Betthy Lee, an' I did. But I don' no more. I want you! I love you, an' I will help Mama take care of you."

B.J. stepped close, got a sly grin on his face, and said, "Patty Ruth, are you gonna be the one who changes little Eddie's diapers?"

Patty Ruth looked at him blankly, then crinkled her nose and said, "Maybe it would be better if Mama and Mary Beth do that."

CHAPTER FOURTEEN

C aptain John Fordham and his dozen men hauled up on a high spot in thick timber about two hundred yards from the Blackfoot village located some ten miles due north of the Box W ranch. The tracks of the herd led straight to the village, and there was a bloody scene as at least a hundred braves were occupied with the butchering.

Both Fordham and Lieutenant Mack Stewart studied the site through binoculars. Fires were burning, and chunks of beef were being turned on spits by the women.

"Well," said Stewart, "the best I can count, the number of dead cattle is plenty close to what Mrs. Wright told Colonel Bateman she had before they were stolen."

"I'd say so," said Fordham. "See that hide they're stretching?"

"Yes, sir. Box W brand. What are we going to do about this, Captain? White Eagle and his men need to be punished for this."

"That's right, Captain," spoke up Corporal Rick Nesbitt. "From what you said Colonel Bateman told you, Mrs. Wright will now lose her ranch."

"But Captain," said a private, "if we're going to administer punishment, we'll have to bring every man in the fort to do it. And even then we'll be outnumbered. We'll have a lot of blood-shed over something that can't be reversed now. The cattle can't be brought back to life."

"I understand that," said Fordham, "but we can't just shrug this off."

"I agree, Captain," spoke up Sergeant Del Frayne, "but we mustn't forget the hard winter we've had in this part of Wyoming. I've been stationed at different forts in Wyoming territory for nearly ten years. In all this time we've never had such a hard winter, and I've never known of the Indians to steal a whole herd of cattle from a rancher. This village has over nine hundred people, and no doubt came close to starving. Should we exact severe punishment on them for this?"

John Fordham sighed, sending a cloud of vapor into the cold air. "Sergeant, I'm in sympathy with anyone who has suffered hunger through this harsh winter, but there's also a principle here. White Eagle and his braves trespassed on the Wright property and stole Carrie's only means of income. Attacking the village with guns blazing wouldn't produce anything but bloodshed on both sides, but White Eagle needs to be confronted and told in no uncertain terms how wrong he was to do this, and what it's done to the young widow."

"You're right about that, sir," said Lieutenant Stewart. "We need to go in there under a white flag and maybe even put some pressure on White Eagle to make some kind of restitution to Mrs. Wright."

"That's exactly what we're going to do," said Fordham, turning in the saddle. "Corporal Nesbitt, affix your white flag to your rifle. We're going in."

Carrie Wright had been keeping herself busy since arriving home. As soon as Marshal Lance Mangum rode away, she started sweeping and dusting the entire house while waiting for news about the cattle.

One minute she was thinking positive thoughts; the next minute she was in despair.

The house was clean and polished by the time the sun began to set, and just as she was putting the broom, dustpan, and feather duster in the broom closet, she heard the sound of horses blowing and hooves pounding the snow-laden ground at the front of the house.

She hurried to the parlor and peered through the lace curtains, then hastily grabbed her shawl and threw it around her shoulders before stepping out onto the porch.

Captain Fordham and Lieutenant Stewart were dismounting. As his feet touched ground, Fordham saw the mixture of hope and anxiety on Carrie's face. During the ride from the Blackfoot village to the Box W, Fordham had prayed for Carrie. She was going to need the Lord's strengthening hand when she heard the news.

Touching his hat brim, the captain said, "Carrie, I would like you to meet Lieutenant Mack Stewart."

Carrie nodded at Stewart, who touched his hat brim and said, "Ma'am."

"Carrie," Fordham said, "we followed the tracks of your stolen cattle from the north edge of your property and found they had been stolen by the Blackfeet, whose village is about ten miles north of here."

"Yes?" she said, eyes wide.

Fordham cleared his throat. "When we got there, ma'am, we found that the Indians had already slaughtered the entire herd and were dressing them out and stretching the hides. They—"

"Oh no!" Carrie's hand flew to her mouth, and tears came quickly.

Captain Fordham moved up onto the porch and laid a hand on her shoulder. "I'm so sorry. Is there something I can do for you?"

Carrie forced herself to calm down and said in a shaky voice, "There's nothing you can do, Captain, but thank you for offering."

"I want you to know that we rode into the village under a white flag and talked to Chief White Eagle about what he and his braves had done. I rebuked them for stealing from you, explaining that your husband had died recently and their theft would cause you to lose the ranch."

"The chief felt bad when he heard that, ma'am," said Stewart. "He explained that because of the severe winter, he and his people have been very short on game. Some of his people starved to death. We saw the graves, which were rocks piled on bodies because the ground is too frozen to dig."

"Oh, those poor people," she said, tightening the shawl on her neck.

"Carrie, you're cold," said the captain. "Can we step inside for a few minutes?"

"Of course. You can bring all of your men inside if you wish."

"We won't stay that long," said Fordham.

Carrie nodded and turned for the door. When she and the two officers were inside with the door shut, she said, "I know the Indians have been on the verge of starvation all winter. I heard about Hannah Cooper giving food to the Crows."

Fordham nodded. "Yes...even though many white people protested her action. Chief White Eagle told me they stole your cattle in the knowledge they might have to face army guns for doing it. But he was desperate after burying more than a dozen of his people."

Carrie frowned. "Captain, I don't want them facing army guns for this. They were only doing what they felt they had to do to survive."

"We aren't going to attack the village," Fordham assured her. "Lieutenant Stewart and I told White Eagle that he and his people should make some kind of restitution to you. He thought on it for a moment, then told us they would share their corn crop with you next summer."

Carrie's lips pressed into a thin smile. "I appreciate his

offer, but I really won't need the corn. I'll—I'll be elsewhere by next summer."

Fordham's features were somber as he said, "I feel so bad that you're going to lose the ranch. But…"

"But what?"

"Well, look at it this way. The Lord could have prevented the Blackfeet from stealing your herd. But as I see it, He allowed this to happen because He has a plan for your life, and the loss of the ranch is part of it."

Carrie bit her lower lip and tried to show that she believed the captain was right, but she was finding it very difficult. "I want to thank you for finding out what happened to my cattle, Captain Fordham. It was very good of you to put forth this effort, and it was good of Colonel Bateman to send you. Please thank your men for me. And until I can do so myself, please express my appreciation to Colonel Bateman."

"I'll do that," said Fordham. "And if there's anything we can do for you—"

"Thank you. If there is, I'll let you know."

Carrie stood at the window and watched Captain Fordham and his men ride away as the last rays of the sun were dying out on the western horizon. When they passed from view, she went to the couch and sat down hard.

Carrie wept as if her heart would literally shatter into pieces. After several minutes, her sobs began to lessen; and finally she stood to her feet and wiped her swollen, red-rimmed eyes with the hem of her colorful apron.

She went to the fireplace and tossed some logs on the fire, then lit the lamp on a small table beside her rocking chair, though it would still be another half hour before darkness fell.

Sighing, the weary young widow sank into the rocking chair, and her glance fell on the well-worn Bible lying on the table. The lamp cast a rosy glow on the pages as she opened the Bible and said, "Lord, I need help."

The pages fell open in Zechariah. She began turning pages, and when she came to the third chapter of Malachi, her eyes fell on verse 6, which she had underlined sometime in the past. Slowly, she read the words: "I am the LORD, I change not…" Next to the verse, she had penciled: Hebrews 13:8. Her shaking fingers turned the pages until she came to that verse, which she had also underlined, and she read aloud. "'Jesus Christ the same yesterday, and today, and for ever.'"

She drew a tremulous breath. "Yes, Lord. You never change. You're the same today as You have always been. And Your wonderful love for me has never changed. Thank You, dear Lord. Oh, thank You!"

Her eyes went up the page to verse 5, which also had the words underlined: "be content with such things as ye have: for he hath said, I will never leave thee, nor forsake thee."

As the revered words made their way into Carrie's distressed heart, fresh tears glistened in her eyes and spilled onto her pale cheeks. These, however, were tears of hope, trust, and thanksgiving for God's abundant grace and promise of provision.

"I don't know how You are going to bring about a solution for my problems, Lord," she said softly. "I only know that I am Your child, that You never change, and neither do Your promises. You have a plan for my life. Help me not to get in Your way while You are working it out."

A deep, settled peace stole over Carrie Wright's heart and soul. Suddenly she felt lighter than she had since the day of Colin's death. Leaving the couch, she went to the kitchen. At the washstand she dipped a cloth in the basin of water and washed all trace of tears from her cheeks. While drying off, she looked at her face in the mirror on the wall behind the washstand. The haggard, worried look she had borne for so long was gone. In its place was a look of peace and confidence.

"Father," she said aloud, "by myself I can't face the loss of the ranch and all it entails. Thank You that I don't have to. I know You will be with me all the way, and with my hand in Yours, You will lead me. Thank You, dear Lord, that You will bring about Your perfect plan for my life."

It had been dark for nearly an hour when Carrie sat at the kitchen table, eating her supper. She was almost finished when she heard a knock at the front door. Lantern light from the big parlor window played across the faces of Pastor Andy Kelly and Deputy Marshal Jack Bower.

"Pastor! Jack!" she said, swinging the door wider. "Please come in. It's nice to see you."

Both men removed their hats as they stepped in and closed the door. While they took off their coats, Kelly said, "Captain Fordham came to the parsonage and told me about the cattle being stolen and slaughtered by the Blackfeet. Jack happened to be at the parsonage at the time, and when I told Rebecca I was going to ride out and see you, he offered to come along."

"That was kind of you, Jack," Carrie said.

"We stopped by the house so I could tell Julianna where I was going," Jack said. "She cried when we told her about the cattle and said to tell you she loves you."

"I love her, too. The coffee is still hot. Would you gentlemen like some?"

Both men said yes, and while they sat at the kitchen table and Carrie placed cups in front of them, Kelly said, "Carrie, you don't look distraught over this terrible loss."

She smiled while filling the cups, then set the coffeepot back on the stove and said, "Only because my precious Lord has given me peace through His Word, Pastor. I was about to fall apart when I sat down and let Him speak to me from the pages of His Book."

"Well, wonderful! Praise His name! I'm here because I wanted to try to comfort you, as did Jack…and to pray with you. I'm so glad to see you in this good state of mind."

"I won't say I'm not upset about it, Pastor, and that I'm not a bit on edge about the showdown I'll have with Karl Devlin, but the Lord will be with me, and I'll make it. I have no idea what God has planned for my future, but I know He will work His will in my life. I want to thank both of you gentlemen for being so kind and caring as to ride all the way out here tonight."

Kelly smiled. "I wanted to remind you of Psalm 84:5–6, and to tell you that in spite of the fact that today you have gone even deeper into the valley of Baca, God has another mountain-top beyond the valley. Only the Lord knows how long you will be in the valley, Carrie, but according to Scripture, you will get through it."

Carrie's eyes misted. "I know you're right, Pastor. And even though the Lord has given me peace about the cattle and the fact that I'm going to lose the ranch, I have to say that the next mountaintop seems a million miles away."

"I'm sure it does," said Kelly. "But this is where faith comes in. As you know, the Bible says faith is the evidence of things not seen. Right now you can't see how the Lord is going to bring you out of the valley and put you in a new phase of your life on the next mountaintop, but by faith you can rest on it and continue to have peace about it."

Carrie nodded and used a napkin to dab at the tears in her eyes.

"Jack and I would like to pray with you," said Kelly.

"Of course."

After both preacher and lawman had led in prayer, they put on their coats and prepared to leave. As they moved toward the door, Pastor Kelly said, "I'll see that someone comes out Sunday morning to drive you into town for church."

"Pastor, that isn't necessary. I can hitch up the team and drive the wagon into town."

"I know you can, but you're not going to. You be ready, and you'll have your ride."

When the two men were gone, Carrie went into the parlor, fell on her knees beside the couch, and said, "Dear Lord, please increase my faith and help me never to doubt You."

The next morning at the Fort Bridger school, Bob Imler was dismounting from his horse when the Cooper children arrived, walking with some of the children from the fort. He caught Mary Beth's eye and hurried up to the group.

"Mary Beth," he said, all the while getting dirty looks from the others, "could I talk to you before you go inside?"

"Of course, Bob," she replied. To her siblings and the others she said, "You go on in. I'll be there in a minute."

Other students who were passing by looked at him suspiciously. Suddenly he blurted out, "Mary Beth, could we talk at lunch time? I mean, right after we've eaten…just for a few minutes?"

"Of course."

When lunch had been eaten and the students were either playing games on the playground or were talking in small groups, Mary Beth and Bob met at a private spot near the road.

"What did you want to talk about?" Mary Beth asked.

"I…uh…I want to ask you to forgive me for the way I treated you after you told Miss Lindgren that I cheated on the test. I shouldn't have hit you."

"I'm glad you see that, Bob. A boy should never hit a girl."

He nodded. "You're right. You see, Mary Beth, my pa hits my mother quite often. He has a hot temper, and when he feels she's got it comin', he beats her good. He's not very good to women."

"I know. I heard about the way he unleashed on Miss Lindgren for giving you that whipping. I also heard about Dr. O'Brien punching your father a good one for treating Miss Lindgren like he did."

Bob nodded. "Yeah. I heard about it, too, when I was ridin' through town to go home that afternoon. When I got home, I saw the bruise on Pa's face. He told Ma a lie about how he got it. When Pa and I were alone in the barn before supper, I told him I knew about Dr. O'Brien sluggin' him because of the way he was hollerin' and cussin' at Miss Lindgren.

"Pa's eyes were fiery. He told me to keep my mouth shut. He didn't want Ma knowin' the truth about the bruise. Problem was…Ma had come to the barn to ask Pa somethin', and before she came through the barn door, she heard enough to know that Pa had lied about how he got the bruise. She told him she wanted to know the truth. Pa knew there was no use lyin' about it anymore, so he told her the story. When she'd heard it all, Ma shamed him for treatin' Miss Lindgren like that. She told him just because he was rough with her, didn't mean he could be that way with other women." Bob's eyes were filled with tears. "Pa got so mad at Ma that he gave her a terrible beatin' right there in the barn."

"Oh, that's awful!"

"I was too scared to try to stop him. But while it was goin' on, I thought about how I treated you that day, and I realized that I was becomin' just like my pa. I don't want to be like him, Mary Beth. I…I'm asking you to forgive me for bein' so mean to you."

A tender expression captured Mary Beth's pretty features. Reaching out and touching his arm, she said, "Bob, I forgive you."

Tears surfaced in the big boy's eyes. "Thank you. I…uh…"

"Yes?"

"Well, you were so quick to forgive me. I figured you'd have to think it over or I'd have to get down on my knees and beg your forgiveness."

"Neither is necessary. You asked me to forgive you and I did. So it's done."

Bob shook his head, then said, "I admire you for not lyin' to Miss Lindgren when I tried to frighten you into doin' so."

"I want you to understand that the reason I told the truth is because I'm a child of God. His Word says we are to be honest before all men, and because I love Jesus, I do my best to obey His Word. You see, the reason it was so easy for me to forgive you is because of the way the Lord Jesus so readily forgave me of all my sins when I opened my heart to Him."

Puzzlement was evident in Bob's eyes.

"Because I was forgiven by the Lord for what I had done wrong to Him, it was only right that when you asked me to forgive you for what you had done wrong to me, that I do it."

A bewildered look captured his face.

"Let me ask you something, Bob."

"Sure."

"Have you ever asked Jesus to come into your heart and forgive you of all your sins and save your lost soul?"

"Uh…no. I never knew I had to do that."

"Well, the Bible says that unless you get saved, you will go to hell when you die."

Bob was trying to think of a reply when the sound of the school bell clattered.

As they started toward the building, Mary Beth said, "You don't want to go to hell, do you?"

"No, I don't! I've heard about that burnin' place. I sure don't want to go there. I thought hell was just where murderers and people like that go. You know. The real bad people."

"It's where all unforgiven sinners go, Bob."

They were near the front porch now.

"Mary Beth?"

"Yes?"

"I'd like to know more about gettin' saved."

"You should come to church and hear Pastor Kelly. He really makes it plain when he preaches."

"But Pa would never allow me to come to church. He hates churches."

"All right, then…you and I will talk every day at lunchtime. I'll bring my Bible and read you some things from it."

A look of relief showed on Bob Imler's face. "Thanks, Mary Beth. That'll be real good. I'll look forward to it."

During the next week and a half, Mary Beth met with Bob at lunchtime and showed him what the Bible said about salvation. On Friday, she felt it was time to press him for a decision. Bob thanked her for caring, but said he couldn't receive Jesus into his heart just yet.

On Sunday morning, Hannah Cooper came to church carrying her new baby. Curly and Judy Charley Wesson were the first to greet her as she and her children came through the door. Others began to gather around.

"Wal, lookee here, Judy!" said Curly. "Little Solomon Edward is comin' to church fer the first time!"

"Yeah!" said the skinny woman, showing her snaggle-toothed smile. "C'n we get a glimpse of him, Hannah?"

"Of course." Hannah peeled back the blanket to expose the baby's face.

"Hey, lookee!" said Curly. "That lil feller looks like B.J.!"

"Good lookin', isn't he, Uncle Curly?" B.J. said.

"Shore is, boy! He shore is!"

"He lookth like Papa, too," put in Patty Ruth.

"That really so, Hannah?" Judy asked.

"Very much so."

"Wal, I'm sure that is a real blessin' to you. So are yuh gonna have him dedicated today, honey?"

"I've already dedicated Eddie to the Lord, but I've made arrangements with Pastor Kelly to do a public dedication after the service this morning."

The Cooper children headed for their Sunday school classes and more people converged on Hannah as she made her way into the auditorium and sat down. One of them was Carrie Wright. After Carrie had cooed over little Eddie, Hannah told her how sorry she was for the loss of her cattle and asked what she was going to do.

Leaning close, Carrie said, "I'm not sure yet, Hannah. The mortgage payment is due April 1, which is next Saturday. I'm waiting on the Lord to either give me the money to make another month's payment, or show me what I'm to do and where I'm to go."

Hannah patted her hand. "I've been praying for you, honey. I have no doubt that when it's time, God will take care of the matter."

Carrie smiled. "Thank you for praying. My life is in God's hands and I know He will take care of me."

At the close of the invitation that morning, Pastor Kelly had one man to baptize. Afterward, he told the people not to leave their seats, he would be right out for a very special occasion.

The people of Fort Bridger's church dearly loved Hannah Cooper and her family, and when Hannah walked down the aisle carrying her new baby, many tears were shed.

While Pastor Kelly held little Eddie in his arms, he told the congregation that Hannah had brought the baby to publicly dedicate him to the Lord. He then prayed over the infant, asking God to bring the boy to Himself as soon as he was old enough to understand about sin and salvation. He also asked the Lord to give Hannah wisdom in raising Eddie, and the rest of her children, without a father in the home. He closed by asking God to use little Eddie for His glory, even as He was using Hannah, Chris, Mary Beth, B.J., and Patty Ruth.

After the service, Hannah was in conversation with Pastor Kelly, Rebecca, and Carrie Wright at the back of the auditorium. Her children stood close by. She was talking about Adam and Theresa coming to Fort Bridger when she saw Chief Two Moons, Sweet Blossom, and Broken Wing coming up the aisle. They stopped to ask if they could see the baby.

After each had taken a good look at Eddie, Sweet Blossom produced a small doeskin satchel tied at the top with a rawhide string and said shyly, "Hannah Cooper, this is a gift for your new little son."

Two Moons and Broken Wing looked on with bright eyes.

Hannah tilted her head to one side. "Oh-h-h, Sweet Blossom, how thoughtful of you." Then to Mary Beth she said, "Honey, will you hold Eddie while I open this gift?"

Hannah moved to the back row of pews and sat down. The others gathered round.

She took out a fleecy white handwoven baby blanket, felt its soft texture, and said, "Sweet Blossom, this is beautiful! Little Eddie will stay nice and warm in this."

A broad smile graced the squaw's dark features. "There is something else, too."

Reaching into the satchel again, Hannah brought out a pair of soft doeskin booties. Running her hand gently over the delicate pieces, she looked up at Sweet Blossom with tears shimmering in her eyes. Laying the blanket and booties on the pew, she stood up and wrapped her arms around Sweet Blossom and kissed her cheek, saying, "Thank you so much, my dear friend. I can see that you put many hours of labor and love into making these beautiful gifts. I will always cherish them."

Sweet Blossom kissed her cheek in return and said, "You have done so much for my family and for our people. In this small way, I try to tell you that I love you."

"You have told me in a wonderful way. Thank you, Sweet Blossom. And I love you too. Very, very much."

CHAPTER FIFTEEN

The next day, Carrie Wright decided to send a letter to Karl Devlin, explaining that her cattle had been stolen and slaughtered by the Blackfeet, and that she had no way of making the April payment on the mortgage. She asked if she could stay on the ranch until Devlin had sold it to someone else since she had nowhere to go. She thanked him in advance for considering this; she would be waiting to hear back from him.

As she folded the letter and stuffed it into the envelope, she said aloud, "Lord, I'm depending on You to show me what to do and where to go before I have to vacate the ranch."

Heavy clouds were coming in from the north and the wind was picking up as Carrie drove her wagon into Fort Bridger. She posted the letter at the Wells Fargo office with Curly Wesson, then went to Cooper's General Store.

Hannah was behind the counter with Jacob. Both were waiting on customers, but they greeted Carrie when they saw her. She noticed that little Eddie was in his cradle behind the counter.

Carrie picked up the food items she needed, and when she returned to the counter, there were no customers in Hannah's line.

"Looks like we've got another storm moving in," Hannah said.

Carrie placed the grocery items on the counter. "I'd say so. I'm heading home as soon as I finish here."

Hannah started sacking the items.

Frowning, Carrie said, "Hannah, what are you doing? You should be tallying these items and putting them on my bill. One way or another, I'm going to pay it as soon as I can."

Hannah shook her head. "What bill, honey?"

"You know what bill. The one Colin and I started running up when you agreed to give us credit. The same bill I've added to since he died."

Hannah looked at Jacob, whose last customer had just walked away with sacks in her arms. "Jacob?"

"Yes, Hannah?"

"Do you know about some bill that Carrie owes us?"

"Nope. Far as I know, there's no bill here with her name on it."

Carrie's lips quivered and moisture collected in her eyes as she said, "Hannah, this isn't right. You have to make a living too."

Hannah leaned over the counter, stroked Carrie's cheek, and said, "The Lord has blessed the store, honey. Last night when I was praying for you, He spoke to my heart and told me I should wipe out your bill. You wouldn't want me to disobey the Lord, would you?"

Fat teardrops ran their course down Carrie's cheeks as she moved around the end of the counter and hugged Hannah.

Moments later, as Carrie picked up her grocery sacks, Jacob said, "Better not tarry, Mrs. Wright. Looks like we're going to get a pretty good storm."

"Maybe you should stay in town till the storm is over," Hannah said. "I'd hate to see you get caught in it."

"I'll be home before it hits us. Thank you again, Hannah."

With that, the young widow hurried out the door.

The storm swept in on southwest Wyoming later that day after Carrie had arrived at the Box W. It lasted for two days, adding some twelve inches of snow to what was already on the ground.

By Thursday morning, the sun was shining out of a cold, clear sky. The weather was frigid, but the sky remained clear through the weekend.

On Monday morning, April 3, the sun was shining once more as Carrie swept and dusted the house. She planned to drive the wagon into town to see if a letter had come from Karl Devlin. She was putting on her coat when she noticed movement beyond the parlor window. Moving closer to the window, she saw that it was a lone rider and he was drawing up to the porch. Sunlight reflected off the badge pinned to his sheepskin coat. His face was not familiar to her.

Carried opened the door just as the lawman was mounting the porch steps.

"Are you Mrs. Wright?" he asked.

"Yes, sir."

Touching his hat brim, he said, "Ma'am, I'm Uintah County Sheriff, Hugo Fisher. I have some official papers to give you. Would you mind if we went inside?"

"Papers?" she said, stepping back so he could enter.

Fisher stomped the snow from his boots and removed his hat as he stepped past her. When she closed the door, he pulled an envelope from his coat pocket. "Yes, ma'am. These are foreclosure papers from Mr. Karl Devlin, and it is my duty to deliver them to you."

"Foreclosure papers?" she said in disbelief.

"Yes, ma'am." He placed the envelope in her hand. "As you will see when you read them, Mr. Devlin has sold the ranch to a Mr. Dean Driskell. You had a payment due in Mr. Devlin's hands as of Saturday. He said he did not receive the payment, nor did he hear from you. The mortgage contract you and your husband signed—which Mr. Devlin showed to me—leaves no room for late payment. Therefore, Mr. Devlin is within his legal rights to foreclose."

"But, Sheriff, I wrote to Mr. Devlin a week ago today, explaining that all my cattle were stolen and slaughtered by the Blackfeet Indians, and that I had no way of making the April payment. I asked him in the letter if I could stay on the ranch until he had sold it to someone else. I told him I would be waiting to hear back from him. A week should be plenty of time for my letter to have reached him."

"Well, in good weather it would be, Mrs. Wright, but we had that storm hit last Tuesday and Wednesday. The stagecoaches weren't running again until midday on Thursday. Mr. Devlin will probably get your letter in today's mail."

"Oh. Of course. The storm. So according to these papers, how long do I have to get off the property?"

"A little less than two weeks, ma'am. You have to vacate the premises by no later than Friday, April 14."

Carrie nodded.

Fisher scrubbed a hand over his mustache. "Mrs. Wright, I'm really sorry about this. I understand that your husband was killed quite recently. I wish there was something I could do, but that contract was a legal one, and I have to uphold the law."

She smiled at the rugged man and said, "I understand, Sheriff. You're just doing your job. I'm a Christian, and I know the Lord will take care of me."

Fisher nodded and said, "I admire your faith, ma'am."

At that instant, they both heard Fisher's horse whinny, and it was answered from a horse farther away.

Carrie went to the parlor window and said, "Oh! It's my pastor and his wife."

Fisher stepped up beside her and watched the oncoming buggy. "Pastor Kelly. I know him. Fine man."

"That he is," Carrie said, heading toward the door.

The sheriff followed her but remained a couple of steps back.

Carrie stepped out on the porch when the buggy came to a stop. "Hello, Pastor, Rebecca."

"I see you have company," Kelly said. "Are we coming at a bad time?"

"Oh, no. It's Sheriff Hugo Fisher. He says he knows you."

When the Kellys entered the house, Andy Kelly shook hands with Fisher, then introduced him to Rebecca. He ran his gaze between the sheriff and Carrie. "Some kind of problem?"

Fisher quickly explained why he was there. By this time, Rebecca was standing beside Carrie with an arm around her.

"I understand that he's just doing his job, Pastor," said Carrie.

"Sometimes I don't like doing my job," said Fisher. "Like right now. Well, I need to get back to Rock Springs. Thank you for your kindness, Mrs. Wright."

"You're welcome, Sheriff."

"You...ah...will be off the premises no later than April 14?"

"Yes, I will, Sheriff."

Fisher bid the Kellys good-bye, mounted, and rode away.

"It'll be all right, honey," Rebecca said softly.

"It isn't that I'm afraid of what will happen to me," Carrie said. "The Lord has given me peace about that. It's just that I feel I've let Colin down."

Pastor Kelly moved closer and said, "Colin wouldn't want you to feel that way. He would know that it would be next to impossible—even in the best of circumstances—for you to run the ranch by yourself. Don't you see that?"

Carrie closed her eyes. After a few seconds, she nodded and said, "Yes, Pastor. You're right."

"The Lord knew this foreclosure was coming and the papers would be delivered to you today. Right?"

"Yes."

"Rebecca and I had no way of knowing that, but we came out here to tell you that God, in His infinite wisdom, has a plan already underway for your immediate future. We have something we want to talk to you about."

Carrie looked from Andy to Rebecca, then said, "All right. Let's go into the kitchen. We'll have some coffee while you tell me."

The sun was sparkling off the glistening snow that blanketed the land, throwing a cheery warmth into the kitchen. When her guests were seated, Carrie poured three steaming cups of coffee, then sat down and said, "All right. I'm listening."

Kelly leaned forward. "You've met Maude Garvin, Glenda Williams's head cook at the café?"

"Yes. She's a very sweet lady."

"And you know that she has an ailing mother back East."

"Yes."

"Well, Rebecca and I learned just yesterday that there are some sibling problems in Maude's family concerning the care of their mother, and Maude is taking an extended leave of absence from the café so she can go back there and help clear up the situation. She has no idea how long it might take, thus the extended leave. So this leaves Glenda in desperate need of a cook. Since Rebecca and I are quite able to testify firsthand that you are an outstanding cook, we thought we'd tell Glenda where she could get someone to fill in for Maude."

"This would provide a decent income for you at least until Maude returns," put in Rebecca. "By then, the Lord will work something else out."

A spark of hope showed in Carrie's eyes. "Do you really think Glenda would hire me just on your say-so?"

Andy and Rebecca looked at each other. "Which of us gets to tell her?" asked the pastor.

"You go ahead, honey," said Rebecca. "I'll tell her the other thing."

"Other thing?" Carrie asked.

"That'll come in a moment," said Kelly. "What I want to tell you is that you already have the job if you want it."

"Pastor, you're joking!"

"No joke. We had a talk with Glenda and told her about your cooking. We told her we were coming out to talk to you, and she said to tell you that upon our recommendation, she will hire you if you want the job. Maude has to leave on the stagecoach for Cheyenne City on Thursday. So the sooner you can start, the better."

Carrie's face lit up. "I can hardly believe this! I'll ride into town immediately and tell Glenda she's got her cook until Maude returns!"

"No need to ride by yourself," said Kelly. "Rebecca and I will take you and bring you back. We'd like to be there when you tell Glenda you're accepting the job."

"Well, all right. Let's get this coffee down and head for town!"

"Let me tell you the other thing," said Rebecca. "Pastor and I talked about this even before we knew Maude was taking the leave of absence. We want to offer you a place in our home until the Lord works out a place for you. We have a spare bedroom, which will be yours, and you can live with us until something better comes along."

Carrie shook her head slowly. "This is incredible. The Lord really does have a plan for our lives, doesn't He? I'm overwhelmed."

"It's because we love you, Carrie," said Rebecca. "You've been through so much heartache. We just want to help you put your life back together."

"Thank you. Both of you. It will be difficult to give up the ranch, as I'm sure you understand. This is where Colin and I dreamed and made plans for our future. Those dreams and plans, of course, are gone. But now that I have at least something to grasp, and I can see the Lord's hand in it, I can leave the ranch with peace in my heart." Carrie's eyes were brimming with unshed tears. "Isn't it wonderful? God is already in my future, just waiting for me to get there." A winsome smile graced her lips. "Let's go to town."

Carrie and the Kellys found the Williamses in Gary's office at the Uintah Hotel. Pastor Kelly told them about the foreclosure papers being served and that Carrie knew of Glenda's offer to fill in for Maude at the café.

"Will you take it?" Glenda said, her big blue eyes fixed on Carrie's face.

"I sure will!"

"Oh, wonderful!"

"Indeed!" said Gary. "Since you'll be carrying the same load that Maude carries, we'll pay you the same salary we pay her."

"Oh, that's very generous of you, but you haven't even sampled any of my cooking yet."

Gary laughed. "Pastor and Rebecca's recommendation is good enough for us! Maude is feeling bad about leaving us in the lurch. I'll go tell her that Carrie has agreed to fill in."

While Gary was gone, the foursome discussed God's hand being so evident in Carrie's life. Only minutes had passed when Gary returned. Maude came with him and thanked Carrie for taking her place on a temporary basis.

"I'm glad to do it. I know it will help you, and it will help Glenda…and it will certainly help me. I know the Lord will have something else for me when you return."

Compassion showed in Maude's face as she said, "Gary told me about the foreclosure papers. Tell you what, since you have to move into town, you can stay at my house. I mean, while I'm gone and when I come back. There's room for both of us."

Carrie looked at the Kellys, then at Maude. "Well-l-l-l, Pastor and Rebecca offered to let me live with them until something else came up."

"I'm sure it would be a blessing to Maude to have someone take care of her house while she's gone," spoke up Rebecca. "If you'd rather stay there, you won't hurt our feelings."

"It would relieve my mind a whole lot," said Maude.

"All right," Carrie said, smiling. "I'll stay at your house while you're gone, and even when you return, if the Lord leaves me in Fort Bridger."

Maude hugged her and said, "We'll pray that He does. Can you go to work right away?"

"I'll have to bring my horses to town and board them at the livery stable. And I'll have to bring my clothing and other things. The furniture came with the house, so it will stay there."

"I can get some men to help with the horses and your things, Carrie," said Kelly. "We can do it yet today."

"I'll be one of those men, Pastor," spoke up Gary.

"Then I can move in with you this afternoon, Maude," said Carrie, "and I can start to work tomorrow."

On Wednesday, April 5, Claude Owens, owner of the *Cincinnati Post,* was sitting at his desk on the newspaper's fifth floor, looking out at the busy street below him.

There was a light tap on the door. Owens, who was in his late sixties, took off his spectacles and said, "Enter."

Adam Cooper opened the door. "Your secretary said you wanted to see me, sir."

"Yes. Come in. Leave the door open. I've sent for Doug, too." Adam was just under six feet tall, had a thick head of sandy hair and dark blue eyes. He was ruggedly handsome as had been his brother, Solomon.

Just as Adam was taking a seat, Doug McClain appeared at the door.

"Come in, Doug!" said the silver-haired Owens.

Doug was just over six feet, with auburn hair and sky blue eyes. At thirty-one, he was three years younger than Adam.

Owens gestured to the vacant chair beside Adam. "Have a seat, Doug."

Owens ran his gaze between the two men and said, "To repeat myself for probably the dozenth time, gentlemen, I hate to lose you. Doug, you're an excellent pressman, and Adam, you're the best editor-in-chief I've ever had. I wanted to let you know that I've hired a new editor-in-chief, so you gentlemen can now proceed with your plans to move to Wyoming."

"May I ask who you hired, sir?" said Adam.

"Of course. Grant Mossman, who at present is editor-in-chief of the *Terre Haute Daily Sentinel.*"

"I've never met Mossman, but I've heard good things about him."

"I'd heard the same things," said Owens, "so I contacted him and made him an offer. His first day at work is Monday, April 24. Adam, if you could stay until that following Friday, you could help Mossman get the feel of things."

Adam glanced at the calendar hanging on the wall near Owens's desk. "That would be the twenty-eighth. Yes, sir. I can do that."

"And you can stay on until that day too, if you want to, Doug," said Owens.

"Fine. Thank you, sir."

Owens sighed. "Well, for the thirteenth time, I sure hate to lose you two, but I can't blame you a bit for what you're doing. I love your pioneer spirit. It's the same spirit that burned in me thirty years ago when I came to Cincinnati and started the *Post.*"

"I'm glad you understand, sir," said Adam. "And thank you for bringing me up through the ranks and making me your editor-in-chief at such a young age."

Owens's eyes crinkled at the corners as he smiled and said, "You earned it, son. And you've done me proud." Then to McClain he said, "Doug, you've done me proud, too, and since Adam is striking out on this venture, I have to say that I'm glad he'll have you at his side. You two will make a great team."

Both men thanked him.

"So, let me ask," said Owens, "is everything in order for you at Fort Bridger? I know you said the loan had been approved by the bank, and the banker and the mayor are both eager for you to get there. But what about a building?"

"The Lord has worked that out for us, sir," said Adam. "Mayor Samuels was able to secure space for us. You see, there's a hardware store and gun shop on Main Street, and half the building has been vacant for a while. Samuels explained in his letter that there was a clothing store in the other half when a man named Justin Powell bought the hardware store and gun shop several months ago, which included the entire building.

"The man who owned the clothing store built his own building several months ago and moved out. So we'll have that half in which to house the paper. Justin wrote and gave me the dimensions of our space, along with a rental agreement to sign. The space will be plenty big enough to hold a large press, the office furniture, filing cabinets, storage, and everything else we need. And Mr. Powell has made the rent quite reasonable."

"Well, that's good," said Owens. "I hope you're a great success."

"It looks good, sir," said Adam. "Mayor Samuels wrote and told me that he and banker Lloyd Dawson have put the word out about a newspaper in Fort Bridger, and the response has been really good. People in both the town and the fort have expressed their excitement, as have many farmers and ranchers and people in other towns within a thirty-mile radius."

"Wonderful!" said Owens. "I'm glad it's all working out for you. I'm sure your sister-in-law and her children are excited about your coming."

"That they are, sir. Since my brother's death, Theresa and I have wanted to go out there and spend some time with Hannah and her family. We received word a couple of weeks ago that Hannah gave birth to her fifth child on March 14. She told us her new little son is the spitting image of my brother. We're excited about being with them on a permanent basis."

"I can understand that," said Owens. "By the way, did you come up with a name for the paper?"

Adam and Doug grinned at each other, then Adam said, "I put a lot of thought into it and just came up with it yesterday. Doug likes it. I figured since the army fort is right there, and the town has the same name, I'd call the paper the *Fort Bridger Bugle.*"

"Hey, I like that! Has a nice sound, and gives it the military touch."

"Glad you like it, sir."

Owens rose from his chair. "Well, I guess I can let you men get back to work."

As both men rose to their feet, Adam said, "Then we'll plan on Friday, April 28, as our last day, sir."

Kathy McClain was in the kitchen when she heard the door open and a familiar voice call out, "Daddy's home! Is Daddy's little girl around?"

Little one-year-old Jenny was playing on the floor near the kitchen table when she heard her father's voice. Kathy smiled as Jenny squealed, collected her little fat legs under her, and pitter-patted toward the parlor.

Kathy stepped to the kitchen door and watched with joy

as she saw Doug hurry to Jenny, sweep her up into his arms and kiss her repeatedly on the side of the neck. The little blond toddler giggled and wiggled. When the kissing stopped, Doug held Jenny close and turned to look at his lovely wife.

"Well," said Kathy, "does Mommy get any kisses, or did Jenny take them all?"

Curving an arm around Kathy's shoulder, Doug bent close and said, "There are plenty left for you."

When he had kissed Kathy several times, he carried Jenny toward the kitchen and said, "I've got good news."

"Oh? Did Mr. Owens find his man to replace Adam?"

"Sure did. Our last day at the *Post* will be Friday, April 28. Adam and I stopped at the railroad station after work and bought our tickets. We'll be leaving Cincinnati on Monday morning, May 1, at nine-thirty."

"Oh, praise the Lord!" Kathy leaned over and kissed the baby's cheek. "Did you hear that, Jenny? It's all set, honey! We're moving to Wyoming!"

CHAPTER SIXTEEN

When Adam Cooper walked into the house, he smelled the aroma of fried chicken. Six-year-old Seth appeared at the parlor door and ran to his father with open arms.

"How's Papa's big boy doing?" Adam said, swinging the boy up into his arms.

"Just fine, Papa! I been helpin' Mama take care of Anna."

"That's a good boy!"

Theresa appeared at the kitchen door. "Hello, sweetheart, have a good day?"

"An exceptionally good day," he said, putting Seth down and reaching into his coat pocket. He took out a brown envelope and held it up. "Guess what's in here!"

Theresa squinted at him. "I have no idea."

"Tickets!"

"Tickets?"

"Yes, ma'am! Railroad tickets to Cheyenne City, and stagecoach tickets to Fort Bridger!"

"Oh, Adam! You mean Mr. Owens hired his new editor-in-chief?"

He gathered her in his arms and kissed the tip of her nose.

"Exactly! Doug and I left work early so we could go to the railroad station and make our reservations."

"Who did Mr. Owens hire? Where's he from?"

Adam kissed her soundly, then said, "I'll tell you all about it while we eat supper. Is my little Anna awake?"

"She was asleep when I last looked in on her."

"Well, I'll just sneak in there and see if she's still asleep."

"I have some good news, too. Would you like to hear it before you check on your daughter?"

Suddenly Adam noticed a special gleam in his wife's eyes. "Sure. What is it?"

"We got a letter today from Mayor Cade Samuels."

Adam's eyes widened. "Did he—?"

"He sure did! We won't need to stay at the Uintah Hotel when we get to Fort Bridger. Mr. Samuels has rented us a three-bedroom house. And he's also rented a house for the McClains."

"Well, praise the Lord! Doug and Kathy will be glad to hear this."

While Theresa put the finishing touches on supper, Adam tiptoed into the bedroom and smiled at his three-month-old daughter who was beginning to stir. He bent over her until she opened her eyes.

"Hi, sweetheart! Papa's home!"

During supper, Theresa placed little Anna on a pallet on the floor next to her, and Adam told her about the man Mr. Owens had hired.

"If we're able to stay on schedule," Adam said, "we'll be boarding a train for Chicago on Monday morning, May 1. That will get us to Fort Bridger late in the afternoon on May 8."

"It's gonna be fun ridin' a stagecoach!" said Seth. "S'pose we'll see some wild Indians, Papa?"

"We just might," Adam said as he reached over and messed up Seth's sandy-colored hair.

Theresa shook her head. "I can't believe we're actually going to go. It's all seemed sort of like an elusive dream until now."

"It's real, honey. The Coopers are moving to the Wild West. We're going to have a wonderful life out there. On the way home from the railroad station, I stopped at the Western Union office and sent a wire to the company in Chicago that we're purchasing the press, office equipment, and paper from. I told them to ship it to Fort Bridger as soon as possible."

"It was such a good thing that Mr. Dawson advanced the loan money for the press and all the rest of the equipment," Theresa said.

"He and Mr. Samuels have been very good to us."

"Yes, and I'm sure the rest of the people in Fort Bridger are just as nice as they are."

"I don't doubt it. Especially Pastor Kelly and the people of the church. Hannah has written so much about them."

"Oh, darling," Theresa said, her eyes bright, "I know we're going to be so happy there. The frontier has to be a wonderful place to live."

That night when Seth was in his bedroom asleep, and Anna was sleeping in her crib near her parents' bed, Adam and Theresa lay awake in their feather bed, holding hands. A full moon sent its silver light into the room.

When Adam heard a tiny sniff, and then another, he turned his face toward Theresa and said, "Honey, you all right?"

He released his hold on her hand and raised up on his elbow to look down into her face. In the moonlight he saw tears slipping from her closed eyelids and across her temples into her hair. "Whatever is wrong?"

Theresa just shook her head.

Placing his palm against her cheek, Adam said, "Now, you know that isn't going to work. I want to know why you're crying. You're hurting over something. Come on. Out with it." As he brushed the tears away, Adam said, "I love you. Whatever is wrong, if it's humanly possible, I'll make it right."

Theresa opened her eyes and saw the love and tenderness in Adam's face. She took a deep, shuddering breath and choked out, "It's not something wrong, darling. It's just hard to leave the only home we've had since we were married. Our children were born right here in this very bed. Now we're leaving it."

Adam nodded. "Tomorrow I'll begin sorting out and packing the things we'll take with us on the train, but of course, the furniture will all stay behind."

After some more tears, she said, "I know they're just 'things,' but they do mean something special to me."

Adam gathered her into his strong and reassuring embrace. Holding her close, he said, "But you are sure you want to make the move, aren't you? We've talked of little else for months."

"Yes, darling. Yes. The Lord has given both of us perfect peace about going to Fort Bridger and starting a new life with our own newspaper. It isn't that I'm wanting to back out on that. I'll be all right. It's just that, well, now that we actually have the railroad and stagecoach tickets in hand, the big move has suddenly become one giant reality. I'm feeling a little fearful of the future and very much nostalgic of the past."

He caressed her back and pulled her even closer. "We know that He will take care of us and provide for us in every way. You believe that, don't you?"

"Yes, darling. With all my heart, I believe that. 'Whither thou goest, I will go' and for me, that means Fort Bridger, Wyoming. I'm fine. I just needed to release a few tears. Sharing my feelings with you has helped immensely."

A sweet smile curved Theresa's lips and Adam pulled her close and kissed her. After a long embrace, they once again lay side by side, feeling a strong sense of peace in their hearts.

Just as sleep was claiming Adam, Theresa snuggled up close to him and whispered, "Thank you, sweetheart, for all that you are, and for all that you are to me. I love you so much."

"I love you too," Adam mumbled, then was fast asleep.

During supper at the Cooper apartment in Fort Bridger, on the same day Adam Cooper purchased the railroad and stagecoach tickets in Cincinnati, Hannah looked across the table at her oldest daughter and said, "Mary Beth, did you talk to Bob during lunch hour at school today?"

"Yes, Mama." Her eyes revealed a hint of sadness. "I read him that passage in Mark chapter 9, where Jesus talked about hell being a place where the fire is never quenched and the worm dieth not. There was even some fear in his eyes while I went over it with him, but he still said he just isn't quite ready to be saved."

"It's the fear of his father, sure as anything," spoke up Chris.

Mary Beth nodded. "As mean as his father is, and as much as he hates anything to do with God or the Bible, I'm sure that Bob shakes in his boots when he contemplates having to face his father and tell him he has become a Christian. I'm praying that the Holy Spirit will make hell real to him, and that he will have more of the fear of God than he does of his father."

"Exactly, honey," said Hannah. "We must pray to that end. It's quite a miracle that Bob came to you, asking forgiveness for the way he treated you. And it's another miracle that he will even let you talk with him about being saved. We just have to ask the Lord to bring the third miracle and put Bob under so much conviction that he will be more afraid to face God without Jesus in his heart than he is to face his father with Jesus in his heart."

On Friday afternoon, April 7, the Cooper children were walking home from school, listening to Patty Ruth talk about what she had learned that day. Chris looked at Mary Beth and said, "How'd it go with Bob today?"

"He's still putting it off. He won't come out and say it, but it's the fear of his mean ol' father. I know it."

"Have you told him you know that's what it is?"

"No. I'm just giving him plenty of Scripture to think about. The Holy Spirit will do His work, I'm sure of it."

The children arrived at the store and moved inside. Jacob Kates was behind the counter, waiting on a couple of soldiers from the fort.

"Hi, Uncle Jacob," Chris said, looking around. "Mama must be upstairs?"

"Yes. She took Eddie up to the apartment about twenty minutes ago to put him down for a nap." He ran his eyes over the foursome and said, "Everybody have a good day at school?"

All four replied at the same time, assuring him it had been a fine day.

When they stepped out the back door, B.J. made a run for the stairs and bounded up them. Chris let his sisters go ahead of him.

Hannah was there to hug and kiss each one, and when she finished with Chris, she said, "I've got good news! I got a telegram today from Uncle Adam. His boss hired a new man, and he and Theresa and the children are getting ready to come to Fort Bridger!"

"When they comin', Mama?" Chris asked.

"They'll be here with the McClains on the afternoon stage on Monday, May 8."

"Wow!" said B.J. "That's only a month from tomorrow!"

"And something else…Uncle Adam told me in the telegram that he's going to call his newspaper the *Fort Bridger Bugle.*"

"Hey!" said Chris. "I like that! Sorta sounds military, doesn't it?"

"Mayor Samuels and Mr. Dawson like it, too," said Hannah. "They also received telegrams from Uncle Adam today. They came into the store just before I brought Eddie up to take his nap and said they really liked the name and had already told lots of people."

"I can't wait for them to get here!" said Patty Ruth. "We're gonna have lotth of fun!"

On Friday, April 14, Glenda Williams walked into her husband's office at the Uintah Hotel and found him poring over a stack of paperwork. Gary looked up and smiled. "Hello, Mrs. Williams."

"Lunch time, Mr. Williams."

"Oh, boy!" he said, dropping his pencil. "I get to eat some more of Carrie's cooking!"

Glenda folded her arms across her chest and tapped her foot, saying with a mock scowl, "I'd really be jealous if I didn't like her cooking so well myself."

Gary laughed and rose from his chair. "Have you noticed how much happier Carrie seems since she went to work for us and moved into Maude's house?"

"Yes, I have. The grief she carried over losing Colin, then the ranch, is lessening every day. I can see the Lord giving her the abundant grace she needed. That sad, haunted look is beginning to disappear, and it's being replaced with an elegant look of serenity."

Gary put his arm around Glenda as they headed for the door. "I'm glad we could have a part in helping her. And of course, I'm glad we have her cooking for us."

"Me too. We would've been in deep trouble if Carrie hadn't been here to take over for Maude."

They entered the back door of the café and stepped into the kitchen. Busy at the stove, Carrie gave them a winsome smile. "Hello, boss. And boss's husband."

"Hello, marvelous cook," Glenda replied.

Carrie chuckled while turning a steak over on the grill. "Thank you, boss, for those kind words."

"Well, I'm just quoting many of our customers who have told me how much they like your cooking."

"Really?"

"Ever since Gary ate in the café on Monday, he wants to eat here all the time."

"Oh, he's just being nice."

"It's more than being nice. I agree with him. I want to eat here all the time, too!"

Carrie's face beamed. "You're both so kind. Thank you for the wonderful way you've treated me."

"It's our pleasure," said Gary. "We're not overworking you with these long hours?"

"Not at all. I love every minute of it. It's best for me to stay busy and keep my mind occupied, as well as my hands. I'll be forever grateful to both of you, my dear friends, for so willingly coming to my rescue."

Glenda hugged her, then said, "Well, dear husband, we'd best get out there and grab us a table before the crowd moves in."

When they had passed through the door into the dining area, Carrie murmured, "Bless them, Lord," then turned back to her work with a satisfied smile on her lips.

In Kearney, Nebraska, on Monday, April 17, Kearney County Sheriff Tom Moyer had just returned to his office from lunch and was sitting down at his desk when the door opened.

A tall, broad-shouldered man dressed in black, with a badge on his chest, stepped inside. He smiled, set cool gray eyes on the older man, and said, "Sheriff Tom Moyer?"

Moyer nodded as he rose from his chair. "Yes, sir."

The man in black—who had a pair of twin jagged scars on his right cheek—said, "I'm Chief U.S. Marshal John Brockman out of Denver."

Moyer's eyes widened. He shook hands and said, "Chief, I know about you, and I very much admire your abilities as a lawman. Let me introduce you to my deputy, Roy Dillard."

Dillard looked at the tall man in awe and said, "Chief Brockman, I too am an admirer of yours. I've read much about your fast draw. I know you've proven yourself faster than any gunslinger who ever challenged you."

Brockman smiled. "I guess that's why I'm still around, Deputy."

"What can I do for you, sir?" Moyer asked.

"Need some information. Are you acquainted with the name Vance Ankum?"

Moyer rubbed his chin. "Well, the name has a familiar ring to it, but—"

"Sheriff, we've got a wanted poster in our file on him," Dillard said. "I'll get it."

The deputy opened the top drawer and flipped through a small stack of posters, then pulled one out and carried it to Moyer. "This is why the name was familiar to you, Sheriff."

Moyer studied the poster and nodded. "Yep." Then to Brockman he said, "Reason it isn't hanging up here on the board with all these other wanted posters is because it says on here that he's wanted in Montana, Wyoming, Utah, and Colorado territories for murder. But there's no mention of Nebraska. So what about him?"

"I'm on Ankum's trail," Brockman said, "and he's riding

hard across Nebraska. I thought maybe you'd heard that he was around, or even had trouble with him. He shot down two men in cold blood in Denver six days ago. Right now I'm short on deputies, so I got on his trail myself."

Moyer frowned. "So he's close by?"

"Has to be. I trailed him to the Kearney area this morning, then lost track of him on the west end of town. I've circled it twice, trying to pick up the trail again, but was unsuccessful. I was hoping maybe he'd had a run-in with you, and you might have him behind bars."

"Wish I did, Chief. I'll be glad to ride with you and help you track him down. Roy can handle the office."

"I appreciate your offer," said Brockman, "but I seem to do better tracking outlaws alone." He extended his hand. "It's been good to meet you."

Meeting the tall man's grip, the sheriff said, "You too, Chief. It's been a real honor."

Brockman shook hands with Dillard, then left the office, mounted his big black gelding, and rode south.

About two miles out of town, Brockman came upon a middle-aged farmer who was working on his broken-down wagon at the side of the road. The left rear wheel was lying on the ground. The farmer was trying to lift the wagon and scoot a large rock under the axle with his foot.

As Brockman pulled rein he said, "Need some help, sir?"

"I sure could use some, Marshal."

Brockman studied the situation. "Wheel just come off, or is it something more serious?"

"That's all. The bolt that holds it to the axle worked loose and I wasn't aware of it. First thing I knew the wagon dropped on that corner, then the wheel went rollin' by me. I just ain't strong enough to lift the corner high enough to get this rock under the axle so's I can put the wheel back on."

"Mind if I help?"

The farmer grinned up at him. "I wouldn't mind at all. Had another feller come by about an hour ago, but all he did was just look at me and keep on ridin'."

"Did he happen to be on a gray roan?"

"Yep."

Brockman extracted a wanted poster from his shirt pocket and unfolded it. "This the guy?"

"Why, it sure is! That's him, all right!"

"You say he passed by here about an hour ago?"

"Yep. Horse was limpin'. Looked like it might've lost a shoe on the right front hoof. He sure can't have gotten too far, Marshal."

"Well, let's get this wheel back on, and I'll be after him." As he spoke, Brockman backed up to the corner of the wagon, got a firm grip on it, and hoisted it upward.

Two minutes later, the farmer was tightening the nut holding the wheel to the axle while he watched the man in black ride away.

John Brockman trotted his horse along the road, following the prints of the rider whose horse had thrown a shoe. Soon he arrived at a small town called Minden, noting that Vance Ankum had gone straight into town. Patting his horse's neck, he said, "Ebony, ol' boy, let's check with the local blacksmith and see if he's seen our man."

At the blacksmith's Brockman learned that the man whose face was on the wanted poster had indeed been there, wanting a new shoe for his gray roan. The blacksmith had told the man he had a team of horses to shoe for a local rancher and wouldn't be able to get to it for about two hours. Vance Ankum swore at him and stormed out.

Back in the saddle, Brockman rode hard, figuring the outlaw would probably look for a horse to steal so he could ride faster. He had ridden no more than a couple of miles when he saw the gray roan a half mile ahead with the killer in the saddle. Ankum was riding the limping horse into the yard of a small farm.

When Brockman put Ebony to a gallop, Ankum spotted him and spurred the roan toward the barn. Brockman skidded Ebony to a halt next to the roan and saw Ankum run into the barn. He dismounted and ran up behind a cottonwood tree and whipped out his Colt .45 Peacemaker. Just then he heard a wagon and turned around to see an elderly farmer and his wife turn into the yard from the road.

When the farmer pulled rein and stopped, Brockman stepped up, keeping an eye on the barn, and said, "Folks, I'm Chief U.S. Marshal John Brockman out of the Denver office, and I've been trailing a killer all the way from Denver. His horse went lame on him, and he just went into your barn. I'm sure he's here to steal one of your saddle horses."

"Our saddle horses ain't in the barn, Marshal," said the old man. "They're in the pasture out back."

"Good. I want both of you to go into the house and lock the doors until I have the man in custody. Will you do that for me?"

"Whatever you say, Chief," said the farmer.

"Thank you. One question…"

"Yes, sir?"

"Does the barn have a back door or side doors?"

"No, sir. There are no back windows either, but there are on both sides. They're near the front, though, so whichever way he would try to come out, you'd be able to see him from out here."

"Good. Now you folks get inside the house."

"Tell you what, Chief. I've got a shotgun in the kitchen. I'd be glad to come out here and help you catch the varmint."

"Thanks for the offer, Mr.—"

"Will Kline. Wife's name is Emma."

"Glad to meet you, ma'am," said Brockman. "And thanks, Mr. Kline, for the offer, but I'll do this alone. Vance Ankum is a coldhearted murderer, and you could get killed. Please go into the house."

Trembling, Emma said, "Let's hurry, Will."

Brockman kept one eye on the barn and the other on the old couple as he watched them enter the house. Then, using the cottonwood as a shield, he shouted, "Ankum, it's over! Throw out your gun, and come out with your hands over your head!"

"You ain't takin' me back to Denver to hang, lawman!"

"I said throw out your gun, and come out with your hands over your head! You're going back to Denver to hang unless you force me to kill you here and now!"

Suddenly the barn door swung open, and Vance Ankum came out with a blazing revolver in each hand, swearing at Brockman and shouting that he would kill him. While his bullets were chewing into bark on both sides of the tree, the experienced lawman dropped down on his belly and took careful aim at the killer's left leg and fired. He fired again, hitting him in the right leg.

Ankum howled and went down, thrashing in agony. He had dropped one of his guns but was trying to bring the other one into play when he found the man in black drawing up with his revolver aimed straight at his face.

"Drop it, or die on the spot!" Brockman said.

Breathing hard and gritting his teeth from the pain, Ankum glared at the lawman.

"I said drop it!"

Ankum let the gun fall from his hand.

Brockman rolled him over, handcuffed him, then examined the wounds. "The slugs went right on through. I'll get the farmer's wife to put temporary bandages on them, and I'll take you to a doctor in Kearney. Then you're going back to Denver to hang."

The sun had set when Chief U.S. Marshal John Brockman drew up in front of Dr. James Jarvis's office in Kearney, riding behind Vance Ankum, whose hands were cuffed behind his back. Ebony snorted as Brockman lifted the wounded outlaw out of the saddle.

A sign by the office door told him that Dr. Jarvis lived upstairs above the office. He sat Ankum down on the board-walk and cuffed him to the post holding up the porch roof. When he came back downstairs, the doctor was with him.

When Dr. Jarvis had examined the wounds carefully, he said, "The slug chipped the thigh bone in the right leg, Chief. The one in the left missed the bone by a fraction of an inch."

Brockman glanced at Ankum, then leaned close to his face and said, "Don't look at me like that, mister. I told you to throw your gun out and come out with your hands over your head. You chose to come out shooting. Blame yourself for those bullet holes in your legs."

Ankum didn't reply.

"I'll do what I can to clean the bone fragments out of this wound, Chief," said Jarvis, "but he shouldn't travel as far as Denver on horseback for at least a month. If he has to sit in a saddle before then, the wounds could open, and he might bleed to death."

Brockman nodded. "How soon can he ride on a train?"

"Well, he could do that in a couple of weeks. Main thing is, this leg with the bone chip is going to need that long to do some healing. And since both legs are wounded, he wouldn't be able to use crutches. Two weeks should be long enough so he can ride a train to Denver."

"All right. You go ahead and patch him up, Doctor. Can

you tell me how to find the sheriff's house? I need to talk to him."

The doctor gave Brockman directions and watched as the lawman handcuffed Ankum to the examining table before leaving.

Sheriff Tom Moyer showed his surprise when he opened the front door and found the man in black standing on his porch.

"Come in, Chief. It's nice to see you again. Did you catch up to that killer?"

"Yes. And I need a favor."

"You name it," said Moyer, whose wife was coming down the hall.

The sheriff introduced Brockman to Darlene, then the men went into the parlor and sat down. The chief U.S. marshal told Moyer about catching up to Vance Ankum at the Kline farm, of shooting him in both legs, and taking him to Dr. James Jarvis.

"Well, I'm glad you got him. So what's the favor you need?"

"Dr. Jarvis says Ankum couldn't travel by horseback for at least a month, but he could travel to Denver by train within a couple of weeks. I need to head back first thing in the morning. I'll be sending one of my deputies to escort Ankum to Denver by train around May 1. I need you to keep Ankum in a cell until then."

"Be glad to."

"Dr. Jarvis will probably have to come and check the wounds and change the bandages periodically."

"No problem. He can come any time he wants to."

"I appreciate this, Sheriff. We'll probably need that cell in the morning. I imagine the doctor will want to keep Ankum in the office tonight. He's shackled to the examining table, so he's not going anywhere."

Extending his hand, Moyer said, "It's a privilege to help out in a small way, Chief."

Brockman shook his hand and headed back to the doctor's office.

CHAPTER SEVENTEEN

All aboar-r-r-rd!" the conductor called as he stood beside the Chicago-bound train. "All aboar-r-r-rd!"

Six-year-old Seth hurried along the platform with his parents and the McClains. "Oh boy, Papa! That's really a neat train! And Papa, look how big it is!"

Adam smiled down at his son. "It really is big, son!"

Adam and Doug carried an overnight bag in each hand, and their wives carried the baby girls.

Passengers were lined up at each coach and slowly climbing the metal steps to file inside. Adam led his group to a line at the first car behind the baggage coach. "This look okay?" he asked.

"One's as good as another," Doug said.

While they moved slowly toward the coach platform, Seth was eyeing the huge engine. The boiler was rumbling and steam was hissing from the bowels of the engine. "Wow, Papa!" he said breathlessly. "I'd like to ride in that! Can I, Papa?"

Adam laughed. "They don't let passengers ride in the engine, Seth."

Kathy smiled at the little boy. "I'd let you ride up there if I owned the railroad company, honey."

"Then I wish you owned it, Aunt Kathy."

"Me too, Seth," said Doug. "Then the rest of us would ride in our own private coach while you were riding in the engine!"

The bell on the engine began clanging. Soon the Coopers and the McClains were aboard the crowded coach.

Adam looked around and said, "Looks like we won't be able to sit close to each other."

"Mm-hmm," said Doug. "You and Theresa grab this seat right here. We'll go back to that one."

The Coopers sat down on the left side of the coach near the front, and the McClains were behind them on the right side, some four or five rows back.

Adam told Seth to scoot over by the window, then helped Theresa get settled with little Anna in her arms. He placed the overnight bags in the overhead rack, smiled at the elderly couple sitting just behind them, then looked back at the McClains and said, "We'll get to sit closer together on the train from Chicago."

Doug and Kathy nodded.

Soon the engine whistle blew, the bell continued clanging, and the engine lurched forward, setting up a chain reaction of heavy thumps between the cars.

Seth was up on his knees as the train rolled out of the depot, his nose pressed to the window. This was the biggest adventure the Cooper family had ever experienced, and Seth was making the most of it. He kept his eyes on the landscape as the train picked up speed and headed northwest toward Chicago. Beneath the coach, the steel wheels set up a steady, rhythmic sound, and little Anna fell asleep.

Across the aisle and back a few rows, little one-year-old Jenny was also asleep. Kathy laid her on the seat between her and Doug, who was by the window, and said, "Darling, I'm so happy."

He reached over and took her hand. "Me too, honey. Something just came to mind that I hadn't thought of in all this excitement about moving to Wyoming."

"What's that?"

"About, oh, maybe two years before we were married, a couple of men came into the *Post* one day. One of them was there to do some kind of business with Mr. Owens, and after they finished their business, Mr. Owens took them on a tour of the plant. When they came into the press room, Mr. Owens introduced them to the pressmen. Turned out the second man was the other man's brother and was visiting from Wyoming."

"Oh, really?"

"Mm-hmm. His name was…ah….Dan Trumbo. His brother's name was Clayton, I think. Yes. Clayton. While Mr. Evans had another pressman explain the operation of the presses to Clayton, Dan and I got to talking. He carried on about Wyoming. Couldn't say enough about it. Went on and on about its mountains, plains, and wide open spaces. He told me that if I ever went out there and saw it, I'd want to stay."

Kathy smiled and squeezed his hand. "Well, I guess you're soon going to find out if he was right."

"Yes, ma'am! Just think, mountains, plains, and wide open spaces. Fort Bridger, here we come!"

"No doubt it's going to take some adjusting, but I'm sure we'll make the adjustment quickly."

"Sure we will," Doug said. "It's going to be a real help to have Adam and Theresa with us."

"Yes, and since Adam's sister-in-law and family are a solid part of the town, it should help Adam and Theresa to fit in, which will help us to fit in."

"Without a doubt. And from what Adam tells me Hannah Cooper has written in her letters about the church, I think we'll fit in real well there, too."

Seth Cooper was still mesmerized by what he saw through the window. The train had passed by several small towns and rolled through farm country where he saw milk cows and horses in the fields.

Little Anna was still asleep in Theresa's arms.

"Honey," said Adam in a dreamy tone, "I've been thinking."

"About what?"

"Well, with all the articles written in the *Post* in the last couple of years about people going West by the thousands, I was thinking that maybe someday—if the Lord blesses the *Fort Bridger Bugle* as we're expecting Him to—I can establish newspapers in towns all over the frontier."

Theresa smiled. "Doesn't hurt to dream. Realities come from dreaming."

"I would have to hire experienced men to run the papers for me, but with the urge to go West capturing so many hearts in the East, and with my many connections in the newspaper business, I probably wouldn't have much trouble finding those men. I really think it's possible to establish a whole chain of newspapers."

"I think it's a wonderful idea, and you're just the man to do it."

The conductor came through, announcing that the train was now in Indiana. Seth let his eyes roam over the rolling hills and small patches of forest. He looked up at his father. "Papa..."

"Yes, son?"

"How come Indiana looks just like Ohio?"

Adam ruffled Seth's hair. "You thought it would look different because it's another state?"

"Yeah."

"Well, you'll notice some difference when we get closer to Chicago. There won't be as many farms, and not so many forests."

With that, Seth went back to gazing out the window. As

he watched the Indiana landscape fly by, he thought of how good it was going to be to live in Fort Bridger with his cousins. He could play with B.J. and Patty Ruth. He loved his little sister, but she was only four months old and wasn't much fun yet.

The train chugged into the large railroad terminal at Chicago right on time, and the Coopers and the McClains disembarked. The layover was just over two hours before the two families would board another westbound train. Adam and Doug soon had their wives and children situated in a comfortable spot close by, then went to the baggage coach to make sure the luggage transferred correctly. While Doug went back to the women and children, Adam went to the front of the station to confirm their schedule, then rejoined the others, who were relieved to know the train was to leave on time.

Seth was in awe of the terminal, taking it all in with gaping mouth and wide eyes. He had never seen so many people all in one place in his entire life.

Theresa and Kathy excused themselves, saying both little ones were in need of diaper attention. When they returned, Adam told them of seeing a nice diner in the terminal. Suddenly everyone was hungry, and they made their way toward the diner.

As the westbound train pulled out of Chicago, the two families found themselves in the second car behind the baggage coach. This time, the McClains were situated in the seat on the left side of the coach that faced backward. The Coopers were in the seat facing them, with Seth once again occupying the seat next to the window.

Soon the wheels were putting out their familiar rhythmic clicking sound, and the babies went to sleep.

While Adam and Doug talked about aspects of their new life in Wyoming, Theresa and Kathy talked about their new homes. Both women were aware of the approximate size of the houses Cade Samuels had rented for them, and they enjoyed discussing how they would decorate their frontier homes and make them warm and cozy. Hannah had corresponded with Theresa, letting her know what to expect in the way of available furnishings, and Theresa had passed on the information to Kathy. They were both relieved to know that lace curtains and colorful draperies were available.

After a time, the women fell silent and watched the landscape pass by the windows, each lost in her own dreams.

On Wednesday morning, May 3, at the Kearney County Jail, Sheriff Tom Moyer and Deputy U.S. Marshal Craig Severs stood outside Vance Ankum's cell while Deputy Roy Dillard unlocked the cell door.

Severs, a man of forty and well built, stepped into the cell and met the glowering gaze of his prisoner. Taking a pair of handcuffs from his belt, Severs said, "Gimme your right wrist."

A sullen Ankum clenched his teeth as Severs snapped a cuff on him, then snapped the other one on his own left wrist.

Ankum looked down at the Colt .45 on Severs's right hip.

Noticing it, the federal man looked his prisoner square in the eye and said, "It's a long trip to Denver, Ankum. I'll give you fair warning. If you ever try to get your hands on my gun, you'll be one sorry dude. You won't like the pain that goes with your failed attempt. Understand?"

Ankum stared back at him but did not reply.

"I said, do you understand?"

"Yeah. I understand."

"Good. Don't forget what I said. You be a good boy all the way to Denver and you'll feel no pain. Try anything funny, and you'll hurt like you've never even imagined. Let's go."

On the bright, clear morning of May 3, the Coopers and the McClains gazed out the windows of the coach to get a good look at the wide, sweeping plains and gentle hills of Nebraska spreading in every direction.

Doug set his eyes on Adam and said, "I think Nebraska became the thirty-seventh state about two years ago, didn't it?"

"Mmm. I think it was more like four years ago. Seems like it happened in '67."

"Yeah. Now that I think about it, that's right. I wonder when the other western territories will seek statehood, especially Wyoming."

The front door of the coach opened, and the conductor stepped in.

Adam shrugged. "May be a long time yet."

"I'd think they'd want to become states so they'd have—"

"Kearney in fifteen minutes!" announced the conductor, moving on through the car. "We'll be in Kearney in fifteen minutes!"

The train started slowing down, and only one man and his wife began gathering their belongings near the front of the coach. Soon the train was chugging into the depot and halted with a hiss of steam and the squeal of brakes.

While his parents talked to the McClains, Seth watched the couple leave the seat across the aisle and head for the door. They had only been gone a minute or two when Seth saw two men enter the coach. They were handcuffed to each other.

"Papa!" Seth whispered, getting the attention of all four adults. "Look there!"

Theresa was holding Anna, who was about to drop off to sleep.

The McClains could see only the backs of the men by then, but Adam and Theresa noted that the husky man wore a badge identifying him as a deputy United States marshal. His prisoner walked with a limp.

Seth's eyes widened at the sight of the gun on the lawman's hip.

Deputy U.S. Marshal Craig Severs ran his gaze throughout the coach and saw only one seat open. It was on the right side of the coach and would put Ankum on the aisle. It wasn't ideal, but Severs decided not to ask anyone to give up a seat so he could be on the aisle. He urged his prisoner toward the vacant seats, then stepped ahead of him and sat down next to the window.

"Looks like we've got us a bad man as a fellow passenger," Doug said in a low tone.

Kathy clutched her baby close and whispered, "I don't like this, Doug."

Seth's eyes bulged as he looked at the two men shackled together just one row back and across the aisle.

Adam patted his head and said, "You don't need to be afraid, son. The man with the badge is a deputy United States marshal. He won't let the bad man hurt anybody."

From their seat, the McClains could look into the faces of both men. When the deputy noticed them looking their way, he smiled and said, "Good morning, folks."

Other passengers in the vicinity listened as the two couples returned the greeting, then the lawman said, "I'm Deputy U.S. Marshal Craig Severs. I work out of the Denver office. I'm transporting my prisoner back to Denver to stand trial. Don't be alarmed. He's handcuffed to me, and he's not going to do anything to be alarmed about. Just relax and enjoy your trip."

Vance Ankum set cold eyes on the two couples. Instinctively, all four looked away.

"Those eyes give me the shivers," Theresa whispered.

"Me too," said Kathy. "I realize the deputy and his prisoner have to ride in one of the coaches. I just wish it was another one."

The conductor was giving the final call to board when the

engine's whistle let out a sharp squeal. Little Anna jerked in her mother's arms and started to cry. Theresa held her close and whispered to her, trying to settle her down. By the time the train was rolling out of the station, Anna was quiet again.

Soon the train was moving swiftly across the plains.

Keeping his voice low, Adam said, "This is just part of it, ladies. Life is different in the Wild West. What you're seeing is no doubt a common thing."

Kathy forced a smile and whispered, "Doug and I were talking earlier on the trip about the adjustments we would have to make. I guess this kind of adjustment hadn't crossed my mind."

"Nevertheless, I'll be glad when we're in Cheyenne City and can get off of this train," Theresa said.

Seth looked up at his father. "Papa, what do you suppose the bad man did?"

"Hard to tell, son. There's no way to know without asking."

Seth thought on it a moment, then said, "Why don't you ask the marshal, Papa?"

"Because it's none of our business, Seth. You don't ask questions like that."

Again Seth was quiet while he thought on the situation. Looking up at his father again, he said in a normal tone of voice, "Are they gonna hang him, Papa?"

"Sh-h-h! I don't know, Seth, and it's none of our business."

When the little boy looked back at the outlaw, the man's pale blue eyes seemed to burn all the way into the boy's brain. Seth blinked and decided to take in the scenery outside once more.

Kathy, who sat with her back to the front of the coach, found her gaze straying to the lawman and the outlaw as she and Theresa talked once again about their houses in Fort Bridger. At one point, Ankum met her gaze with a malevolent stare. A cold hand seemed to clutch her heart, and she quickly looked away. She kept her eyes riveted on Theresa as they continued to talk.

Soon Jenny interrupted her mother's conversation by waking up and immediately beginning to fuss. Turning to Doug, Kathy said, "Honey, I need to take her to the washroom and change her diaper."

"I think it's about time for Anna, too," Theresa said. "We'll go with you."

Both women felt Vance Ankum's eyes on them as they got up from their seats.

When Kathy's hands started shaking, Doug said, "What's the matter? You're trembling."

Kathy leaned down and whispered, "That outlaw across the aisle keeps giving me dirty looks."

The husbands looked at each other, then Adam said, "You ladies go on to the washroom. We'll handle this."

Both Adam and Doug noticed Ankum trying to catch the eyes of their wives as they carried their babies toward the washroom.

Adam stiffened and started to get up. Doug was instantly out of his seat. He laid a hand on Adam's shoulder and said through tight lips, "You stay with Seth. I'll handle it."

Adam watched as Doug stepped across the aisle. Both Ankum and Severs looked at him as he leaned down and said to Ankum, "Keep your eyes to yourself. You're frightening my wife. Got that?"

Ankum gave Doug a cold look and said, "I don't know what you're talkin' about."

The deputy gave a quick yank on the handcuffs, getting Ankum's attention and growled, "Quit it, Vance."

"I ain't done nothin'," Ankum said.

"The man's wife wouldn't be frightened if you weren't giving her reason for it. You keep your eyes away from her!"

Doug leaned down and put his nose less than an inch

from Ankum's. "You'd better obey the deputy, fella, or else."

Ankum started to retort, but Severs yanked on the hand-cuffs again, giving the man a sharp pain in his wrist. Ankum winced, then closed his eyes and sat back in the seat.

Doug went back to his seat. As he sat down, he sent a hard glance at Ankum, who was staring at the floor.

"Maybe that'll be enough," said Adam, who had Seth on his lap.

"Better be," Doug said. "I think it might be best if you and I sit together on this seat and let Kathy sit with Theresa."

"Sure," Adam said, standing up with Seth in his arms and sitting down beside Doug. "Good idea. Kathy won't be facing him now."

When the women came back with the babies, both hus-bands stared at Ankum, but he was looking across the aisle and out the window.

"I had a little talk with that outlaw," Doug said. "Told him to keep his eyes to himself. The deputy told him the same thing. But Adam and I figure it would be best if you ladies sit together on that seat, so Kathy's not facing him."

"Good idea," said Theresa as she slid toward the window.

"That bad man better not look at my mama anymore," spoke up Seth, "or Papa will pound him good."

Doug raised his eyebrows. "Really, Seth? How do you know that?"

Theresa chuckled. "Seth has heard me tell about a man in Cincinnati who said something bad to me."

"Yeah! And Papa beat him up, didn't he, Mama?"

Theresa glanced at her husband and said, "Yes, he did."

Adam's features tinted. "Well, he had it coming."

The train rolled on, sending its smoke toward the sky.

Vance Ankum did not venture a direct look toward the

two couples across the aisle, but he did watch passengers as they moved back and forth in the coach. His attention was drawn to the men who wore sidearms as they walked past him. Sometimes their guns were within arm's reach.

After a while, the conductor came through the car, announcing that the train would be in Lexington in fifteen minutes. Soon the train was slowing down, and Vance Ankum noticed a man go past him toward the washroom with his gun holstered on the left side.

Ankum kept his eyes peeled on the door of the washroom ahead as the train started to slow down. Minutes later, the train pulled into the Lexington station and ground to a halt. He swore to himself. The left-handed man hadn't returned.

Soon the train was on the move and pulling out of Lexington. Just as Ankum was trying to figure out what had happened to the left-handed man, he saw him come out of the washroom at the same time the conductor was entering the door of the coach. They stopped and talked to each other for a few seconds, then walked side by side down the aisle. The conductor was on the man's left, blocking any opportunity for Ankum to yank the gun from the holster.

He cursed the conductor under his breath.

Across the aisle, the Coopers and the McClains were talking about the church in Fort Bridger. Hannah's letters had conveyed a lot of information about it, and now the Coopers were talking about Pastor Andy Kelly and how much Hannah thought of him. She had written about some of the sermons, giving details of their content and their eloquent delivery.

"Sounds like Pastor Kelly does a lot of studying and has a true pastor's heart," Doug said.

Across the aisle, Vance Ankum stiffened when he saw the left-handed man walk past him again.

CHAPTER EIGHTEEN

At the same time the train carrying the Coopers and the McClains was rumbling across the plains of Nebraska, Patty Ruth Cooper was watching her mother pour hot water into a small galvanized tub on the kitchen table. Her stomach had given her some trouble during the night, so Hannah had kept her home from school.

Baby Eddie lay on a blanket next to the galvanized tub. Hannah set the teakettle on a cool part of the stove, then picked up the water pail and poured cold water into the tub. When she had poured in a good amount, she dipped her bare elbow into the water to test it.

"Still a little too warm, Eddie," she said, looking at the baby, who was kicking and squealing.

While Hannah poured in more cold water, she said, "Patty Ruth, did that peppermint oil make your tummy feel better?"

"Mm-hmm."

"That's good, honey."

She dipped her elbow in the water again. "Okay, Eddie. It's just right."

As she began removing the baby's sleep clothes and diaper, Patty Ruth frowned and said, "Mama, how come you put your elbow in the water to thee how hot it ith? Couldn't you jutht uthe your finger?"

"The skin on my elbow is much more tender than the

skin on my fingers, honey. My fingers are used to being in very hot water because of doing dishes and washing clothes. The skin on my elbow is more like Eddie's skin, and I can tell how hot the water will feel to him."

"You're really thmart, Mama."

Hannah smiled as she dipped the baby into the warm water. Little Eddie had already learned to love his bath. While his mother was washing him, he splattered water as he kicked and splashed water with his hands.

When some of the soapy water struck her face, Hannah chuckled and said with a twinkle in her eye, "Eddie Cooper, you're a little imp!"

As though he understood, Eddie beat the water with his fists and kicked his feet, splashing her more.

This time, even Patty Ruth got splattered. She echoed her mother's words to the little boy and Hannah laughed harder. "See, Eddie, even your little sister says you're an imp!"

"Mama…"

"Yes, honey?"

"What'th an imp?"

"It's a mischievous child, honey."

"What's m—mith—mithch—"

"Mischievous?"

"Uh-huh. What'th that mean?"

"It means naughty. A mischievous child is a naughty child."

Patty Ruth giggled. "That Eddie ith naughty!"

"He is when he splashes his mother and little sister," Hannah said.

The little redhead nodded and concentrated once again on the bath. Pretty soon she said, "Babieth are a lot of work, aren't they, Mama?"

"They are, honey, but they're worth it."

"Did I thplash you when I wath a baby?"

"Yes, you did."

"Did I futh and cry like Eddie doth?"

"You did. All babies fuss and cry, especially if they're hungry or need a diaper change."

There was a knock at the door and Hannah said, "Would you see who that is, please?"

Patty Ruth jumped off the chair and dashed to the door. Water dripped as Hannah took Eddie from the tub and laid him on the towel.

"Mama," Patty Ruth called, "it'th Uncle Curly!"

Curly stepped in hurriedly and closed the door.

"Good morning, Curly," Hannah said as she dried the baby. "What can I do for you?"

The skinny little man pulled a yellow envelope out of his coat pocket. "It's what I can do for you, Hannah. I have a telegram here from your parents in Independence, Missouri."

"Oh, wonderful! They probably want to know how their newest grandson is doing now that he has finally arrived."

"Mm-hmm. And I'm shore they're longin' to see the li'l feller. You want I should stay 'til you read this and see if'n you want to send a reply?"

"Oh yes!" She hastily finished drying Eddie and said, "I'll be just a minute."

The little man chuckled. "Take yore time. I ain't in no hurry. 'Sides, I gotta ask this purdy li'l redhead somethin'."

Patty Ruth took her usual stance, looked up at the bald-headed little man, and waited.

Widening his eyes, Curly looked down and said, "Whut's yore name, li'l girl?"

Patty Ruth and her Uncle Curly were into their regular routine, which ended up with her getting a big hug and returning it lovingly.

Eddie was now dressed. Hannah kissed his cheek and placed him in the cradle, which she had put on the kitchen table. She opened the envelope, and as she read the telegram from her parents, Ben and Esther Singleton, tears flooded her eyes.

Patty Ruth's face twisted up. "Mama, what's wrong?"

"Nothing's wrong, honey. It's good news. *Very* good news. Grandma and Grandpa are coming to visit us this summer!"

Patty Ruth clapped her hands and danced around, saying, "Oh, boy! Oh, boy! Oh, boy!"

"I thought that'd make you happy, Hannah," said Curly. "You want to send a wire back?"

"Yes."

He pulled a slip of paper and a pencil stub from his shirt pocket and licked the tip of the pencil, then said, "Shoot!"

As soon as Hannah had dictated the reply, Curly hugged Patty Ruth again and moved to the kitchen to pinch Eddie's cheek and tell him what a big boy he was, then left.

As she cleaned up after Eddie's bath, more tears moistened Hannah's eyes. She sorely missed her parents and desperately longed to see them. What a blessing it would be if her parents lived close to her and the children.

I'm getting way ahead of myself, she thought. *They're only coming for a visit.* She pondered it for a moment, then thought, *But Dad is retired, and we're the only family he and Mom have. It sure wouldn't hurt to pray about it. Maybe the Lord would lead them to move here to Fort Bridger. All things are possible with God.*

Later, Hannah took Eddie to her bedroom to feed him, then put him down for a nap. All the while, she asked the Lord to put it on her parents' hearts to want to move to Fort Bridger. She prayed about it even as she cleaned the apartment. When the cleaning was done, Hannah sat down at the kitchen table and began writing a letter to Betty Walford, one of her close friends in Independence. She and Betty had gone through school together, and Betty and her husband were still in the church there. They kept in touch by writing each other periodically.

Patty Ruth had gone off to play with her dolls.

Hannah was almost finished with the first page of the letter when she heard footsteps on the outside stairs, followed by a knock on the door. As she was getting up to answer the knock, she heard Eddie making noises in the bedroom.

Patty Ruth appeared in the hallway and called, "Mama, Eddie'th awake."

"You go check on him, honey," Hannah said, moving toward the door. "I'll be there in a minute."

Hannah opened the door to find Carrie Wright, who looked a bit pale.

"Why, Carrie, how nice to see you. Please come in."

As she passed through the door, Carrie said, "I was down in the store picking up some things for Glenda. I asked Jacob if he thought it would be all right if I came up to see you for a few minutes."

"Well, I'm glad you came up. Here, let me take your coat."

As she hung up the coat, Hannah said, "You look troubled, Carrie. Is something wrong?"

"Not really wrong. I mean, it's nothing new. I'm just having a difficult time missing Colin. I thought since you're the only young widow in Fort Bridger, and you've been without Solomon longer than I've been without Colin, maybe we could talk."

"Of course. You sit down over here in the parlor. Eddie just woke up from his nap and I need to get him. I'll be right back."

A few minutes later, Patty Ruth came into the parlor. She walked up to Carrie, who was sitting on the sofa, and said, "Hi, Mithuth Wright. Mama ith changin' my little brother'th diaper. She thaid for me to come and thee you for a minute, 'cauthe I have to go play in my room when she'th talkin' to you."

Carrie smiled. "Well, it's nice to have a moment with you, Patty Ruth. Are your new teeth starting to grow in yet?"

Patty Ruth nodded and opened her mouth, pointing at the vague whiteness along the edge of the upper gum. "Thee?"

"Well, sure enough. Have any of your other teeth started to loosen?"

"Not yet, but Mama thayth they'll be doin' it pretty thoon."

Hannah came into the room, carrying Eddie. "All right, Patty Ruth, you go play in your room now."

"Yeth, ma'am. It wath nithe to thee you, Mithuth Wright."

"You, too, Patty Ruth."

When Hannah sat down in her rocking chair with Eddie in her arms, Carrie left the couch to stand over them. "What a precious baby, Hannah. Do you think he'd let me hold him for a minute?"

"I don't know why not. He loves attention." As she spoke, Hannah lifted the baby toward Carrie.

She carefully took him into her arms and sat down on the couch, gazing into Eddie's face. "Oh, you're such a handsome little man! I wish—" Carrie's eyes filled with tears. "I wish I could have a little boy like you."

Hannah left the rocker and bent over Carrie to hug her. "I know it's only natural for you to want to be a mother, and I have to be honest and say there's no joy compared to it. But the Lord has His will for your life all worked out, and whatever it is, it'll be perfect."

"I keep holding onto that fact, Hannah. I've really been doing better, but I guess I still have a long way to go."

"Of course you do. You've been through so much."

Carrie kissed little Eddie's forehead and said, "I'll let you go back to your mother now, sweetie pie."

Hannah took the baby and sat down again in the rocking chair. She set her compassionate gaze on Carrie and said, "How can I help you about your lonely feelings for Colin?"

"I just need to know how you've coped with Solomon's

death, Hannah…how you stand it with him gone, missing him as I know you do."

Hannah lightly rocked in the chair and said, "Let me share some things with you."

She told Carrie about how she had to learn to let the Lord fill her loneliness with His own presence, and explained how she often talked to Solomon as if he were listening from heaven.

"Somehow," she said softly, "just sharing both the good and the bad things, as if Solomon could hear me, really helps a lot. It relieves that empty spot in a real way. Try talking to Colin like that. I believe it will help you, too."

Carrie nodded. "Thank you, Hannah. Your words of wisdom have given me strength. Just talking to you has done me a world of good."

"I'm glad, Carrie. I'd like to pray with you before you go."

When they had prayed, Hannah rose from the rocker and said, "The Lord is going to bring happiness back into your life. The Lord loves you, and He wants you to be fulfilled."

"I know He does." Carrie looked down at little Eddie. She stroked his cheek and said, "You're such a precious little boy." Then she gave Hannah a quick hug and left.

Patty Ruth stepped into the hall as Hannah passed her room. "Did Mithuth Wright leave, Mama?"

"Mm-hmm. I'm going to bring Eddie's cradle into the parlor, honey. I want you to take care of him while I finish writing my letter."

"Oh, boy! I like takin' care of my little brother!"

"Is your tummy still feeling all right?"

"Uh-huh."

"That's good."

While Patty Ruth hovered over the cradle, Hannah finished the letter. She was blotting it when Patty Ruth tiptoed up to the kitchen table and whispered, "Eddie'th athleep, Mama."

"Good." Hannah folded the pages and slipped them into the envelope she had already addressed. "You're a good little mother."

Patty Ruth grinned. "I hope when I really am a mother, I'll be ath good a mother ath you are, Mama."

Hannah leaned over and hugged the bright-eyed child and kissed her cheek. "Thank you, sweetheart. To me that's a real compliment."

The sound of soft footsteps on the staircase outside met their ears. Rising from the chair, Hannah said, "You know who I think that is?"

"Who?"

"Sounds like soft-soled, Indian deerskin boots to me."

Patty Ruth's eyes widened. "Really?"

"I think so." Hannah went to the door and pulled it open. After welcoming Chief Two Moons and Sweet Blossom, she embraced the Indian woman and invited them inside. She told them little Eddie was taking a nap so she would take him to the bedroom. Both Indians nodded and looked at the sleeping baby as Hannah carried the cradle past them. Patty Ruth followed, and Hannah told her to stay in her room and play while she talked to the chief and his squaw.

When Hannah returned, the Indians were still standing. She gestured toward the couch and told them to be seated, then sat down in her overstuffed chair.

"You have such a beautiful baby, Hannah Cooper," said Sweet Blossom, her dark eyes shining.

"Thank you. He looks so much like his father."

"I would like to have met your husband, Hannah Cooper," said Two Moons. "I know he was a very special man."

Hannah smiled. "That he was, Chief. But one marvelous thing about it, I will be reunited with him one day in heaven. And there, you will get to meet him yourself."

Two Moons nodded. "That is very good to know. Sweet

Blossom and her husband are so glad to know that we are going to heaven. We thank you again for talking to us so many times about Jesus Christ."

"Well, now you know why I kept talking to you, don't you?"

Two Moons nodded again. "Umm. We feel same about our people as Hannah Cooper felt about us. We want them to be saved like us."

"That's the way it works, Chief. Is there something I can do for you?"

The chief and his squaw exchanged glances, then Two Moons said, "Would you have time to answer some questions from the Bible for us?"

"Of course," Hannah said, smiling from ear to ear.

"Two Moons apologizes for him and Sweet Blossom bothering you with our questions, Hannah Cooper. We would go to Pastor Andy Kelly with them, but we know he is very busy."

"There is no need to apologize, Chief," Hannah said. "You're right. Pastor Kelly is quite busy, but he would never be too busy to talk to you. However, I'm honored that you would come to me. Now let me get my Bible, and I'll see if I can answer your questions."

When the question and answer time was over, the Indians thanked her, saying she was a good teacher.

Hannah walked them to the door. "How are things going in the village in regard to you two having become Christians?"

"Very good," the chief said. "Our God has worked in their hearts. No one is showing any rebellion about it, not even the medicine men. They see the joy we have, and they know it would be foolish to speak against our God."

"Our hearts are so heavy for them," put in Sweet Blossom. "We very much want them to know Jesus Christ."

"Of course," said Hannah, "and you must pray daily that the Lord will give you wisdom to know how to talk to them.

You are very young Christians and have much to learn. If you need help in explaining about Jesus and His salvation to them, Pastor Kelly would be glad to come to the village and help you. This would make him very happy."

"We are glad to hear this," said Two Moons. "When we see that even a few of our people show interest, we will ask Pastor Andy Kelly to come."

As soon as Hannah closed the door behind them, Patty Ruth came in and said, "Ith it all right if I wath lithenin', Mama?"

Hannah hugged her. "Of course, honey. It was nothing secret. I just thought it best if you were not in the parlor while they visited with me."

"I'm thure glad I'm thaved, Mama, 'cauth I'll get to thee Papa in heaven too…jutht like Chief Two Moonth and Thweet Blothom will."

A tear formed in Hannah's eye, and she quickly wiped it away. "Me too, sweetheart. Me too."

As the train raced across Nebraska's rolling prairie, Vance Ankum's eyes were pinned on the left-handed man as he started down the aisle from the washroom.

Kathy watched little Jenny as she lay on her father's lap, then said to the others, "It's so wonderful to have the Lord with me every step I take in this life. I don't know how I stood it before I was saved."

"I think that's the case with the rest of us, too," said Theresa. "It's hard to remember how I faced life when I didn't know the Lord. I'm so glad He's always with me."

Kathy nodded. "I love Hebrews 13:5: 'I will never leave thee, nor forsake thee.' This makes my life here on earth a peaceful one. Jesus won't forsake me here…and when it comes my time to leave this world, He won't forsake me when I step through death's door." Tears surfaced in Kathy's eyes. "What a wonderful, wonderful Saviour He is!"

Across the aisle, Vance Ankum noted that Deputy U.S. Marshal Craig Severs was looking out the window at a band of Indians galloping over a hill. Most of the people on that side of the coach were pointing at the Indians and talking excitedly.

Ankum turned back to the aisle. The left-handed man was almost to him, and Ankum tensed up, focusing on the gun, his heart pounding. Timing it perfectly, he moved with the speed and precision of a striking rattlesnake. Deputy Severs felt a slight tug on the handcuff and brought his head around in time to see his prisoner grab the revolver and snap the hammer back in one smooth move. He lunged across Ankum's body and seized his wrist.

Adam Cooper and Doug McClain looked on wide-eyed as the two men struggled for dominance.

Just as Theresa and Kathy were turning around to see what their husbands were looking at, the gun roared. Kathy jerked from the impact of the slug as it plowed through the back of her seat, then she slumped into a heap. Doug pulled Jenny to his chest and dropped to his knees in front of Kathy. The bullet had passed through her body and dug into the seat between Doug and Adam.

Theresa, who had been frozen in shock, regained her composure and bent over Kathy as Doug called his wife's name.

Vance Ankum cocked the hammer again, but the husky deputy managed to grab the barrel and twist the muzzle toward his prisoner's midsection. The gun roared again, and Ankum doubled over, collapsing on the seat.

As Theresa examined the exit wound in Kathy's chest, the deputy U.S. marshal removed the handcuffs from himself and the dead outlaw.

Smoke filled the crowded coach, and windows were shoved open in spite of the cold air that swept in. Just then the conductor came in and was told what had happened. When he saw Kathy, he pulled the brake cord. Immediately, the train began to slow down.

"Is there a doctor on the train?" Doug asked, looking up at the conductor. He had eased back from Kathy to give Theresa room to work.

"I don't know of one, but I'll sure find out."

Theresa looked up and choked out the words, "It won't make any difference now. Kathy is dead."

CHAPTER NINETEEN

Doug's face twisted at Theresa Cooper's words. He clutched little Jenny to his chest and bent over Kathy, his eyes wide in disbelief. He let out a strangled cry. "No-o-o! No, Kathy, no-o-o!" When Theresa took the wailing baby from Doug's arms, he threw himself across Kathy's body and sobbed.

As the train eased to a halt, the powder smoke began drifting out the windows recently opened. The sounds of weeping could be heard throughout the car. The conductor hurried out the door to find the engineer and fireman and explain why he had stopped the train.

Deputy U.S. Marshal Severs stood in the aisle, looking down at the heart-wrenching scene of the man grieving for his dead wife.

A woman stepped up to the group, asked if she could help, and Theresa placed little Jenny in her arms, then bent down and took her own daughter from Adam so he could concentrate on comforting Doug. She turned toward Seth, who had backed up as far as he could against the window. Huge tears were rolling down his face. She hugged her son with her free arm and spoke to him in a soothing tone.

In a few moments, the conductor returned and enlisted two men to carry the dead outlaw's body to the baggage coach.

When Doug regained some control of his emotions, and

Adam helped him off his knees and onto the seat, Craig Severs bent over Doug and said, "Sir, I want to tell you how sorry I am. My prisoner had the man's gun out of his holster so fast that all I could do was try to get the gun out of his hand."

Doug set bloodshot eyes on him. "It's not your fault, Deputy."

Severs cleared the lump in his throat and said, "Thank you."

The conductor entered the car again and moved up to Doug. "Sir," he said, "I won't hurry you on this, but with your permission, we will place your wife's body in the baggage coach."

Doug looked at Adam, asking with his eyes what he should do.

"All things considered, I think it would be best," Adam said.

Doug remained silent for a few moments, then said, "I know you need to get the train moving again. I'll carry her."

"I'll help you," said Adam.

"It's all right. I can carry her."

"Then I'll just go with you."

Inside the baggage coach, the conductor provided a blanket for Kathy's body. Adam stayed at Doug's side while he tenderly laid her on the floor next to a stack of luggage. Ankum's blanket-covered body lay at the other end of the coach, next to some wooden crates.

Doug's shoulders sagged as he started to cover her, then he bent over and kissed her forehead, whispering, "I love you," and slowly pulled the blanket over her face.

As the conductor walked the two men back to the coach, he said, "Are you traveling together?"

"Yes, we are," Adam said.

"And your names are...?"

"I'm Adam Cooper. This is Doug McClain. We're on our way to Fort Bridger, Wyoming."

"I see." The conductor cleared his throat. "Mr. McClain, I'm thinking it would help you if you didn't have to return to the coach where…well, where your dear wife was shot. It's a long way to Cheyenne City. Would you rather ride in another coach?"

Doug nodded. They were drawing up to the front platform of the second car from the baggage coach.

Stopping, the conductor said, "You two wait right here. I'll be back in a moment."

As he watched the conductor hurry away, Doug said, "It's nice of him to consider my feelings. I hadn't even thought about…" His voice trailed off and he clamped his lips tight as his chin began to quiver.

Adam laid a firm hand on his shoulder and squeezed.

The sound of the conductor's feet on the metal steps met their ears. When they turned, he said, "I've got you all set in this car, in the same location as the seats you had, so you can face each other."

"Why don't you go ahead and board, Doug," said Adam. "I'll get your things, along with ours, and bring them."

When the train was once again rolling westward, the other passengers frequently glanced at the small group sitting in facing seats, knowing that Doug was the man whose wife had been shot and killed in the next car.

Fresh tears welled up in Doug's eyes. He took a shuddering breath and tried to speak, but the horror of it all settled down on him, and he closed his eyes, letting the tears stream down his cheeks.

Little Jenny saw her father's tears, twisted in Theresa's arms, and reached toward him, saying, "Da-da. Da-da."

Doug opened his eyes at the sound of her voice, wiped away the tears, and took her from Theresa's extended hands. He cradled his little girl close to his heaving chest and wept all the more.

Jenny pulled back in his arms, and with little chubby fingers touched his wet face, saying, "Da-da."

Doug kissed her tiny hand. "Oh, Jenny, Daddy loves you! Daddy loves you!"

The Coopers sat silently, praying in their hearts for Doug. After some time, he said, "Oh, Adam, Theresa, what am I going to do? Kathy was my life. Everything I did, I did for her." His words caught on a sob.

"Doug," Adam said softly, "I know you're too much in shock right now to comprehend this, but I'll say it and maybe the words will register in your mind. The Lord knew this tragedy was going to happen. He will make a way for you. He will not leave you, nor will He fail you."

Doug swallowed hard and nodded. He caressed little Jenny's head on his shoulder and said, "I know God doesn't make mistakes. I know His way is perfect. I...I am so thankful He saw to it that you and Theresa were with Jenny and me when this happened. You're both so kind and loving."

"We love you and Jenny, Doug," said Theresa. "We want to help you in any way we possibly can."

Doug eased Jenny back and looked into her eyes. He gave her a tentative smile to calm her fears and kissed the tip of her little button nose. In turn, she dimpled back at him with a smile.

Adam touched Doug's arm. "This may sound easy for me to say, since I still have Theresa, but God is already in your tomorrow. He has a plan for your life, and He's already out there in the future, waiting for you."

Doug looked at his friend, and said, "What a beautiful way to put it, Adam. Being the eternal God, He most assuredly is already in my future. Thank you for reminding me of that."

Theresa's eyes were misty as she said, "I was just thinking of Kathy's words, spoken only a few minutes before she went to heaven. Remember? She said, 'It's so wonderful to have the

Lord with me every step I take in this life.'"

The young widower nodded.

"And then she quoted Hebrews 13:5 and said, 'This makes my life here on earth a peaceful one. Jesus won't forsake me here…and when it comes my time to leave this world, He won't forsake me when I step through death's door. What a wonderful, wonderful Saviour He is!'"

Theresa brushed tears from her cheeks and said, "She's with her wonderful Saviour now, Doug."

"Yes. She's safe in His strong arms."

Soon the train was pulling into Brady, Nebraska. The clang of the engine's bell echoed across the prairie, and a few people in the coach rose from their seats.

Little Jenny McClain wiggled in her father's arms and began to fuss. By the time the train came to a stop, she was crying. While the passengers were getting off, Theresa said, "She probably needs to be changed, Doug. As soon as we pull out, I'll take her to the washroom and change her."

Doug managed a weak smile. "I'd appreciate that, Theresa."

Moments later, an older couple entered the coach and took the seat directly across the aisle from where Doug was sitting. They waved at someone on the depot platform. The man continued to look out the window, making some kind of hand signals, but the woman, who sat on the aisle, turned and scowled at Jenny, who was still softly crying.

Soon the train was pulling out of Brady, and the silver-haired pair across the aisle waved to their people on the platform once again.

Theresa handed Anna to Adam, saying she would take Jenny and change her. However, Jenny was still crying when Theresa brought her back.

Doug took her in his arms and cuddled her close, saying, "You need to take a nap now, sweetheart. Let's see how fast you can get to sleep."

Still Jenny cried. Doug kept talking to her in low tones, doing what he could to make her happy.

The couple across the aisle kept shooting hard looks their way.

Anna was now fast asleep in her mother's arms, and Adam had lifted Seth onto his lap. The little boy was unusually quiet and his face had a disturbed look.

"Son," Adam said, "I know what you saw was a terrible thing, and I wish you hadn't seen it. But you need to understand that Aunt Kathy is in heaven now, with Jesus. She is very happy there with Him. Nobody in heaven is unhappy. It's a wonderful place."

"They don't have bad men there who shoot people, do they, Papa?"

"No, they don't. Nobody shoots anybody in heaven. Everything that happens there is good. Do you understand?"

"Yes, Papa."

The boy finally laid his head against his father's arm, and soon the steady clicking of the wheels settled him into slumber.

Still Jenny cried.

By this time, the couple across the aisle were scowling at the weeping child. Doug saw their expressions but paid them no mind.

After a few more minutes, Theresa said, "Doug, maybe a woman's touch would help."

Adam carefully laid Seth, who was still sleeping, on the seat beside him, and said, "I'll take Anna, honey."

When Theresa took the crying toddler in her arms, Jenny wailed loudly and cried, "Mama! Mama!"

"Let's see if walking her will help," Theresa said, rising from the seat.

Jenny wailed all the way to the end of the aisle, no matter what Theresa did. When she sat down with Jenny on her lap, the older woman across the aisle got up and gripped the back of Theresa's seat to steady herself, saying, "Ma'am, it's quite obvious that the child wants her mother. My husband and I are getting very tired of listening to her cry. Where's her mother?"

Doug set his dull gaze on the couple and said, "Her mother is dead…in the baggage coach. She was shot and killed between Kearney and Brady by an outlaw being transferred to Denver by a federal marshal."

The woman's face turned paled. Her voice was faint as she said, "I'm so sorry. I didn't know."

The woman's husband, who had stood up beside his wife to complain, now looked Doug in the eye and said, "Please forgive us." He took his wife by the arm. "Come on, Myrtle. Let's sit down."

Just before noon, Theresa took Anna to the washroom to feed her, and upon returning, pulled food from the supply they had brought on the train and fed the group.

When lunch was over, it wasn't long until Jenny was asleep, along with Anna. Seth sat by the window next to his father again and watched for any movement he could see on the plains.

The afternoon passed quickly, and soon the sun was setting, pushing deep shadows into the low spots and the gullies. The flat land between them was alive with red-gold light.

Once again Doug was holding his daughter, who now sat quietly on his lap, and Adam was holding little Anna.

Doug sighed. "I've been thinking about what to do concerning Kathy's body. I really have no choice but to have her buried at Cheyenne City. Carrying the body all the way to Fort Bridger for burial would not be sensible, even if the stagecoach company would haul it. Which I doubt."

"You're right," said Adam. "Best thing would be to have a service for her and bury her at Cheyenne City."

"I wonder if there's a Bible-believing church there. I sure want the right kind of preacher to do the service."

"I guess there's only one way to find out," said Adam. "We'll get us a couple of hotel rooms this evening, then check out the churches in the morning."

"Honey," said Theresa, "once we get to Cheyenne City and know what we're doing about the service and all, we need to wire Hannah and let her know what happened, and that we'll be a day or two later getting there."

Adam nodded. "We'll do that."

The train was late arriving at Cheyenne City on Wednesday evening, May 3. The Coopers and Doug checked in at the Pine Ridge Hotel, which was on Cheyenne City's Main Street a couple of blocks from the railroad station. Everyone ate a little food, and they all went to bed early.

The next morning, when Doug stepped out into the hall with Jenny in his arms, Adam and Theresa were there to meet them, along with Seth and little Anna.

As they headed down the hall, Adam asked, "How did you and Jenny sleep, Doug?"

"It was a little rough to begin with. Jenny cried herself to sleep, calling for Kathy. Once she got to sleep, she stayed there until dawn. I slept in short increments. How'd your night go?"

"Seth and Anna slept quite well," said Theresa, "but Adam and I were like you."

While they were eating breakfast, Theresa said, "I'll stay with the children while you men check out the churches."

Deborah Corbett opened the parsonage door in response to the knock and smiled at the two men standing there. "Good morning, gentlemen."

The man who had knocked, touched his hat brim, returned the smile, and said, "Mrs. Corbett?"

"Yes."

"My name is Adam Cooper, ma'am, and my friend is Doug McClain. We're from Ohio, on our way to Fort Bridger. We've had a tragedy. Is the pastor here?"

"Yes. Please, come in."

Both men removed their hats as they stepped into the small parlor.

"Please be seated. I'll let my husband know you're here."

Less than a minute had passed when a tall, slender man in his midthirties appeared. "Good morning, gentlemen. I'm Pastor Shane Corbett. My wife said you wanted to see me. You're on a trip to Fort Bridger from Ohio, and you had a tragedy, she said."

Adam and Doug rose to their feet and shook hands with the preacher, introducing themselves, then Adam said, "Sir, the sign in front of your church has the inscription: 'Except a man be born again, he cannot see the kingdom of God.'"

"That's right."

"Before we go any further with our request, Pastor, please tell us how a person obtains the new birth."

Corbett smiled. "By repentance of sin, putting your faith in the Lord Jesus Christ and Him alone for salvation, and receiving Him into your heart as John 1:12 and Ephesians 3:17 bear out."

Adam and Doug smiled at each other, and Doug said, "That's what we believe, too, Pastor Corbett. May we talk to you?"

"Certainly. Let's go over to my office at the church."

When they were seated in the pastor's office, Adam explained about Kathy's death on the train, and the need to bury her in Cheyenne City.

The preacher agreed to conduct the burial service—which

would take place on Friday morning at the grave site—then took Adam and Doug to the town's undertaker to arrange for Kathy's body to be claimed at the railroad station.

Next, Adam and Doug went to the Wells Fargo office. The agent reserved seats for them on the stage that headed west from Cheyenne City on Saturday afternoon. After many stops, and the nights spent at stage stops, they would arrive in Fort Bridger on Wednesday, May 10, late in the afternoon.

From there, the two men went to the Western Union office where Adam sent a telegram to Hannah. He gave her the time they were scheduled to arrive in Fort Bridger and asked that she advise Lloyd Dawson and Cade Samuels of the delay in their arrival. He also gave her the name of their hotel in case she needed to contact him.

In Fort Bridger, on that same Thursday morning, Carrie Wright entered Glenda's Place and went to the kitchen. Glenda was busy at the stove, cooking breakfast for her customers. When she saw Carrie, she gave her a mock frown and said, "Dear girl, what are you doing here? This is your day off."

"Well, I just wanted to come by and tell you that if I'm needed, I'll be glad to work. I'm supposed to eat breakfast with Hannah, but I could come back as soon as I'm finished and take over for you."

Glenda sighed and cocked her head. "Honey, it won't hurt me to do the cooking one day a week. Like any normal human being, you need to rest. Now, I want you to disappear. Thursdays will be your regular day off. Got that?"

"Glenda, you're so good to me. I—"

"If this is being good to you, it's because I love you and I care about you. Now, do as the boss says. Git!"

Carrie laughed. "Okay, boss."

Glenda flipped flapjacks in a skillet. "You mentioned yesterday that you and Hannah might spend the day together. Is that what you're going to do?"

"Looks like it, since you won't let me work."

"Great. I've noticed that you two are becoming close friends."

"Mm-hmm. There's a special bond between us because we're both widows. I'm also developing a closeness to Hannah's children—especially to little Eddie. I get to hold him a lot when I'm in the Cooper home."

Glenda smiled. "I know you and Hannah can be a real blessing to each other, and I'm glad for you." She hugged her, then laughed. "Of course, I'm Hannah's best friend, you understand. And don't you forget it!"

Carried grinned. "Oh, I wouldn't think of trying for that spot!"

When Carrie arrived at the Cooper apartment, Hannah and Mary Beth had breakfast almost ready. They welcomed her with hugs, then Carrie said, "Well, where's my little man? I'm sure he needs a hug from Aunt Carrie, too."

Hannah chuckled. "Eddie will just have to wait for his hug, Aunt Carrie. He had his breakfast and now is fast asleep."

They sat down at the breakfast table, and after Chris had asked the blessing on the food, Hannah said, "It's nice of Glenda to give you Thursdays off, Carrie."

"It sure is. The Williamses have been so good to me."

"They're wonderful people."

Patty Ruth slipped a chunk of biscuit under the table to Biggie. "We got thome wunnerful people comin' nex' Monday, too! Uncle Adam, Aunt Theretha, an' Theth, an' Anna will be here!"

"I'm sure all of you are excited about that," said Carrie.

"We sure are," Mary Beth said. "You'll really love them, Aunt Carrie. I'm looking forward to meeting Mr. and Mrs. McClain and their little daughter, too."

"We all are, honey," said Hannah. "And from what Adam and Theresa have written about the McClains, I'm sure everybody in town will love them."

"It's going to be really good to have the newspaper here," Carrie said.

Hannah nodded. "Everybody I've talked to seems to think so. And they all like the name—especially the army people. Colonel Bateman talks about it every time I see him."

B.J. looked across the table at his brother. "Are we gonna ask her?"

"Oh yeah!" said Chris. "Mama, Luke and Joshua Patterson want us to go home with them right after school today, so we can see their new calf. It was born on Tuesday. Is that all right?"

"Of course, just so you're home between five and five-thirty. Your Aunt Carrie doesn't know this yet, but she and I are going to the Powell home at three to have tea with Julie. Mary Beth and Patty Ruth are coming there right after school. We'll be back by five."

Carrie's eyes lit up. "Oh, that will be great! When did you set this up?"

"Yesterday afternoon when Julie came into the store."

"Mama, I got to thinking about it," said Mary Beth. "I'll have to come on home after I bring Patty Ruth to the Powell house. To earn extra credit I'm doing a special project about education in the United States, so I'll need to come home right after school and get started on it."

"That will be fine, honey."

Carrie set her soft eyes on Mary Beth. "How's your witnessing to Bob Imler going?"

"I believe he's real close to getting saved, Aunt Carrie. I've been talking with him a lot about the wrath of God and the horrors of hell. He's still afraid of what his father will do if he becomes a Christian. Our family has been praying that the Holy Spirit will convict him so strongly of his lost condition that he will fear the Lord more than he fears his father."

"And I believe that moment is very near, Mary Beth," said Hannah.

"Yes, Mama. Me too."

"Well, I guess we'd better get the dishes done and the kitchen cleaned up. It'll soon be time for all my students to leave for school."

Half an hour later, when the Cooper children were bundling up, there was a knock at the door.

"I'll get it," said Chris, buttoning up his heavy mackinaw and heading for the door. When he opened it, Curly Wesson stood there with a yellow envelope in his hand.

Curly's features were ashen as he said, "Chris, I have a telegram for your mother."

"Come in, Uncle Curly."

Hannah was at the kitchen cupboard with her back toward the door, but upon hearing Curly's voice, she turned. The gray color of his thin face sent a shiver down her back.

"Is it bad news?" she asked.

"I'm afraid so."

Hannah hurried toward him. "Who's it from?"

"Adam Cooper."

"Has something happened to them?"

"I'll let you read it for yourself, sweet Hannah."

CHAPTER TWENTY

Hannah Cooper ripped open the yellow envelope. "It can't be about Adam if he sent the telegram. Is it Theresa? Seth? Anna?"

"No, it's the family travelin' with 'em," Curly said. "You'll see."

The Cooper children and Carrie Wright gathered close.

Suddenly Hannah cried out, "No! Oh no!"

"What is it, Mama?" Mary Beth asked.

"It's Mrs. McClain…Kathy. She's dead!"

"What happened?" Carrie asked.

"Let me finish." Hannah's eyes ran the lines rapidly. Tears trickled down her cheeks as she looked at the small group and said, "Kathy was shot on the train when it was in Nebraska. An outlaw being transported to Denver got hold of a gun, and there was a struggle. A bullet hit Kathy. Oh, poor, poor Doug. And that little baby. Oh, dear God in heaven, be with them in a special way."

"Why don't we pray right now for him and his little baby?" Carrie asked.

Hannah nodded. "Curly, would you lead us?"

"I shore will."

Curly's words touched every heart as he prayed for Doug McClain and little Jenny.

When he finished praying, Chris looked at his mother

and said, "Does Uncle Adam say when they will be arriving here, Mama?"

"They're burying Kathy in Cheyenne City in the morning. They're booked on the westbound Saturday afternoon stage, and they'll arrive here Wednesday on the late afternoon stage."

"That's the one," said Curly. "Unless the weather slows 'em."

Hannah looked back at the telegram. "Curly, would you send Adam a telegram? You can word it for me. Let him know we received the message of Kathy's death, and ask him to tell Doug we're praying for him, and to tell them all we will be expecting them next Wednesday. Also, tell Adam that I will pass the message to Lloyd Dawson and Cade Samuels and tell him I'll talk to Pastor Kelly about it so he can have the church praying for Doug and Jenny, too."

"I'll do it right away."

"Thank you, Curly. Bring me a copy of what you send, and I'll pay you for it then."

The Cooper children lined up to hug and kiss their mother before leaving for school.

Mary Beth was last. "Mama, I don't understand…"

"What, sweetie?"

"Why would the Lord let Kathy McClain be killed?"

"I can't answer that, Mary Beth. The only thing I can tell you is that just the same as the Lord had a plan in allowing your papa to die on the journey here, and in allowing Colin to die when he and Carrie were just getting their ranch started, He took Kathy to heaven for a purpose we don't have to understand. We just have to trust Him and believe He never makes a mistake. Even if we don't understand the things God causes or allows, we have to love Him and serve Him because He so loves us and has a perfect plan for our lives."

Carrie put an arm around Mary Beth's waist. "Believe me, honey, I've had my battles with doubts about God's goodness, but now I have perfect peace that all is well, and the Lord has never forsaken me."

Mary Beth nodded thoughtfully and followed her siblings to the door. She paused and said, "Mama, Aunt Carrie, would you have a little prayer meeting right now and ask the Lord to let me lead Bob to Jesus today?"

"We sure will, sweetheart," Hannah said. "Bye. I love you."

"I love you, too, Mama. And I love you, too, Aunt Carrie. Bye."

Carrie shook her head in wonderment. "What a precious girl. What a precious, precious girl."

"She's a special one," said Hannah. "God has blessed me with five very special children."

"That He has. And I haven't had my morning hug from number five."

"Tell you what. After we pray for Bob Imler, I've got to go down to the store and see if all is well with Jacob. Eddie will probably wake up while I'm gone. You can get all the hugs you want then."

After praying for Bob's salvation, Hannah left the apartment and went down to the store. Carrie tiptoed down the hall and peeked into Hannah's bedroom. The baby was sound asleep in his cradle. Smiling at him, she whispered, "Okay, snookums. You go ahead and sleep a while yet. But wake up pretty soon, will you?"

Carrie went to the kitchen and looked for something to do. When she opened the silverware drawer, she decided to polish every last piece of silverware.

Soon she had hot, soapy water in a pan and was giving the silverware a good cleaning and polishing job. She prayed for Doug McClain, asking the Lord to give him the same perfect peace she now had in her own heart over Colin's death.

She was humming a gospel song, her hands deep in the hot water, when she heard what sounded like whimpering coming from Hannah's bedroom. She paused and listened. Nothing. "Hmm, I thought for sure I heard him. Well, maybe I did, but he's gone back to sleep."

A few minutes passed, then there was a distinct wail, loud and clear. Carrie quickly dried her hands and hurried to the bedroom. She lifted Eddie into her arms. "It's all right, sweet one," she whispered to him. Her hand went to the diaper. "Oh. No wonder you're upset. Let's get you changed."

When Eddie was wearing a clean, dry diaper, he was happy again and smiling at Carrie as she tickled his cheeks. "How about we sit down here in your mama's rocker for a while, sweetie?"

Carrie cuddled the baby close to her breast, talking to him in a soft, loving voice.

Hannah climbed the stairs to the apartment, noting how easy the stairs were now compared to the difficulty she had during the last three months of her pregnancy. When she stepped inside, her gaze went to the kitchen where she saw the silverware spread out on the cupboard counter. Carrie was nowhere to be seen.

Smiling to herself, Hannah headed for her bedroom. About halfway down the hall, she picked up Carrie's soft voice as she talked to Eddie. When she eased up to the open door and peered in, her eyes smarted with unshed tears.

Carrie was holding Eddie and looking into his pink little face, telling him how much she loved him.

Hannah sighed and said, *O Lord, she would make such a good mother. Please bless her with Your love and give her what she needs to take the place of motherhood.*

As Hannah stepped into the bedroom, Carrie looked up at her sheepishly. "Oh. Hi. He's acting sleepy again. I'll put him back in the cradle." As she spoke, she left the rocker and moved toward the cradle.

Hannah bent down and kissed her baby's forehead and said to him, "I think your Aunt Carrie would spoil you if I'd let her."

Carrie placed Eddie in the crib and tucked a second blanket around him. "There you go, sweet stuff. Thanks for the hugs and kisses."

The two women moved into the hall, and Carrie turned to Hannah. "I promise I didn't go in and wake him up. He started crying, so I checked his diaper, and he needed changing. Honest."

Hannah gave her friend a quick hug. "Carrie, dear, don't worry so. You may hold Eddie anytime you want. I just appreciate the help you've been to me. And I noticed that you were doing a polishing job on the silverware when Eddie interrupted you."

"I hope it's all right."

"All right? I've been meaning to polish the silverware for the past six months and haven't gotten to it yet. How about a second cup of coffee before we finish the polishing job?"

Carrie chuckled. "I'll go for that."

Spring had finally arrived in Wyoming, and it was a beautiful sun-filled day. The students at the Fort Bridger school ate their lunches, then busied themselves in various ways for the next half hour until Miss Lindgren would ring the bell.

As had been the case for several weeks, Mary Beth Cooper and Bob Imler stood near the road, out of earshot from the others. As they talked, Mary Beth could plainly see that the Holy Spirit had Bob under deep conviction.

After reading Romans 10:13 aloud for probably the fiftieth time since they had started these sessions, she looked into his eyes and said, "Bob, do you want to call on the Lord to save you…right now?"

"Mary Beth, I really want to but…"

"But what?"

"Well, I just can't."

"What's standing in your way? Whatever it is, the moment after you die you'll wish you hadn't let it keep you from being saved. Now what is it?"

Bob started to speak, then swallowed hard. "Mary Beth, I…"

"Go ahead."

"Well, it's not something that's standin' in my way. It's someone. It's my pa. I'm scared of what he'd do if I got saved."

Mary Beth opened her Bible and turned to Proverbs chapter 29. "Look at verse 25 and read it to me."

Bob focused on the page and read it aloud: "'The fear of man bringeth a snare; but whoso putteth his trust in the LORD shall be safe.'"

"You know that a snare is a trap, don't you, Bob?"

"Yes."

"Many a soul has been snared by the devil, using their fear of what some other human being will think, say, or do if they get saved. And now they're in hell. Please don't let your fear of your father trap you in hell. Let me show you another verse." Quickly, Mary Beth turned to Proverbs chapter 9. Putting a finger on verse 10, she said, "Read me what it says right here."

Bob set his eyes on the verse. "'The fear of the LORD is the beginning of wisdom: and the knowledge of the holy one is understanding.'"

"All right," said Mary Beth, a prayer burning in her heart, "we have the fear of the Lord and the fear of man. Are you going to be God's wise man or the devil's fool?"

Bob lifted his cap and ran shaky fingers through his hair.

When he did not reply immediately, Mary Beth said, "Bob, I read to you a few days ago about the awful White Throne Judgment in Revelation chapter 20. Remember? If you leave this world a lost sinner, the day will come when you'll be brought out of hell to stand before God. The book that has all your sins recorded in it will be opened. Included in that book will be all the times I've talked to you and showed you about salvation in the Bible and you've rejected Jesus. You'll stand guilty before God for having died without His Son. Will your father be there to stand beside you and defend you? Will he be there to fend off the wrath of God and keep Him from casting you into the lake of fire?"

Bob was squeezing his hands together so hard the knuckles were shiny white. All the color had left his face. "No. Pa won't be there to defend me, Mary Beth."

"You'll have to face God alone, right?"

"Yes."

"Then isn't it wise to keep that from happening by having the fear of the Lord, and not the fear of your father? Without Jesus in your heart, you will face the wrath of God and spend eternity in the lake of fire. But if you'll let Jesus save you, He'll wash all your sins away in His precious blood and make you a child of God. God's born-again children won't even have to stand before the White Throne Judgment."

"All right, Mary Beth. I'll face whatever my pa does to me, but I want to be saved right now."

Mary Beth's throat constricted with a hot lump. She forced it down and said, "Wonderful, Bob! Let's bow our heads and close our eyes." As she spoke, she laid a hand on his arm.

With Mary Beth guiding him, Bob Imler called on the Lord Jesus Christ to be his Saviour.

After praying, and with joy bubbling in his heart, Bob said, "I'm saved, Mary Beth. I'm saved! Jesus told me in His Word that He would save me if I asked Him, and I know He has saved me!"

"Yes," she said, wiping tears from her cheeks, "and now your next step of obedience to the Lord is to be baptized." She was showing him verses on baptism when the bell rang.

As they started toward the schoolhouse, Bob said, "Mary Beth, I want to be baptized, but I know Pa will never allow it."

"I've prayed for your salvation, Bob, which is the most important thing. But I will be praying now that your father will let you be baptized and that he will allow you to come to church."

Bob shook his head and sighed. "You have an awful lot of faith, Mary Beth."

She giggled. "What I have, Bob, is a powerful God."

When school was out that afternoon, Bob Imler put his horse to a gallop, heading home as fast as the animal could carry him. Though he'd told Miss Lindgren and the Christian young people at school about inviting the Lord into his heart, he just had to share it with his mother.

As he slowed the horse to a trot and turned off the road, heading down the lane toward the house, Bob noted that the barn door was standing open a few inches. No doubt his father was doing some work in the barn. He hauled to a stop at the back porch then he stepped through the door into the kitchen. His mother was kneading dough at the kitchen table and looked up at him and smiled. "Hello, son. You're home early. Get out of school ahead of time?"

"No, I just rode extra fast. I have somethin' to tell you."

"Oh? What's that?"

"Ma, I got saved today. Mary Beth Cooper has been talkin' to me a lot about becomin' a Christian. She helped me to call on the Lord at school."

Cordelia nodded, forcing a smile. "Well, if that has made you happy, it's fine, son."

"Ma, she showed me that after a person gets saved, he's supposed to be baptized. I'd really like to do that, but I'm afraid Pa won't let me."

Rufe Imler stormed into the room, his face red with anger. "What a stupid thing to do, Bob! And you're right. No son of mine is gonna be baptized, nor is he gonna be one of them fool church members!"

"But Pa, I—"

"Shut up!" Flecks of spittle were on Rufe's lips as he shouted, "Outside! I'm gonna beat the Christianity right outta you!"

Cordelia was trembling now, but she said, "Rufe, please don't beat him. He only—"

"You shut up too, woman!"

Then Rufe spun back to his son and said, "On second thought, I'll get you later. Right now I'm goin' to town and tell that little snip, Mary Beth Cooper, what I think of her for makin' a religious fool outta you!"

Mother and son watched through the kitchen window as Rufe entered the barn, swearing to himself, and moments later came out leading his horse. Still swearing, he mounted up and galloped away.

Mary Beth was alone in the apartment, sitting at the kitchen table and doing her extra school work, when she heard thundering footsteps on the stairs outside. Before she reached the door it began to rattle under the power of the fist pounding on it.

Her heart went to her throat as she grasped the knob and pulled the door open.

Rufe Imler glared at her and he was breathing heavily.

Before he could get a word out, Mary Beth said pleasantly, "Mr. Imler. How nice to see you. Please come in."

The huge man stomped inside, and Mary Beth said, "You know, I really like your son, sir. Bob is—"

"Enough of that!" he bellowed. Profane words issued from

his mouth like a flood as he swore at her for turning his son into a religious fanatic.

Mary Beth prayed for strength and courage, and her prayer was answered immediately. She remembered the Scripture promise that the Lord would not forsake His own. His presence was obvious to her and she stood her ground, saying calmly, "Mr. Imler, you are mistaken, sir."

"Mistaken about what?"

"There is a big difference between a religious person and a saved person."

Rufe spewed out another string of profanity and said, "They're exactly the same thing, girl!"

"No, sir. God's Word makes it clear that there's a difference."

"I never heard of such a thing."

"Well, sir, you know who the apostle Paul was, don't you?"

"Yeah."

"In one of his letters he told how as a religious man he persecuted God's born-again people because they stood against his religious traditions. He testified how the Lord saved him by His grace. The book of Acts tells how when Paul got saved, it was such a shock to everybody. Then it tells about the change that came into his life. And in Galatians chapter 1, Paul said that he now preached the faith that once he destroyed."

Rufe guffawed. "All he did was change religions."

"No, sir. The religion did nothing for his soul, but when he—"

"Aw, c'mon, girl. You're tryin' to fill my head with nonsense."

Mary Beth lifted her graceful chin. "If you will quit butting in, I'll show you how wrong you are, Mr. Imler."

"Okay, okay. Go ahead."

"As I was saying, sir, Paul's religion did nothing for his

soul, but when he opened his heart to Jesus Christ and became a Christian, he knew his sins were all forgiven and that he was going to heaven when he died. He didn't hope he was going to heaven, he *knew* it. Just as your son knows it now. Religion bases its teachings on human works and religious deeds, but true Christianity is all based on the finished work of Jesus Christ in His death on the cross, His burial, and His resurrection. We become saved by putting our faith in the Lord Jesus for our salvation. When we do that, we're not religious, we're saved."

Rufe remained silent.

Looking up at him, and meeting his hard gaze, Mary Beth said, "Do you understand the difference now, Mr. Imler?"

"Well, I guess so. I just don't grab why Jesus Christ would have done this for us."

In her heart, Mary Beth thanked the Lord for working on the man and calming him down. "It's because of His love for us. His love is greater than our sin."

Rufe asked a couple more questions, and Mary Beth answered them to his satisfaction, though it all seemed a bit like a fairy tale to him.

She asked him to tell her the difference between religion and salvation. When he repeated it back to her sufficiently, she said, "All right. So you see, Mr. Imler, Bob is not a religious fanatic. He is not religious at all. He is a newborn child of God who knows his sins are forgiven and that, without a doubt, he is going to heaven."

Rufe shook his head. "Little girl, I have never heard it explained like this before."

"Well, sir, if you had come to church and heard Pastor Kelly preach, you would have heard it."

Rufe cleared his throat. "Well, uh, Pastor Kelly came to my house to talk to me 'bout bein' saved, but I wouldn't listen to him. I sent him away before he could get much of a start."

"Let me ask you this, Mr. Imler: Do you want to go to hell?"

Rufe cleared his throat again and muttered, "I'm not sure there is a hell, girl."

"Really? Well, when you were swearing at me, you used the word three times. If you don't believe in hell, why do you use the word?"

Rufe had no response.

"You need to turn to the Lord and let Him save you, Mr. Imler. Hell is a place of eternal fire and torment."

The big man frowned and said weakly, "Well, I…I'll have to think about all you've told me."

"While you're thinking about it, will you let Bob come to church this Sunday and be baptized? According to the Bible, that's what he's supposed to do after being saved. It's God's command. You wouldn't want Bob to disobey God, would you?"

"Well, all right," Rufe mumbled. "If that's what Bob wants, I'll let him be baptized."

"Will you also let Bob come to church from now on?"

With a frown wrinkling his brow, he said, "Little girl, you drive a hard bargain. I'll have to think on that, too."

"All right, sir. Thank you for saying you'll let Bob be baptized on Sunday."

Shaking his head, Rufe turned and opened the door, mumbling to himself, "I must be crazy. See you later, girl."

Rufe closed the door behind him and started down the stairs.

Mary Beth opened the door softly, stepped out onto the landing and watched him lumber his way down. Jacob Kates was approaching the staircase just as Imler touched the ground.

Jacob gave him an inquisitive look and said, "Hello, Mr. Imler."

Rufe was still shaking his head. "That Mary Beth! She should be a preacher."

Jacob watched the big bear of a man walk away, then moved up the steps and gave Mary Beth a puzzled look. "What did you say to the man?"

"I just told him about being saved," she said, shrugging.

Jacob's face turned pale.

"I think I gave him something to seriously ponder," she said.

"Ah, honey, is your mother back from the tea party yet?"

"No. It'll be about five o'clock before she's back. Is there something I can do for you?"

"Josh Campbell and his wife are in the store. They need a little credit till they can sell some more of their calves."

"Well, I'm sure it'll be all right to extend them credit, Uncle Jacob. Mama has done it for them before."

Jacob grinned. "Knowing your mother and her kind heart, I felt sure she would approve it, but I didn't want to do it without her say-so."

"You go ahead and do it. I'll take the responsibility. Don't keep the Campbells waiting."

"Thank you. You know, Mary Beth, you're a whole lot like your mother."

"Uncle Jacob, you could pay me no higher compliment."

CHAPTER TWENTY-ONE

B ob Imler and his mother watched Rufe ride into the
yard and trot his horse to the barn. As they waited for
him, Cordelia laid a hand on Bob's shoulder and said,
"Now's the time to learn to trust your God, son. If He could
save your soul, surely He can protect you from your father."

Bob nodded. At the thought of facing the man who had
beat him more times than he could count, he whispered,
"Please, God. Don't let him beat me."

Turning from the window, Cordelia said, "Bob, would you
go out on the back porch and bring in some more logs for the
kitchen stove, please?"

"Yes'm."

When he stepped out on the back porch, his glance
flicked to the barn. His heart pounded as he gathered several
logs in his arms and carried them into the kitchen.

Cordelia busied herself at the cupboard counter, preparing to cook supper.

While Bob was on his knees, placing the logs neatly on
the floor beside the stove, he heard familiar footsteps on the
back porch. He felt a sinking sensation in his stomach as the
door opened. When he turned to look at his father, he did a
double take.

Cordelia's face also registered shock at the expression on
her husband's face.

Bob rose to his feet, and mother and son waited silently for Rufe's first move.

The smile was still on his face when Rufe took off his hat, hung it on a wall peg, and said, "What's for supper, Delie?"

Mother and son exchanged glances, then Cordelia said, "Corned beef and cabbage."

"Sounds good."

"Did you...see Mary Beth Cooper?"

"I did, and we had quite a talk. I'm tellin' you, that's some girl." He sat down at the table.

"What do you mean?"

"Well, that little gal stood right up to me and met me head-on. She explained the difference between what she called saved people and religious people. Never heard such before."

Bob spoke up. "Then Mary Beth explained about me bein' saved, Pa? That it's not just a religion?"

"Yeah. She made sure I understood that. And she told me that you're supposed to be baptized after you get saved."

"Yes, sir."

"Now, boy, I want you to understand that I don't believe all this salvation, open-your-heart-to-Jesus stuff, but since you've chosen to embrace this Christian faith, I'll allow you to go to church this Sunday and be baptized."

"Really?"

"Yep."

Bob licked his lips nervously. "Pa?"

"Yeah?"

"Thank you for givin' me permission to be baptized."

"Well, boy, you owe it all to that pretty little gal. She's really somethin'!"

That night, Bob Imler lay in his bed, amazed at the change in his father, and thanked the Lord for answered prayer. His mind went back to the moment earlier that day when he and Mary Beth were walking toward the schoolhouse after she had led him to the Lord, and he'd told her his pa would never allow him to be saved.

Sleep was trying to claim him as he said, "Thank You, Lord, for your power, and for answered prayer. And thank You for Mary Beth."

A dismal sky hovered above the little group gathered beside an open grave in a windswept cemetery. The dark clouds were as heavy and dark as those that covered Doug McClain's heart.

Little Jenny rested in her father's arms. She studied his sad features and looked around for a familiar face she hadn't seen in days. Her daddy's tears did something to Jenny, and she began to whimper. Doug pressed her little head against his chest to comfort her. Consoled by the rhythmic beat of his heart in her ear, she found solace as well in the plump, dependable thumb that found its way into her waiting mouth. She snuggled deeper into her daddy's arms and watched the scene around her with wide eyes.

Pastor Shane Corbett finished reading from his Bible, then led the tiny group in prayer. When he finished, Doug said, "Thank you, Pastor, for the beautiful service. What do I owe you?"

"Absolutely nothing. I'm just glad I could do it for you." Then laying a hand on Doug's shoulder, Corbett said, "I want you to know that I'll be praying for you and this precious little girl."

"Thank you."

As they walked out of the cemetery, Doug's mind went back to the day in Cincinnati when he and Kathy were talking about their move West, and he had said that the move to Fort Bridger would be the mountaintop of their lives. *Instead of a mountaintop,* he thought to himself, *it's a valley. A very deep valley.*

On Wednesday morning, May 10, the sun shone out of a cloudless sky, and the birds twittered in the trees along Main Street as Andy Kelly, Cade Samuels, and Lloyd Dawson entered the Wells Fargo office and were greeted warmly by Curly and Judy Charley Wesson.

Kelly said, "We wanted to check and see if the stagecoach due in this afternoon is on schedule."

Curly showed them his nearly toothless smile and said, "It shore is, Pastor. The way station whar the stage stopped last night wired me 'bout an hour ago, which is what they're s'posed to do. They said the stage left on schedule this mornin'."

Lloyd turned to Cade. "Then we can proceed with the plans to set up the big welcome for the Coopers and Doug McClain."

"Yes, sir! Let's do it!"

Judy showed her single snaggletooth in a gleeful smile. "This is excitin'! I'm glad everybody is wantin' to show a special welcome to the folks who will give this town its own newspaper!"

The stagecoach pulled away from its last way station just after lunch and rocked and weaved along the road leading to Fort Bridger. As usual, little Seth Cooper had stationed himself next to a window and was looking with wonder at the vast open country, hills, and mountains of southern Wyoming. Doug was sitting directly across from Adam, holding a sleepy Jenny.

"I know you'll love living in Fort Bridger, Doug," Adam said. "Hannah can't say enough about it in her letters."

Doug managed a smile. "I'm sure I will."

"The Lord still has a plan for your life that I know will be magnificent," said Adam. "That's the way He works."

"And Adam and I will do all we can to help make your life a happy one," Theresa said.

He set soft eyes on her then on Adam and said, "You two are such a blessing. No one could have better friends."

As the hours passed, Seth saw a herd of buffalo, a herd of antelope, and two bald eagles making loops in the sky. With each sighting, he let out wild, happy squeals. When the eagles had finally flown out of sight and the boy eased back on his knees in the seat, Adam said, "There's no question about Seth. He most definitely is going to love his new home!"

The sun was low on the horizon when the stage topped a long hill and the majestic Uintah Mountains came into view. The golden light kissed the jagged peaks and broken battlements, causing everyone to gasp in wonderment.

"Oh, my!" Theresa said. "Have you ever seen anything so beautiful? Truly our heavenly Father is an artist!"

"For sure no man could paint it like that," Doug said.

Adam nodded. "I'm loving the West more every minute."

"Me too, Papa," said Seth. "I really like it here."

"Fort Bridger, straight ahead!" the driver's voice called above the sound of pounding hooves and the rumble of wheels.

Seth focused on the uneven rooftops of the town and the flag flying above the gate tower of the fort, and shouted, "Oh, boy! There it is, Papa, Mama! There it is!"

When the stage turned onto Main Street, Theresa said, "Oh, look, everybody!"

Near the Wells Fargo office a block ahead, a huge banner was stretched over the street that declared in bold red letters:

WELCOME TO THE ADAM COOPERS AND DOUG AND JENNY McCLAIN!
HOORAY FOR THE FORT BRIDGER BUGLE!

A large crowd was filling the street, and adults and children alike were waving at the stage as it rolled toward them.

Seth squealed when he saw the fort's brass band clustered in the center of the street, playing a patriotic tune. Little Jenny felt Seth's excitement and let out a squeal of her own.

When the stage rolled to a stop, Curly and Judy stepped up close. "Howdy, folks!" Curly said as he opened the door.

"Welcome to Fort Bridger!" said Judy. "We're Mr. an' Mrs. Wesson, the Fargo agents here."

Just behind them were Hannah and her children. Little Eddie was in his mother's arms.

When Curly helped Theresa out, Hannah rushed up to embrace her and little Anna. Adam and Seth were next, and the hugs began, starting with Patty Ruth, then Mary Beth, then B.J., followed by Chris. By this time, Hannah was embracing Seth and his father.

When Doug stepped from the coach with little Jenny in his arms, Hannah and her brood gave them a warm welcome and introduced Pastor Andy and Rebecca.

Suddenly the brass band struck up a loud tune, and from the porch of the Wells Fargo office, Cade Samuels waved his arms and said, "Mr. and Mrs. Cooper, and Mr. McClain, I'm Cade Samuels, Fort Bridger's mayor and only barber. I want to give you an official welcome from this town and tell you that we are very happy to have you here. We are all very excited about the *Fort Bridger Bugle*!"

Applause broke out, punctuated with cheers and whistles.

Adam and Theresa, who were standing between Hannah and Chris, looked at each other and smiled.

When the applause died down, Lloyd Dawson mounted the porch. The mayor introduced Dawson to the newcomers, then the banker spoke his own words of welcome.

A uniformed army officer then moved up as Dawson stepped off the porch to shake hands with the Coopers and

Doug McClain. When Colonel Ross Bateman was introduced, he gave an official army welcome and said, "Mr. Cooper, Mr. McClain, I want to tell you how happy we army people are about the name you've given your newspaper. We think the *Fort Bridger Bugle* is most appropriate, and we wish you the very best as the paper is established."

After Marshal Lance Mangum, and his deputy, Jack Bower, spoke their words of welcome, Cade Samuels motioned for Pastor Kelly to step up on the porch.

Kelly set warm eyes on the Coopers and Doug McClain and said, "The ladies of the church have prepared a special supper for you at the fellowship hall. All the church members will be there. Even Glenda's Place—the town's only café—will be closed for the evening so the owners and their employees can attend the supper."

The band played another brief, rousing number, then Mayor Samuels looked at Adam and Doug. "Would you like to say anything?"

"You go ahead, Adam," Doug whispered.

When Adam mounted the porch, the crowd broke into applause. He ran his gaze over the friendly faces and said loud enough for all to hear, "I thank you on behalf of my family and my associate for the wonderful welcome. Whew! We never expected anything like this!"

There were cheers, and some people applauded again.

"We haven't met most of you yet," said Adam, "but let me take just a moment to introduce ourselves to you."

After Adam pointed out each member of his family, he pointed to Doug, who was holding Jenny, and said, "Folks, I want you to meet my best friend, Doug McClain, who will be my pressman. In his arms is little one-year-old Jenny."

There was more applause, then all eyes were fixed on Doug and his squirming daughter. Astounded at the warm welcome, Doug let a smile touch his lips as he said, "Thank you for this wonderful gesture toward us. I know we will all become good friends."

Doug's smile hid the shadow of grief he felt at the thought of Kathy. When Jenny saw that the people were looking directly at her as they clapped, she was delighted with the attention and opened her mouth wide, showing four little teeth in a big smile. She clapped her hands, mimicking the crowd around her.

When the applause finally waned, Doug looked to Adam, his eyes asking him to take over.

Adam's voice broke as he said, "I know that all of you have…have been informed of Kathy McClain's death on this trip. I want you to know that Kathy was a fine Christian lady. She will be terribly missed by Doug and Jenny, of course, but also by my family. And I also want you to know that Doug was one of the leading pressmen at the *Cincinnati Post*. I'm so grateful to have him with me. I wouldn't be able to establish the *Fort Bridger Bugle* without him."

"We're glad to have all of you, Mr. Cooper!" came a man's voice from somewhere at the back of the crowd. "God bless you!"

Adam waved. "And God bless you, sir!"

The mayor spoke up. "I want to thank everyone for being a part of the welcoming committee. Let me remind you that these people need to head on over to the church for supper, so please do not detain them by trying to meet them personally at this time."

The luggage had been taken off the stage by the crew and left beside the Wells Fargo building. Pastor Kelly stepped up to the newcomers and said, "I have some men of the church who will take your luggage to your houses now. After the meal, we'll deliver you to your new homes."

Hannah and her children walked with Adam, Theresa, and Doug toward the church. When they arrived, the meal was not quite ready.

Hannah said, "I know you're all tired from your long trip. Come over here and sit down."

When she got them seated at a table, she said, "There are some special friends of mine who are eager to meet you." As she spoke, she waved at Gary and Glenda Williams and Carrie Wright, who stood close by, looking on.

Hannah made the introductions, explaining that Gary and Glenda were the owners and operators of the Uintah Hotel and Glenda's Place. She pointed out that Carrie was their chief cook at the café.

Hannah looked toward the kitchen. "I want to see how much longer it'll be till the ladies are ready to serve supper. Nobody stray, all right? I'll be back in a minute."

During the lull, other church members came by and introduced themselves to the newcomers and offered personal words of welcome.

When Hannah came back, she said, "They tell me it'll be at least another twenty minutes. So, Carrie, I'll see about fulfilling your request right now."

Hannah leaned close to Doug and said, "Carrie was widowed back in February. She has asked for the privilege of speaking to you alone. Is that all right?"

"Of course." Doug smiled at Carrie and stood up with Jenny in his arms.

Hannah indicated a corner of the hall and said, "You can go over there in that corner; nobody will bother you there."

When they were alone, Carrie said, "My last name is Wright, Mr. McClain."

"Yes, ma'am."

Jenny studied Carrie while she told Doug the story of Colin's untimely death, the loss of the ranch, and how the Lord had worked in her life up to this time, increasing her faith even in the midst of her grief. When Jenny reached a hand toward her, Carrie smiled, took hold of the little girl's hand, and kept talking.

When Carrie finished her brief story, she said, "I wanted you to know, Mr. McClain, that I understand your loss and the pain that goes with it."

"You sure do," he said.

"I've been praying for you ever since the news came to Hannah, and I will continue to pray for you."

He adjusted Jenny on his arm. "Mrs. Wright, thank you for sharing your heartache with me, and thank you for your understanding and your prayers."

Carrie had been offered Jenny's hand again, and while she squeezed it tenderly, she said, "I'm able to be a help only because of Hannah Cooper. She became a widow last year and was a wonderful help to me. If I can, I just want to be the same kind of help to you."

"You already have been, ma'am."

Jenny squealed and smiled at Carrie. Carrie responded by shaking Jenny's arm up and down, making her giggle.

When Carrie let go of the little girl's hand, she said, "Such a sweet baby, Mr. McClain. You must be very proud of her."

"I am, believe me."

Jenny reached her hand toward Carrie again and said rather timidly, "Mama…"

"Oh, bless her heart," Carrie said.

Even as Doug smiled, the word spoken by his little daughter brought a stab of pain to his heart.

Suddenly, Jenny reached both arms toward Carrie, saying louder, "Mama!"

Carrie gave Doug a questioning look. When he nodded, she opened both hands to the little girl and gathered her close to her breast.

A joyful cooing sound came from Jenny's lips.

"Well, will you look at that?" said Doug. "It looks like Jenny feels right at home with you. Thank you, Mrs. Wright."

Carrie flashed him a smile. "It's my pleasure," she said as

she wrapped the baby in a tight embrace.

Doug glanced toward the other side of the hall and saw the people taking their places at the tables. "Looks like they're about ready to start serving. Guess we'd better get back."

During the meal, while Carrie sat with the Williamses at a table across the room, Hannah told Adam and Theresa about Carrie's sorrows and her temporary job at the café, then asked that they and Doug pray for her.

When the meal was over, and Pastor Kelly had led in special prayer for Doug and little Jenny, Doug walked over to Carrie and said, "Mrs. Wright, I want you to know that I'll be praying for you, too. Especially about another job when the regular cook returns."

"I appreciate that, Mr. McClain."

Jenny cooed, set her big blue eyes on Carrie, and said, "Mama."

Carrie blushed, kissed the little girl's hand, and said, "You'd better keep a close eye on her, Mr. McClain. I just might become a kidnapper."

As Doug walked away, Jenny was still reaching back for Carrie.

When Adam and Theresa entered their new house, they fell in love with it. Theresa was glad to see nice, well-kept furniture; even the windows had delicate curtains and draperies.

Doug was equally pleased with his house. That night, after Jenny was asleep, he lay in his bed and wept, wishing Kathy were there to share the new home with him.

On the next Sunday, the Adam Coopers and Doug McClain walked the aisle at invitation time to put their membership in the church. Bob Imler was baptized, though his parents were not in attendance. At the close of the service, the people welcomed Bob and the newcomers into the membership.

When Mary Beth Cooper approached Bob later, she said, "It sure was wonderful to see you baptized. I only wish your parents had been here."

"Well, Ma wanted to come, Mary Beth, but Pa wouldn't let her."

"We must pray hard that the Lord will work on your father's heart. If we can get him saved, reaching your mother will be pretty easy."

"Mary Beth, I want to thank you again for caring about me, and working with me till you brought me to the Lord."

She gave him a sisterly hug.

Miss Sundi Lindgren stepped up with Dr. Patrick O'Brien at her side and said, "Bob, I just had to come by and tell you how happy I am that you've become a Christian."

"Well, Miss Lindgren, now that I'm a new man, I won't be a problem to you anymore."

Sundi hugged him. "I'm sure you'll be a blessing."

Within ten days the printing press arrived on a wagon supply train, along with the office furniture and equipment and supplies. The men of the town and fort helped unload the shipment, and within a few more days, Adam and Doug had the press rolling. During the ten-day waiting period, Adam and Doug had painted a large sign and placed it over the front door of the *Bugle* office.

The first issue of the *Fort Bridger Bugle* was a smashing success. Adam planned to put out one edition a week until he could garner business for his classified section, which would bring in the better part of the paper's income. He would then make it a biweekly publication.

Within two weeks, Adam was getting responses from people of nearby towns where the paper was being sold, and from farmers and ranchers.

Theresa was taking care of Jenny during the day so Doug would be free to work at the paper. He had been given a standing invitation for evening meals at both the Adam Cooper home and Hannah Cooper's. He took them up on it at times but also began to eat a lot of his evening meals at Glenda's Place.

CHAPTER TWENTY-TWO

On a Tuesday evening in mid-June, Doug McClain entered Glenda's Place with little Jenny in his arms. He noticed the Lindgren sisters having dinner with Marshal Lance Mangum and Dr. Patrick O'Brien. He chose the table next to them. After they exchanged greetings, waitress Paula Forbes drew up, carrying the usual high chair for Jenny.

She set the high chair up to the table, and said, "Here's your throne, Princess Jenny."

The baby smiled back at her and made a cooing sound. Paula took Doug's order, writing it on a pad, and made her way behind the counter. When she laid the order on the shelf below the open window, she looked into the kitchen and said, "Carrie, you-know-who is here with her father."

Carrie was frying potatoes at the stove. She gave Paula a pleasant look and said, "Thanks, honey. I'll get out there and see her as soon as I'm done with these potatoes."

Doug was chatting with the two couples at the next table when he heard Jenny squeal and cry out, "Mama!"

His head whipped around and he saw Carrie threading her way amongst the tables. As she drew up, she spoke to Doug, then to the two couples while lifting Jenny out of the high chair. She kissed the little girl's fat cheek and said, "Hello, sweetheart. I've missed you. It's been two days since I've seen you."

After hugging the baby good, Carrie put her back in the

high chair and said to Doug, "Don't let up on praying for me about another job. Glenda told me this afternoon that she just received a letter from Maude Garvin. Her mother died, and she will be back a week from today."

Doug nodded. "I won't let up. I'll pray about a new place for you to live, too."

"Well, that seems to be taken care of already."

"Really?"

"Glenda told me Maude said I could live with her. The Kellys have told me that I'm welcome to live with them, too, but Maude's house is larger, and I'll have more room there."

"Well, that's good. I'm sure the Lord will provide the job soon too."

"Carrie," Sundi Lindgren said, "we couldn't help overhearing what you just told Doug. Everybody in this town loves Maude. She sort of has the reputation of being everybody's adopted mother. You'll love living with her."

Carrie smiled. "Sounds good to me, Sundi. I can use that kind of atmosphere right now." With that, Carrie excused herself, saying she needed to get back to the kitchen. Before she left she bent down to kiss Jenny's cheek.

Maude Garvin arrived in Fort Bridger on June 20, and after taking her luggage home, she went to the café. Paula welcomed her back and told her that Glenda was at the hotel.

Moments later, Maude and Glenda were seated in the hotel office. Glenda brought her up to date on happenings in Fort Bridger, including the arrival the previous month of the Adam Coopers and Doug and Jenny McClain. The *Fort Bridger Bugle* was doing even better than Adam Cooper had expected in such a short time. In the latest edition, Adam had announced that the paper would come out twice a week beginning the first of July.

"Well," said Maude, "sounds like there's been plenty of good stuff happening while I've been gone."

"Yes, but it's also good to have you back."

"Did you tell Carrie I want her to live with me?"

"Yes, I did."

"And?"

"You've got a permanent guest, Maude. Gary and I wish we could come up with a job for her here in the hotel, but there just isn't one."

"Well, I'm sure the Lord will take care of that," said Maude, rising to her feet. "I didn't go back to the kitchen when I went in the café to see you. I'll go over now and talk to Carrie."

Carrie was busy at the stove when she saw Maude come through the door. She smiled at the older woman, thinking that Maude was everyone's idea of a typical cook. She was round in all the right places, with a plump, rosy face that was usually wreathed in a bright smile.

After they embraced and Carrie gave her condolences regarding Maude's mother, the older woman said, "Glenda told me you've accepted my invitation."

"I sure have. Thank you so much for the offer. I'll be actively seeking a new job, now that you're back. I've put enough money aside that I can pay you the first month's rent and groceries."

Maude shook her head. "There will be no charge for rent, honey. Once you're working elsewhere, I'll let you help with the grocery bill, but the rent is free."

"Thank you, Maude. You're so kind. When will you start back to work?"

"Tomorrow. I'm going to rest these bones the remainder of today."

That evening, Paula's face appeared at the kitchen window in the café, telling Carrie that Doug and Jenny had just come in. There was a temporary lull in the kitchen, so Carrie went out to greet them. As soon as Jenny saw Carrie, she reached both chubby arms toward her.

After Carrie hugged and kissed the baby, she placed her in the high chair and said to Doug, "This is my last day here. Maude will be back tomorrow. I'm going to put an ad in the *Bugle* and go to every merchant in town, too. Surely the Lord has a job just waiting for me."

Doug grinned. "I know of a job that's available."

"Really? What is it?"

"That's something I need to talk with you about. How soon can we do that?"

"How about right after work tonight?"

"All right. You're usually done about nine, aren't you?"

"Yes."

"Okay. I'll be here at nine."

When Doug and Jenny were ready to leave the café, Carrie came out from the kitchen, kissed Jenny's cheek, and said, "Bye-bye, little darlin'."

Jenny made a happy, gurgling sound and patted Carrie's face.

"Be back at nine," Doug said and headed for the door.

Jenny looked over his shoulder and extended a hand toward Carrie. She broke into sobs and cried, "Mama! Mama!"

Carrie was waiting at the café door when Doug appeared at precisely nine o'clock. Behind her, Paula was sweeping the place with a broom. Carrie turned and told her good night, then stepped out to meet Doug. "Where shall we go?" she asked him.

"I'll walk you home. We can talk on the way."

"All right."

As they started down the boardwalk, Carrie said, "Did you leave Jenny with Theresa?"

"Mm-hmm. And speaking of Jenny brings up the job I told you about." When Carrie gave him a puzzled look, he said, "Let me start from the top. As you know, Theresa keeps Jenny for me during the day so I can work at the paper. Well, Adam has Theresa quite busy keeping the books for the *Bugle*. She does it at home, but having her own two children to take care of, I know it's making it difficult for her to take care of Jenny too. Not that she has said anything of the sort. Theresa is a kind and generous lady, but I can see that she's overloaded."

They reached an intersection on Main Street and took the side street toward Maude's house. As they walked in the near darkness, Doug offered his arm to Carrie.

"What I want to do," he said, "is to hire you to take care of Jenny at my house during the day, while I'm at work. I can afford to pay you as much as you've been making at the café."

Carrie turned her head toward him again, and in the vague light, he could see perplexity on her face.

"The reason I know that is because I asked Gary Williams how much you were being paid."

Carrie laughed. "Oh, you did, eh?"

"It's just good business," he said, chuckling. "Will you accept the job?"

"I sure will."

"Good! Now…I know how attached Jenny already is to you. And it looks like she's going to continue to call you Mama. I hope that won't be a problem for you."

"I certainly don't mind her calling me that. How could caring for such an adorable child ever be a problem, Douglas McClain?"

"Well, I just thought—"

"I've already lost my heart to that precious baby. Taking care of her will be my joy and a wonderful privilege."

"Thank you! This really relieves my mind."

"Tell you what," Carrie said. "I'll also do the housecleaning for you, plus the washing and ironing."

"Oh, I couldn't let you do that. The pay's too low for you to do all those things."

"Why don't you let me be the judge of that? The main thing is that I have become as much attached to Jenny as she has to me. I will love being able to spend all that time with her."

Doug shook his head and grinned. "Then who am I to argue? The job is yours. Can you start tomorrow morning?"

"What time do you want me there?"

"Well, let's say 7:30. I have to head for work by 7:45."

The next morning, Carrie arrived at the McClain house at 7:20. When Doug answered her knock, he was still chewing a mouthful of his breakfast.

"You're early," he said.

"It's a policy I have," Carrie said, running her gaze over the part of the house she could see. "Your house is beautiful, Doug."

"Mm-hmm. Mrs. Dawson and Mrs. Samuels did the decorating."

"That sweet baby still asleep?"

"Yes," he said, heading toward the kitchen with Carrie at his side. "She's had to get up earlier than this since I needed to get her to the Cooper house before I went to work. She's probably enjoying a few extra winks."

Doug excused himself while he picked up his plate and finished the small amount of scrambled eggs on it. When he started to pick up the dishes to carry to the cupboard counter,

Carrie said, "Don't bother with those. I'll take care of cleaning up the kitchen. You go on to work."

Doug looked at her and smiled. "I wish I could adequately tell you what it means to have you here with Jenny."

"And I wish I could tell you what it means to me to be with her, Doug, but there aren't enough words in the English language. Just relax at work and enjoy your job. I'll be enjoying mine."

Carrie happily tidied up the kitchen, keeping her ears open for any sounds from the baby's room. Still, all was quiet when she finished the job. Unable to wait a minute longer, she tiptoed into Jenny's room. The baby was awake and lying wide-eyed, playing with her fingers.

Jenny looked up and focused on the smiling face bending over her. "Mama!" she said, rolling on to her knees.

"Hello, sweetheart. My, my! Look at you!"

Jenny was using the side of the crib to pull herself up. A bright smile lit up her face, which was all rosy from sleep.

Carrie took the adorable child from the crib, kissed her warm little cheek, and said, "I love you."

Jenny giggled and said, "Mama…"

Cuddling the baby close to her breast, Carrie kissed her again and said, "No, sweetheart. I'm not your mama. But I'm going to care for you as though you are my very own."

After changing the baby and dressing her, Carrie took her to the kitchen and placed her in her high chair while she cooked some breakfast for her. When the baby's breakfast was ready, Carrie sat down in front of her and spooned warm oatmeal into her mouth and gave her little bits of buttered biscuit. They laughed together when most of the oatmeal spilled right back out, only to be spooned up again. When Jenny was full, Carrie left her in the high chair while she readied her bath.

Jenny had always loved her bath, and she giggled and slapped her open palms on the soapy water, splashing both herself and Carrie. When the water cooled, Carrie lifted Jenny from the water and quickly toweled her off. A few minutes later, Jenny was powdered and clad in a gingham dress, and her little natural curls were dancing on her head.

"You are as pretty as a picture, my little one."

Jenny patted Carrie's cheek and said, "Mama."

Carrie's heart expanded with love for the little girl. She playfully pinched her little button nose and said, "You don't listen, do you?"

She made a pallet of a blanket and placed Jenny on it, giving her some toys from her cradle, then began cleaning the house.

Jenny gurgled in her own baby language as she played with the toys, and Carrie marveled at how good she was. She paused to watch the baby for a minute and said, "Lord, this is the best job I could ever have. Thank You for Your abundant goodness."

Carrie was almost finished with her housework when she passed by the baby once more. Jenny hadn't made any sounds for a few minutes. The toddler's eyelids were drooping and her little lips were working silently. Her eyes opened when she sensed Carrie's presence, and she made a grumpy sound.

Carrie picked her up and went into the kitchen. She gave Jenny a drink of milk from a small tin cup, then carried her into the bedroom that had been converted into a nursery and changed her diaper.

There was a rocking chair in the room and Carrie sat down with Jenny in her arms. The baby laid her head against her breast. Rocking her gently, Carrie sang in a low, soothing voice, and all too soon for Carrie, the baby was fast asleep.

Keeping the rocker in steady motion, Carrie let her mind wander to Colin and thought about what their little daughter would have looked like if they could have had one. She tried to picture him as a father and told herself he would have been a good one.

Jenny moaned in her sleep and shifted position, interrupting Carrie's reverie. Rising carefully, Carrie carried Jenny to the crib and softly kissed her soft curls, then laid her down and covered her with a light baby blanket. "Sleep well, my little angel," she whispered. "Because of the love you have shown me, I know a little bit of what a mother feels."

Little Eddie Cooper was a happy baby. His siblings loved him very much, especially B.J., who felt a special attachment to him. The other siblings each made time for Eddie, but it was B.J. who spent the most time with him. And as B.J. had predicted, he and his little brother were becoming buddies.

On the same day that Carrie began her job in the McClain home, Hannah sat in her favorite overstuffed chair in the parlor, waiting for her children to come home from school. When they came in just before 3:30, they found her all smiles.

"Well, Mama," said Chris as he bent over and kissed her, "you look happy. Did Eddie say his first word?"

Hannah chuckled. "No, but I do have some good news for all of you. However, I get hugs and kisses first."

When everyone had readily complied, she ran her gaze over their faces and said, "We got a letter today from Grandpa and Grandma Singleton. And guess what! They're coming to see us next month, and they're going to stay till sometime in September."

For Carrie, it was a blessing to know she was helping Doug and having a part in forming little Jenny into what she would grow up to be. The job kept her days filled to capacity, and when she pillowed her head at night, she fell immediately to sleep, feeling satisfaction in what she was accomplishing.

One day in late June, Carrie put Jenny down for her afternoon nap, and took the rugs outside to clean them. It was a hot day, and sweat beaded her brow as she beat the rugs and the dust flew. She mopped her brow with her apron, then carried the rugs back into the house and placed them on the floors she had polished. Then she went to the kitchen and sat down at the round oak table. She rested there, listening to the birds chattering in the trees outside the kitchen window.

Her mind began to wander and took a road she hadn't allowed before. She imagined herself as Doug McClain's wife and Jenny's stepmother. After pondering this for a few minutes, she shook her head and admonished herself for taking such a flight of fancy.

"It's too soon for either of us," she scolded herself aloud. "But maybe…just maybe, someday such a thing might be God's will for us." She drew a deep breath. "In the meantime, young lady, you just be a blessing to Doug and Jenny and let the Lord have His way in your life."

As she rose from the table, she scrubbed a hand over her face, but it didn't wipe away the secret smile on her lips.

In the first week of July, the *Fort Bridger Bugle* came out with two issues—on Tuesday and Friday. Tuesday was the Fourth of July, and the paper carried an article by Adam about America's great ninety-fifth celebration of Independence Day. On Friday, Lloyd Dawson entered the *Bugle* office, carrying the day's paper in hand. Adam and Doug were bent over a work table, discussing an upcoming issue when they saw the banker come in.

"Good afternoon, gentlemen," said Dawson. "Congratulations on the paper! That article on Tuesday was very good, Adam, and the one you wrote for today's issue about the great migration to the Wild West is superb. How are sales going of late? I see your classified section is beefing up."

Adam smiled. "The *Bugle* is doing well in every way. Circulation is constantly increasing—nearly everybody in town and fort has subscribed to it. And now, some of the neighboring towns are catching onto it. The paper's being delivered by stagecoaches all over southwest Wyoming and parts of Utah, Colorado, and Idaho."

Dawson pointed to the classified section. "I notice that nearly every merchant in Fort Bridger is advertising, as well as merchants in other towns. I want you to know that my bank customers are raving about the news coverage—both the nationwide news and that of Fort Bridger. And the women, they're really excited about the articles you've got Theresa writing in her column. Let me tell you, gentlemen, you're doing a marvelous job. And Adam…you've even made payments ahead on your loan. You're looking at one happy banker who is plenty glad he made an investment in Adam Cooper and the *Fort Bridger Bugle*!"

On that same day, Hannah Cooper and her children gathered at the Wells Fargo office to meet the five o'clock stagecoach. As Hannah and her brood sat on the benches in front of the office, B.J. was holding Eddie and keeping his attention.

Hannah thought about how much she had missed her parents since she and Solomon drove away from Independence almost a year ago. During those painful months, she would not let herself dwell on how much she missed them. Now that the day was finally here to see them again, she and her children were almost beside themselves with excitement.

It was a hot day, and the lowering sun was beating down on Hannah and her little family. As she glanced up the street once more, hoping to catch sight of the oncoming stage, an errant breeze wafted its way along Main Street, giving a brief respite to the heat.

Suddenly the stage rounded the corner a block away. Patty Ruth saw it first. "There they are!" she shouted, jumping up and down and clapping her hands. "They're here! They're here!"

Hannah stood to her feet when the stage rolled to a halt. A stranger stepped out first, then reached back in to help the lady behind him. It was Esther Singleton.

Taking Eddie from B.J.'s arms, Hannah rushed up to her mother, and at the same time, Ben Singleton stepped down. Both Hannah and baby were folded into a tight embrace by her mother, while the other children rushed to their grandfather.

When there had been hugs all around, the grandparents studied little Eddie with tears in their eyes and agreed that he was the spitting image of Solomon, and also looked a great deal like B.J. This made the nine-year-old pop out his chest.

"Oh, Mama, Papa, I really didn't know how much I've missed and needed you until I saw you!"

The parents hugged their daughter once more, then Hannah said, "I have the Fargo agent ready to take your luggage to the apartment."

"Then let's go!" said Ben.

Curly Wesson came out of the office and took the Singletons' luggage from the stage crew. Placing it in a small cart, he followed the happy group down the street.

As they walked along, Ben sidled up to his daughter and put an arm around her shoulder. "I've missed you so much, honey," he said.

Tears sprang to Hannah's eyes once again as she said, "Papa, I'm so glad you're here. I don't think I can ever let you leave!"

The silver-haired man tweaked his daughter's ear and said, "Well, we'll just have to see what we can do about that."

Whatever did he mean by that statement? Hannah thought.

Patty Ruth was walking a step ahead of the rest of them and teasing both her older siblings about the romance in their lives.

"Patty Ruth," said Chris, "drop it."

"Drop it?" the child said with a giggle. "Why, Chrith, I think Grandpa and Grandma should know that you and Abby Turner are goin' thteady!"

Ben Singleton chuckled. "Is that really so, Chris? You've got a steady girlfriend?"

Chris set grim eyes on Patty Ruth, then looked at his grandfather. "Well, sort of."

"Thort of!" Patty Ruth said. "I heard you tell Luke Patterthon at school that you and Abby are goin' thteady!"

"Okay, okay. But it's none of your business."

"And my big thithter hath a crush on Bob Imler! They talk a whole lot together durin' lunch and retheth!"

"P.R.," Mary Beth said, "you don't have to announce it to the whole world."

The little redhead giggled. "I didn't! I jutht told Grandpa and Grandma!"

Ben laughed and said to Hannah, "Looks like romance is budding in the Cooper household!"

"Well, Papa, it's not just the Cooper household. Romance is in the air this summer in Fort Bridger. Things are looking serious between our marshal, Lance Mangum, and Heidi Lindgren, who owns the town's dress shop. And it's looking just as serious between Heidi's sister, Sundi—who is our school-marm—and young Dr. Patrick O'Brien. There is even talk among the townspeople that there might be a double wedding someday soon."

CHAPTER TWENTY-THREE

One afternoon in mid-September, Carrie Wright was sitting on the back porch, holding little Jenny on her lap and talking to her. Jenny responded with smiles and words that she alone understood.

Though there had been a couple of cold snaps, Indian summer was holding on in Wyoming, and the weather was still moderately warm.

Doug McClain walked toward his house, having been given the afternoon off by his employer. He decided he would use the time to hoe some weeds that had taken root in the flower garden by the front porch. As he walked alongside the house toward the rear, his ears picked up Carrie's voice. He slowed his pace and moved up to the corner of the house to peer around it.

Carrie lifted the baby off her lap, hugged her tenderly and kissed her cheek, saying, "I love you so much, sweetheart. I wish you were my little girl. I wish that when you learn to talk big people's language, you could call me 'Mommy.'"

Jenny responded with a smile and said, "Mama."

At the same moment, Carrie heard a knock at the front door. She left the chair with Jenny in her arms and hurried through the kitchen door.

Doug waited at the corner of the house until Carrie was

well inside, then went to the toolshed to get the hoe. Just as he was coming out of the shed, Carrie walked out to the back porch with Mary Beth Cooper, who was carrying Jenny.

Carrie's attention was drawn to Doug as he closed the door of the toolshed. "Oh!" she gasped. "I didn't know you were home."

"Just got here," he said, smiling. "Hello, Mary Beth."

"Hello, Mr. McClain."

"You got off early, Doug," Carrie said.

"I got caught up on all my press work, so Adam told me to take the rest of the afternoon off. Thought I'd get rid of those weeds in the flower garden out front."

"Oh. I'd have done it for you if I knew the weeds were there. I hadn't noticed them."

Doug shook his head. "You do more than you should around here as it is. You're not going to hoe my weeds."

Carrie chuckled. "Oh yes, Mr. McClain. I really slave around here, don't I?"

He grinned and headed toward the front yard. When he reached the flower garden, Doug could hear Carrie and Mary Beth playing with Jenny. The baby was giggling happily. As he began to chop weeds, Doug thought of what he'd heard Carrie say before Mary Beth knocked on the door. He let her words echo in his mind.

It only took a few minutes to finish the job. He came back around the corner of the house and drew up to the porch. "How long can you stay, Mary Beth?"

"I don't have to be home for a couple of hours. Is there something I can do for you?"

Doug nodded. "I need a favor."

"Certainly."

"Will you watch Jenny for about an hour so Carrie and I can take a walk?"

"I'll be happy to do that."

"Okay, Carrie," Doug said, smiling at her. "Let's go for a walk."

When they went toward the front of the house on the way to the street, Carrie gave Doug a strange look. "Where are we going? And what is it we need to talk about?"

"I have a special place I want to go for our talk. It's not too far."

Carrie shrugged. "Whatever you say, boss."

"Boss?" he said, laughing as they reached the street and turned west. "I may employ you to take care of my daughter and the house, but we both know the boss around here is that chubby little girl who owns both of our hearts."

"Can't argue with that."

Soon they were out of town and walking across a wide field of wildflowers, heading due west. Moments later they stopped at the edge of a broad, sweeping valley that ran all the way to the towering Uintah Mountains to the southwest. A soft, warm breeze toyed with Carrie's blond hair.

She ran her eyes over the scene before her, and said, "The first time I saw this valley and those magnificent mountains, they captivated me. They still do. What a splendid display of God's handiwork!" She turned to him. "What did you want to talk about?"

"Well, to begin with, let me tell you what triggered my desire to talk to you. When I came home today, I headed for the toolshed, and as I drew near the rear of the house, I heard you talking to Jenny. You said you love her so much and that you wish she was your little girl."

A tint appeared on Carrie's cheeks. "Well, I—"

"And you expressed your wish that when she learned to talk big people's talk, that she could call you 'Mommy.'"

The tint on Carrie's cheeks grew darker and spread over her face. "Doug, I…well, I didn't mean…that is to say—"

"Please don't be embarrassed." Doug took hold of her

hand. "I think it's wonderful that you feel that way about Jenny. I'm glad you love her that much."

"Oh. Well, I'm glad you're glad." His firm grip on her hand made her want to squeeze back, but she refrained.

He looked deep into her eyes and grinned. "Know what?"

"What?"

"I'm sure that if Jenny could use big people's talk right now, she would say to you, 'I want you for my mommy.' Just think of how often she calls you 'Mama'—even in her baby talk. I'm sure she does it when I'm not around, too, right?"

"Well, yes."

"See what I mean? So just imagine that suddenly she could tell you what's in her heart. She's obviously very fond of you." Doug squeezed her hand. "Carrie, I have to admit that I've grown very fond of you myself."

His words took away her breath and she turned to face the valley.

Doug's brow puckered. "I didn't mean to upset you."

Carrie turned back and said, "Don't be sorry, Doug. You didn't upset me. It's just that…well, that I've grown very fond of you, too. I didn't know till now that you felt that way about me."

"I've wanted to tell you how I feel…I just hadn't found the right time. But when I heard you talking to Jenny, I decided this was the time. I realize that it's been a short time since both of us lost our mates, and we must use discretion in all of this, but when sufficient time has passed, it just might be the Lord's will that we…well, that we…"

Carrie smiled, shaking her head in wonderment. "Doug, as long as we're confessing things, you might as well know that I've had exactly the same thoughts."

"You have?"

"Yes."

"And as the days pass, you believe that the Lord will let us fall deeper and deeper in love?"

"Now that I've heard how you feel, I'm absolutely sure of it."

"And one day, when we both have peace from the Lord that it's time, you'll let me present you to Jenny as her real mommy after we say our vows?"

"Oh yes!"

Before they knew it, they were in each other's arms, holding on tightly and agreeing that God had a plan for their broken lives, and He was now revealing it to them.

After a long moment, Carrie eased back in his arms and said, "I want to tell you about a sermon Pastor Kelly preached right after Colin's death. It relates to this very thing we're talking about. Have you ever read in Psalm 84 about the valley of Baca?"

"Yes...the valley of weeping."

When Carrie had finished telling Doug about Pastor Kelly's sermon, he said, "That's beautiful. I've read that psalm many times but never realized that the only way to get to the next mountaintop is to go through the valley."

Carrie nodded. "Yes. A powerful illustration of the Christian life. Not long after Pastor preached the sermon, I was having an awful time over Colin's death. Pastor talked to me about it and told me that one day the Lord would take me beyond the valley to the mountaintop." She reached up and touched his face with her fingertips. "Doug, both of us have been in the valley of weeping since we lost our mates."

He shook his head in wonderment. "Let me tell you what I said to Kathy just before we left Cincinnati. I told her that our move to Fort Bridger would be the mountaintop of our lives. I had no idea, of course, that the Lord would take her to heaven on the trip and plunge me into the valley of weeping. It's a very deep valley, Carrie, which I don't need to explain to you. Yes, now I see that both of us have been traveling these many months in the valley of Baca."

"Yes, we have. Doug, I've never told you that I'm unable to bear children. Will that change anything?"

"Absolutely not."

Carrie smiled. "I have so desperately wanted to be a mother."

"I can see that, just by watching you with Jenny."

Tears filled Carrie's eyes. "Oh, Doug, just think of it! When the time comes that we marry, I will be Jenny's mother! Praise the Lord; I'll be a mother! Oh, thank You, Lord Jesus!"

They joined hands and turned to gaze out over the vast valley toward the mountain peaks. The grass, trees, and flowers in the valley were already taking on a hint of fall colors.

Carrie looked up at Doug, then set her eyes on the valley and the beautiful looming mountains. There was elation in her voice as she said, "Doug, I can now see beyond the valley!"